L. P. Hartley (1895–1972) w   vid
Cecil as 'One of the most disti   the
most original'. His best-known work is *The Go-Between*, which was made
into a 1970 film. Other written works include: *The Betrayal, The Boat, A
Perfect Woman* and *Eustace and Hilda*, for which he was awarded the 1947
James Tait Black Memorial Prize.

He was awarded the CBE in 1956.

L. P. Hartley

My Fellow Devils

JOHN MURRAY

First published in Great Britain in 1951 by James Barrie

This paperback edition first published in 2013 by John Murray (Publishers)
An Hachette UK Company

1

A CIP catalogue record for this title is available from the British Library

ISBN 978-1-84854-866-4
E-book ISBN 978-1-84854-867-1

Typeset in Sabon by Hewer Text UK Ltd, Edinburgh

Printed and bound by Clays Ltd, St Ives plc

John Murray policy is to use papers that are natural, renewable and
recyclable products and made from wood grown in sustainable forests.
The logging and manufacturing processes are expected to conform
to the environmental regulations of the country of origin.

John Murray (Publishers)
338 Euston Road
London NW1 3BH

www.johnmurray.co.uk

To Mary MacCarthy

Whoso is partner with a thief hateth his own soul.

Proverbs

I

THE first time that Margaret Pennefather saw Colum McInnes on the films she was not attracted by him, indeed she was repelled, even more sharply repelled than she expected to be. She had heard of him, of course, for who had not heard of this latest tough guy of the screen? On the hoardings she had seen his squarish face, with its blunt features and over-animated eyes, staring at her, and the revolver which he nearly always carried, threatening her – 'Watch out, babe!' – many times, and had always turned away. She did not care for that sort of thing; she did not care for the cinema at all, and had hardly been since before the war, when she some-times let herself be taken to an Austrian film at the Academy or a French film at Studio One. She was serious-minded.

Too serious-minded, her friends told her. She had a good many friends, most of them women, and most of them, though of this she had no idea, a little in awe of her. Her mother had died when Margaret was five years old and she had been brought up by her father, a fairly prosperous merchant in the city. He had retired when the war came, having attained the age of sixty and being in rather delicate health; and now their roles were reversed; it was she who looked after him. This was by no means a whole-time job but it absorbed her affectionate instincts and developed their protective side, so that at the age of twenty-eight she had never fallen in love or given much thought to men. The men she saw most of were her father's contemporaries who shared his interests and treated her rather as the lady of the house, to whom bread-and-butter letters should be addressed. She had another reason for feeling older than she was; her father had divided his fortune with her, she was financially independent, and could have walked out of the house at any time and lived comfortably on her own. She didn't dream of doing this but it was a fact that insensibly influenced her attitude to herself and other people's attitude to her. In a small way she was an heiress, for whom the material stability of marriage had no appeal. She had a position of her own, she was an independent sovereign, and when she visited her cousins who belonged to a large family and were normally occupied with the manifold emotional experiences of growing up she felt the difference between herself and them. She gave them her news and they gave her theirs, but the transactions were made in different currencies; they were token presents, manifestations of family solidarity, rather than an interchange of confidences. Her cousins felt strange with her and she with them; perhaps there was a touch of wistfulness on both sides – on theirs for her security and on hers, less analysably, for the daily and hourly uncertainties which somehow enriched their lives.

But she was far from being discontented or shut up in herself. She had a great deal to give; and in the small town where they lived, within easy reach of London yet surprisingly not a dormitory town, she found outlets for it. War work while the war lasted; and after the war, municipal bodies and charitable enterprises. She had a gentle dignity of manner that was innate, so that although she was generally the youngest member of the committees on which she sat she never seemed, or indeed felt, out of place. Listening to stories of crime, hardship and poverty she learned a great deal about the world at second hand. At first it horrified her, brought up as she was in surroundings where such things never happened; but gradually, and increasingly as she herself was called upon to investigate cases, lighten loads and adjust disagreements, she found herself thinking in terms of other standards, in which there was no place for feeling shocked.

Whatever righteous indignation she felt at first soon melted when practical measures had to be taken. Yet when she got home from interviewing some family whose entire behaviour seemed devoid of good-will, decency and commonsense, she could be quite critical of domestic lapses – a cobweb the housemaid had overlooked, or too much salt in the soup. She had trained herself to see cases of severe illness and to go without flinching where infection was; but she still worried when her father sneezed, in case he should be going to get a cold. If she had been introspective or gifted with a keener sense of humour she might have wondered at or been amused by the different standards she kept for her home life and for the world outside. As it was she did not even notice they were inconsistent.

Most of the friends she made in the course of her public work were, like her father's, older than herself, and the bond between them was vocational rather than personal; she did not visit with them much or see them socially. But with a few, both on and off committees, she was on more intimate terms, and they, unlike her, did not think that filial piety and attention to one's station and its duties constituted the be-all and the end-all here. Her air of detachment, and the suggestion of primness they professed to find in her, were a challenge; obscurely they felt she ought to be more involved, and by involved they meant involved in affairs of the heart. It was characteristic of her position that her friends tended to be drawn from different walks of life. People met in her drawing-room who, except on committees, would not perhaps have met elsewhere; but even those who were not socially homogeneous had the same thought, and discussed it among themselves, though they did not quite know how to broach it to Margaret, in the face of her apparent indifference to the exciting and tender side of life, well as she was acquainted with its more sensational manifestations among the humbler townsfolk of Dittingham.

Afterwards, no one could remember who first had the idea that the solution to the problem might be found in Colum McInnes' latest film, nor by what reasoning it was arrived at; but they remembered vividly that by common consent the task of approaching Margaret had been allotted to Diana Crossthwaite.

Besides being one of Margaret's closest friends Diana had a natural impetus of personality developed by much social experience, and at this moment made all but irresistible by the fact that she had become engaged to one of the most eligible young men in the place. Stuart Tufton was his name.

'He isn't everybody's choice, of course,' said Diana, who had brought him, at Margaret's request, to a small cocktail party she was giving. 'I wish he had been more like a film-star, but nowadays one has to be content with what one can get.'

She looked at him with fond possessiveness. Stuart Tufton was a tall young man with a pink complexion and a small, fair moustache. In speaking he sometimes tried to overcome what seemed to his interlocutor a disdainful expression, partly natural, for he was conventional and there was much he disapproved of, partly assumed to disguise the babyish cast of his features. But once he had disposed of this protection he was pleasant enough.

Remembering his cue, he put off his hauteur and shyly said to Margaret,

'Who is your favourite film-star?'

Margaret, who was measuring out the drinks, a task she performed with painstaking exactitude as if they were libations to the god of hospitality, hesitated a moment and said,

'Greta Garbo, I think.'

'But my dear she was before the Flood!' exclaimed Diana. 'And he doesn't mean that kind of film-star. If I can say it without sounding coarse, he means a man.'

'Oh, a man,' said Margaret vaguely, and began to search her mind.

'Yes, a man,' repeated Diana, defiantly. 'Colum McInnes, for instance.'

At the mention of his name, a hush fell on the company. Then one girl said, 'I think I've seen him in every film he's been in.'

'My dear, I've seen him six times in every film he's been in.'

'Do you remember him in *Rogue Richard*?'

'Shall I ever forget? It was too cruel when they caught him. I cried and cried.'

'I think I almost like him better when he's the villain than when he's the hero.'

'Oh, but he's always the hero.'

'Oh yes, if all murderers were like him they'd be simply irresistible.'

'I'm afraid I've never seen him,' said Margaret, trying not to sound chilling.

'Not seen him? Not seen Colum McInnes?' Murmurs of incredulity ran round the room, glancing off the shining china, dusted by Margaret's own hand, that crowned with domes and spires the long, low bookcases. 'Not seen him?' repeated Diana. 'Not even in *Kiss The Highwayman*?'

'No.'

'Then your education has been neglected. We dote upon Margaret, don't we?' Diana appealed to the company, who chorused assent. 'She's the backbone of the place. We should all go to pieces without her. Everyone in Dittingham would give themselves to a life of vice. She has only one fault or she'd be perfect.'

They all stared at the paragon, whose comely, softly-blooming face began to expand into an awkward smile.

'What is it?' she asked.

'She hasn't seen Colum McInnes, of course! Look, she's blushing, and no wonder. But we'll soon put that right. We'll make a party next week to go and see him in *Put Paid to It*.'

'I hope he won't be smoking a cigar,' said someone plaintively. 'In *Under the Lilac*, it quite spoilt his profile.'

'Oh but you could see round it,' said Diana. 'Now what about dates?'

'Next week I'm afraid I'm rather—'

'Now, now, no excuses, Margaret darling, and no looking at little books,' for Margaret was automatically opening her bag. 'We'll take no denial. Honestly, dearest, you *must* come. You're so serious about most things, but you're positively flippant about the films. How can you go on being a godsend to people, when you don't know what's happening in their minds? You'll get like one of those social workers in books, you know, very well-meaning, but—'

Margaret's face clouded over and she looked a little frightened.

'Of course, you never could,' pursued Diana, 'but after you have seen Colum McInnes, it would be still more unthinkable.'

The cloud slowly faded from Margaret's face. She raised no further protests, and before the party broke up arrangements for the expedition had been made.

When the film was over they walked back to the parking-place where Stuart Tufton had left his car. Diana and he went on in front, their profiles almost touching. The other man, who was a friend of Stuart's lagged behind, and said,

'I'm afraid you didn't enjoy that very much.'

Margaret looked at him in surprise and some dismay. How could he have known? Sincerely she hoped the others had not noticed. 'Oh,' she said, 'I did enjoy it quite. Please don't think I didn't. It's only that I'm not very used to films . . . of that kind.'

'Films of violence, you mean?'

Margaret nodded.

'I don't know that I'm all that keen on them myself,' he said.

Margaret immediately felt drawn to him. She had had little

opportunity of talking to him, for she had only met him in the foyer of the cinema. All through the performance she had felt at a disadvantage by being out of tune with the spirit of the film. She did not, of course, admit that to her hosts, but she was afraid that her professions of enjoyment had sounded a little false. It was a relief to know that someone else felt about it as she did.

'I didn't like it when he shot the policeman,' she said.

'No.'

'Or when he broke that other man's arm.'

'No. But the audience enjoyed it. The more red-handed he is, the better they like him.'

'I suppose people would say we were prigs,' said Margaret.

'Yes, but it's rather nice being prigs together.'

She smiled at him and felt the sense of their companionship deepen almost into conspiracy.

'I wonder,' she began, 'Mr—?' She reddened and glanced at him in confused inquiry.

'Burden,' he told her. 'Nicholas Burden. I'm usually called Nick.'

'I am so sorry,' she said. 'I mean,' she blundered on, 'I don't usually forget people's names.'

'Well, please don't forget mine,' he said quite sharply. 'But I interrupted you. You were going to say?—'

With an effort she recollected herself.

'I was going to say I wondered what made men take to playing parts of . . . of that kind.'

'Oh,' said Nick, 'he was always a tough little gangster.'

'You knew him then?' exclaimed Margaret. 'You know Colum McInnes?' Even she could not keep the awe out of her voice.

'Yes, I was at school with him. But that isn't his real name.'

'What is his real name?'

'Does it matter?' Then, unwillingly, Nick told her.

7

'Oh,' Margaret's voice sounded disappointed. 'So he's not a Scotsman?' She had always felt romantic about the Scots.

'No more than I am.'

'Oh,' said Margaret again. She couldn't understand why she felt deflated. But soon her interest began to revive. 'Do tell me what he was like,' she begged him.

'Oh, much the same as he is now,' said Nick rather shortly.

'Do you mean as he is in the film or . . . or in real life?'

'Well, in the film. In real life I don't know. I haven't seen him much for several years. But they say he's turned over a new leaf. He doesn't smoke or drink – he's the Bayard of the film world now.'

'Is he married?' Margaret asked.

'Yes, but only once, and he's my age, nearly thirty. It's quite a remarkable record for a film star. But he's divorced now, or has managed to get rid of his wife – I don't know how, as he's a Roman Catholic.'

'Was it his fault?' Margaret asked.

'I've no idea – I'm not in the secrets of his later life.'

Margaret considered. Her companion had been a little curt in his replies, but she found she did not want to let the subject drop.

'Was he a bully at school?' she asked.

'No, I can't honestly say he was. He was vain and wanted admiration, liked you to feel his muscles, and so on, he threw his weight about a bit and wasn't popular with the masters. He used to get into scraps and scrapes. But no, you couldn't call him a bully, he was too detached for that.'

'Was he – er – good at games?' persisted Margaret.

'Oh yes, he was in both elevens, I think. But he never had much team spirit. He was a cabotin sort of character, always playing a lonely part – the Ulysses type, which so many men want to be, or to be thought – you know, full of wiles, and god-like, or goodly, or whatever the word means.'

8

'But not godly?' Margaret was pleased with this quip.

'Oh no, not nearly sure enough of himself for that. He may be now – everyone says he is. I suppose that sort of character is really rather vulnerable – always pretending to be something that you're not and wondering what effect you are making.'

'Was he a friend of yours?' asked Margaret.

Nick hesitated, and looked away. 'Yes; I suppose he was. For a few terms we used to go about together. But I'm a struggling barrister and he—' Nick spread out his hands. 'He wouldn't know me now, he's much too grand.'

There was a touch of finality in his tone, which restored Margaret to a sense of their relationship, lost sight of during her inquest into Colum McInnes' past life. She wondered if she had been a little rude, but she could not let the subject – which she obscurely felt must not be referred to again – die away completely.

'Fancy your knowing him all the time,' she said, 'and never telling us!'

At that he turned towards her, and she saw how charming his face was with its wide smile and the wrinkles of amusement that radiated from his eyes. They had reached the car-park, and Diana and Stuart were busy with their car, showing the renewed animation of face and movement that reunion with a beloved car often brings.

'They might want me to introduce them to him,' he said. 'Don't tell them that I used to be a friend of his. Promise.'

'Yes, if you promise not to tell them that I didn't enjoy the film.'

They had just time to smile at each other over their shared secrets before the others joined them and Nick took his leave.

2

COMING downstairs next morning Margaret was conscious of a change. Everything that she looked at bore witness to it. Almost for the first time she felt dissatisfied with her home. She saw it as someone else might have seen it, but as she herself had never seen it before. It announced itself as a suburban villa, of vaguely Tudor descent, the sort that cartoonists and high-brow writers poked fun at. The twinkling white bannisters, the brown beams of the lounge hall, where no one ever lounged, the high bosomed doors leading off it, so discreetly – only the one which led to the kitchen regions showed signs of wear – all this made her feel critical. And now the spotless upholstery of the drawing room – smooth, rounded blobs of pink confined in lines of gold, curved or straight, with the gilt looking-glasses multiplying them. And what an air of tidiness, and emptiness, and silence, and even a faint whiff of stuffiness, though the casement windows, so solid and close-fitting, were open to the spring air, as they should be. Nothing for the housewife to complain of; not a speck of last night's ash on the glass ashtrays; all was swept and polished: Lily never scamped her work. Yet somehow Margaret did criticize it; or rather she felt ill at ease with it; it no longer made a framework for her thoughts, it spoke another language, and she would have been glad to find some evidence of imperfection – a chair out of place, or even a slight, a very slight, breakage.

But what had taken her into the drawing-room at all? she suddenly wondered. It was clean contrary to her daily routine to begin her tour of inspection until after breakfast; some spirit in her feet must have guided her away from the dining-room, where breakfast was always laid and where her father was even now awaiting her. He would not mind waiting for her – like everyone else he recognised her independence of action, her touch of royalty, and encouraged her in it. If he was the master she was the mistress of the house. But where were the feelings, the time-honoured feelings, much too elusive to analyse, but impossible not to miss, which should have been hers when she laid her hand on the door-knob, ready to receive his morning kiss? They were not there, they had flown, leaving a stranger on the threshold.

Her father's morning greeting had an edge to it.

'Well, my dear, and how did you enjoy the frolic?'

Margaret considered a moment. He would be disappointed if she had said she had not enjoyed it.

'Oh, it was all right, Daddy. It was quite exciting. I'm not sure how much I like that gangster stuff, though. It's so unreal, for one thing. Crime isn't a bit like that, as I know from my small experience. Besides, it isn't really good for people, especially children, to fill their minds with ideas of that sort. They get to think crime's glamorous, which it isn't.'

'What did you think of the great McInnes?' her father asked.

'Fancy your remembering his name.'

'Well, I'm not such a back number as all that.'

'Of course you're not, Daddy.' She hated having made him even momentarily feel old. But putting off his question hadn't made it any easier to answer. 'Oh well,' she said, 'I can see what people admire in him, of course. Well, not admire, but get sort of fascinated by. But I'm afraid he's not my type.'

She was rewarded by seeing her father's face relax, and, was it possible? a thin flush stained his cheeks, which were sometimes a little papery in the mornings. He stretched out his long vein-embossed hand for the toast, and gave a little sigh.

'So you didn't fall for him, as they say. Who else was there?'

'Stuart and Diana, of course, and a friend of theirs called Nicholas Burden.'

'Nicholas Burden? I've seen that name somewhere.'

'He's a barrister.'

'Ah, that must be it. I sometimes read the Law Reports. What was he like?' The anxious look had come back into her father's face, intensifying his regard.

'He seemed very nice,' said Margaret. 'He told me he was a friend—' She checked herself, remembering she had promised not to betray Nick's secret.

'A friend?' her father prompted.

Margaret hated telling the smallest fib. She had to go through a long process of justifying it by appeals to social usage and the obligation to protect other people's interests before she could utter it. 'Oh, not of anyone in particular. He . . . he must have a lot of friends. But we didn't have time to talk much. He lives in London, you see, and I came back with Stuart and Diana, and dined with them at Diana's, as you know. Stuart brought me home, I didn't get in till half past eleven, quite late for me.'

'Was there anyone else at dinner?'

'Just Diana's mother and father.' Margaret felt she was being very dull and non-committal. 'They talked quite a lot about me being made a J.P.,' she said with a rush.

Her father looked at her proudly. 'Well, it is rather an achievement at your age.'

Margaret coloured, whether at the reference to her achievement or her age, she could not tell. They both sat in silence for a minute or two.

So it was safely over, his daughter's brief sally into the world where they marry and are given in marriage. Safely over, without leaving, so it seemed, a ripple; an incident so little charged with meaning that it did not disturb the usual tenour of breakfast-table conversation. Social requirements had been met; something had been done, but nothing had been felt. It was all eminently satisfactory. He was safe until the next time.

But was it really satisfactory? Mr Pennefather's heart was not strong, but it had by no means ceased to beat and it gave a different answer. True, she is your daughter, said his heart, but she is also a woman and when you are no longer here she will be sitting at this table alone, wondering how it happened that she gave the best years of her life to looking after an old man. For a moment he seemed to see her greyheaded behind the coffee-pot; the hint of sternness that sometimes showed itself behind her eyes had settled into a look that was almost sour. He imagined her thinking of him; but her face did not soften at the memory, it grew more bitter. Selfish old man! she was thinking; if it hadn't been for him I shouldn't be sitting here, at this same old table by this same old coffee-pot, I should be – and his mind lost itself in a vision of the domestic felicities which would inevitably fall to Margaret's lot if she cut herself adrift from him.

But Margaret, the Margaret of the present moment, had no such notions in her mind. On the contrary, she was thinking how reassuring it was to be restored to her old self and to her old, comfortable awareness of her surroundings. Her rapprochement with the coffee-pot, the certainty that it meant to her exactly what it meant before, was particularly precious. And this return to the status quo had been achieved so simply: just by giving her father a plain account of the previous day's outing. The fond look she gave him plainly said: 'May our loving, happy relationship last forever!'

He asked her rather brusquely: 'Stuart and Diana getting on all right?'

Torn away from her thoughts she answered almost mechanically,

'Oh yes, Daddy. People in . . . in their position always do.'

I ought to tell her that they sometimes don't, he thought. But his mind could not help rejoicing at her ignorance of the heart; she went by rule and did not know the smallest thing about its workings, nor did she seem curious to know. Yet still he was haunted by the thought that the flower, so softly glowing now, might wither on its stem, and he said tentatively:

'Perhaps we . . . you . . . ought to give them a return party sometime.'

'Who, Daddy?'

'Well, Stuart and Diana and—'

Margaret looked surprised.

'Oh, I don't think so, Daddy. I don't think it's a bit necessary. The Crossthwaites live for that sort of thing, of course. I'm not criticizing them, but there *are* other things. We did have them in for cocktails the other day. But I will invite them, if you want me to.'

The troubling coloured vision of another future for Margaret faded from his mind, nor was he loath to see it go. Well, he had made his protest.

'I only thought you might be finding it a little dull, my dear, shut up with your old father,' he said lightly.

'Dearest Daddy, you must never say that,' she said, and got up and kissed him for the second time.

But a seed may lodge and germinate in a stone wall and before the day was out Margaret found her thoughts veering of their own volition to the idea of a return party. As a pleasure, as a recreation, she would not have entertained it, perhaps. But as a return for benefits received, it had the sanction of an obligation and to the claims of obligation Margaret was extremely sensitive. And she liked things to be orderly. For her, the mute inglorious cry of cutlet for cutlet was the expression of a higher claim, affecting the balance of life. Looking back, she thought she saw the balance of entertainment tilted against her; she was known to be well off, and in dismay she wondered whether her friends had thought her mean. It was a twinge of conscience that had made her call them frivolous.

But what form was the party to take? A dinner party at Fair Haven was her first idea; it would bring her father in and she did not want him to feel left out. But no, to be a real return it must be a party for youth, a young party. Margaret frowned. She was uneasy in the presence of youth, and the young people of Dittingham knew each other so much better than she knew them that she would feel a stranger at her own party. But Diana and Stuart must be asked, of course. Perhaps a quartet would do; but who would be the fourth?

It did not take Margaret long to make up her mind to invite Nicholas Burden; had she been more familiar with her own mental processes she might have felt them steering towards him sooner than she did. She found his address in the telephone book and wrote to him then and there, naming a day next week. She would not ask the others until she knew his answer. If he could not come she would let the party slide. She saw no flaw in the logic of such a course.

But it must not be a repetition of the other party. Not a cinema; she did not really care for cinemas. They would go to a play and have supper afterwards, then Nicholas could have it with them. If it meant stopping the night what matter? She would have plenty to do in London the next morning.

She took up the paper and scanned the list of plays. A good play it must be, something worth seeing. Being out of touch with the theatre, the titles she saw did not convey a great deal to her. Nothing by Shakespeare, nothing by Shaw, nothing even by Noel Coward. But what was this? 'Newgate Theatre. Commencing April 10th. Colum McInnes in *The Robber Chief*. Book Now.' She smiled, shrugged her shoulders and read on. But she found nothing in the rest of the list that attracted her, and her eyes strayed back to the Newgate Theatre.

Of course, she mused, she ought to consult her guests' taste as well as her own. Her guests would certainly enjoy seeing Colum McInnes in *The Robber Chief*. Even to her inexperienced eye it seemed an unsophisticated piece, possibly meant for children. Perhaps she could bring herself to enjoy the simple thrills, and she could shut her eyes at anything she didn't like.

It didn't matter about her; the great thing was to give pleasure to her guests. If it was Colum McInnes, she needn't even bother to ask them their opinion. There was Mr Burden, of course. He professed not to like Colum McInnes, but he might have said so simply in order to agree with her. He was an agreeable and agreeing man, and she thought that in his company she would be able to sit through the performance without too much discomfort, supported by the thought that the others were having a good time. It would be much safer to choose something that was sure to please two of the party than to risk a pig in a poke.

Oddly enough the 10th was the very day she had chosen for the party. It was most unlikely that she would be in time to get tickets for a First Night (illogically this thought gave her confidence) but she could try. And when she had failed as she certainly would fail, she would ask Stuart and Diana to choose for her.

She did not fail, however. Everything went swimmingly. The agent produced four returned tickets for the first row of the stalls; Nicholas Burden said he would be delighted to come. Margaret had not told him which play they were going to in her letter, indeed at the time of writing she did not know herself. Now she could write to him again, would have to write to him again. Diana received the news with screams of laughter, which echoed down the telephone. 'But my dear, did you know? That's Colum McInnes's new play!' Margaret said rather soberly that she did know, but thought that this might be rather different from his films. 'Different!' exclaimed Diana. 'What makes you think so? I hope not.' 'Well, a play is different from a film, isn't it?' argued Margaret feebly. 'I mean, you see the man himself. He wouldn't be so . . .'. She stopped, wondering what on earth she was going to say. 'So Colum-ish?' suggested Diana. 'I should have thought he would be much, much more.' 'You haven't seen him in a play before?' asked Margaret. 'My dear, he's never *been* in a play before! Do you mean to say you didn't know? That's what makes it so unbearably thrilling. We shall see him in the *flesh*!' 'Oh,' exclaimed Margaret, feeling herself grow pink, and thankful that Diana couldn't see her. 'Of course we needn't stay if we don't like it.' 'Not stay? You must be mad . . . Who did you say was coming with us?' Margaret hadn't said, and feeling rather ashamed of the paucity of her acquaintance, and the unoriginality of her ideas, she brought out with an effort, 'Mr Burden.' 'Nick? He *will* be pleased. I'm glad you liked him.' The conversation drifted into other channels, arrangements for the evening, and the local gossip at which Margaret was never very good.

Nicholas Burden did not at once reply to Margaret's letter telling him what the play was to be; and his answer, when it came, struck her as being less cordial than the one in which he had thanked her for her invitation.

3

BUT as it turned out Margaret's intuition, though founded perhaps on wishful thinking, proved to be correct. As the Robber Chief, Colum McInnes was a different character from the low-grade gangster of *Put Paid to It*, he was more like a latter-day Robin Hood. True, he was dirty and unshaven and very quick on the draw; his gun protruded like an extra finger, and once he used it, after a (to Margaret) agonizing quarter of an hour during which the weapon seemed likely to go off at any moment. But to some extent the steel had gone out of his voice; he no longer spoke in smooth, deadly monosyllables with a strong trace of American accent, calling his victims 'pal' or 'chum' with a subdued but ferocious irony. He was often quite articulate and once, when explaining the cruel circumstances of his childhood and youth which had made him take to his present career, almost eloquent; he even dashed away a tear, and the audience dashed away many. Moreover as a softening and ultimately a redeeming influence there was a little girl who turned up, most inopportunely, at dead of night when he was cracking a safe; her artless questions turned him from his purpose and her promise not to tell on him led to further meet-ings, in the Park, at a teashop, and finally in the very house he had been burgling where, smart and spruce for the first time, she persuaded him, as a friend she had picked up, to meet her family – father, mother, and an older, prettier sister who soon felt for him what Robinetta felt. It was this that gave the play its twist and touch of pathos – for Robinetta had to stand by and watch the flowering of a maturer love. Needless to say he did not at once give up his evil ways; suspicion fell on him in the very quarter where his heart most dreaded it; and it again fell to Robinetta, by an equivocation which was very near a lie, to allay their misgivings and preserve for her sister the love which burnt so steadily in her. It was a touching moment when, at the close of the play, she came in and, finding them together, tiptoed out again.

To Margaret's inexperienced ear the applause sounded terrific and she found herself clapping as loudly as any. Unconsciously she identified Colum with the gangster, believed that the audience as a whole shared her delight in his reformation, and felt, as she did, that virtue burned more brightly because of his conversion to it. The actors were recalled many times; the white sheep and the black, their enmity laid aside, came hand in hand and wreathed in smiles. Presently they were reduced to three: Colum McInnes stood between the sisters, bestowing a lover's glance on one and a brother's on the other. At last, as the enthusiasm of the audience was still unsatisfied, he appeared alone, receiving with a touch of his old truculence, and the curt nod that delighted everyone, the undivided homage of the house; and it was then that he looked down and recognized his old friend in the front row of the stalls. His face, which had been wearing its grimmest behind-the-pistol look, suddenly relaxed and the naughty schoolboy's smile which he gave Nick embraced with equal warmth Margaret who was sitting beside him.

'Well,' said Diana when they were at supper afterwards, 'it's all right for once in a way but I don't think he can get away with that old-fashioned stuff again, do you? People won't take it, even from him.'

'I expect he's having a good laugh in his sleeve,' said Stuart.

Margaret found herself unwilling to accept this cynical view.

'I know,' she remarked, 'that actors and actresses aren't supposed to feel the parts they act in, and they would be quite worn out by the emotional strain of it if they did, but don't you think the parts they play must have some sort of influence on them, both for good and bad?'

'How sweet you are, Margaret,' said Diana, 'I believe you would really like to think that Colum McInnes is a reformed character who works for the Charity Organization Society in his spare time.'

'We don't know that he isn't,' said Nick. Surprised to hear himself say this, but encouraged by a grateful look from Margaret, he went on:

'But whatever his moral state is, you may be sure that to-night's audience will go home feeling more kindly disposed towards little girls.'

'And burglars, perhaps,' put in Stuart.

'Well, perhaps burglars, too.'

'You should know more about burglars than we do, Nick,' said Stuart. 'Your work takes you among them, I expect.'

'So does Miss Pennefather's,' Nick said.

Thus appealed to Margaret found her thoughts difficult to sort out.

'Of course their home life,' she began. 'It nearly always starts with that.'

'You couldn't tell how a fellow like Colum McInnes was brought up, could you?' said Stuart. 'I don't want to sound snobbish, but I don't suppose he's got much background.' He paused and Nick gave Margaret a warning glance. 'A chap like that is pretty sure to be a bit hairy-heeled.'

'Please don't talk about him in that way,' cried Diana. 'You're suspicious of anyone who doesn't belong to at least four clubs.'

'Well, nobody obliged him to play gangster parts,' said Stuart reasonably. 'One would suppose he must have some sympathy with that sort of thing, or he wouldn't have chosen to represent it on the stage.'

'Darling, it would be too exciting if he really was one.'

Margaret frowned a little.

'Perhaps he was, and has now been rescued by a good woman's love,' said Stuart. 'That's why he made such a success of his part to-night.'

'Or a little girl's,' said Diana, laughing.

'He may be that kind of man, we don't know.'

'But it was a success, wasn't it?' put in Margaret, childishly anxious to have this confirmed.

'Well,' Diana said judicially, 'I wouldn't call it an overwhelming success, but it was a personal triumph and we can't thank you enough, can we, Stuart? And think of having been at the first night! We shall be able to dine out on it for months! Now we really must be getting back to dear old Dittingham, and you, Nick, must be a proper cavalier and see Margaret back to her hotel.' Diana couldn't help taking charge.

Margaret called for the bill. She frowned over it a little, wondering what tip to leave: women were accused of being mean over such matters. Feeling touched and protective, Nick watched her silent painful calculations. Having made up her mind she pushed the plate away from her with a decided little gesture. They all rose and gently threaded their way through the now emptying tables to the restaurant door. Stuart and Diana went off to their car, leaving Margaret and Nick together.

'May I really see you back to your hotel?' he said. 'I can protect you from any Robber Chiefs that little way.'

'But of course.'

When they were in the cab she said,

'I hope you did really enjoy the evening.'

'Yes, I did, – to tell you the truth, more than I expected to.'

'I'm so glad. So did I.' She added thoughtfully, 'I found him much more sympathetic to-night.'

'Who?'

'Well, Colum McInnes.'

'Oh yes,' said Nick absently. 'He certainly was on his best behaviour.'

'You think he isn't really like that?'

'Like that?'

'Like . . . he appeared to be to-night.'

'How can I tell? He may be . . . it's so long since I saw him.'

'But he must have remembered you, by the way he smiled at you.'

'So he did! I'd quite forgotten.'

'I wonder the others didn't notice.'

'I expect they were too busy thinking of each other,' Nick replied. 'Do you like staying at the Regina?'

'Oh yes, we've always stayed there.'

There was a pause, then he asked awkwardly, 'Next time you come up, will you let me know?'

'Indeed I will,' said Margaret.

'We could go to a play or a film or something.'

'I should enjoy that very much.'

'I don't know that there's a great deal to see in London just now. You wouldn't want to see Colum McInnes again, would you?' he said smiling.

'Well, of course, I . . .'.

'Perhaps we could just dine together without going out. I know a little place where the food doesn't poison you.'

Margaret heard the urgency in his voice. She had lived until the age of twenty-eight without hearing it in any man's voice except on the stage, as she had heard it to-night; but until to-night she had only heard the tone, which somehow jarred on her, she hadn't been receptive to the feeling behind it. During the play she had felt what it could mean, when Robinetta's sister was its object, and still more, perhaps, when it was used to Robinetta herself, for the Robber Chief – who should blame him? – had been very tender to the little girl. Now that she heard the note again, in a mood so softened and transformed by the evening's emotion, she found nothing strange or repellent in it: quite the contrary.

'I should like to dine with you very much,' she said.

The taxi turned into the street where Margaret's hotel was, and started to slow down.

'In that case,' said Nick, 'perhaps you could suggest a day when you might be able to come up.'

His voice, instead of plunging about through all the notes of the register, as it usually did, was quite level now, and suggested that it was struggling in a strait-jacket of good manners that he would have fain thrown off. The sense of strain and almost physical conflict in him were so apparent that Margaret heard the words without taking in their import and sat staring at him.

With increasing difficulty of utterance he repeated: 'Perhaps you could tell me a day when you might be coming up to London.'

Almost hypnotized by the anxiety in his voice, but restrained by a deep-seated instinct against committing herself she answered almost at random,

'Would Tuesday week do?'

Even in the darkness of the taxi she could see his face fall.

'Must it be so long?' he muttered.

The driver had got down and was opening the door, but becoming aware of the tension within – a tension with which he must have been familiar – he considerately closed it again.

'Very well,' she said, hunting about in the confusion of thoughts which gave no precedent of how to deal with such a situation, but anxious to calm him, 'shall we say next Tuesday?'

She was rewarded by seeing the return of happiness light up his face.

'Tuesday would be perfect,' he said in a voice more like his own. 'I'll write to you about it.' He opened the door for her and they stood for a moment on the pavement.

'You won't forget?' he said, anxiety once more reducing his utterance to a mutter.

'No,' she answered. 'I . . . I . . . I promise.'

4

SPRING had turned to summer before Nick and Margaret announced their engagement. It was Margaret who hung back. Indecision was a state of mind most unusual to her. It was not, she believed, that she was uncertain of her feeling for Nick. It was the break with her old life – the snapping of the innumerable threads that bound her to Dittingham. Her deep sense of obligation was touched and wounded at a hundred points. All her public and charitable work, on which her very sense of her identity depended, must she give it up? Must the whole fabric of affection and respect that she had built up for herself in the district be relinquished? Were the many people who relied on her to rely on her no more?

But most of all, of course, she dreaded the thought of abandoning her father. He was old and frail for his years; it would be like signing his death-warrant. There was an unmarried sister, Margaret's Aunt Charlotte, who might be persuaded to keep house for him, but he had never greatly cared for her and she had a bridge-playing, croquet-playing life of her own which she would be unwilling to give up – which it would be unfair to ask her to give up. All the little things that he counted on to make him happy – the maintenance of the routine so precious to the elderly – were things that she only could supply.

Still, she knew that however important filial duties were, conjugal duties came first. She could not, she felt, ask Nick to settle down in Dittingham, more than an hour's train journey from his work. Though he was not really delicate and had powers of quick recovery he was easily tired; he was working very hard at the Bar and getting on well; it would be cruel to saddle him with this heavy handicap. Together they would have plenty to live on, even in the post-war world; she could not plead lack of money as an excuse for setting up a joint establishment at Fair Haven. She did not talk it over with her father, she did not talk it over with Nick; she allowed herself, for the moment, to eat her cake and have it.

The cake was very sweet, and Margaret lived in an enchantment which enabled her to enjoy the present without providing for the future, like a happy healthy person who sees but does not feel the need to make a will.

But the wish to tell her happiness was stronger than the prudential or humane considerations which would have bade her keep it to herself. Moreover she disliked concealment and did not want her father or anyone else to stumble on the real reason for her increasingly frequent journeys up to London.

Yet how hard it was when the moment came! Each approach, as she tried it over in her mind, seemed more brutal and wounding than the last. To think that one kind of love, that of its nature could so well include another, should by the circumstances it raised be compelled to make the other of none effect.

'Daddy,' she said.

'Yes, my dear?' It was half past six, an hour when he sometimes allowed himself a whisky and soda, and the day seemed to renew itself in the assurance of an untroubled evening.

'There's something I want to tell you.' Her voice trembled and the happiness she had been feeling for so many days was changed to pain. He drew a longer breath than usual which expired in a sigh.

'You needn't tell me, my dear, let me tell you.'

She was ashamed of the relief she felt. Profiting by his unselfishness, thankful to be spared the passing pain of breaking unpleasant news, she had lost sight of the lasting sorrow she was giving him.

He went on:

'I've known it for some time, and if you hadn't told me I was going to tell you how happy I am for your sake.'

Margaret's eyes filled with tears and she could not speak.

'There's nothing to feel sad about, nothing,' he assured her. 'Before, it was a little sad, perhaps?' She shook her head violently. 'Well, I used to think it must be. But now!' He laid his hand on hers. 'My dear I can't tell you what a difference there is between a life you make for yourself out of your aspirations and your sense of duty and . . .', he lifted his eyes to hers, 'and your affections, and a life which is created for you by a mutual love . . . May I know who the lucky man is?'

All in a rush Margaret began to tell him about Nick. Like her, he was an only child, but he was an orphan; both his parents were dead, he had made his way by scholarships and the little money they were able to leave him. Young as he was, only two years older than herself (and this seemed young to Margaret, brought up so much amongst her elders) he was already doing well at the Bar and beginning to make a name for himself. This she had learned not from him but from Stuart who had known him at Oxford, where he had always been looked on as a coming man. He was serious-minded and ambitious, but not austere, and he liked his pleasures to be rather highbrow. Margaret paused; the thought of how she had taken him to see Colum McInnes was incongruous now; her mind recoiled from it, for it did not fit into the pattern of her happiness; yet how could she regret it when she and Nick had been brought together by the warmth of feeling it engendered? She would have to look up to him, she told her father; she might even be a little afraid of him but she did not mind that.

'And what do you talk about when you are together?' he asked her.

'Oh,' she said, and thought a minute. Her father sometimes asked her this question about parties she had been to, and she was never very good at answering it. But surely she must know what she and Nick talked about?

'We talk about books, for one thing,' she began.

'But you never read any!' her father exclaimed.

'I have been doing lately,' said Margaret, turning pink.

'Yes, I saw them lying about, and wondered . . . And what else do you talk about?'

'Well, films and plays.'

'But you never go to any!'

'I have been doing lately,' repeated Margaret, turning redder.

'But surely he doesn't approve of Colum McInnes and that blood-and-thunder stuff?'

A shadow crossed Margaret's face. 'No, I think he doesn't. Nor do I, of course, really. But,' she added, brightening, 'some highbrows do you know. They enjoy them in inverted commas.'

'In inverted commas?'

'Well, that's a phrase Nick has for knowing a thing's not really good but enjoying it all the same because you find it amusing.'

'I see. And what else do you talk about?'

Margaret frowned. Much as she had wanted to tell her father about Nick, she almost wished this inquisition would stop. She didn't seem at all able to give the flavour of their intercourse together. It was unlike her father to show so much curiosity, and the animation in his manner was quite new. He seemed to be more excited than she was. His cross-examination reminded her of the way Nick sometimes talked to her. But then Nick was a barrister . . . Perhaps all men were the same . . . Most people respected her reserve. There was something sweet and exciting in the knowledge that they . . . men . . . wanted to know about her for her own sake, for herself; but all the same she could not subdue a slight feeling of resentment.

'We talk about each other's past lives.'

'And do you say you were never happy until you met each other?'

Margaret reflected.

'He has said something like that, several times, I think. I don't think I have.'

She had only spoken the truth, so what was her surprise to see tears in her father's eyes, and his face light up with a rainbow smile. A second later he looked serious again.

'Still I think you should tell him so sometime.'

Dutifully Margaret made a mental note to do so, but the language of love did not yet come easily to her and besides she had a feminist streak and felt that though men should always be made comfortable they must not be too much indulged.

'Do you ever talk about money?' Mr Pennefather asked. 'Or is money too mundane?'

But Margaret disregarded the irony in his voice.

'Of course we do, Daddy,' she said seriously. 'We went into it thoroughly. In fact,' she coloured, 'one reason why we haven't got engaged is because he thinks I have too much money.'

'Too much money?'

'Well, more than he has. But as I pointed out to him it isn't more than he earns, or as much. He's afraid people will think he wants to marry me for my money. I don't understand why he's so sensitive about it. I wanted to bring him down to see you but he said no, not until I had told you of . . . of the difference between us in that way.'

'Well, that was nice of him,' said her father, though not quite so enthusiastically as she hoped. Men, even the nicest men, even her father, were apt to be odd and secretive and unaccountable where money was concerned. 'And is that the only difference between you?'

'The only difference, Daddy?'

'Yes, have you no other differences besides the discrepancy between your respective unearned incomes?'

She hesitated, but his smile encouraged her.

'No, I honestly don't think we have.'

'No quarrels about trifles?'

She thought, and shook her head.

'Well, that's a good thing anyway.' Yet somehow he sounded less satisfied than the words implied. 'You always agree with him about books and such things?'

'Well, nearly always, you see he knows so much more about them than I do. Sometimes I think his taste is a little . . . severe.'

'But you don't tell him so?'

'Oh no, we respect each other too much – we are much too fond of each other.' said Margaret gravely.

Her father sighed. She wondered why. Did he think they ought to go in for lovers' quarrels? His animation seemed to desert him; it was as though the exhilaration that the thought of his daughter's happiness had brought him, making him feel young again, had worn off, and he now began to realize how his own life would be impoverished. With a return to his old, diffident manner he said,

'You say you talk about the past. Do you also make plans for the future?'

This was another moment that Margaret had been dreading.

'Yes, we do.'

'Will you like living in London, do you think?'

Margaret glanced at him, and again felt as if a physical weight had been lifted off her. So she would not have to break this to him either. Her heart went out to him in gratitude.

'I shan't like it, but I think I shall get used to it.'

'Of course you will,' he said stoutly. 'It's high time you enjoyed your youth. All the things you do round here – the public work I mean – belong to somebody much older than you are.'

Margaret pondered. In Dittingham she was somebody; in London she would be nobody – she would have to start again, as Nick's wife, entertaining for him, making friends with his friends, some of whom she had met and found rather formidable; always, for a time at least, on trial, making good. Here her position was secure; she had her friendships, her relationships with the world of Dittingham and outside, just where she wanted them; every tradesman in the place was an old friend, and ready to do her a post-war favour. In no department of living had she to exert herself *pour se faire valoir*. Whereas in London! – She tried to forget what the change would mean to her, and concentrate on facing it.

'It may not be very easy at first, but every woman has to go through with it,' she said, unconsciously falling into her habit of thinking of women as downtrodden. 'Of course I shall miss it all here – the house, the garden' – she looked out wistfully at the rose trees, which would soon be in bloom. She had spent many patient, pleasant hours removing their dead heads, and never understood why some people professed to find the task a bore; for her the ingredient of duty in work was like a spice. Here, outside the circlet of Nick's love, home-ties tugged at her irresistibly. Elsewhere he created his own context and it was compelling; here, even he was an intruder.

'I've been thinking about it,' said her father, 'ever since I saw that it was likely to come. Don't you think it would be a good plan if I sold this house which is much too large for me alone, and bought a smaller one – big enough for you to come and stay with me, as I hope you often would – but less of a white elephant? What do I want with three acres of garden and six or seven spare bedrooms? I should rattle about like a pea in a pod.

I could get ten thousand pounds for this house, I'm sure, and buy another for six; and then I could give you the difference as a wedding present.'

'Oh but you *couldn't* leave Fair Haven, Daddy,' she cried.

'My dear, I not only could but I think I should rather like to. I may have a good many years before me, I am not too old to make a fresh start. I think I should be happier in new surroundings when I am on my own.'

Margaret was appalled. The image of Nick receded and, clothed in the hues of filial impiety, became almost hostile.

'I couldn't let you!' she cried. 'I should never forgive myself if you did!'

He looked at her puzzled, and his finger moved to and fro lightly brushing the arm of his chair, a habit he had when he encountered an unexpected obstacle.

'Don't make it difficult for me, my dear,' he said. 'I'm sure it would be for the best.'

Margaret didn't believe him and didn't really want to. Love of home was still her most deep-seated feeling, for it was bound up with her love for her father, her tender memories of her mother, and the unbroken sequence of her feelings since childhood – her very identity depended on it. She could never, she now felt, have contemplated the step of getting married if she had not known that Fair Haven would be at her back like a sheet anchor, an assurance of continuity in the flux of things.

'I can't let you!' she repeated. 'I shall tell Nick that he must live with us, and do his work from here. After all, you always did; why shouldn't he?'

'You forget, my dear, that a barrister's work is different from mine – it has to be done often under pressure, and late at night. And then there are all sorts of contacts, seeing people at short notice, and so on. I don't think you ought to ask him to put himself at such a disadvantage.'

These were arguments with which Margaret was familiar; she had used them herself. Now that they were being turned against her she knew the answers to them.

'Well, then, he must keep on his room in London,' she said (Nick lived in a bed sitting room), 'and stay there if he is too busy to come here. Think what an economy that would mean! Surely in these days when everything is so expensive one ought to try to avoid running two households!'

Her father shook his head. He was old and tired and the arguments his daughter had put forward appealed to his heart though they did not convince his head. Nevertheless, he still felt impelled to take the other side.

'I don't think it would be fair on him,' he said. 'A man ought to have his own home: I always did. I liked your grandparents but I shouldn't have wanted to live with them and it wouldn't have answered.'

'Oh, but that was different!' cried Margaret. 'You couldn't have done your work from Bath.'

Her father nodded. This was undeniable.

'Besides,' Margaret went on, 'Nick is quite used to being alone . . . just as . . . just as I am. He is really very independent, that is one of the things I like him for.'

'But he would miss you in countless little ways.'

'He's lived all this time without missing me,' said Margaret robustly.

'I know, but being in love creates all sorts of needs that weren't there before,' her father said. 'He would want you to help him, naturally.'

Margaret frowned a little.

'I don't think he would, Daddy, he's not a helpless kind of man, and I shouldn't like him as much if he was. He's used to looking after himself.'

'That doesn't mean he won't want to look after you.'

33

This was a new idea to Margaret. She couldn't imagine herself being looked after; her habit of responsibility was ingrained.

'No,' she said. 'But I'm sure he wouldn't like a clinging wife. And I could look after him much better here than I could in London. There's Dr Ellery, for one thing.'

'Oh, I wasn't thinking of his health,' her father said. 'His health's good, isn't it?'

'Yes, except that he gets rather easily tired, and that upsets his nerves. He's rather highly-strung.'

'Nerves?' exclaimed Mr Pennefather horrified. 'Does he suffer from nerves?'

'Oh, only sometimes,' said Margaret, 'when he gets over-tired. Many people do, Daddy; he isn't the only one.'

'And don't you think that going up and down to London every day will tire him more?'

'But he will have the week-ends here!' cried Margaret.

'Yes, he will.' Again her father sighed, and this time his sigh was a capitulation. It seemed so ironical and topsy-turvy that he should be urging her to live away from him, and she should be urging him to let her live with him. But since she wished it so—

Margaret prevailed, for she had the stronger will and, *au fond*, both their minds were possessed by the same vision – a continuance of the life they enjoyed at Fair Haven, with only one small innovation to disturb its wonted rhythm, Margaret's husband, Nick.

5

Nick proved unexpectedly amenable. He was so much in love with Margaret that any request of hers only made her dearer to him, and if the request seemed capricious or wilful or unreasonable, it only made her dearer still. Margaret had come to him primed with arguments but prepared to give way if he should refute them, for she respected his mind and was besides uncertain where the justice of the matter lay; she did not forget that until she had talked to her father she thought she had no right to ask Nick to make such a sacrifice. But he, strange to say, did not seem to regard it as a sacrifice. It would solve so many problems, he said; house, housekeeping, staff, some of the greatest material problems of modern life, would be automatically solved. Smiling he said that he had expected to marry into his wife's family; what would have grieved and disappointed him would have been if Mr Pennefather had shied at the idea of having a stranger to live with him. 'And perhaps when he sees me,' said Nick, 'he won't want to after all.'

But Mr Pennefather was delighted with Nick; he had never liked a young man better. He had meant to get out his best wine in any case; now he wished it was even better than it was. He knew a good deal about the Bar; Nick knew a good deal about business; and as it turned out they discovered common acquaintances in both fields, so that their men's talk, which might have been boring to Margaret, was liberally besprinkled with names, many of which, having often been mentioned by both parties, meant something to her. Moreover she herself was a business woman; her work had brought her into contact with affairs; she had the respect for the practical issues of life that most women have, and an ability to grasp them beyond the reach of most women. As she listened to them talking, she felt a touch of maternal amusement, as if she were already a mother watching her children playing with their toys; but she also felt, and perhaps more keenly, a pride that they could understand so well, and talk so interestingly, about the things that were at the heart of a man's life – things which to understand, and be good at, made the difference between success and failure. Her father had been successful in his business; Nick was earmarked for success; here she was between their two outstanding capacities, like a figure in one of the allegorical groups that Nick had shown her at the National Gallery, glancing at each in turn, flattered to be the mirror in which they saw their success reflected, the presiding divinity who could award them each a prize.

Indeed, in the course of that enchanted week-end, Nick appeared first as a son-in-law and then as a son, the son Mr Pennefather had never had; and it was not surprising – so suggestible are our emotions at such times – that Margaret began to feel for him something of a sisterly affection, as if he had been the brother that she had never had. And as a sister she felt some of the fondness that is not altogether akin to love, being protective and admiring and responsible, but self-preserving rather than self-annihilating, a conscious recognition of the familiar, rather than a bewildered confrontal of the strange. Nick at Fair Haven was the Nick of the Inner Temple, a place she still thought of with awe almost as a foreign country; but he was not the stranger who had come to her out of the unknown, with its thick darkness on him lit only by fugitive gleams that came she knew not whence; he was irradiated by a steady glow, familiar and controllable as the electric light of Fair Haven, which answered to the switch so punctually and showed a prospect of white and pink and gold with which she had grown up. It was wonderful, wonderful, that he fitted in so well; but the feeling of wonder passed, or began to pass, and with it some of the mystery of Nick's otherness. He had ceased to be a foreign country to her, that she must gropingly and tremblingly explore, and become a guest, a beloved guest; but with a guest's liability to make himself agreeable, to observe the ways of the house, to take on its atmosphere, to be grateful for its hospitality, even to be criticized by its standards. Within a few hours she began almost to take him for granted with the rest of her surroundings, and she had some excuse, for he seemed to take her for granted too, and did not always look up, much less stand up, when she came into the room, so deeply engaged was he in conversation with her father.

In reality Nick was not so adaptable as he tried to appear. He had no thought beyond Margaret and believed that the nearest way to her heart lay through her father. Had Mr Pennefather been an ogre he would still have played up to him. The relief of discovering that he was not made Nick even more attentive to him than he might otherwise have been. The idea of becoming an inmate of Fair Haven had not appealed to him when Margaret proposed it. He had taken the long view and the long view did not make it seem attractive. Now the long view was hidden by the short view – Mr Pennefather's amiability, the solid comforts of the house, and even the house itself, which could be appreciated in inverted commas. The fear that in the long run the arrangement would not work ceased to trouble him; it was enough that it worked to-day; and the swing-over in his feelings was as exhilarating as a sudden escape from danger. Moreover he felt quite sure that by identifying himself with Margaret's background he was doing what would please her most.

*

Stuart and Diana came to dinner on Sunday night. The occasion was discreetly festive, the air began to tingle, and a conversation developed of a type never before heard in the dining-room of Fair Haven – little jokes and innuendoes charged with mysterious meaning. Stuart and Diana were the ringleaders in this. The others were a little shy of it at first but they felt it would be ungracious not to follow where the devotees of Hymen led, and Stuart and Diana were privileged people, already radiant with the pearly nimbus of approaching marriage. Margaret and Nick had meant to break the news of their engagement later in the evening; it was to come like a bomb-shell; but in the first five minutes the demeanour of their guests showed that however it came it would not come as a surprise. All the same it was fun to keep up the pretence that this was a perfectly ordinary occasion, to postpone the revelation, and meanwhile to enjoy the conversation and parry the innuendoes – the honey-seeking, honey-laden words, fluttering like butterflies round a buddleia-bush. So with demure eyes and in all senses of the term disengaged faces Nick and Margaret maintained their role of an unattached couple until, after dinner, a kind of lull, a warning sense of imminent anti-climax, told Nick that the game had been played out. He caught Margaret's eye and waited for her to speak, but she could not, so he turned appealingly to her father. Dislocated by these manoeuvres the conversation faltered and ceased and Mr Pennefather said, 'I think Margaret has something to tell us,' but Margaret could not trust her voice and it was left to Nick to make the announcement.

After the congratulations and exclamations, the unblushing inconsistencies between feigned surprise and protestations of having known all along, healths were drunk and speeches called for. The latter were not forthcoming and for a few minutes the conversation degenerated into an almost imbecile babble in the course of which even Mr Pennefather was conscious of saying things so inept, remarks recalling baby-clothes and rattles, that afterwards he blushed for them. Laughter and giggling and even backslapping went on, and the room hummed with inarticulate noises all somehow suggestive of the happiness to come. But gradually a kind of order was restored, the mind to some extent resumed its sway, and the revellers, blinking and ashamed, began to think of something sensible to say. Diana was the first to recover herself. She addressed herself to her host. Suddenly she realized that what was fun for the younger generation might not be fun for him. The realization did not damp her spirits but expressed itself in the form of an apology.

'It's our fault, Mr Pennefather,' she said, her voice and features still not quite steady. 'You must blame us. We did it. None of this would ever have happened if we hadn't taken Nick and Margaret to see Colum McInnes in *Put Paid to It*.'

The wedding was fixed for the middle of July and insensibly, as the days passed, all Margaret's energies began to be directed to that event. Her meetings with Nick took on the nature of conferences between two generals making plans for a battle. Their own relationship was a little dulled and overshadowed by these preliminaries, they could no longer live for each other, they had somehow become the world's property and had to satisfy the world's demands by making a public sacrifice of their privacy. The intervention of Stuart and Diana's marriage, which at first seemed a distraction, soon increased the tension; they were next on the list, and must acquit themselves as well as or better than their predecessors. The exact amount of pomp to aim at was not easy to gauge. Mr Pennefather and Margaret were old-fashioned people who did not want a great deal of display. Stuart and Diana's wedding was a smart affair, in London; theirs would be at Dittingham – more homely, more regional, more rustic. This would mark a difference, do away with any disagreeable notion of competition: it would have the added recommendation, for Margaret, of advertising to her, as to everyone else, that she was not leaving her old home.

Yet how unreal, somehow, did she feel in the bustle of this pre-nuptial dream, in making all these practical arrangements that had so little to do with her true feelings, that often exhausted and diminished them! To have to meet Nick with a list of things to tell him, and remember afterwards all that she had forgotten to tell! He did what he could, he was kind and patient, but his work had first claim on his time and energy, and most of the details fell on her.

They decided to give a cocktail party before the wedding, a small flourish to bring together the friends and relations of the bride and bridegroom. Between them they managed to muster about eighty names, and the labour would not be thrown away, for the same list would serve the wedding invitations. Margaret found herself sending cards to friends she hadn't seen for years. One of these, a school-friend now married, had seen the announcement of Margaret's engagement in the paper and had written her a letter of congratulation phrased so movingly that it brought tears to her eyes. 'I shall love to come to your party,' the friend wound up, 'but as I've absolutely nothing to wear I must go to London for a day or two. Dearest Margaret, couldn't we meet and do a matinée? I'm such a country cousin I've no idea what's good, but I've always had a secret longing to see Colum McInnes and if you think you can bear it I'll get tickets for *The Robber Chief*. I won't ask your young man because I shall want to talk to you about him.'

Margaret, who was always punctual about answering letters, sat down at once, and it was quite clear to her what she meant to say. Thanks for the letter as heartfelt as she could make them, a warm acceptance of the invitation; but might it be another play instead of *The Robber Chief*, because she had seen that?

As she was coming to the last point, however, her pen stopped. To see the same play twice was money thrown away. One saw a play and talked about it, and then one saw another play and talked about it. That was what Nick and his friends did; that was the form.

But people *did* see the same play twice if they wanted to; sometimes they went many times to the same play. It would not hurt her to see *The Robber Chief* again; and it would be too bad to disappoint her friend, whose heart was obviously set on seeing it.

So Margaret said yes and as the time – it was only a day or two ahead – came nearer, she found herself thinking of the prospect with excitement. Not the play, of course, but the meeting with her old friend.

Even so, their reunion was unexpectedly emotional; they opened their hearts to each other as only women can; and when the curtain rose on the thieves' kitchen such resistance as Margaret had to the play's sentimental appeal was already undermined. Her friend, who, unlike Nick's friends was not a sophisticated playgoer, enjoyed it uncritically and wept through most of the last part; and Margaret, after a half-hearted struggle to maintain the stiff facade which had never sat comfortably on her, surprised herself by weeping too – she who never cried. She was dimly aware that she was weeping for something that was not in the play, for some sense of loss that the sight of Colum McInnes gave her.

Afterwards she could never remember at what point the turmoil in her labouring feelings gave birth to a resolve. Nick must invite Colum McInnes to their party, he must, he must. She had an intuition that he would not want to; how could she make her craving to meet the film-star plausible? The strength of her desire lent her subtlety. Nick lived in a world, or on the fringe of a world, at whose parties celebrities were welcome *qua* celebrities. It did not matter if they were strangers to their hosts. Bait was spread and they were angled for; and if they were hooked and landed the satisfaction of the anglers, though decorously concealed, was lively. Their presence made the party a success.

One or two very minor celebrities had already accepted invitations to their party, but no star of the magnitude of Colum McInnes.

Several times Margaret brought the subject to the tip of her tongue but could not get it further. Meanwhile she was aware of a change in her attitude to the party and even to the wedding itself. The meaning seemed to have gone out of them; their radiance was dimmed by a brighter, nearer light. She went about her preparations for them like an automaton. She asked herself what she really wanted, and replied, I want to meet Colum McInnes just once. I do not want to meet him ever again. But unless I meet him I shall have no heart for what lies before me. I shall be like someone going on a long journey with a message, who starts off without knowing what the message is. All of me that matters will be left behind on the further shore. I shall have lost the key to my personality, I shall travel without myself.

Margaret was unused to introspection and totally without experience of the power of an obsessive thought. Nick soon noticed that she was not looking well.

'I'm afraid all this excitement and rushing to and fro are wearing you out, my darling,' he said.

Margaret could not meet his eye.

'I don't feel quite well. Perhaps it's the heat.'

'Couldn't you knock off for a bit and take a rest?'

'I don't think I can. There's still a lot to be done.' She spoke listlessly; but suddenly she had an idea and said, with more animation, 'We haven't sent out all the invitations to the party yet.'

'Oh, I thought we had.'

'No, there are still one or two . . . Nick?' Her mind was awhirl with shooting lights, clouds of grey vapour coiling and uncoiling, and a noise like the thunder of waterfalls.

'Um?' he said.

She ventured shakily, 'I wonder if we could ask Colum McInnes?'

She saw him stiffen.

'Colum McInnes? But why should we ask him?'

'Well, he used to be a friend of yours.'

Nick looked across at her and then down at his plate. They had finished luncheon and in a moment the waiter would be bringing them their coffee. Nick shrugged his shoulders and a look of obstinacy crept into his eyes.

'If he came, it would spoil the party.'

'Oh why? I should have thought it would be the making of it.'

'But don't you see? Apart from the fact that I don't like him and don't think you would, either, he'd throw the whole thing out of focus – people would be staring at him and wanting to be introduced to him. He'd be lionized. We shouldn't get a look in. It would be his party, not ours.'

'Oh, I don't think so, Nick, he isn't as famous as all that.'

'And besides he wouldn't come.'

'We can't be sure unless we ask him.' Their coffee appeared, and Nick moodily scooped into his cup the exiguous post-war sugar-ration.

'He's not our sort at all,' he said.

'Yes, I know . . . and I . . . I remember what you told me. But among so many people we should hardly speak to him.'

'Then why bother to ask him?' The arguing, almost hectoring tone, which he so seldom used, edged his voice. It was a sign of nerves, she knew, but she disregarded it.

43

'I was thinking,' she said desperately, 'partly of your career. It's good for you to be known by as many people as possible, isn't it? And specially by important people. Having him would be a sort of . . . feather in our cap. We have asked several people you don't know very well because they . . . well, have influence.'

'He's not the sort of feather I should want to wear,' Nick said. 'And what would he think of me, asking him after all this time, just because he's famous? I don't want to get the reputation of a tuft-hunter, and I don't suppose you do.' It was almost the first time he had spoken unkindly to her, and horrified she realized they were on the verge of a quarrel. But though she had exhausted all her arguments she could not let the matter drop.

'Oh Nick, I . . . I don't know why, but I feel so strongly about it. I feel as though we should be missing some great opportunity . . . It's such a small thing . . . just to send a card. Please, please do it for my sake.'

Nick tossed his head back and let his hand fall hard against his thigh.

'Really, Margaret, I hate to disappoint you, but I'm afraid I must say no.'

He turned away from her, so as not to see her downcast face and reproachful eyes in which the tears were already glittering.

Later in the afternoon Margaret went home. Tired and tear-stained she let herself quietly into the house and went straight to her blue-upholstered writing room. On the table lay a pile of invitation cards. She took one. 'Miss Margaret Pennefather and Mr Nicholas Burden request the pleasure of——'s company at the Dorchester Hotel.' With trembling fingers she wrote 'Mr Colum McInnes' in the blank space. She knew where to send it, for she had long ago looked up the address in the London Telephone Directory.

6

Alternating fits of elation and misgiving succeeded this defiant deed. Elation came first: she had acted, and that is in itself a powerful sedative. She would never have to reproach herself with a missed opportunity. She would meet Colum McInnes and say a few words to him and that was all she wanted.

But soon a voice whispered to her that he would not come. Nick had said he wouldn't, and why should he? Vaguely she believed that actors whether on the stage or on the films were endowed with endless leisure; but why should he want to come to a party where he would know nobody?

And how much better, really, if he didn't come! Nick was right: their party would not be nearly grand enough to assimilate such a formidable morsel. Hitherto she had been looking forward to it with mixed feelings, of which fear was certainly not one: it was just another preliminary to be gone through, a stepping-stone to the great event that was to take place a week later. It had needed some organizing and would confer the sense of satisfaction that a successful piece of organizing gives. It would not seriously disturb the rhythm of her being, cherished and conserved for twenty-eight years. At least it wouldn't, if Colum McInnes didn't come. And of course he wouldn't; she knew that now as well as if he had written to tell her so.

But supposing he did come? Ah then! This was a picture which, as often as she evoked it, was liable to end in exultation or in dread. Sometimes she had an intoxicating conversation with him, the other guests, forgotten, looking on; sometimes he just pushed past her on his way to Nick, whose hand he grasped, overwhelming him with so much public attention that all the other guests decided to instruct their solicitors to send him briefs; sometimes she never saw him but was told, afterwards, that he had just walked into the room and, bored, walked out.

Yet through all these moods of hope and fear persisted the fantasy of Colum McInnes, a rough little boy with ragged clothes and pleading eyes, a juvenile delinquent with a bad home background, who had never had a chance, but who had been brought up before her and to whom she was now going to lend a helping hand. No, he should not go to an Approved School if she could help it; she was going to try what kindness could do. She would, in a sense, adopt him; take him into her comfortable pretty house; and there, with Nick and her father helping, she would reform him, teach him to be clean, orderly, affectionate, and honest; and after years, many years, of good food, good example and good treatment and good education, he would emerge into the world, a good citizen.

So many goods! They warmed Margaret's heart whenever she thought of her small protégé, and she almost hypnotized herself with them.

She did have some twinges of conscience at the thought of having deceived Nick, if deceived was not too strong a word. She remembered uneasily that he had never refused her anything before. But she did not believe that he would really mind. He would not try to take the offence out of its context, and the context was trivial. He as a barrister, no less than she as a Justice of the Peace, knew that small deceptions were the stuff of everybody's lives. Moreover, she was used to getting her own way, and healthily enjoyed doing so; there was an added zest if her will prevailed over a man's – fascinating, necessary, but spoilt and mistaken creatures that they were.

*

Nick, she thought – and her thoughts of him went on, under or perhaps above the fantasies of Colum McInnes that sported in another department of her mind – was not a man who needed help. In external, practical things, yes, and she had gladly relieved him of most of the arrangements for the wedding. She had even taken their tickets for Brittany, where they were to spend their honeymoon: Nick had once been there on a reading party; he was a man of habit and wanted to revisit it. She had gone into the question of hotels and reserved their rooms. She had made arrangements for the car her father had given them as a wedding present to be taken under the protection of the A.A. at Southampton (Mr Pennefather's chauffeur was to drive them down to catch the night boat after the wedding). Sometimes she had consulted Nick, but sometimes, on small points, she had acted on her own account. She didn't think that many details had escaped her. It was thanks to her that Nick, who was very busy, had been able to work uninterruptedly through all the time of their engagement.

But in other less material ways he did not need her help. He needed her, she knew, but that was different. He did not need guidance or support from her, he did not need his personality building up or his self-esteem reviving; he did not need scolding or comforting or praising or excusing. In those ways she could do nothing for him. He was not and could never be an object of shame or pity. He might hold her hand and often did, but he would never put his head in her lap, for the sake of the comfort she could give him. And did she want him to? No, of course not; she was proud of his self-reliance and of the steel-tempered spirit that was sheathed in such a fragile envelope of flesh. And as the days passed this image ousted the other, and when the day for the party came, she hardly noticed, and certainly did not care, that Colum McInnes had not answered her invitation.

*

Margaret found herself enjoying the party far more than she had expected to. It did not affect her, as she thought it might, like a bazaar or a flag-day, with a sense of achievement triumphing over weariness; it was not a social effort from which she herself remained detached. It had a spirit and personality of its own which excited and transformed her. Never again, except on her wedding day, would so many people smile at her and seem pleased to see her. One can only feel like an idol by being treated like one; and Margaret rightly felt herself an object of devotion. Nearly everyone who knew her liked her, sometimes at a respectful distance, but she had been marked out as an old maid, and this sudden reversal of her rôle had a piquancy that gave a special flavour to the party, as though some goddess vowed to singleness had suddenly changed her mind. Margaret, unconsciously aware of this, had never looked prettier; her soft face glowed, and to her natural dignity was added a shyness that gave it grace. She was not a natural hostess, she had too anxious a sense of everybody's claims; she always felt she talked too much to one and not enough to another. But now she seemed to have got the way of it. She rescued the friendless from their nooks and corners and established them in conversations; she seemed to know instinctively when to break in and when to leave alone. Eyes turned towards her, and where she went the throng always seemed thickest.

Too tired after a hard day's work to make much social effort, Nick watched her dominate the scene. Almost for the first time in his life, he felt in harmony with himself and with the world. Latterly his life had been a succession of small triumphs, but they were all provisional – rungs on the ladder of ambition which, if they showed the ground receding, did not show the summit coming much nearer. Moreover they increased his responsibilities and his fear of falling. But now, in a sphere that meant much more to him, he had reached the top; he was absolved from further effort. And this success had been achieved at nobody's expense; nobody grudged it him; indeed, delight in his delight was written on every face. Gratitude to Margaret, to life, swelled up in him, obliterating the defences of his mind, disarming him entirely. Longing to share and testify to his happiness he looked round. Mr Pennefather was standing by himself. Nick went to join him.

'There's no doubt who's the centre of attraction, is there?' he said.

'Well, my boy,' said Mr Pennefather with a smile, 'I think the honours are pretty evenly divided.'

Nick shook his head. 'I'm not a glamorous figure,' he said. 'They can feel my wig and gown even if they can't see them. But Margaret—'

'She has blossomed out, hasn't she? her father said. 'But whose is the credit for that? Not hers, I think, and certainly not mine.'

Nick looked at him gratefully.

'Sometimes,' he said, 'now, for instance, I feel it's all too good to be true.'

'You may be sure we feel the same.' It had become second nature to Mr Pennefather to speak for his daughter as well as for himself. He turned his head. Some late arrivals were being announced.

'Mr Stanley Porteous!' roared a voice. They both watched Margaret going to the door to greet him. 'I must go too, I suppose,' Nick said, but before he had time to move he heard the voice cry even louder, and with every overtone of empressement as if this was indeed the climax of the party:

'Mr Colum McInnes!'

Mr Pennefather did not appear to take in the significance of the name, but nearly everyone else turned round, their faces lighting up with curiosity; and something like a hush fell. Nick went pale, and muttered, more to himself than to Mr

Pennefather, 'How the devil did that fellow get here?' With face transformed and fascinated eyes he watched Margaret greet the uninvited guest. Most of the party had retreated from the doorway, and were covertly staring at the film-star who, accustomed to the limelight, stood in an easy position that Nick remembered well, looking down at Margaret with a provocative smile, half mocking, half amused. A jagged flash of hatred tore at Nick. 'By God, I'll turn him out,' he said, and strode across the floor. McInnes saw him coming, and disengaging his eyes from Margaret moved to meet him with a frank and boyish smile that showed his teeth.

'My dear fellow,' he said, 'this is a pleasure!'

Nick just touched his outstretched hand and said in a low voice, 'How did you know that we were giving a party?'

'How did I know, my dear chap?' McInnes's voice, extraordinarily flexible and clear, registered amazement. 'Why, you invited me! I have your card on me, as it happens.' And very deliberately, with a curious fulness of gesture as though he was practising the movement, he pulled the card out of his breast-pocket and handed it to Nick.

Nick stared at it wonderingly; then, raising his eyes, he saw Margaret coming towards them with slow steps. She gave him a look half reproachful and half guilty and he completely lost his head.

'What does this mean?' he thundered, thrusting the card at Margaret but not looking at her.

'I think it must be a card you didn't know about,' murmured Margaret wretchedly.

'Know about it, of course I know about it, and I specially asked you not to send it!'

He threw out his hands with a gesture of mingled exasperation and despair and the card slipped from his fingers and fluttered down on to the floor between them.

'Excuse me,' the film-star said, and stooping down he picked the card up. Smiling at them both he carefully restored it to his pocket. 'It is mine, isn't it?' he said, 'and proves I'm not a gate-crasher?' Every word was audible to the onlookers. He bared his teeth a little, his eyes glittered dangerously, and the magnetism that had made him what he was surged through the room and rebounded from the walls. 'I have every right to stay,' he said, enjoying himself, 'but should not dream of doing so when my presence is distasteful to one of my hosts. To the other I tender my most sincere apologies.'

He turned and with his steel-sprung stride was making for the door when he heard a sound, a soft flop, too gentle for a thud. He stopped, and before anyone else had time to reach her he lifted Margaret in his arms and carried her to a gilt-framed, pink-upholstered sofa that might have come from the drawing-room at Fair Haven. There was a general movement in the direction of the sofa, but he checked it with his hand. 'Please give her air,' he said. Nick stood alone in the middle of the room, a picture of misery and irresolution. Then Mr Penne-father came to his side and gently guided him towards the sofa where Margaret, her head pillowed on Colum McInnes's arm, was already opening her eyes.

7

MARGARET saw Nick several times again after this, but the interviews were painful to them both. Both saw themselves as at once in the right and in the wrong, than which no state of mind is less likely to lead to reconciliation. The sense of being in the wrong wounds one's pride, the sense of being in the right inflames one's moral indignation. Nick was not a barrister or Margaret a J.P. for nothing. Both defended themselves; both felt that a question of principle was involved. Wives must not be deceitful and disobedient; husbands must not be bad-tempered and cruel. Soon it seemed that they cared more for their arguments than for each other. Long wearisome altercations took place as to whether Margaret had been deceitful or merely disobedient; whether Nick had been cruel and beastly or merely hasty and ill-mannered. As a result of this verbal wrangling each of them began to take up a position from which it was difficult to withdraw without loss of face. If they had not been so fond of each other they would have found it easier to forgive each other.

It was a deadlock. To the last Mr Pennefather struggled on the side of reconciliation and his counsels might have prevailed had not the papers taken up the incident and given it much prominence. For the most part they ignored the rights and wrongs of the case and concentrated on its sensational and romantic aspects. Not only the three chief participants, but Mr Pennefather and other guests as well were solicited for interviews by reporters. Margaret and Nick gave garbled and unwilling versions, but Colum McInnes was much more forth-coming, and in most of the accounts appeared not only the in-jured party, which he was, but a hero and knighterrant, the Bayard of the film world. While her curmudgeonly fiancé had stood looking on, he had rescued Margaret and rendered her first-aid. Exerting his natural authority he had kept the crowd back, thereby facilitating her recovery.

Margaret, too, had a good Press. The Portia of Dittingham, one newspaper called her, in allusion to her precocious appoint-ment to the Bench; and she was variously described as the Lady Bountiful and Fairy-godmother of the district. Her public spirit and readiness to help the needy were much insisted on; also her fair good looks, which pleased every reporter. Nor was the fact that she was an heiress omitted, indeed it was dwelt upon with enthusiasm, and magnified. Even left-wing papers did not hold it against her, so closely was it associated with public service. The reporters were gallant men and though Margaret told them, with shamefaced truthfulness, that her fiancé had forbid-den her to send the invitation, they left this out, or represented it as a natural weakness which any admirer of Colum McInnes could easily forgive. Margaret, it was suggested, was one of his most whole-hearted fans; and who could blame her for wanting to have him at her cocktail party?

Nick came out of it very badly and might have come out worse if he had not been a barrister and therefore presumed to under-stand the law of libel. 'Film-star rescues heiress: fiancé looks on' was one of the least wounding headlines. For his own sake as well as Margaret's he did not want to dwell on having banned McInnes from the party; it would make him look insanely jeal-ous. So he contented himself with saying that he had wished the party to be for their personal friends, of whom McInnes, though it was true he had known him at school, was never one. When he saw the uninvited guest he lost his temper, as other people had done in similar circumstances. Had he known Miss Pennefather had invited McInnes he would, he said not quite truthfully, have minded very much less. No, he did not know how the incident would affect their future relationship. That was still under consideration.

The plea of jealousy would have gone down better with the public, who now saw Nick simply as a weak, irascible man quite unworthy of his delightful bride. Several people whom he did not know wrote to tell him this. He would never get on at the Bar, they assured him, unless he learned to control his temper, and they advised him to take up another calling, and even to go to another country. Whoever they employed to do their legal business for them, they intimated that it would not be Nick – and they were sure that all right-minded people felt as they did.

But if Nick smarted under the lash of publicity, Margaret found its caresses hardly less distasteful. To have her Christian name bandied about (for she was always 'Margaret' to the story-hunters – assuming for a day or two the prerogative of the Princess), her private mortification advertized, her eligibility enlarged upon, her home life dragged into the lime-light, it was too much. Scores of strangers wrote to her expressing sympathy and not a few proposed immediate marriage. 'I may not be up to much,' one of them said, 'but if you marry me you can give drinks to any film-star that takes your fancy.'

She who had only once before been seriously worried by nerves, now began to develop all kinds of neurasthenic symptoms – loss of appetite, loss of sleep, and most inconvenient of all, an invincible repugnance to putting her foot outside the garden gate. She had few close friends in Dittingham; she was on terms of nods and smiles and little chats with almost everyone she met; and thinking of the different greetings she would now receive – the shy looks and expressions of embarrassed sympathy, she simply could not face them. If she ran the gaunt-let she suffered afterwards from nervous tremors, lasting sometimes for an hour or two.

But she could not take to her bed for there was too much to be done – too many letters and telegrams to be sent. All the edifice of happiness so laboriously built up with loving touches, now had to be pulled down piecemeal. She might have asked Nick to do this for her, or some of it; but she had been the organiser all along and he would not know where to start. Besides she did not want to be beholden to him for help, she did not want to write to him, and also – for she still kept her conscientiousness and her sense of the paramount importance of a man's career – she did not want to interrupt his work. When she thought of the biggest task of all, the return of the wedding presents with which the house was stacked and which still continued to dribble in, she felt as though the current of her life had reached an impassable obstacle and would stop.

Diana, who would have come to her rescue, and somehow, she knew, put a less hopeless and gloomy complexion on the affair was abroad on her honeymoon; indeed one of the minor crosses Margaret had to bear was Diana's ecstatic letter from Rapallo, dilating on the joys of her married life and auguring the same for Margaret.

But perhaps her chief concern was for her father. Mr Penne-father had taken the whole thing very hard and looked years older. He had been, and still was, devoted to Nick; and though he gave his daughter all the sympathy he could, she knew that in his heart he felt she was a good deal to blame. He was her only confidant; her tongue itched to talk to him – if only she could have done that for hours and hours, whenever and wher-ever she felt like it, so that from sheer weariness and boredom she would never have to think of them again! But though he listened patiently to her outpourings they seemed to drain him physically, increasing his pallor and brittle, fragile look. She could not bear it that he did not see the thing from her angle; they had never had a disagreement of the heart before.

'But I didn't deceive him!' she wailed. 'I only disobeyed him. I never promised him I wouldn't send the card. Even he admits that.'

Her father sighed and said,

'But what has all this got to do with love?'

A hunted look came into Margaret's eyes and the tremors threatened to begin again.

'You shouldn't blame me,' she said, 'if I'm old-fashioned enough to think that love *does* depend on mutual respect. At least that's one important condition of it. How can Nick and I love each other properly if he's always thinking I deceived him, and if I think he's unreasonable and bad-tempered and small-minded and inconsiderate and—'

'All these are arguments,' her father broke in. 'Love isn't a question of settling an argument, much less of winning one. It's a state of mind and heart and senses. Do believe me, my dear, all you have had is a lover's quarrel – I only wish you had had more of them, and sooner. They are safety-valves invented by Nature to preserve a difficult relationship. Your dear mother and I had a great many.'

'But yours didn't get into the newspapers,' Margaret took him up, for the conversation was following a pattern only too familiar to her.

Her father passed his hand across his eyes. 'I agree that makes it more difficult for you both, my dear, but it doesn't change the situation radically. The Press has a great deal of power, we know, but it can't forbid you to make up a quarrel.'

'You talk as if it was only I who wanted to break off the engagement, Daddy,' protested Margaret, her voice struggling with tears. 'It's him just as much as me. More, really. And it's nonsense to say the papers haven't affected the situation fundamentally – they have. Nick says that everyone now thinks he is a fortune-hunter trying to marry me for my money. It's most unfair on him of course, and may ruin his career.'

'Did he tell you so?'

'No, but isn't it obvious?'

'I don't think it is at all obvious,' said her father with more animation than he had yet shown. 'In my view it would be far worse if a few people, whose judgment you respected, thought so unjustly of Nick. What does it matter what the riff-raff say? They'll forget all about it to-morrow.' He glanced at his daughter interrogatively, and finding no response looked away, unhappily aware that the more they argued the further from each other they became. 'I wonder how it got into the papers at all?' he said, to change the subject.

'I told you, Daddy. Quite a lot of Nick's friends are journalists and they were all at the party. It might have been any of them, he says. He says he'll never trust a journalist again,' she went on, seriously. 'He can't tell – that's partly why he's so unhappy – he has to suspect them all. It might be them and it might be . . . it might be . . .' – she stopped.

'Who?'

'Well, Colum McInnes.'

Her father's face stiffened with dislike. 'I think that's much more probable. A man of that sort must have his finger on every pulse in Fleet Street. If they have pulses,' he added vindictively.

'Somehow I don't think it was him,' said Margaret. 'Surely it wouldn't be worth his while. And he seemed so nice.' Her father said nothing, then tried a last appeal.

'My dearest child, do try to think of it all as an illness that will pass and leave you as you were before. You know how it is with a toothache – you feel it is the only reality and you will never be free from pain. But you are – you are. Suddenly the pain stops and you are yourself again and it all seems like a dream. You and Nick were in love with each other, I am sure you were. From the way you talk about him I can tell that you still care for him. Surely that is the only thing that matters? And I could swear that the real reason that he speaks and feels bitterly, as you say he does, is *not* what happened at the party, or afterwards, it is the temporary interruption to his love for you that makes him unhappy, the fact that his true self is hidden from him – as one's health is hidden from one in a fever – and he can't find it. That's what upsets him – to be forced to behave out of his real character. I'm sure if you could see him now, sitting in his chambers, all of him – except perhaps the surface of his mind, which is covered with spots like measles – is really thinking of you and longing to be with you, and cursing the infection which makes him strange to you and to himself. Have faith – you must have faith.'

He stopped, almost breathless. Margaret tried to see the image as he evoked it but her mind and feelings were too tired and strained to entertain it. She was imprisoned by the circumstances of the Now, and could not imagine them different, any more than a lost traveller can imagine the sun at midnight.

Mr Pennefather realized that his appeal had failed, but he went on, 'At any rate promise me that you will see him again before you decide to do anything irrevocable.'

Margaret promised, and the next day lunched with Nick in London. Both were very considerate to each other; both refrained from the recriminations which had marred their previous meetings. They talked rather sadly, like old friends who have been overtaken by a common misfortune. But everything between them, they felt, was controversial, and avoiding that they had nothing to say to each other. The minutes dragged, heavy with defeat and frustration.

'My father is very sad about us,' Margaret said at length. 'I . . . I do so hate to disappoint him.'

'So do I,' said Nick.

'Could we, perhaps . . . ?' A quiver of hope trembled in her voice.

They looked at each other, at the faces which no longer kindled to each other's glances, responding only to some dreary monitor from within.

'I don't think so, Margaret. I don't believe either of us really wants it.'

Hearing him say this, she believed it to be true. The longing for finality that had been besieging her for days returned with overwhelming force; she drew off her diamond engagement ring and said,

'Then may I give you this?'

He nodded and almost absently slipped it into his trouser pocket.

8

THE uncertainty had been the most immediately torturing thing, and when it was over Margaret felt more herself. Decided by nature, she was particularly unfitted to flounder in the quicksands of half measures. Now that her life had regained its forward movement, the actual processes of living came easier. To cancel was better than to postpone. The nervous strain was over.

But when the life of Dittingham began to stir around her, making its familiar voices heard, and she took out the diary that for weeks she had used to record such different engagements, she began to realize what she had lost. Freed from nervous stresses, her emotions began to reassert themselves. They had been enlarged and strengthened to meet experiences she had not known before. Unexercised now, they yearned and ached over a void which the busy miniature world of Dittingham, with its insistent calls on her attention, could not fill. Love is irreplaceable by other activities and refuses substitutes. Her manifold avocations in Dittingham did not add up to, could not even compete with, the treasure she had lost. The chatter of a flock of sparrows gives no comfort to an ear that has listened to the nightingale.

Habit and routine are powerful anodynes, but only when they yield an irreducible minimum of spiritual support. Whoever seeks their solace must be content with narrow horizons. Accustomed to wider prospects, Margaret was always looking over the edge of hers, and trying to use, for jobs which only needed an undivided mind, the spiritual force created by her love for Nick.

She felt a misfit, and the process of adjustment to a life of little things went slowly. She had grown so used to thinking of herself as a married woman that she had come to look on spinsters with a kind of pity. This pity she now felt turning on herself and was horrified, for self-pity was an emotion she had no use for, and indeed until recently had had no need of. In trying to banish it she was helped by a healthy reaction against those who let their pity for her show itself too plainly. A certain tartness of manner, designed to keep sympathisers at arm's length, was noticed by her friends and commented on. She saw that a woman who had, in effect, left Dittingham as a bride to return to it a maid might well excite compassion. But away with it! Better a virgin queen in Dittingham than a struggling bachelor's obscure consort. Her thoughts turned often towards Nick, for only to him could they turn with something of their old fulness. Yet they never quite reached him, so many barriers still stood between. With her father, the only other human being who might have wooed her from herself, she was still uneasy. They felt guilty and constrained in each other's presence.

But lacking a wind to raise them the Atlantic rollers began to die away; soon they might moderate to the ripples required for tea-cup storms. Sometimes she welcomed this contraction of her being as a sign that the savour was returning to the life she had resumed, a life in which, now, the happiest moment was the moment when she turned out her bedside-lamp and shut her eyes.

One morning, about a fortnight after the public announcement that her marriage with Mr Nicholas Burden would not now take place, a letter came for Margaret. With their gradual discontinuance she was beginning to lose her dread of letters addressed to her in an unknown hand. This one intrigued her by the size of the envelope and the thickness of the paper, on which her name appeared in a dashing scrawl. She opened it and read:

Dear Miss Pennefather,

As the unwitting and unwilling author of your misfortunes I have long felt I owed you an apology, and I should have written before to express my regret had I not felt that in certain circumstances silence is the kindest thing. Also, although I was innocent of any wish to hurt you, I have seen enough of human nature to know that we do not always forgive those who, however inadvertently, have been the means of wounding us. And perhaps in your eyes I am not so guiltless as I should like to appear, having unintentionally committed the discourtesy of failing to answer your invitation. For that I think I did apologize during the few words which were permitted to us, and I still hope you have overlooked it as the lapse of a very busy and hard-working man, for busy and hardworking we are, whatever the public may think about us.

Nick is an old friend of mine, whose reception of me at the party I find difficult to account for, though God knows! not difficult to forgive. I can less easily forgive him for what I feel you must have suffered on and since that day. Our brief but tantalizing talk and the small service I was able to do you then perhaps hardly entitle me to make the request I am going to make, but I shall make it all the same. After all, one invitation excuses another. Will you do me the honour to lunch with me one day at my flat – I say my flat because there we shall be perfectly private and I am sure we neither of us desire a renewal of the attentions of the Press. Whether you feel able to accept or not, whether you reply or not, I shall still be

   Your injurious but invited guest
               (*with an indescribable flourish*)
                              COLUM McINNES

P.S. Please forgive my illegible handwriting. For reasons you will appreciate I preferred not to dictate this letter to my secretary.

P.P.S. Any day you care to name I shall make a point of keeping free.

Margaret's immediate reaction was to thrust the letter back into its envelope and hide it beneath the bedclothes. Ashamed of this childish behaviour she took it out, re-read it more slowly and, as she believed, more realistically. She reminded herself that she was twenty-eight, that she had just undergone an experience which showed her the danger of straying outside the habitual orbit of her thoughts and feelings. How had she got into her present position? By accepting an invitation to lunch with a strange man in London. Romance was always a dangerous draught, but Nick had seemed a much safer vessel for it than Colum McInnes would be. Better let her feelings alone to regain their normal tone. Dittingham was the true measure of her emotional capacity.

But surely she deluded herself? Was there anything romantic in the letter, except the adventitious aura of a film-star's name? Was it not, in the circumstances, only civil of him to write? Though he had nothing to reproach himself with, he had done what any magnanimous, imaginative man might do – given the circumstances. No doubt it was the price he paid for his celebrity, that every letter he wrote to a woman should have the effect of a love-letter. How vulgar-minded to suppose that it was anything more than an ordinary communication! He had far more excuse to ask her to lunch than she had had to invite him to her party. And as regards the incident itself, he was the only one of them whose conduct had been blameless.

Not to answer would be unpardonably rude. But how should she answer? She must not be caught again. Just a note of thanks, saying she was too busy to go up to London at present?

Margaret already had the writing-paper in her hand, and her pencil was trying out experimental sentences. 'So I am very sorry that in the circumstances I cannot accept your most kind invitation.' 'In the circumstances I feel I cannot accept your invitation at present.' 'It would be a great pleasure but I'm afraid for the present I must say no.'

So far her pre-breakfast self; but when the meal had run its course, outwardly indistinguishable from scores of others, but inwardly maimed by her awareness of her father's disappointment, which revived her own, she felt that to refuse would be to throw away a life-line. All the same, her letter of acceptance was as colourless as she could make it.

The flat was one of many whose uniform windows she had seen from below in a cliff-like soot-blackened brick wall. A manservant in an immaculate white coat announced her: his manner was so impersonal, so completely devoid of human attributes that she was surprised to hear him speak. 'Mr McInnes told me to say that he is very sorry but he may be a little late. Will you have some sherry or a cocktail?' he added in a routine voice. Margaret said she would like a cocktail. 'A dry Martini, a Bronx, a Manhattan or an Old-fashioned?' the man intoned in an indifferent sing-song, devoid of interrogation. 'A dry Martini,' said Margaret firmly. He bent down over the low table and mixed the drink in a glass jug with incredible deftness and speed; before she had time to think he was handing it to her, and before she had time to thank him he was gone. She sank down into a chair, so deep and soft she felt she would never get out of it, and looked round.

The room was a good size but not a good shape: the ceiling was low and seemed to press down on her. But what chiefly struck her was its air of highly organized disorder. On the table at her elbow was a collection of shiny American magazines;

two or three of them were open, casually as it seemed; but when she looked she saw pictures of films, and they were all films in which Colum McInnes was taking the chief part. Soon she discovered that his face, scowling, threatening, languishing, appealing, sad, sunny, wistful, was looking at her from all over the place. 'What can he be really like?' she thought confusedly; 'Which of them is he?' and the thought had scarcely crossed her mind when she heard his voice behind her.

'Good morning, Miss Pennefather. Am I dreadfully late?'

She started violently and struggled to get up out of the chair.

'No, no, *please*.' His expressive hands implored her to remain seated. 'I am so sorry I startled you,' and his square face lengthened in a look of intense concern. 'It's so bad for one to be startled, it upsets one for the day.' Gratefully Margaret sank back into the chair, and he went on, 'It's all my fault – you see, I have to practise so many noiseless entries I forget how to behave like an honest citizen.' He stamped his feet once or twice and the room shook. 'There, that's better. Now you know I'm here. And did Richards give you a drink? Yes, I see he did, and left some for me too. I don't drink much but this is a special occasion.' He raised the glass, looked over it and said, 'Now, what shall I wish you?'

Every idea that came into Margaret's head had to be at once discarded.

'Well,' he said, before she had time to feel embarrassed, 'I'll wish you happiness – that can do no one any harm.'

'And I'll wish you the same,' said Margaret.

At once his face saddened. 'Ah,' he said, 'you don't know what you say. But all the same!—' He tipped his head back slowly, revealing in all its beauty the line of his throat and jaw. From some impulse of imitation, Margaret also drained her glass.

'Good,' he exclaimed admiringly. 'You did that very well. Now we can have another. But first tell me, how do you like my room?'

'I really haven't had time—' Margaret began.

'I saw you looking at my photographs,' he said. 'This is the latest. What do you think of it?'

She recognized at once the features of the Robber Chief in mid-conversion, as it were. The mouth, under its thin line of moustache drooped sternly at the corners, but the eyes had a puzzled and defenceless look. The cheeks certainly needed a shave and the whole face would have been better for a wash.

Margaret glanced from the photograph to the original and smiled.

'Oh, it's no good comparing us,' the film-star said. 'It's not me, it's the Robber Chief. The public likes me with a two days' growth of beard. I think it's too sentimental, don't you? Not good box-office. I shall have to go back to the real rough stuff.'

'But *The Robber Chief* has been a great success, hasn't it?'

Colum McInnes shrugged his shoulders and threw his hands out.

'It took them unawares,' he said. 'They didn't quite know what to make of it. And it got me a section of the public I'd never had before – you know, the tender-hearted. I get lots of letters from them congratulating me on turning over a new leaf. But I get more from my old fans, saying "For God's sake cut out the Sunday School treat and go back to being a Borstal boy." Are you a film-goer, by the way?'

Margaret had to confess she wasn't.

'Good. I somehow thought you weren't. Now just for a moment try to imagine that you are, and tell me which of these you'd rather go and see.'

He went to the table, chose three or four more likenesses apparently at random, and gave them to her. Margaret tried to hold them fan-wise like a suit of cards, but they were too big, and she laid them side by side on both arms of the chair.

66

They all portrayed the actor in grim mood, and from what he had just told her she supposed he meant her to choose the one in which he had a scar on his face and a patch over his eye, or the one in which some of his teeth appeared to have been broken. She did not do this, however, but selected one in which the undeniable gaol-bird look was redeemed, for her, by a stubby pipe in the corner of the mouth and a sardonic twinkle in the eye.

'Bravo,' he said, 'I was hoping you'd choose that. It's one of my favourites. I'm sure your judgment is very sound,' he went on. 'I wasn't asking you just to let you study my manly beauty. But would you like one, by any chance?'

'I should indeed,' said Margaret.

'Then I'll give you a proper likeness.'

Suddenly his face grew very grave. He opened a drawer in a cabinet, found what he wanted, took it to his writing-table, scratched away a moment, and then as solemnly as if it was a prize, he gave it to her. 'So that you won't forget me,' he remarked.

He had written diagonally across the right-hand bottom corner, 'To Miss Margaret Pennefather from Colum McInnes.' She reddened and was too confused to take in more of the photograph than that it represented the subject in an ordinary lounge suit, looking radiantly handsome. She thought it was too big to go into her bag, but after some fumbling it just fitted. The clasp clicked on Colum McInnes.

'Thank you very much,' she said, breathlessly.

'The pleasure is mine,' said he. 'By the way, do you like being photographed yourself?'

With a pang she remembered the photograph she had had taken for Nick after their engagement, and wondered what he had done with it.

'Well,' she said, 'it's a little like going to the dentist.'

'Oh, you can't have been to the right man,' McInnes said. 'Try mine. Just say I sent you and I'll guarantee he'll do you something that you'll like. It's absolutely essential to have a good photograph for Press purposes. The one in the papers wasn't half good enough.' Margaret's face clouded over at the remembrance, and involuntarily she shook her head. Colum McInnes mistook her meaning and said earnestly, 'Of course, no fee . . . no fee. They'll be only too glad to do it gratis – for my sake . . . and for yours. No financial responsibility whatever! But I should like to make one condition, though.'

'What is it?' asked Margaret, apprehensively.

'That you will give me one of the photographs.'

'Oh yes,' said Margaret, relieved that it was a request with which she could so easily comply.

'Luncheon is served, sir,' said a voice behind them.

The Moselle was almost as colourless as water, and Margaret did not notice how often Richards was refilling her glass. The conversation seemed like an emanation of the wine, so subtly and revivingly did it penetrate into the thirsty corners of her being. Almost everything that Colum McInnes said surprised her, and by surprising pleased. This, too, was an intoxicating experience, for of late most of Margaret's conversations had followed well-worn lines, and she had come to think that the way of platitude was the only safe way. McInnes himself was a continual surprise. His face was never the same for two minutes together, it seemed to have a life of its own, independent of what he said. Margaret, too, felt her facial muscles stretching and contracting in a most unwonted manner. And this was not to be wondered at, for the questions with which he plied her, sometimes without waiting for the answers, were such as no one had ever put to her before. Most people respected her reserve; Colum McInnes did not, he ambushed it, and surprised out of her all sorts of preferences, prejudices, likes and dislikes that she did not know she possessed. More than once she suspected herself of inventing them in order to satisfy his curiosity, and to make herself appear more interesting than she was. Timidly she tried to copy his technique and make him talk about himself; but what seemed natural to him sounded, she thought, impertinent in her, and his life in all its bearings was so utterly remote from hers that she did not know where to drop her plummet. She did, however, gather from his answers, that he was far more interested in his present than in his past; he seemed to think that what he had been was of little consequence compared with what he was – and indeed she might have been excused if she had concluded that no episode in the thirty years of his experience had been so important to him as this one of lunching with her.

Her confidence grew as she saw her mood reflected in the hexagonal Venetian wine glasses, honey-coloured and faintly iridescent, and a thought insistently recurred – if only he would speak to her of Nick! There was as much dread as there was curiosity in the thought: she could not, she could not broach it to him; it was much too delicate, and whatever he said, she felt, she would resent for Nick's sake; but the wish to speak of it, and hear him speak of it, was as imperative as the instinct that takes the tongue to the sore place. So that when, with the appearance of a dish of peaches, he said, 'You know, I can't tell you how sorry I am for what happened between you and Nick,' she made no effort to check him, or, later, the tears which came into her eyes.

After luncheon, in the sitting-room, she did not refuse a thimbleful of brandy, so anxious was she not to lose the confidence of her confidences, or draw upon herself that cool, externalizing perception of what she was saying that would have summoned the policeman, reticence, from round the corner. Oh to keep her powers of self-criticism and of general censoriousness forever in abeyance, as Colum McInnes's seemed to be: for in the affection he felt or professed to feel for Nick there was no hint of disapproval. Indeed, he seemed to think that the emotions were a law unto themselves; people were as they were, and must be accepted as such. Even at school, he said, Nick was morbidly sensitive to public opinion: to be singular in any way was abhorrent to him, to be marked out for public censure was unbearable. 'He was like that, you know. Our friendship was a friendship of opposites. It couldn't have gone on after we left school.'

'I can understand that,' said Margaret. 'What I can't understand is . . . well, you know . . . his getting so angry at the party.'

By now she had told Colum McInnes everything that had led up to the incident, from her first sight of him in *Put Paid to It*. She had concealed nothing, not even the aversion she had then felt for him.

This seemed to amuse him. 'So you didn't take to me at first?' he said. 'I hope I'm making a better impression now.'

Margaret admitted that he was. 'You have been so generous about Nick,' she said. 'I feel I understand him much better than I did.' This was true; but it was not so much that she understood him better as that her view of him was softened by her admiration for his chivalrous opponent.

'You don't feel you could make it up with him?' the film-star said. 'Surely that would be the best thing to do?'

He bent his gaze on her in half teasing inquiry and Margaret thought: it might be a good thing perhaps, but not the best. Suddenly he put two fingers to his chin and seemed to ponder deeply.

'Supposing I asked him to meet you,' he said, 'do you think he would come?'

'You mean the three of us?'

'Well, yes, unless you preferred me to go away. Two's company, isn't it?'

Margaret agreed. 'But I don't think he would come,' she said. 'He seemed so—'. She stopped, unwilling to frame the thought, much less to utter it. And though she had felt so much more kindly to Nick, and indeed to all the world, only a moment before, every instinct she had cried out against Colum McInnes's proposal.

'He seemed so?' – the actor prompted her.

'Well, so set against you. I couldn't understand it.'

Colum McInnes chuckled, a hollow, almost staccato chuckle. His devotees would have known, what Margaret did not know, that it was a danger signal; when his enemies heard it, they knew they must watch out.

'I dare say I could explain that to you sometime,' he said. 'Not now, though. But if he won't meet me again, will you?'

'Yes,' said Margaret.

'You aren't prejudiced against me any more?'

'No.'

It seemed so natural for him to take her hand. When he had let it go, she sat still, looking at it, as if it was a stranger's. The pulse beat at her wrist, but the pulse of time beat too. She struggled to her feet. 'I had no idea—'

'Nor had I,' said he. 'And I don't like it now I have it.' He did not try to detain her, however. 'When shall I see you again?' he said.

But being back in time she felt the chill of time's realities.

'I'll write, I'll write,' she murmured.

'Mind you do,' he said. 'And don't forget the photograph, either. That's two things to remember.'

He escorted her to the door and closed it on her; she felt she had never been shown out of a room before, and it was not until the lift came softly to rest on the ground floor that she remembered she had not thanked him for her luncheon.

9

CLEAN breaks are sometimes easier to make than compromises: the spirit rebounds from opposition with vigour unimpaired, whereas to struggle through an undergrowth of half-hearted resistance saps its strength. Having once decided to marry Colum McInnes, Margaret felt she could make light of the obstacles.

She was very much in love with him, that was one reason – so much in love that she wondered whether she had really been in love with Nick at all. But she still thought she had; and just as the image of Colum had obsessed her with a secret longing through all the period of Nick's courtship, so now, in a very different way, she often thought of Nick. She did not long for him nor did she regret him; he seemed very remote from her in time, remoter than her far more distant past; yet he did not recede beyond a certain point, and she was conscious of him as something that had happened to her, irrevocable, with a claim on her that, though dormant now, might one day revive. She found she could talk about him without embarrassment to Stuart and Diana, who were in touch with him, and was relieved to hear that he was getting over his black fit, and finding solace and success in work. Her intense regard for the sacredness of a man's career was thus appeased; she could have almost better borne to hear that he was heartbroken than that his work had suffered.

She was relieved, too, that they did not blame her for what had happened; on the contrary they saw it, as she was trying to see it, as inevitable – an avalanche that had fallen on the mountaineers, through no fault of their own.

She did not, however, tell them about Colum McInnes for he had sworn her to secrecy; and though she suspected that he had let it out to some of his friends, or they had guessed it, she was resolved to stick to her side of the bargain. One thing she stipulated, and this he granted her, that she should tell her father.

She did not find this as difficult as she feared, for her emotions had grown tougher and the idea of crossing other people's wishes or hurting their feelings did not seem to her so terrible as it had. On the Bench she had always been able, without feeling too miserable, to take decisions which would be painful to other people, but then she was responsible not to herself but to abstract justice. The two departments of behaviour, the personal and the administrative, had been kept separate in her mind. At home she was one person, on the Bench another, and she had totally distinct standards for each. What would have shocked and horrified her had it happened to herself or anyone she knew would scarcely have made her turn a hair had she listened to it in her capacity of magistrate or social worker. At home she had been quite a severe moralist; on the Bench hardly a moralist at all. It was not so illogical after all, for the things that happened in the outside world did not happen in Fair Haven, or they had not happened, during twenty-eight years.

But now, to her comfort, she found she could borrow and appropriate to her private use some of the standards that hitherto she had kept exclusively for her administrative side, and the idea of telling her father that his daughter, having broken off her engagement with a serious, hard-working young man he thought the world of, was now going to marry a film-star notorious for his success in playing the parts of gangsters, crooks or worse, did not really appal her. Such things went on in the outside world, the world of the Bench and of social service committees, things far worse than that went on; and was it so frightful if a whiff of them now drifted through the closely fitting casements of Fair Haven, that had hitherto admitted nothing more strong-smelling than the scent of flowers?

Mr Pennefather had been a business man and a man of the world, but he had given that up fifteen years ago: he was seventy-five and the harsh sounds of the world were becoming indistinct to him. Moreover the world he remembered was the world before the second war, in which his standards were still respected, if they did not still prevail: it was the world before the Atom Bomb, the Concentration Camp, the Labour Camp, and the increase in crimes of violence and juvenile delinquency. It was a world in which people did not do these things. When Margaret broke to him her intention of marrying Colum McInnes he was horrified.

He even, reverting to the feelings of his youth, put on the heavy father; almost he forbade her to marry the film-star on pain of drawing down a father's curse. When this did not move her he tried other ways. Privately he made inquiries into the facts of Colum McInnes's past life. These facts, in spite of the actor's celebrity, were not very easy to come by, but Mr Pennefather unearthed a few. Did Margaret realize what kind of man it was whom she meant to marry? – a man of dubious antecedents, educated at a good public school but after that, what? Three years of 'travelling' all over the world, in the course of which he had been a sailor, a ship's fireman, a journalist, a lumberjack, a gold-prospector, and 'down and out in London, Paris, New York, Chicago and Buenos Aires'? Apparently the book of reference in which Mr Pennefather found these biographical curiosities gloried in them; but did they constitute the background of the kind of man one would want to marry? Margaret explained that she had heard all this and much more, from his own lips. 'He doesn't conceal anything – he isn't ashamed of his past life.'

'Evidently not,' said her father, almost with a snort. And he proceeded to read out a list of the films that Colum McInnes had taken part in from *Red-Handed*, *Kiss the Highwayman*, *The Grey Gangster*, *The Gangster's Girl* to *Put Paid to It*. Did they inspire confidence?

Margaret told him that she had seen very few of Colum's films. She had seen all she could, naturally, but most of them were out of commission; she would have to wait until they were revived to see them. 'And do try to believe, Daddy,' she said – for latterly she had been obliged to take a rather pompous tone with her father, his arguments against her marriage had seemed to her so childish – 'on the stage or on the screen, there really is no connexion at all between the sort of parts a man plays and the sort of man he is. Any actor or actress will tell you that. Do you suppose that writers of detective stories are likely to commit murders, just because they write about them? You enjoy books of that sort very much, or you used to – much more than I did. I'm sure you wouldn't have minded me marrying' – she instanced two of her father's favourites – 'if they'd asked me. Why object to Colum? It's just the same thing.'

'The writers you speak of would be too old for you,' her father was disingenuous enough to say, 'and on that ground alone I should be unwilling for you to marry them. But I don't think it is the same thing. A writer remains outside his book, an actor cannot remain outside his part.'

'But they do, Daddy, they do! Do you suppose that Ellen Terry, whom you used to admire so much, became like Lady Macbeth when she played her?'

'You have chosen a bad example,' her father said, 'and one that helps to prove my point. Ellen Terry was wonderful as Portia and Rosalind, she was not so good as Lady Macbeth, for the simple reason that she could not imagine herself being that kind of woman. And besides' – for he saw that Margaret was about to interrupt him – 'the legitimate stage has altogether different standards from the films. They have their peculiarities, and their laxities, of course, I should be the last to deny that, but they are real, solid people such as you might meet in ordinary life.'

'But Colum is on the legitimate stage!' cried Margaret, 'and he's very real and solid, as you'll see when you meet him.'

'I don't want to meet him, I don't want to meet him,' said Mr Pennefather, shaking his head fretfully. 'And there's another thing you forget. You may say what you like, but gangster films, or whatever they are called, do have a bad effect on the minds and morals of young people. Only this morning I was reading a letter in the *Times* to the effect that juvenile delinquency is enormously encouraged by the glamour attaching to crime in films of the type we have been discussing. You, as a Justice of the Peace, should know that.'

'But it's just what we *don't* know!' Margaret cried. 'Statistics are almost impossible to come by, and the evidence, such as it is, is contradictory and inconclusive.' She paused, for this was one of the few points which, whenever her father brought it up, left her uneasy. But she was beginning to feel that even this was just part of his bad case, his ridiculous old-fashioned prejudice against the cinema. She forgot that only a few weeks before he had been more open-minded about the cinema than she was; by trying to uproot his prejudices, she had uprooted her own, and even this stubborn one about the naughty children was beginning to lose its hold.

'And anyhow,' she said, 'no one can say that this last play isn't edifying. You see, he's quite converted and well . . . it would take too long to tell you, but I do wish you'd let me take you to see it. If you saw him in that you'd feel quite differently about him, I know you would.'

Mr Pennefather shook his head and shifted rebelliously in

his chair. 'I don't want to see him,' he repeated, 'I don't want to see him. Oh if only—!' he closed his eyes and drew a long breath. He felt himself old and impotent and disliked the obstructionist part he felt called upon to play. All this argument – he could not refrain from it, though he could see it was confirming his daughter in her folly. Words, words, how they betrayed the feelings, stripped them of their dignity and importance and seriousness. In all this bickering and taking sides the vital issues that were at stake got lost to view. Nick and Margaret had missed their certain happiness that way. The heart's reasons were silent; the mind's were woefully articulate, and could only express themselves in altercation. So he thought and so he believed; but what he said was:

'And I suppose you know that he's a Roman Catholic and has been married before? I thought that divorce wasn't permitted in the Roman Church?'

He had never taunted Margaret with this before, and as soon as the words were out he regretted them. No doubt Margaret did know; but if she didn't it was a cruel way of telling her.

'Of course I know, Daddy,' she said, and perversely he at once felt relieved. 'He makes no secret of it. But it was only a civil marriage . . . which doesn't count as a marriage with them. He's been legally divorced and will be free to marry me once certain formalities have been gone through.'

Mr Pennefather clenched and unclenched his fingers in distaste.

'And on the same terms, I suppose?'

'Oh no, we should be properly married.'

'Properly!' Mr Pennefather's scorn dwelt on the word.

He looked away from Margaret and let his eye dwell lovingly on the pink and gilt room, with all its cheerful, neat, expensive, comfortable appointments, and said,

'And what is to become of me?'

Margaret should have felt the pathos of this – the plea which he had never made before, which indeed he had violently repudiated when it was a question of her marrying Nick. Then, he had unselfishly embraced the lot of a lonely widower, for Nick's sake and hers. But now he flung his unhappiness at her, as if it was an ace of trumps that he was slamming on the table, or a form of blackmail she would be unable to resist; and the grief and bad conscience she felt about leaving him, lessened by her newly arrived at conviction that one could not make an important move in one's life without wounding someone, was swallowed up in a gush of indignation that he should take this unfair way of working on her feelings.

'Oh Daddy, you know how welcome you'll always be,' she said, 'to us in . . . wherever we are; and we shall come here often, if you'll only let us.'

She jumped up and almost ran from the room.

She was not, she was not a Goneril or a Regan: to that charge her heart gave her a ready answer. What did give her pause, in her father's catalogue of comminations, was a less obvious one.

That Colum was a Roman Catholic hardly worried her at all. Colum's religion was his own affair. She had been brought up in her father's creed of enlightened rationalism, and religious tolerance was one of its tenets. To Roman Catholics one must be specially tolerant, since they were so intolerant themselves. She had no Roman Catholic friends. Marrying Colum would be a little like marrying a foreigner. Each would have the other's neutrality to respect, and respect was a powerful and stabilizing factor in any relationship. Margaret was a great respecter of respect. 'My husband's an R.C. you know: I hope it won't be inconvenient, but he'll want to go to Mass on Sunday morning,' she would hear herself saying to a weekend hostess.

Then there were the promises she must make on behalf of her children, that they should be brought up Roman Catholics. About this she had felt more doubtful, for here her responsibility would begin. It was one thing to marry a Roman Catholic: it was another to bring perhaps several more Roman Catholics into the world. For the moment she would shelve her personal feelings. Was the Roman Church a good thing? Margaret gave much anxious thought to this question. A very Protestant nurse had brought her up to think that it was not; her father was prejudiced against it: he said that every Papist was a persecutor at heart. All the history books she had read at school proclaimed the Reformation as a deliverance. She had only to say the words Rome and Reformation over to herself to feel how the one chilled and the other warmed her. Roman Catholicism was a totalitarian religion and allowed the individual no liberty of conscience.

But times had changed. The world had recently seen new forms of totalitarian government, crueller far than the Papacy at its worst, governments which disavowed and disallowed morality, even of the rather debased and suspect kind which she believed to be taught by the Roman Church. The new alignment of the world, she had been told, might well be Communism versus the Roman Catholic Church. On which side would she enrol herself?

Well, it would be time to consider that problem when it arose, if it ever did. But there was an aspect of the subject which had an important bearing on the present, and one which Margaret had had many opportunities of observing at first hand – the unsatisfactory condition of children whose home life had no religious background – the little hooligans whose crimes of theft, arson, violence and wanton destruction were becoming an increasing anxiety to the public and the Bench. Statistics seemed to show – though Margaret, in common with her older colleagues was inclined to shake her head over the value of statistics – that this lamentable phenomenon of delinquency, or anti-social behaviour, as it was euphemistically termed, was less common among children whose home life had a religious background. It was undeniable that Roman Catholic children had more home life (for did not the Church insist on the importance of family ties?) and presumably more religious background than the others. She must try to find out whether they were also better-behaved. The only example she had to form a judgment on was Colum, and she couldn't think clearly about him. One part of her mind saw him proudly as the Bayard of the cinema world; another, more fondly perhaps, as a little boy of gangster propensities whom it would be her task in life to reform. In any case he was an exception. He had told her this himself – not that she wanted telling – when asking her if she minded making the promises for the children. 'I had no home life,' he said, 'I was just dragged up, you mustn't go by me.' What could Margaret do but kiss him and tell him she hoped that all her children would grow up exactly like him?

But when she was alone she still had doubts, and wondered whether religion was necessary for a religious background. The State seemed to think – and Margaret was much influenced by current official opinion – that the benefits of religion could be be obtained without religion. They could be produced synthetically by the efforts of psychiatrists to readjust the children to their social environment. Freed from the warping effects of early maladjustment they would not want to do these things. And this was undoubtedly the better way; far better to lead a good life (if such an old-fashioned term was permissible) as the expression of a free, unencumbered, socially integrated personality than to succeed in keeping out of the law courts by submitting to a so-called supernatural compulsion based on bribes and threats. Yes, but the psychiatrists' method was still in its experimental stage, and slow in showing results: what harm could there be in trying out the older way, even if the State was lukewarm towards it and science disowned it? If religion really was the price of a religious background, then the price must be paid. Margaret did not really believe it was, and of course in the case of her children the miracle would already be achieved; they would have a home-life, she would see to that, and they would have a religious background, for Margaret would hand on hers. Besides, the implications of the name 'Fair Haven' were sufficient guarantee that a child would be brought up properly; it would be surrounded by love, incoming love, and outgoing love, love of home, love of parents, love of friends, love of—

The word love seemed a solution and her mind did not bother to carry the idea any further. It did remind her that her children's upbringing might not take place at Fair Haven; but, her sanguine outlook told her, any home she made would be Fair Haven to her, and to them. Their moral state was already provided for by love – the love she felt for them in advance, the love she bore to Colum. And if he wanted this extra safeguard, if she could not have him (as it seemed she could not) without accepting for his children a framework of dogmatic Christianity, she would accept it. Even at the price of having religion imposed on a religious background, a flagrant case of putting the cart before the horse. It might make a slight barrier between her and them – this swinging of censers, jingling of rosaries, these solemn ritualistic antics, in which she had no part, conducted by spiritual directors garbed in black with whom she would never feel at ease; but for them it would only be a laborious and unnecessary process of painting the lily, and for her, a slight sacrifice of her natural dignity and authority. Sacrifice, self-sacrifice were words to conjure with; they made Margaret feel happier about the whole thing. Yes, she told Colum, she would gladly sign the promises.

And there for a time the matter rested. But one evening, after dinner, which as usual they had had alone – for the announcement of their engagement had not yet been made public and Colum still did not want them to be seen about together – he began to talk for the first time of their wedding, a subject that excited Margaret so much, and caused such confusion in her feelings, that she could hardly take in what he said. Venice, Venice, she kept hearing. And then it gradually came through to her that he was proposing that they should be married in Venice, at a church which had always specially taken his fancy. At first she could not catch the name, so he repeated it several times, almost with impatience, for he disliked being asked to repeat anything – 'the Salute, the Salute, Santa Maria della Salute. Everyone knows it.' Margaret humbly reminded him that she had never been to Venice; he had spoken to her of Venice before, as a possible place for their honeymoon. 'Honeymoon? Oh yes,' said he, as if someone else had made the proposal: 'everyone honeymoons in Venice. But very few people are married there.' Margaret said she supposed Venetians must be. At this he laughed heartily and generously: he never snubbed an attempted joke. 'But very few English people are,' he said, 'and don't you see, my darling,' suddenly he was very serious, 'that it would be ideal in *every* way?' Margaret said she didn't. Colum never resented her bewilderment; he liked his proposals to come as a surprise. 'But don't you see, we don't want to be married in London; it's so banal for one thing, and I have a hundred reasons for not wanting to be married in London. And you don't want to be married in Dittingham, so you say.' This was quite true; Margaret had not a hundred but several reasons – her father's attitude was one, the memory of her broken engagement another – for not wanting to be married in her home town. 'Don't you see we couldn't be married in England,' he went on, 'except perhaps at Gretna Green, and you wouldn't like that.

No, Venice is the place, and then we shall be right on the spot for our honeymoon. I don't mind spending our honeymoon in Venice as long as we can be married there.' She looked at him doubtfully: she knew the force of his caprices; they appeared to be much stronger than his long standing intentions or desires.

And why after all shouldn't they be married in Venice? It would be much nicer to be married in Venice in a church, and apparently a beautiful church, than in a registry office in England, in dismal secrecy, as if they had done something wrong, whereas they were each victims of circumstance, like scores of other people. Being with Colum had taught her to mistrust her habit of instinctively saying 'no' to any proposal that had the flavour of the unexpected; he was often right about what was enjoyable – a midnight drive down to an island in the Thames to bathe, for instance: how strongly she had opposed it and how madly she had enjoyed it! He said you should take life by surprise and she was beginning to believe that he was right.

'Of course I'll be married in that church,' she said, 'I'll be married anywhere you like. But how can you arrange it?' Her mind flew at once to ways and means and she remembered that a wedding takes a lot of planning: a church needs wooing like a bride before a bride can rustle down its aisle leaning on her father's arm.

'Oh, I'll manage it all right,' he said, 'I know someone in Venice who'll fix us up in a jiffy.'

Margaret was by now so well used to the idea of locked doors flying open at Colum's touch that she did not doubt his ability to perform this minor miracle. Why then did his mobile countenance still look so discouraged?

'What's the matter, dear?' she asked, tempted to adopt a wifely manner with him. 'Is there a snag you hadn't thought of?'

'There is a snag,' he answered. 'But I had thought of it. I've been thinking of it for some time.'

83

'What is it?'

'You're not a Catholic.'

Margaret was much relieved that it was nothing worse.

'But darling, you said it didn't matter as long as I made the promises.'

'I know, I know,' said he, 'it doesn't matter, except that if you're not a Catholic we can't be married in a Catholic church, at least not in the way I want to be. It will have to be a mixed marriage, with maimed rites, a few mutterings, hardly any music, a sermon telling us to behave as well as we can do in the circumstances, and then the church cleaners coming round with brooms to sweep us out.'

'What a shame!' said Margaret, her Protestant blood rising at the thought of this indignity.

'Yes, isn't it? And think – if you were a Catholic – that marvellous church, packed with distinguished and amusing people, all craning their necks. And the golden haze over the altar – thousands of dancing motes like tiny fire-flies – perhaps we could persuade them to use wax candles instead of those electric makeshifts that switch on and off. The nuptial mass is the most beautiful service – I don't think I could ever feel I had been properly married without it. It evokes all kinds of feelings, Margaret, that you didn't know were there but have always been there, for they are part of our religious inheritance.'

Margaret was moved by his calling her by her name, which he seldom did, using it rarely, like a jewel; and touched by the way he seemed to associate her experience with his, forgetting she was not of his religion. But his words went no deeper than that; they did not affect her present state of mind and feelings any more than if he had been an angel telling her what would have happened had there been no Fall.

'And think of the effect it would have!' he was saying. 'I don't mean the advertisement – that's a sordid word – but the réclame the wedding would give us, over the whole world! We should be in every picture paper in Europe and America!'

He glanced at her unresponsive face.

'I see you don't like that,' he said, 'nor do I, of course, really. But don't you see the picture of us walking down the broad flight of steps to our gondola, with the great door of the Salute open behind, and the dome rising above us – if they could get that in – it would reach quite a different sort of public from the one that thinks of me just as any old crook or gangster – it would give us another context altogether.'

He looked at her again and this time Margaret, though still regarding his eloquence as a decoration to an academic theme, showed that she felt more sympathy with it.

'It's you I'm thinking of more than myself,' he told her. 'I shouldn't want the world to get the idea that you were a sort of gangster's Moll – the sort of woman I associate with in my pictures. They couldn't – you know how strong suggestion is – if they saw you in that setting. And it's the only one that's worthy of you – it really is,' he vehemently declared.

Margaret smiled at him as she might have smiled at the pretty fancies of a child.

'And there's another thing,' he went on, 'you must forgive me for boring you with all this, but it means a lot to me. I'm not a good Catholic, Heaven knows, but I should like to do something – it may sound hysterical and superstitious to you – something to show I'm really on the side of the angels, something to glorify the Church, or if you don't like that, something to glorify God. It would be vulgar, I suppose,' he admitted, his voice changing as though with recognition of the type of human material that nowadays one has to work with – 'theatrical, cinema-stuff, but how else can one get an idea across, except by vulgarizing it? The idea would still be there, and the beauty too, and if I'm only Colum McInnes, a film-actor with no meaning of my own, you are the real thing – it might be a sham if I was the centre of a . . . a religious celebration, but it wouldn't be if you were!'

His voice rang with appeal, and at last Margaret realized that he was asking her to become a Roman Catholic. It was a great shock, the first real crisis they had had. She sat quite still, to recognize it, to face it, and then said,

'Darling Colum, I couldn't, you know, I really couldn't.'

Colum dropped the subject at once. As his face changed, so apparently did his thought. The rapt look disappeared; the lover's look came back. They talked of other things, silly things, in the tender language which Nick, a less accomplished mentor, had not known how to teach her. They mentioned Venice, quite casually, and not in connexion with the wedding: Colum said he was hoping to take a flat there for the honeymoon. They talked of her father, of his opposition to their marriage, and of devices by which his opposition might be overcome. These grew more and more fantastic: one of them was that Mr Pennefather should be offered a part in the film that Colum was to act in when *The Robber Chief* came off.

'What did you say it was to be called?' asked Margaret.

'*The Devil is so Distinguished*,' answered Colum, grinning.

'What is it about?'

'Oh, I couldn't tell you now, you wouldn't like it, but I'm in the name part and I'm a proper devil, I assure you, not a half-hearted one, as I am in *The Robber Chief*. People won't stand for that, you know.'

They both laughed, Margaret a little ruefully.

'I shall always think of you as "The Robber Chief",' she said.

'Well,' he teased her, 'the Devil's more distinguished.'

So the evening passed, an evening which, like other evenings with Colum, seemed to have no length in time, only a measureless content of delight. But just as something – some clock-tick in her unconscious mind – was warning her that it must soon be over, Colum suddenly said gently,

'Darling, I'm sorry if I worried you with that stuff about our wedding. It was all nonsense, really. Of course I wasn't asking you to become a Catholic just for the sake of a posh wedding. You understood that, didn't you?'

Bewildered by this sudden reopening of the subject Margaret told him she had understood.

'I oughtn't to have asked you, even in fun,' he said. 'It was a poor sort of joke. I hope you don't think the worse of me?'

'Dear Colum, no,' she assured him.

'The Church would be down on me, you know,' he said reflectively. 'We aren't encouraged to try to make converts – except of our wives, and you aren't my wife yet. Protestants think we are, but we aren't.'

'I don't see why not, since it's your religion,' Margaret said, perversely feeling called on to defend his Church.

'Yes, I know, but we aren't, and I shouldn't have, even in fun. The thing is, you see, I'm a bad Catholic, and somehow I felt—'

'Yes?' said Margaret.

'I oughtn't to say this either.'

Margaret smiled. 'Even if the Church forbids it, you have my leave to go on.'

'Well, I thought that if you were one too, a whole lot of things would be easier for me.'

Margaret thought a long time and then said, for the sake of saying something,

'What sort of things?'

'Oh!' he smiled at her. 'I could tell you more easily if you were a Catholic. Then we could share them; and what fun that would be for you! I'm the only Catholic that you know at all intimately, aren't I? And such a bad one, not an example that you'd want to follow! But you'd make a very good Catholic,' he added with conviction.

'Should I?' said Margaret.

'Yes, you would.'

At their next meeting Margaret told Colum that she might become a Roman Catholic after all.

10

DIANA TUFTON, as she now was, listened to Margaret's recital with her blue eyes popping from her head. It went on all teatime, and long after, to an accompaniment of ohs and ahs and other sounds more explosive and less articulate, in the very modern drawing-room, furnished with highly polished light woods bent into surprising but comfortable curves, of Stuart and Diana's new house. 'The Starting Point', they had facetiously called it, and it bordered the racecourse about three miles from Fair Haven. To begin with Margaret could hardly get any sense out of her friend, so overwhelmed was she by the romantic aspects of Margaret's engagement; but being practical and a woman of the world she presently emerged from this phase and began to regard Margaret's position from a more realistic standpoint.

'But you won't tell anyone else, will you?' Margaret begged, 'Colum said I could tell you but he doesn't want any one else to know.'

Diana nodded vigorously several times.

'But I expect they do know,' she said, 'you couldn't keep a thing like that secret.'

'There's been nothing about it in the papers,' said Margaret.

'So he's known how to muzzle the Press,' said Diana. 'That shows, doesn't it?' She meant, what an amount of influence Colum had; but both their minds flew back to Margaret's earlier engagement, which the Press had done so much to break up.

'Do you ever think of Nick at all?'

Margaret coloured.

'Yes, but not emotionally. I . . . I want him to get on and make a name. I should love to hear that he's doing well.'

'He is, Stuart says he is. He's working harder than ever. He gets a lot of work. Do you know, Margaret, I was wretched when I heard about it, for both your sakes, but now it seems to have been an inevitable stage in both your lives – you weren't meant for each other, that's clear, but without Nick you wouldn't have got into – how shall I say? – the Colum McInnes state of mind, and without you Nick wouldn't be going ahead as he is, by all accounts. Probably he's a natural bachelor – he must be, or he wouldn't have let that little rumpus at the party upset him so much. No real man would have let it influence him.'

'Daddy seemed to think it was my fault.'

'Masculine solidarity, my dear, masculine solidarity. Men always hang together. Your sweet Colum really *had* something to complain of and look how well he behaved. He might almost have been on the stage.'

'Yes,' breathed Margaret. The mere mention of Colum's name still had power to thrill her.

'But you say he doesn't let you see many of his friends. That's odd.'

'Well, I've met a few, but mostly people he doesn't know very well – he has such an enormous number of acquaintances. But not his cronies. He says they'd spread the news all over London.'

'The darling! I'm sure he's right. But you'll have to meet them sometime.'

'Oh yes,' said Margaret, uneasily.

'Oh well, I don't expect they'll eat you, but they're bound to be rather jealous. You must expect that. You must sharpen your claws, Margaret dear. And now he wants you to become a Roman Catholic. I think that's the oddest thing of all.'

'Why?' said Margaret, defensively.

'Oh, I don't know, it seems so incongruous in a film-star. If he'd wanted you to become a Mormon!—'

'I see what you mean,' said Margaret. 'But what would you do in my place?'

Diana fixed her eyes on vacancy and drew an audible breath. 'Have you told your father about it?'

'No, I couldn't discuss it with him. He's so unfair about Colum, as it is.' A thread of indignation quivered in Margaret's voice.

'If you became a Catholic Colum couldn't divorce you.'

'No.'

'But he divorced his first wife.'

'Yes, but it was only a civil marriage, and she wouldn't have any children.'

'What an awful woman. She can't have cared for him in the least. Do we know anything about her?'

'Only that she's married again.'

'The monster. I pictured her a vague divorcée. I hope she has a hundred children,' Diana said vindictively. She thought a moment and said in a different voice, 'It looks as if he was really fond of you, doesn't it, wanting to tie himself to you?'

With suitable casualness Margaret said she thought he was.

'But that mustn't prevent us being practical,' said Diana crisply. 'What is sauce for the gander is sauce for the goose, if you'll excuse my farmyard language. If you're a Catholic, you won't be able to divorce him either. Had you thought of that?'

Emotion thickening her voice Margaret was understood to say she had thought of it, but the question was purely hypothetical, it could never arise.

'I don't want to wound you,' said Diana, 'and you know I loved Colum McInnes long, long before you had even heard of him. I often tell Stuart he was the only man I ever loved. And as

91

long as I'm about, unless you keep him under lock and key, you'll never be really safe. But I must warn you, Margaret, that film-stars have been known to stray, and their wives have worn a highway to the divorce-court – Packards, Hispanos and Rolls Royces are skimming down it all day long.'

But Margaret didn't want to be caught up into the flippant tone of her friend's conversation. 'I shall never want to leave him,' she declared, 'unless he wants me to.'

'In that case,' said Diana, 'why don't you give way to him in this small matter?'

Feeling a change steal through the atmosphere of the room, Diana waited for her friend to speak.

'He doesn't insist on it,' Margaret said at last. 'He doesn't insist on it at all. He asked me as a kind of favour. I can hardly tell you – it was all very personal, something to do with the difficulties of his private life. He said that by becoming a Roman Catholic I should help him. He said he was a bad Catholic.'

'That sounds rather bad,' said Diana, shaking her head, and unconsciously adopting Margaret's serious tone.

'I expect it means something different with them, I don't think it means that he's a bad man. Whatever he did mean, I feel I can't disregard it. And yet I *don't* want to be "converted" – I mean, you know what I'm like – I go to Church but I'm not at all religious. Daddy's an old-fashioned agnostic and I suppose I take after him. If I was giving up something I really valued I should find it easier – if you understand me. Then it would be a sacrifice – now it feels like a betrayal, I don't know of what. I feel it would be a mockery and no good would come of it. And yet there it is, since Colum told me, I can't get it out of my mind. It's as if he'd started something that keeps nagging at me.'

Diana looked concerned and patted Margaret's hand. 'My dear,' she said, 'I really have no experience of these things *at all*.

It's quite left out of me. If Stuart had been a Hottentot and insisted on my being baptized one I should have just let them lead me to the font, or whatever they have. But if you have a conscientious objection to becoming a Roman Catholic, I see how difficult that is. Of course many people have,' she went on, looking round the room as though she could see them. 'You aren't peculiar in that respect. It's he who seems peculiar to me. I think you'd better *ask* somebody about it.' She dwelt heavily on the work 'ask'.

'Yes, but who?'

'Why not try Father McBane? He's rather a pet, by all accounts. My R.C. friends simply swear by him. He'd get you in in no time.'

'But I'm not sure I want him to,' wailed Margaret. 'In fact, I'm sure I don't.'

'Well, it wouldn't commit you just to give the old boy a trial,' Diana said. 'They all say he's a perfect lamb, except for just one thing. He doesn't like sin. He's much more down on it than some of them are, I gather. Penelope Carstairs cried for days after she'd confessed to him some little peccadillo that she'd done. Truly, she was a perfect *sight*. But she adores him just the same. You can consult him like a specialist, you needn't follow his advice. And he has this advantage – he lives in London, so no one need see you crossing his threshold and put it about that you are going over to Rome.'

'Could you get me his address?'

'Of course, darling, I'm only too glad to help in any way I can. Everything you've done lately has been a surprise, but this is the most unexpected development of all. I'm afraid it isn't really up my street.'

August was now well advanced. Colum did not again bring up the subject of their wedding, but Margaret knew he wanted it to be in September and there was little time to lose if she was to—

But was she? A mood of exasperated frustration seized her. Why, of all things, should this have happened to her? With whom did she feel irritated? Certainly not with Colum, indeed she liked him the better for what he wanted her to do, and liking is a delicious and not an inevitable concomitant of love. She could not be more in love with him but she was decidedly fonder of him. Was she then annoyed with herself? No, the situation had been forced on her, she had done nothing to bring it about. With the Roman Catholic Church? Well, perhaps a little, but apart from the futility of being annoyed with such an ancient and venerable institution, she could not pretend that it had done anything to put her in her present plight.

Destiny, destiny was to blame; but how ridiculous to feel, as certainly she did, a sense of personal grievance with what was surely an impersonal force? She was not so superstitious as to believe that destiny was hunting her, Margaret Pennefather, with special malevolence. Nor, though chafing at the restlessness and mental inconvenience it caused her, did she feel the force itself to be malevolent. She would be ready, in a way, to meet its wishes if only she could be certain what it was. It was not the force, she thought, that she resented, but the pressure it was putting on her to make her mind up. She did not want to make her mind up, and she lacked the necessary qualifications. It was as though she had been required, quite kindly but very firmly, to give her opinion on the merits of an unknown racehorse – to make a strong, positive, public declaration about something which she was totally ignorant of, and which was indifferent to her. Well, perhaps not quite indifferent, or why should she be so preoccupied by it?

The Rector of Dittingham was a good friend of hers. Every month or so he dined at Fair Haven. Sometimes he teased her for her rather perfunctory attendances at Church. He was the natural person to consult, and had she been a more regular church-goer she would perhaps have consulted him. But how could she expect him to believe in her spiritual needs? Her behaviour as a member of his flock had never given him the slightest reason to suppose she had any. He would require all his good manners to conceal his scepticism. And how could she ask a clergyman of the Church of England whether he recommended her to join the Church of Rome? As well ask a Roman Catholic priest whether he would advise her to join the Church of England. She knew in advance what he would say. But the attempt to clarify her position did not make it any easier to take action: rather the opposite.

At any rate if she went to Father McBane she would be spared some of the purely local and superficial embarrassment of a visit to her parish priest. She would be almost anonymous. It would not be Margaret Pennefather who was undergoing this penance (penance, what a word!) but just any woman.

She made the appointment by telephone, and kept it punctually. The street was not dark but the houses were tall and of a uniformly sombre hue. Still feeling aggrieved, she knew not with whom, she pressed the bell in the Gothic doorway. Oh, that this was over, she thought. A maid showed her into a study, not too well lighted, and Father McBane got up from his writing table and begged her to sit down. He was not an old boy but a sallow dark-haired man in early middle life, with eyes that kindled quickly. Overwhelmed with distaste for her mission, she could not tell whether she liked him or not.

'You came to see me?' – he said.

Margaret had rehearsed some of her part of the interview, and though she was nervous she had had too much experience of speaking to forget her cues. She proceeded, feeling gradually less strange.

'My fiancé, Colum McInnes – perhaps you know his name—'

'Oh yes,' the priest said, hurriedly, 'I don't live out of the world to that extent, you know. I've seen his pictures like everyone else. He is an interesting actor.'

At this Margaret felt more comfortable with him, more elastic in mind and speech, and readier to depart from the letter of her programme. But she still felt vaguely resentful and some of her resentment, she was sorry to find, seemed to be centred on this nice and sympathetic young man. He did not appear to be aware of this, however, and contented himself with making encouraging noises of understanding and assent until she had said her say.

'And what is it you want to ask me?' he said at last. It was the very sentence she had been dreading, for she did not really know.

'I suppose it is what you think I ought to do,' she said, her tone giving an ungracious inflection to the words.

He paused and said, 'Are you sure you have not made up your mind already?'

Have I been so rude? thought Margaret, conscience-stricken. What must he think of me? After all, this interview was of my seeking, not his. A busy man, he is giving me his time for nothing and I can't even be civil to him.

She said hesitatingly, 'No, no, Father' (the word, often rehearsed, came creakingly from her tongue), 'I didn't mean to give you that impression. I came for guidance. I have no prejudice or almost none against your Church; if I had, it would be easier for me. It's easier to turn from something to something than from nothing to something. I hope I shan't shock you if I say so, but I seem to have no religious impulses at all. It is that which makes me hesitate. Don't think that I wouldn't welcome them . . . if I had them, or that I hang back from any other motive.'

'What do you want to do?' the priest asked her.

Margaret puckered her face in the effort to answer this question truthfully.

'I wish I knew. As I told you, when he asked me it seemed utterly impossible. I never even gave the thing a thought. And though I naturally want everything he wants, I was slightly repelled by his thinking I should turn Catholic in order to have a . . . a grand wedding.'

'You were right to be,' the priest said.

'Oh, do you think so? It seems so natural to me now. He likes display, you see, and . . . and imposing spectacles, it's all part of his life. He can't help setting great store by appearances. And he knew that I have very little religion of my own, so he thought it wouldn't make any more difference to me than well . . . changing trains at a railway station.'

'Paris is well worth a mass.'

Margaret knit her brows.

'Yes, but he isn't cynical. He said afterwards that he'd only asked me in fun – to become a Catholic for the sake of the wedding, I mean – but I didn't quite believe him. I think he wanted me to become a Catholic for his sake.'

She hoped the priest's eye would light up at this, but all he said was, 'It is no doubt a better reason than the other.'

'Oh, but, excuse me,' cried Margaret, disappointed. 'Surely it is a *good* reason?' Then she produced her trump-card. 'He said he was a bad Catholic and that if I became Catholic—' She couldn't finish the sentence, the conclusion sounded too presumptuous.

'You would help him to be a better one?'

'Yes,' said Margaret, relieved that Father McBane had said it for her. Then she remembered something. 'What does it mean to be a bad Catholic, Father?'

'It means a Catholic who is lax in the performance of his religious duties.'

'Oh,' said Margaret, feeling as though a tooth had been drawn out, 'Only that? Nothing worse than that? You could be a bad Catholic but a good man?'

Father McBane took some time to answer this question. 'I don't say you couldn't,' he answered carefully. 'But no Catholic would regard it as a recommendation to be told that a co-religionist was a bad Catholic.'

Margaret's face fell, then brightened again. 'But surely all the more then I ought to try to help him, if it's going to be for his good,' she pleaded. 'It seems such a small thing to do for him.'

The priest shook his head. 'It isn't a small thing,' he said.

'I know, I know,' said Margaret, all contrition. She felt she had committed a breach of manners and the priest's feelings would be hurt by her slighting reference to matters which to him were of supreme importance. 'But I hope I've proved to you,' she said, 'that I really am serious, and not so . . . so frivolous as to come to you with my mind made up.'

'I don't think you're in the least frivolous,' the priest said. 'But I still think you came here with your mind made up, and that perhaps it's my duty to try to help you to unmake it.'

Margaret stared at him, and despite the warm August afternoon she felt a chill spreading from her spirit through her body.

'What do you mean?' she said.

'I mean,' said the priest, 'that you came here fully intending to make this . . . this sacrifice for the man you are going to marry.'

Margaret opened her eyes wide.

'I'm almost sure I didn't,' she said.

'I may be mistaken, of course,' the priest said gently, 'but that was the impression you gave me. And don't you now feel disappointed because I don't think you would be doing the right thing?'

In every nerve Margaret felt that this was true. She nodded.

'Well, then. It isn't that I think your reasons for wishing to become a Catholic are inadequate. Many people have had worse reasons for wanting to join our Church than yours. But you will forgive me if I say they are not quite the right reasons.' He looked at her interrogatively. 'You would not have contemplated taking this step if you had not met Mr McInnes?'

In this guise Margaret hardly recognized her adored Colum. 'No,' she said.

'Nor, even then, would you have thought of it unless he had asked you as a personal favour?'

'Oh,' cried Margaret, 'surely it was more than that! It was to help him to be . . .' the words stuck on her lips but she forced herself to say them . . . 'a better Catholic.'

Father McBane nodded. 'What I said was unjust. What I meant to say was, you were going to do it for love of him, not for the love of God.'

Margaret felt at once the truth of this, and it surprised her that the phrase 'the love of God' should have so much weight and meaning for her. It would not have had, a short time ago. But her disappointment stung her anew. Was she to be cheated out of this office of love for Colum, on the performance of which, with the bliss it was to bring her, she now realized she had set her heart, simply because of some fine theological distinction? Could not she love God through Colum? she asked the priest.

He would not quite say no.

'And,' she said, emboldened by this partial dialectical success, 'you said that it wouldn't have entered my head to try to join your Church if I hadn't fallen in love with Colum. That may be so. But doesn't the impulse towards religion always have to come from somewhere? Isn't the seed carried by the wind? And even if my motives were not the best, does it mean I couldn't become a good Catholic? *He* said I should be a good Catholic,' she added naively.

She hoped that Father McBane would say, 'Of course you would.' But he didn't; he sighed and suddenly looked sad and careworn. 'I wish we could leave him out of it,' he said. 'What are the alternatives before you, Miss Pennefather? You have told me so much about yourself, I feel you will not mind my asking you this question.'

Margaret's face showed her astonishment.

'To marry Colum, either as a Catholic or as . . . a Protestant.' Her voice grew shrill. 'It seems to me you would rather I married him as a Protestant,' she accused him.

'There is another alternative,' Father McBane said. 'You might not marry him at all.'

Margaret was furious. The whole interview had been so disappointing, so different from what she had expected; and now he was presuming to advise her about something which she had never asked him about and which was no concern of his. A twinge of conscience – for she had never satisfied her conscience that she ought to marry Colum – only added fuel to her wrath.

'Perhaps you would rather I was his mistress!' she exclaimed.

The priest confronted her outraged stare with gentle eyes. 'My daughter,' he said, and her heart heard but did not heed the beauty of the words, 'if you did not marry Colum McInnes, would you still wish to be a Catholic?'

Thoughts poured through Margaret's mind, tossed to and fro by emotions until they became unrecognizable. She started up in her chair.

'No!' she cried. 'Never! I would not dream of it.'

If it cost the priest anything to bite off a retort, he showed no sign.

'You are angry with me,' he said, 'and naturally. But, Miss Pennefather' (and she was almost disappointed that he did not again say 'my daughter'), 'do not think that I speak irresponsibly or that I enjoy putting difficulties in the way of someone who wants to join the Catholic Church. I could easily say, "Begin your instruction to-morrow," and I should like to, I should like to,' he repeated. 'But instead I must say that I think you would do well to wait, wait until you see your way more clearly.'

'Until after our wedding, you mean,' said Margaret.

'Yes, until some time after your wedding – your wedding to Mr McInnes, whose acting I so much admire.'

Margaret's anger had by now almost entirely evaporated under the influence of the priest's quiet authority and her own well-developed sense of fairness. She was having, she reminded herself, a consultation with a specialist – a free consultation: this fact did not fail to weigh with her – and could one be angry with a specialist for speaking plainly? She was ashamed of her outburst, of having lost control of her feelings and her manners. But there was nothing more to say; his time no doubt was precious and she must bring the interview to an end. 'I am very sorry, Father,' she said, 'that I spoke rudely to you just now. I'm afraid I got carried away. I am most grateful to you for your advice.' She reached out for her bag as though to rise, but the priest leaned back in his chair.

'You have been most patient,' he said, 'and under great provocation. And I should tell you now that another priest might give you another answer: we do not all think or speak alike.' He stopped to moisten his lips. 'And in spite of what you said,' he added, 'I don't think your wish to become a Catholic rests solely on your wish to serve your fiancé in the way that you rightly feel would be most valuable to him, nor do I think (may I say this?) that even if you didn't marry him you would lose it.' He looked at her hard. 'You told me you felt resentful.'

'I did for a moment,' Margaret said, 'and I apologize.'

'I didn't mean that. You told me at the outset that you felt resentful – not towards yourself, not towards your fiancé, not,' he smiled, 'towards me or towards the Church, but towards something – the force that had made you question yourself about these matters, that was urging you to take a decision about something you didn't want to decide about, that wanted something of you that you did not want to give, that was troubling your spiritual life. Am I right?'

'Yes, I did say so.'

'And that you didn't know whom you were feeling resentful towards?'

'I still don't know,' said Margaret.

'Then I think I can tell you, Miss Pennefather. It was God,' the priest said flatly.

'But why should I feel resentful towards God?' Margaret asked.

'Because He wants to bring you closer to Him,' said the priest.

He looked at her for a moment, his face impersonal and remote, and then turned away.

Margaret rose to her feet. She could think of nothing to say and merely to shake hands seemed inadequate. Suddenly she remembered the last item in her schedule, from which she had departed so widely, and began to fumble in her bag.

'For any charity you choose,' she said, offering him some notes.

'Thank you,' he said, almost automatically. 'I shall give it to the Poor Clares.' His face was exhausted and as soon as she had gone he dropped on his knees in prayer.

11

MARGARET dreaded Colum's visit to Fair Haven but she was determined it should take place. He, on the other hand, did not seem to dread it at all. 'I know I shall like your father,' he said, 'and I think he will like me when he sees me.' Margaret felt more than doubtful about this; Colum was nothing if not self-confident, and self-confidence was a quality her father did not care for either in men or women. 'I see,' said Colum, when she told him this, 'I will just be reasonably self-reliant, and no more.'

One of the reasons why she got on well with Colum was that it was easy to say no to him. Nick, with whom she sometimes compared him, was a difficult man to disagree with. He felt a minor disagreement as if it was a breach; he seemed to think their whole relationship threatened if he did not see eye to eye with her in the smallest matter, and he was too sensitive not to show it. Hurt, he appeared at his worst; sulky and spoilt, which he was not. His behaviour after the party had looked like an exhibition of pique, but Margaret was more and more convinced that what had really upset him was not so much his wounded feelings as his inability to hide them. Happy in her love for Colum she was able to make allowances for everybody, and Nick benefited retrospectively.

With Colum disagreements and refusals went like water off a duck's back. He would insist on having his own way, or would let her have hers, and the operation was as clean and antiseptic as if a surgeon had done it – no inflammatory edge was left behind. There were no sore places in their relationship.

So that if she had to tell him that on second thoughts she had decided not to become a Catholic (she would never tell him the real reason) she would have no cause to dread an 'inevitable unpleasantness', for there would be none. Her own disappointment at being deprived of the opportunity to do him a service would be the thing she would have to reckon with. But still she could not quite make up her mind – unmade for her, as she now realized, by the priest. Detached from his presence his persuasiveness had lost some of its force. With one hand he had taken from her something tangible – the hope of being of use to Colum; with the other he had given her something between a threat and a promise – the sound of a wind blowing in her mind, a footstep that might come nearer, an inarticulate voice that might one day speak. Was she still resentful towards it? She scarcely knew. The only sure way she knew of helping herself was to help others. It might not be as crude as the daily good deed of a boy scout, it might even be quite impersonal, as her public work was. But to give her spiritual satisfaction it must be the expression of a desire to be of advantage to other human beings. The idea of being in need of help herself was always a little distasteful to her; the idea of being in need of help from something not a person, for some inadequancy of which she was unaware, was completely alien. Yet the priest's words lingered in her mind.

At last the fateful Sunday came. Stuart and Diana were there to help her, but she was too nervous to talk much to them, and they were nervous too – even Diana had lost some of her aplomb. But most nervous of all was Mr Pennefather, who in the course of the morning twice changed his suit, from his habitual dark Sunday wear to a sports coat and flannel trousers, and then to an old suit of tussore silk which had not seen the light for many years and smelt of moth-balls. Margaret besought him to take it off but he was obdurate: in his heart he believed it had some kind of spiritual affinity with Hollywood.

At last they heard the gravel scrunch and Diana, who could not resist going to the window, saw a chromium and grey car drive up, sleek, shining and stream-lined, fulfilling her every expectation. Out jumped a chauffeur, whose grey uniform, matching the car, gave a new and even more formidable meaning to the word smart, and whose movements suggested quicksilver under strong control. The door was opened with the precision of a military exercise and Colum stepped out. He, too, was wearing grey – an ash-grey check. The check was not offensive but Diana's keen eye noticed that the suit fitted him almost too well, making him look over-dressed. But being an impartial judge of clothes, she allowed for the fact that in the films and on the stage Colum was nearly always dressed in any old clothes a gangster could get hold of. Without a leather belt and a patch here and there and pockets ominously bulging he was almost bound to look too soigné.

The chauffeur dived into the car and produced a square parcel the size of a large hat-box. After a short discussion as to which of them should carry it the chauffeur took it, looking over the top of it with the outraged air that men who value their appearance sometimes wear when carrying a parcel. With measured tread he followed his master to the door, and out of Diana's sight. A moment later the parlour-maid announced the film-star.

Looking at him through their eyes, Margaret saw another Colum, a man hardly above middle height, shorter indeed than Stuart or her father, aggressively clean and healthy, whose vitality of movement and vividness of expression made him at once dominate the room. His hair grew in a natural V above his temples. It was a valuable asset – as valuable as the lurking shadows in the hollows under his cheek bones – when he wanted to look sinister. But that was not his object now. He carried himself as if he was a flag – something that everyone would want to look at, and he went through the introductions as though he was making a present of himself to each in turn, though his manner with each was different; courtly with Diana, breezy with Stuart and deferential – a decided dimming of the headlights – with his host. To Margaret he just bowed. One and all they felt their importance magnified and their awareness sharpened. That acquiescence in mediocrity and obscurity which dulls our faces and which we come to think of, however unwillingly, as a protection, was momentarily lifted, and they saw themselves not as well-to-do suburban nobodies, who would never be anything else, but as people with the world's spot-light on them, people worth watching. Colum was generous in many ways, but especially in his readiness to invest with his own lustre anyone he talked to. When he spoke of the celebrities he had met he managed to imply that the rest of the company had met them also; so that instead of these important names being a barrier to fence him off and arouse envy in the breasts of the less fortunate, they became a common meeting ground on the high places of fame.

Of Diana Colum did not have to make a conquest – from the first she was his slave, and even Stuart, after the inevitable interval of wondering whether he was quite a gentleman, concluded that it didn't greatly matter if he wasn't. If either of them thought of the parallel occasion, not many months before, when they had met to hail Margaret's engagement, they did not think of it with regret, still less with irony. Not from disloyalty to Nick, but from an unconscious respect for the decrees of life, which take no count of stragglers. And for Margaret the other celebration was as dim as a faded photograph beside a bright one. Only Mr Pennefather thought wistfully of it. Partly it was that he did not altogether relish being impressed in his own house, and partly too because the qualities that impressed were foreign to him. He had a predilection for the well-worn and the shabby, for things whose gloss had been rubbed off, revealing the sterling stuff below. Of this he had caught more than a glimpse in Nick; and Nick had fitted in; with Nick in it the house was like itself. But now he felt he might be anywhere. Everything was sharpened and accelerated and accentuated; everything was hard and bright and brittle; the very quality of the light seemed to have changed. It was a question of catching up, of being on time, of looking, laughing, answering, all at the right moment, and Mr Pennefather was not built for speed.

When they rose to go into the drawing-room for coffee, Colum asked his host if he might use this breathing space to give him a small present – 'not very small in size,' he said, approaching the parcel – for he had timed his inquiry to coincide with the exact moment when they would pass through the hall – 'but I'm afraid of very little intellectual content.' Permission given he lifted the parcel in his arms, incidentally demonstrating how the unwieldy cube could be carried with perfect grace, and glided behind it into the drawing-room. Here he immediately saw the one place where it would stand and not look awkward; and almost before they had time to wonder what was in it, or lament their cooling coffee, the wrappings fell away, to disclose what they at once saw was a cigar-cabinet. But a cigar-cabinet with a difference; for instead of the air of opulence, subdued or unabashed, that such objects usually have, this one with its glass knobs, its delicate grey colour, the fine lines ruled across its face, seemed effortlessly to proclaim the superiority of workmanship to wealth. It combined the charm of a model with the magnetism of a toy; and in some mysterious way, as presents so often do, it recalled in miniature its donor. Lost in admiration they crowded round it, touching it, exclaiming at the polish, the finish, the close fit of the little drawers; and when they looked up, there was Colum beside them, but the litter that bestrewed the floor had vanished.

Next morning it was found in the waste-paper basket, but how it got there was a mystery. No messiness, no fuss: the floor looked as though a carpet-sweeper had been over it. Even the box was nowhere to be seen. Later they wondered why they hadn't seen it, but at the time only the cabinet was visible and real: the conjuror's accessories had disappeared.

Margaret had told Colum of her father's weakness for cigars, so there was nothing miraculous in the aptness of his gift. No doubt Mr Pennefather guessed this, and was not too much startled by his prospective son-in-law's acumen. But as he sat inhaling one of the best cigars that the post-war world could offer, in the ceremonious silence demanded by such a treat, he did not feel inclined to look Colum's gift-horse in the mouth. It was much too pleasant in his own, for one thing, and, for another, Mr Pennefather had, for some time past, been steadily losing his opposition to the match. He accepted it as inevitable, and besides, his nature craved a return to his old relationship with Margaret. Any olive branch that Colum offered he would have met half-way. Here was the olive branch, a veritable pipe of peace. His mind grew too drowsy to choose its metaphors. Life is not a matter of smoking cigars, but while one is in the act of smoking them it seems so, and there were hours and hours of pleasure stored up in the cabinet. Even the most suspicious father-in-law cannot feel the same after a present as before it; if Colum was not the man he would have chosen for his daughter's husband, he was a lively, likeable, handsome fellow. And it was a pleasure to see, through the fragrant smoke, how admiringly she looked at him, and he at her. The glances she exchanged with Nick had been less lover-like.

After he had gone to bed, Margaret and Colum sat talking – both rather drowsily, she trying to memorize the nice things he was saying about her father, to tell him the next day. 'I didn't expect to find him quite such an old darling,' Colum said. 'He seemed to swallow me hook, line and sinker. He even told me it would do you good to marry a Catholic. He said you hadn't had enough religion in your life, and it was his fault.'

'Did he really?' said Margaret, pleased. Imagine her father saying that.

'Colum,' she said.

'Darling, you say my name so nicely.' It seemed a shame to take him at a disadvantage, almost as vulnerable to her stroke as Sisera to Jael's; but it would be best to get it over, and Margaret felt that what she had to say was too important to await a favourable moment: it was tact-free, and dictated its own context.

'Should you mind very much if I don't become a Catholic?'

'Become what, darling?' he asked sleepily.

'A Catholic – I mean, not just at once.'

'Of course not, darling. Why should I mind?'

Had she heard him right? she wondered.

'Well, you asked me to, you know.'

'Did I darling? If I did, it was the most awful cheek.'

Her feelings warred between relief that he had taken it so lightly, and disappointment that something that she had worked herself up about, and that had come to mean so much to her, should mean so little to him. But relief predominated.

'Would you turn Protestant if I asked you to?' she said.

For answer he sat up and carolled in a resonant baritone,

> *'Bid me to live and I will live*
> *Thy Protestant to be!'*

'Sh! you'll wake my father.'

'Darling, that reminds me—', he said, and took her in his arms.

*

Colum left early on Monday morning. Impossible as it seemed for such a powerful vehicle, the car crawled to the garden gate and Margaret walked beside it, holding Colum's hand through the window. He kissed it before he let it go, and she only waved half-heartedly, for fear the wind might blow the kiss away.

Later in the day the Victorian pin-cushion – an octagonal affair of variously coloured velvet, made in segments like an orange – which had always stood on her dressing-table, was discovered to be missing. It had been her mother's and she cherished it. A thorough search was made, but the pin-cushion did not turn up. The only explanation seemed to be that a poltergeist had taken it. But the mind accepts the miraculous more easily than it is sometimes thought to, and Margaret had quite ceased to wonder about its disappearance when two or three days later she came across it, looking oddly out of place, in the middle of Colum's writing-table.

'Why, there's my pin-cushion!' she exclaimed.

'Yes, my dear, I wanted something of yours. Did you miss it?' he asked innocently.

'Of course I did! I hunted high and low! I never thought you were a thief!'

'Well, now you know,' he said.

WELL, my darling, it is all over now and I will try to tell you about it. First of all, Margaret looked too pretty for words. She had a dress of white angelskin and quite a *short* veil, and a sort of little Portia cap, but spreading out more at the sides and relieved from looking *hard* (which wouldn't have suited her at all) by a band of flower petals sewn into it, petals of tuberoses they were, and they smelt too divinely. It wasn't *quite* what I should have chosen for her – it was a little too straight for her very English type of prettiness – but Colum (he has asked me to call him Colum) wanted it. But why do I tell you all this? You won't understand a word of it.

She had two 'attendants' – a little girl and a little boy – the children of one of Colum's Lido friends. They were dressed – but I won't go on wasting words on you. I wish you were more interested in clothes, though. I'm sure you could be if you tried.

Colum pulled strings and managed to *get hold* of the Salute, as they call this large domed church which is nearly opposite our hotel. It is rather like St. Paul's and considered to be very fine, which in a way it is, outside; but inside it's too like an architectural drawing for my taste, and chilly. Not Margaret's church at all, if you understand me; our old St. Peter's at Dittingham would have suited her much better – but of course Colum's a Catholic and he had set his heart on it. However even he couldn't persuade the Patriarch (as the head of the Venetian Church is called, only of course he's under the Pope, as they all are) to let them be married in the church proper – the main building, I mean – just because she's not a Catholic. Even Colum thought it was rather mean of him and said a few words under his breath. So they were married in the sacristy – but, please, darling, disabuse your mind of the idea of an English sacristy. This one was a great high room like a hall, lined with pictures – the one over the altar was by Titian, I was told; so was the ceiling. But somehow I don't fancy pictures in a church, do you? For one thing, you can't see them and one of them I would really rather *not* have seen – David with Goliath's head, too realistic by half, and not at all religious, though I suppose it comes into the Bible. But one couldn't connect darling Margaret with scenes of that sort. The Marriage at Cana, on the opposite wall, was much more suitable. I couldn't see it properly from where I was, but at any rate the people were all properly clothed which they aren't, by any means, in some old pictures. Of course in Italy people do not cover themselves up as much as we do – we noticed it in Rapallo – and the Venetians being mostly poor, as far as I can see, and spending half their lives in boats, must save quite a lot on clothes.

Well, I only tell you this to show you I do use my eyes, which you sometimes say I don't. How I wish that Mr Pennefather had been well enough to come, and that you hadn't been too busy (but I suppose I ought to be glad of that). But there was no one to give poor Margaret away and that seemed so sad somehow: she has always been so surrounded by protectors and protectresses, and you know what I mean – a deep layer of affection. And here she was in this foreign place, very beautiful, no doubt, but where nobody knew her, or what it meant to *be* her. She was just any bride. But of course, the Italians are a warm-hearted people and they like brides – they like *all* women (do they *not*? even I, my dear, have been *followed* in the street, at a respectful distance) and they crowded on the steps of the church (which I must say are very beautiful, so *shallow*). Somebody said that Colum had arranged for them to be there, but I don't believe it. Well, of course he was the first to leave the hotel, in a black and gold gondola, and gondoliers with blue sashes, with his best man, Alastair Milsom (I needn't tell you who *he* is) sitting beside him, and he looked just as you would expect – perhaps a shade sure of himself and his hat too far back on his head, but I could never wish him other than he is, as you know. There were a lot of guests and waiters on the terrace of the hotel to watch him go and he gave that little shrug which he sometimes does on the films in moments of great danger, and they recognised it and laughed.

The gondoliers rowed very slowly across the Grand Canal, and he walked very slowly up the steps of the church – it was all slow motion but everything goes slow in Venice.

All this we saw from the window of Margaret's sitting-room, but I don't think she took in much of it, she was so miserably nervous. I've never seen her *really* nervous before. She usually gets over it at the last. Only of course it has been a strain for her seeing so many new people, not brought together in a good cause, but in a purely social way – which she has never greatly cared for. I was amused and interested to see so many people I'd heard and read of, but I'm not sure I should have been, if I'd known they might be my companions for life – for believe me there were some fairly tough types among them – especially the women, who have a way of looking at you that I found quite disconcerting. I don't suppose that Margaret has ever been looked at in that way in her life – you know, not with that moist-eyed and affectionate interest that a bride expects, but quite hard, and up and down, and through and round. 'Why don't you *tell* us when you're going to get married?' one of them said to Colum, just as if it was something he did every day, and poor Margaret, who was standing near by, and didn't seem to be included in the remark, turned quite pink. But I dare say there are some quite jolly girls among them.

Where was I? Oh yes, we were watching Colum and his escort from the window. Then of course it was Margaret's turn and you know how she hates to keep anybody waiting so we went down and started almost at once. Her gondola was even grander than Colum's and had lots of white ribbons fluttering from it and at the back a huge picture basket of Madonna lilies crowned with white chiffon – terrifically bridal. Besides the two gondoliers half the people in the hotel tried to help her into the boat and she kept looking shyly round and saying '*Grazie*' which is the only Italian word we have either of us learnt so far. Then she sat down and spread out her dress which looked too pretty against the black leather, and smiled. She couldn't help it with all those faces smiling at her, as if the whole world was one smile. The sun came out, and all the water glittered – which it doesn't always do, by any means. I wished I could have gone with her, but she had to go alone, and I followed in another gondola.

There were only about a dozen of us in the sacristy, and they did seem to hurry through the service, just as Colum said they would. No music, no flowers – it didn't seem like a real wedding until it was over and then of course it *did* – it's the fact that counts, isn't it? Colum led her away from the sacristy as if there were twelve hundred people instead of twelve, and through the empty church, and when we got out on to the steps where the crowd was thicker than ever, and cameras flashing and snapping, and all that watery Venetian glitter – I longed for a pair of dark glasses. At last they were together in the same boat, after all the artificial business of being kept apart so long, as if they were in quarantine and might give each other something – and off they went to this apartment that Colum's taken, on the

Zattere, wherever that is. I haven't seen it yet, but I shall, when I lunch with them to-morrow.

Meanwhile I'm at a loose end, hence this long letter. I shall write to Mr Pennefather too but I shan't tell him everything I've told you – because *really* the whole thing was a great success – Margaret looked so very pretty and they had all the publicity that Colum wanted. It was just that I felt uneasy, having known Margaret all my life, to give her up to so much strangeness – strange people (in more ways than one) in a strange place. But I'm sure we haven't really lost her. I told her again and again, when she was so agitated just before the wedding, that she could always count on us.

What are we to say to Nick? That worries me a little. I know he's taken the whole business of Margaret's marriage very badly and I'm afraid he will think we've been disloyal. But what could we do? We haven't taken sides. It isn't as if it was either of their *faults*. It was just too unlucky that it should have been Colum – whom Nick apparently hates with a deadly hatred – which is not surprising, all things considered. But if it was Nick who had got married to someone else, instead of Margaret, we should have gone to his wedding, shouldn't we? I mean, life has to go on. But somehow I don't think he will get married – not for a time anyhow. He never was quite the marrying sort, was he, and now he seems to be taken up with his work, to the exclusion of all else. Well, if he asks about it, which I don't suppose he will – a woman would want to know, but men aren't curious, or pretend they aren't – tell him it all went off quite nicely. Of course one doesn't know, does one, how strong the wedding-bond is in the case of film-stars, and this one did seem tied in a rather flimsy way and Nick may even be hoping . . .

There was a knock at the door.

'Come in!' cried Diana. She said it more than once, but no

one came, so she opened the door and found on the threshold a small page dressed in white.

'Scusi, Signora, ma c'è la Signora Maccus che vuol parlare con lei.'

Diana couldn't understand him.

'Signora Maccus?'

'Si, si,' said the boy. 'Signora Maccus. Dico che venga su?'

Still not knowing what he meant or what to expect, but wanting him to go away, Diana nodded, and returned to her letter, in a provisional state of mind.

And of course she isn't a Roman Catholic, which would make it easier. All the same, I shouldn't encourage him to wait, for I do think that men are happier married, don't you, Stuart dearest, and as soon as the soreness has had time to wear off . . .

Another knock. This time the boy did not wait but opened the door and announced with much *empressement*,

'Signora Maccus.'

'Margaret darling, I didn't recognize you by that name!'

They flew to each other and embraced.

'But darling, why aren't you with Colum?' Diana asked.

'He was on his way to the Piazza to see some people, so he dropped me.'

'Dropped you?'

'Oh, it was my idea,' said Margaret, smiling. 'I felt I wanted to see you. But I'm going on to join him in a minute or two.'

'Who's he meeting this time?'

'Mrs Belmore, I think, that rich old American lady that he's always going about with. I don't take to her very much, do you?'

'If you ask me, I think she's quite the dregs. I wonder Colum doesn't see it.'

'Oh he does', said Margaret. 'But he said to me, "I've got to keep in with the old devil. She has a lot of influence in the film world".'

'I should have thought that Colum could afford to ignore her.'

'Well, you see, the film world is so tricky, as he says. And the stage, too. *The Robber Chief* started off well, but didn't keep it up, or we shouldn't be here. The public wants something new from him, he says.'

'*The Robber Chief* was new.'

'Yes, but not really new. There was too much sugar in its system, it was diabetic, Colum says. One paper even said he had taken sugar off the ration.'

'I thought it was a bit on the sweet side.'

'That was what I liked,' said Margaret wistfully. 'But Colum says that it's no good. A drop of bitters is what they really want from him he says.'

Diana noticed with some amusement that the mysteries of Colum's calling were now invested with the utmost awe for Margaret. She spoke of them with bated breath; she referred to the film world with as much reverence as if it had been the next world, and quoted Colum as if he were its prophet. And it was odd that she should be so dazzled: for in the sphere of human affairs that she understood – and it was no inconsiderable one – the sphere of public affairs and social work, she was just as unimpressed and hard-headed as her colleagues.

'And what is his new film to be about?' Diana asked.

'*The Devil is so Distinguished*? He hasn't told me yet, he says he's superstitious about talking of his films until they have reached a certain stage . . . But I gather that he's going to be well . . . a pretty bad hat, you know, only suave and elegant and kid-gloved, so to speak, not rough and tough and ragged as he used to be.'

Diana considered this.

'And properly shaved.'

'Of course. In ordinary life, you know, he always is.' Margaret blushed and looked at her friend shyly.

'Darling,' Diana said, 'how has it all gone?'

Margaret drew a long breath.

'Blissfully.'

13

17th September

It is six o'clock in the evening. Diana has just gone. Colum and I went with her to the station. It was wet and windy and our smart gondola looked all bedraggled. The gondoliers had taken away the lovely dark blue carpet that covers all the floor, and put a strip of old stair carpet in its place. The *tenda* they put up for bad weather flapped about and didn't keep the rain out properly. I was afraid Diana might start her journey wet, but Colum asked her to change places with him, it was drier where he was sitting, on the spare seat, facing us. All the same, I was sorry that her last impression of Venice should be such a dreary one, after all the lovely days we've had. When she was in the train, standing at the window, she seemed already far away – half way to England. Colum says we both cried, but we didn't really, I'm sure. Colum begged her to stay with us in our London flat, and she promised to.

I've never kept a diary before, and I don't suppose I shall keep this one long, but Diana's going away did seem a turning-point, almost as if she was taking away my old life with her. She is so *English* – I see that now – and the people round us, even when they are English, don't seem very English to me. Of course one doesn't go abroad to see English people, but it was nice to be able to discuss them with her, which I can't do so easily with Colum, since most of them are his friends.

*

In a way I was longing for her to go, so that I could be alone with Colum, and I'm still joyful when I think of it, though of course we aren't alone together a great deal, there are so many parties we have to go to – it's essential to Colum that he should, because of his work. He's gone to a cocktail party now, at Mrs Belmore's – Mrs Bel, they all call her, so I'd better. I may follow when the gondola comes back, though he didn't seem to think I need, and perhaps I ought not to ask the gondoliers to go out again in the wet. He said he wouldn't be wanting them, as Mrs Bel will send him back in her launch. It seems she will do anything for him. I think I shall sit here and wait till he comes back. We are dining alone, thank goodness.

I oughtn't to say that, for now I'm beginning to get used to them, I think I shall like some of them very much. Diana told me they might be jealous of me; but they don't seem to be, even Lauriol Sorensen, who is so beautiful and has known Colum so much longer than I have. She is a Swede – or says she is, she doesn't speak with any accent – and was on the stage, I think; I ought to know all about her, but I don't. She has an offhand manner, as they all have – it seems to be the fashion. Of course they all know each other and about each other, partly from reading in the papers, I suppose. They can't know much about me from the papers, and what they do know . . .

Wondering what impression Colum's friends might have got of her from the papers, Margaret stopped. Someone had described her interlude with Nick as 'a gallop with another man'. It wasn't meant unkindly but she didn't like it. If only she had met Colum before she had met Nick! She went to the window and looked out. Twilight was falling and the air was resonant with the clangour of church bells. It was a sound that always saddened her, this clashing tumult that every evening saluted the setting sun. The Giudecca Canal was dark and turbid, and the few craft that were stirring seemed to be pushing their way with difficulty through the driving drifts of rain. She turned back to the room again. It was long and lofty; the furniture looked miniature against the towering walls, and the painted ceiling, which depicted, in Tiepolesque manner, the apotheosis of a doge, was almost lost to view. She switched the lights on and admired again the flush of pink in the deep crimson of the brocaded walls. But all this grandeur did not help her to dicover her own position in the midst of it. She went back to her writing table.

And what they do know doesn't amount to much. I wish they did know more about me, in a way; but what would my life mean to them? Our values are so different. All that we have in common is Colum . . .

In common: Margaret did not like the phrase for was she not at the centre of his life, and they at its furthest edges? If she doubted this, where was she? A mood of panic seized her, and she longed for Colum to come back. Perhaps putting down her thoughts would steady her.

Of course, it's only in Venice, and for a week or two, that we shall lead this deck-chair life. I want to be busy about something, and I know that Colum does. They all tell me that when he once starts working I shan't see anything of him, and what shall I do then? It's the conversation – the conversation that I can't keep up with. It somehow doesn't *give* me anything. I rather enjoy listening to it, it's so quick and slick and lively; but it seemed intended to give you the feeling that nothing is worth while. And it's funny, but I can't get used to their positions. They never sit or stand, they always lie. They make one ashamed to be on one's feet, as if one was doing some sort of physical exercise – 'Why are you so strenuous?' Lauriol once said, and I was only standing talking to her. It oughtn't to, but it puts one at a disadvantage to be looked up at, and it doesn't suit me to recline, I know, my clothes won't settle and I can't relax. It's all because I'm not an artist, I expect. If I were I should know, as Colum says, that the artist gives himself entirely to something that, for the ordinary purposes of life – just isn't *there*, and has to be created out of nothing: that's the reality to him, and the rest is a kind of make-believe, to be got through somehow – as Art is to me, I expect. I regard Art very highly, of course, but not as one of the most important things in life, except when it's somebody's career, as it is Colum's.

Naturally I expect them to talk a great deal about love, I was prepared for that and should be disappointed if they didn't. Also I have no doubt they have irregular relationships – I'm quite used to such things, at Dittingham they happen all the time, and no one turns a hair. Besides it's a tradition in the film world and on the stage. Nothing that they could ever do would shock me, of course; I've seen so much of the seamy side of life. I could tell them stories – but they wouldn't want to listen – they never want to hear or say more than three or four words running. Colum says they quarrel a great deal, but I can't think what *about*, because they don't seem to *mind* anything enough to quarrel. You can't quarrel without caring, and they don't care. 'I couldn't care less,' they're always saying. Perhaps Nick and I wouldn't have quarrelled if we hadn't cared so much. I could never quarrel with Colum, not because he doesn't care but because he wouldn't let me.

I wish I knew what he sees in them. When he's with them he talks like they do, but he has another way of talking to me, even when they are there. I hope he won't lose it! How glad I am we had that long time alone together, and perhaps we shall again, when we get home – not that I want to go home – it's so heavenly here.

18th September

Horrified by what I wrote yesterday and have only not destroyed it because I want it to be a lesson of how *not* to think and feel in future. Also, there is a right and a wrong way of doing everything; diaries should be written in a sort of shorthand. Diana's going away must have affected my spirits more than I was aware of – that's my only excuse. Colum came back long before I expected him, he couldn't stay another minute, he told me, he missed me so much and was so bored at the party.

Went to Murano, Burrano and Torcello in Mrs Bel's motor-launch. Would rather have taken one ourselves, but as Colum says, why pay when somebody else wants to. Admired glass-blowers' absorption in their work, as indifferent to spectators as lions at the Zoo. Mosaics at Torcello seemed to me too stiff. Colum said this was Byzantine stylization, and the tall blue Madonna was his favourite woman in the world. I said I wished I was taller. C. warned me against looking for a personal reference in works of art. I said I should try to see them through his eyes. C. said I musn't and we laughed a good deal.

Came back by San Francesco nel Deserto. So fresh and green and *living* after Torcello. Liked the pine trees and the brown-robed monks – friars, Colum said they were. He told me a little about the Franciscans and said he had once thought of becoming one.

Dined with Mrs Bel and about sixteen guests. Sat next to an Italian and talked of polo. Englishman on the other side knew Dittingham and had heard of me! Asked if I found opportunities for welfare work in Venice and looking round the table said, 'You might begin here.' C. said I flirted with him disgracefully. Enjoyed this dinner more than any I've been to, but forgot to ask Mrs Bel how the sweet was made. Colum said 'Never mind, we'll ask her in London.' I didn't know she had a house there too.

19th September
Glorious day. Spent morning on the Lido, bathing and sunbathing. C. sunbathes with a stop-watch, adding ten minutes every
day. He has beautifully even tan; mine rather blotchy. I burn and
turn red. Perhaps I ought to stop it. Everyone takes sunbathing
very seriously and compares progress. Lauriol said 'I'm not
everybody's woman by any means, but with the sun I am a
general favourite.' I envy her her pale gold skin, which goes
a deeper honey-colour every day. Sunbathing bores me anyhow;
I don't know what to think about while I'm doing it. Colum
said 'You can always think of me,' and since then I haven't
found it quite so boring.

20th September
Started out early in the gondola and saw the Frari, Sant'
Alvisè, Madonna dell' Orto, S.S. Giovanni and Paolo, San
Francesco della Vigna and several other churches. Getting
more used to Venetian churches now and they don't always
strike me as being too bare or too ornate. There is a very nice
Bellini in the Frari – I'm getting to love his pictures, and wish
there was one in every church. Colum says they are too 'good'
for him, but he likes me to like them. He sometimes genu-
flects on entering a church but there are so many of them that
often he forgets, to my secret amusement. Don't like to seem
lacking in respect, so sometimes give altar a distant bow.
Colum amused by this. 'I told you you ought to have become
a Catholic,' he said. I asked him if he'd been to Mass since we
came to Venice? and he confessed he hadn't. I said 'Will you
go if I go?' and he said 'Anything to please you,' so we
arranged to go to Mass at St. Mark's on Sunday. It's not for
me to prompt him, but I feel he should take his religious
duties more seriously.

21st September

Went to the Bank and cashed my last Travellers' cheques. Luckily wine is cheap but the weekly bills here are enormous. We haven't entertained much – English people can't. Of course it's different for Mrs Bel, she is an American and has her money free. I got into rather a panic, and said to Colum, 'What shall we do now?' I didn't like to ask him whether he had also cashed his Travellers' cheques. He laughed and said, 'Oh, there are ways and means, and there are a lot of kind old creatures here who wouldn't let us starve.' Suddenly remembered our wedding reception and what it must have cost. 'Oh don't worry about that,' he said. But I couldn't help feeling anxious, I shouldn't like to think we were being paid for by Mrs Bel or somebody like that.

22nd September

Frightfully worried this morning – can't find the diamond bracelet that Colum gave me as a wedding present. Didn't dare to tell him at first, but had to in the end, because we were going to the Lido and I could not bear to leave the house with all that hanging over me. The whole flat seemed transformed – quite different from what it used to be – alien and hostile. I'm sure I left the bracelet on my dressing table when I went to bed, and Colum says he saw it too. I didn't discover it was missing until after the servants had done the room. It was frightfully careless of me, of course, I should have locked it up. I turned out all the drawers a dozen times – and oh the miserable feeling of tidying them after each upheaval, and then going back and untidying them again! Colum was so sweet about it – he didn't blame me in the least, and went through all the drawers with me, and thought of places where it hadn't occurred to me to look. He kept telling me 'It doesn't matter, it's insured,' but I felt it was like losing part of *him*, and the mere fact of theft is so upsetting –

it creeps under one's skin and sets one's mind on edge. 'You'll know another time,' he said. 'You can't really trust Italian servants, they're very pleasant, but they're all light-fingered. Now let's be off.'

It was bright sunshine on the Lido, but the cloud on my mind wouldn't lift, and I couldn't help telling everyone what had happened, over and over again. They were very nice about it, and nearly everyone had had a similar experience, which somehow made me feel better, and less selfish. The only one I didn't tell was Lauriol, for I'm never certain how she feels towards me, she's such an old friend of Colum's and I shouldn't be surprised if she was jealous of me. She was lying on her back sunbathing, some distance from the others, with a pale blue handkerchief wrapped round her head. She called out to me: 'Did I hear you'd lost something?' I went over to her and told her the whole story – I couldn't keep it off my tongue. 'How maddening for you,' she said, 'but are you sure it's stolen?' 'What else could have happened to it?' I asked. 'Well, things do get lost sometimes,' she said. 'Tell Colum to look behind the door.' I couldn't see her face because of the handkerchief, but I felt sure she was laughing at me, and I went back to the others, feeling hurt. Colum was deep in conversation with Mrs. Bel.

After dinner Colum and I drifted round the little canals in the gondola. We held each other's hands – I didn't want to at first, it seems in such bad taste – but somehow it adds to one's happiness to share it with the world. It wasn't very public, because some of the canals were so high and dark and narrow you could see nothing, but then suddenly one turns a corner and finds oneself in a blaze of light from a restaurant by the water's edge, and all the people staring. I had always worn my bracelet in the evenings and at first I felt a kind of bareness on my wrist, a cold, naked spot that almost hurt, but with his hand on mine I soon forgot it. We went under the Bridge of

Sighs, it was a thrilling moment, for that canal is very dark and fearsome with sheer walls like cliffs and not a lighted window. Colum heaved a deep theatrical sigh and I felt quite angry with him. Then we were out in the open water and the gondola began to rock and Colum let my hand go and I remembered about the bracelet. We didn't get in till after midnight.

24th September

Such an extraordinary day. Woke feeling acute sense of loss, as if something had settled on my heart like ice. Stretched out my hand to feel for Colum's head very gently, so as not to wake him, and it wasn't there! Jumped out of bed and saw that it was nearly ten o'clock. There was a note on my dressing-table which said 'Good morning, darling, you are a sleepy-head. I'm going out now to do one or two things. If you wake up in time, meet me at Florian's at twelve.'

Suddenly I felt very happy, as I always do when Colum asks me to meet him. I love being with him but I love meeting him almost more. To think that he is somewhere waiting for me! I lingered over my breakfast and dressed slowly: it was like doing something to a tune, only 'meeting' isn't really a tuneful word. I was ready by eleven o'clock. Two hours had seemed too short to wait to see him, an hour seemed much too long. Suddenly I thought: why not pray to St. Anthony of Padua for the return of my bracelet? Colum had been talking about him – that gave me the idea. He said that in all Venice there was only one church dedicated to St. Anthony, and that was a small one. An elephant got loose and went mad with fright and finally was shot in it, he told me. He also said that the people of Padua didn't like St. Anthony at all, and sometimes cursed his name! I shall never get used to the familiar, joking way some Catholics speak of their religion. I shouldn't if I was one, it would be too wonderful to be sure such things were true.

Then I wondered if he would like being prayed to by a Protestant, but surely a pious Protestant deserves to be heard as well as an irreverent Catholic. I thought the prayer would be most effective in St. Anthony's own church, but the idea of the elephant being killed there somehow put me off it, so I went into the nearest one, which is called San Trovaso – not a three-star church, by any means, but very light and airy, with worn but beautiful carved pews. I knelt down, but I couldn't help feeling I was somehow an impostor, with no right to be there: and though I prayed, I couldn't get any meaning into the words. I didn't like to say 'diamond bracelet'; it seemed all wrong, in a church, to be asking for the return of something so material and worldly, so I said 'what I have lost' instead, hoping that St. Anthony would know what it was. But still I could not get any sense of communication and the feeling of being there on false pretences increased. I wondered if I was bringing down a curse upon myself and all sorts of morbid thoughts went through my head.

Suddenly I saw a young woman with a dog on a lead walking down the aisle. In spite of my unwelcoming looks she sat down in my pew, and the dog, a small black Pomeranian, at once stretched itself out on the knee-rest, as though it was perfectly church-trained. Well! I thought, if a dog can come in here, surely so can I, and immediately the distressing baffling sense of dumbness, deafness and unworthiness passed away and I felt confident and happy in my prayer; and my petition seemed to fly away from me like a homing pigeon. What joy that was! I repeated the prayer once or twice, just to make sure, and each time with the same effect, as if a flock of pigeons was flying to St. Anthony! It seemed ungrateful to leave the church at once, so I sat on in its clear amber glow – while the Pomeranian made eyes at me, being anxious to please – like most Italians. Before I left I genuflected to the altar, rather awkwardly – anyone could see I wasn't a Roman Catholic – but I felt I had to.

Such a heavenly feeling too, on leaving the church, at peace with myself and everyone. I took the vaporetto at the Accademia, and quite forgot, so happy was I, Colum's warning to keep tight hold of my bag; one cannot be too careful, these little steamers are full of thieves, he says. But it was there all right when I got out.

I didn't see him at once in the Piazza. Florian's has so many chairs and there was a sprinkling of people there already. Then I saw him sitting quite alone – that was why I didn't see him sooner, I think – it was almost the first time I'd found him alone in Venice. I felt as if St. Anthony had granted me an extra prayer and I ran to join him before anyone else could. I can't remember what we said – it was all so foolish, we might have been parted for ten years. Then I told him about praying to St. Anthony and how I felt sure I should get the bracelet back. He smiled and said he was sure St. Anthony would do his best, but he would have his work cut out to keep track of all the thieves in Venice. I felt a little dashed and said, 'Well, perhaps he'll do it for your sake. Surely there must still be places where we haven't looked?' He shook his head. Then I remembered what Lauriol had said, and added laughing, 'Behind the door, for instance.' 'Behind the door?' said Colum. 'What made you think of that?' So I told him that Lauriol had said he was to look behind the door. 'Lauriol said so?' and he looked quite startled, as he often does at quite a trifle, for his face registers everything. 'Yes,' I said, 'she was only teasing, of course; I'm afraid she doesn't like me very much.' He looked thoughtful and said. 'Not like you? I shouldn't be surprised if she likes you more than she likes me.' I laughed, because I didn't think it possible for her or anyone else not to like Colum, and we both said 'Darling!' together, and that ended it. One or two people stared at us, and whispered to their neighbours, but nobody joined us. I think it was the most wonderful morning I've had in Venice.

And the most wonderful evening too. I'd been looking forward to it because we were going to a party at an Italian house (of course they are all Italian, but this one was lived in by a Venetian family who had always owned it and there are very few such in Venice) and a famous violinist was to play. We were to dine with Mrs Bel first, which was a pity, and go on afterwards. About seven o'clock I went to my room to dress; the shutters were all closed as usual, and it was rather stuffy, so I went straight across and opened them. Then I remembered that light attracts mosquitoes, and I went back to the door to turn it off. I was afraid of falling over something, it was so dark; but down the room the windows glimmered and I couldn't wait to get back to them.

Such a marvellous sight! The lights of the Giudecca were reflected on the water in thin broken lines of gold, like the spokes of a wheel, and they all converged, it seemed, below my windows. The lights aren't regularly spaced and between them were great blocks of shadow, dense and black, almost solid. There was a full moon, and where it struck the water, close to the further shore, it made a sort of agitation of bluish silver, as if the water was seething – yet all round it was absolutely calm. And coming towards me, not a pathway of light like the moon sometimes sends, but a few scattered splinters, like silver feathers, dropped in haste. Along the shore, on this side, the boats and barges and little steamers were moored close together, sometimes packed three deep, tucked up for the night – not a stir of life on them, they might have been asleep. The evening bell-ringing was over, and though the people below talked and sang and shouted as they always do, breaking the silence, somehow they didn't disturb the peace. I don't know how long I sat watching, trying to fix the picture in my mind, and just when I was feeling I could take in no more I thought I heard a sound in the room behind me, and turned round to make sure. It was nothing, but it broke my mood and reminded me that it was time to dress. Still half in a dream I closed the shutters and went back to the door and turned the lights on. And there, on the dressing table, lay my bracelet.

I could hardly believe my eyes, I was so astonished, and feelings rushed through me in such violent waves they almost hurt, as if they were breaking down adhesions that had formed across my mind. The bracelet had such power for me I dare not touch it: I could only call, 'Colum Colum!'

He came straight to me from his dressing-room.

I pointed. 'Look!'

I shall never forget his face, how mischievous it was.

'I wondered when you were going to see it,' he said.

'But, Colum!'

'You mean how did it get there? Darling, I found it with St. Anthony's help.'

'But where?'

'More or less where Lauriol said, behind the door.'

'Please show me, Colum.'

'It's St. Anthony's secret,' he said teasingly, 'only you must be more careful another time.'

'Where did I put it?'

'Ah!' he said. 'I know where I shall put it.' He fumbled with it, pretending not to understand the catch; I love his cave-man moods, though of course he's not a cave-man really.

Afterwards came the dinner and the party, and though I enjoyed them both, the dinner much more than I thought I should, it was a good deal because of finding the bracelet. For some reason, I value it now much more than when he gave it me. I couldn't help looking at it every now and then, to gloat over it, and Lauriol, who sat next to me at the party said, 'Well, I see you've got it back. Congratulations. Did you tell Colum what I told you to?' I didn't quite like the way she said it, rather as if Colum had been her property, and answered, 'Oh yes, but it wasn't he who found it really, it was St. Anthony,' which was quite true.

25th September

Rather a disappointment. Colum didn't want me to go with him to St. Mark's. He said it would have been different if I'd been a Catholic, but as I wasn't, he would all the time be wondering what I thought about it, and wouldn't be able to give his full attention to it. I said I wanted to thank St. Anthony for what he'd done for us; but Colum said I needn't go into a church for that. Of course it may be a ruse to get me to join the Church; but I don't think so – being an actor he has an actor's temperament, and I swore to myself when I married him that I would never, never resent any manifestation of it. And I never will. I asked him if he minded me going to another church, alone, and he said, 'Of course not,' so I did – to our nice, friendly church of San Trovaso, but it wasn't the same thing and I didn't understand what it was all about. I couldn't follow the movements of the priest, and the sudden sharp ringing of the bell somehow alarmed me. I felt as if it was something very important being said in a foreign language – which I suppose it was. If Colum had been there, I should have felt its meaning through him, but perhaps that was exactly what he didn't want, to be a kind of channel, instead of receiving it all into himself. I came away not disappointed or disillusioned, but puzzled and with whatever feeling it was that took me there unsatisfied. I must go again. Afterwards we all met at Florian's, and some of them pretended that Colum hadn't been to Mass at all and he wouldn't say he *had* – he's sometimes a little secretive about himself and I don't blame him, for I don't think they would have appreciated his motives for going. Everybody *very* nice about my getting my bracelet back. I think I've been unjust to Colum's friends.

Somebody asked me how I'd spent the morning. I said I'd been to church, and Colum said 'She'd make a much better Catholic than I am' which is nonsense, of course – one couldn't become a proper Catholic overnight – I know enough to know that. I don't suppose I shall think about it so much when I get back – unless it thinks of me! Colum seemed a bit subdued and sad. I hope it's nothing that I've said or done. Perhaps he doesn't like me barging in with my semi-religious suggestions. It's maddening for amateurs to air their half-baked notions when it's something that one really knows about – I feel it over the few things I know something about, like how *not* to treat delinquent children. Colum I'm sure knows something about religion – or he wouldn't have said he was a bad Catholic. I'm not so ignorant as to think that religion only expresses itself in what one *does*, either in ordinary life or in church. I must make that clear to Colum – he need never apologize to me for what he does. Besides he does *live* his religion, or he wouldn't be so sweet to me, and everyone else.

I wish I could take more interest in his work – but there again I'm such an amateur. And anyhow he doesn't like to talk about it except in a general way – though I gather he isn't altogether happy about *The Devil*.

26th September
Churches, churches, churches. I can't make out whether I really want to see them, or whether I go because the guide-book says there is a Tintoretto above the second altar on the left. Sometimes I think it's they who want to see me. Colum says I'm church-mad, and asks me what I'll do for churches when I get to England? Of course there are plenty of churches in England, and I still think that, as buildings, they have more religious feeling than these have, and are more awe-inspiring. But these in a way are more like home: it's the difference between paying

a formal call and dropping in on someone. I'm not fond of paying formal calls. When I get home I shall have to find something else to occupy me. Somehow I never envisaged marriage as a woman's career! Colum told me this, and it's quite true. He's told me quite a lot about myself I didn't know. He's very observant – much more so than I am. I don't suppose I could tell him much about himself that he doesn't know. But I don't want to – I love him for what he is. I've never been curious about people. Mine is a stationary love whereas his, he declares, is dynamic, and grows with each discovery that he makes about me. Somehow I never expected to be an object of *interest* to anyone! and am perhaps only just finding out what it means to have an emotional life. We have talked a great deal about love. Colum doesn't think I was ever really in love with Nick; I thought I was, because he was the first man who paid any attention to me. Colum says that Nick was really in love with him! at school – a schoolboy attachment, he called it – and Nick was ashamed of it and wanted to forget it, and that was why he was so angry when Colum came to the party. I couldn't help being a little shocked, and Colum was shocked at me for being shocked – and I suppose it was ridiculous when I think of all the things I've heard about, without turning a hair, at the Bench and on Committees. But somehow it seems different when it happens among people one knows! It didn't make me feel angry with Nick, though, or despise him – rather the opposite, for I see now why he acted as he did and it seems much less unreasonable.

Colum says I really fell in love with him the first time I saw him, in *Put Paid to It*, when I thought I so disliked him. 'Darling, I *hated* you!' I said, but he shook his head and declared it really was a form of love which 'softened me up' (hideous expression!) and made me fall for Nick. 'Your real bond was that you both loved me,' he said with such an insufferably complacent expression that I smacked him, though not hard, and told him he thought that *everyone* was in love with him. 'But they are!' he said, and I suppose it's true, for even here he has to have a secretary to deal with his fan mail.

28th September

The weather has broken and I'm not as sorry as I should be, for Colum's three weeks is up the day after to-morrow. More than any place I know, rain alters Venice. It blackens it, for one thing. All the light goes from the sky; the walls and roofs are dark with rain – looking down from my window (what a lot of time one spends in Venice looking down from balconies and windows) I see the men in oilskins, the women hidden under umbrellas, and nearly everybody in goloshes, black and shiny, like beetles. The creepers, and those poor tufted struggling ailanthus trees along the Zattere, blow about and shudder in the most distressing way – and even inside in our great entrata, wet streams down the walls and glistens on the flagstones. There is a feeling as though everything has gone irreparably wrong, and never would come right. The sirocco-laden air fills one with dread. One thinks of Venice as a place to be happy in, and I've been wonderfully happy here – but I'm not sure it is. In the sunshine it seems to be happy in spite of you, and in the rain unhappy because of you. What I should like to take away with me are the reflections – under bridges and on walls and ceilings – the bars, ribbons, rope-ladders of light, racing towards you or away from you, cork-screws of light, spinning round – all that restless wavy flicker, and the sparkle on everything. I've been happy in that way too, but surely one's feelings need a point of rest, and that's what I'm looking forward to when I get back to England.

Mrs Bel is giving a farewell party for us to-morrow night – I shan't try to describe it, for I know just what it will be like, and it won't be one of the things I want to remember, though I'm not saying that I haven't enjoyed our social life. We've been most royally entertained, for Colum's sake I know, but I haven't been made to feel unwelcome, far from it. As Lauriol said to me in a candid moment, 'It would have been far worse if you had been one of us.' And I have loved writing this diary, which is a sort of record of my happiness, which never seemed worth writing about before, nor did I ever seem so important to myself – I owe all that to Colum. I have a hundred joys I never had, but I also mind a great many things I used not to mind – words and looks not coming exactly as I hoped they would, and so on, a whole domain of 'being hurt' – or something like it – which I've always looked on as a dreadful female fault. I never used to cry and now I've grown into a cry-baby. I'm not at all the stoic that I thought I was, and I didn't know how capable I was of being spoilt, until Colum started spoiling me! I couldn't get rid of the feeling that he was tough and hard, like the parts he acts in; but he never is, except in play, never with women, at any rate, certainly never with me. It may be something to do with his religion, which doesn't encourage people to be hard on each other or even on themselves. That's why he doesn't mind saying he's a bad Catholic – though I wish he wouldn't – or wasn't. In a way Venice has meant more religiously to me than it has to him, which is natural enough for he knows all about it whereas I am only discovering it – if I am.

Perhaps when I get back I shall go to Father McBane again, and ask him if he still thinks I ought to wait.

And now I must bring my journal to an end, for I shall be too tired to write after the party. And I have another reason too, for giving it up. I don't think it's healthy to put down all one's thoughts on paper. One ends by making a sort of image of oneself, which one feels one must live up to. It retards and makes one static. A mistress told me that at school and I'm sure it's true. I can imagine myself one day getting quite jealous of the Margaret in this diary – though I hope not – or thinking her a fool, which would be worse. I remember the same mistress telling me she had made a rule for herself and copied it out on paper: 'I must not take my spiritual pulse,' – and I never have, until now, and even then I meant it to be a record of my sight-seeing, which many people keep who go abroad – Daddy, for instance, who can't possibly be accused of being egotistical or introspective.

And I have another reason, too, for dropping it. Somebody has been reading it! Last night I found some grains of tobacco-ash between the leaves, and it smelt just faintly of cigar-smoke. Colum hardly ever smokes, but when he does, it's a cigar. I have no secrets from him and don't mind him reading it a bit. All the same it wasn't meant for him – I don't quite know whom it was meant for, but certainly not for him. And how did he find it? It was much more carefully put away than my dear bracelet! I wonder if I should tell him of my detective work? I don't think I will – he'll think I was angry with him, and I'm not, I'm not, I'm not. I never could be.

14

STUART and Diana did not think they had taken sides by giving their approval to Margaret's marriage. They meant to go on seeing Nick as before, if he was ready to see them. It was not their quarrel. On the other hand they had indirectly been the means of making him unhappy, and exposing him to ridicule and humiliation, experiences which he was temperamentally more unfitted to bear than most men. He was bound to blame them a little. This they did not take too much to heart, for Diana was resilient and happy-go-lucky, and Stuart's public school conventionalism enabled him to put the episode into a drawer labelled 'Bad Business' or 'Bad Show', in which it was isolated and unable to spread into another smaller drawer labelled 'Hard Feelings'. Stuart's code made him an unsatisfactory confidant; Diana could tell him quite a lot in writing; she could even be expansive to him on the telephone; but en tête-à-tête he was apt to imprison gossip in good form; he would not surmise, he would not make conjectures, he refused to wonder whether Nick was 'getting over it', whether he wanted to know if Margaret was happy, whether he loved her in his heart and was pining for her, whether he hated Colum and given the opportunity would try to do him down. To such questions Stuart would return the baldest answers. 'Don't know. Can't imagine. I suppose the fellow's feelings are his own affair.' And Nick's behaviour, when he met them, bore this out. He would not talk about the films or the local affairs of Dittingham, and any conversational approach that might lead to Margaret or Colum he carefully avoided.

But all the same he had changed. The chagrin and disappointment he had suffered touched some nerve in him that intelligence and ambition and industry had never reached. Only the diffidence and self-distrust which had endeared him to his colleagues had prevented him from going still further than he had. But now the unwillingness, amounting to inability, to press his advantage, or take up the kind of point that some barristers did not scruple to take up, fell from him. Each time that he pressed a point and made it, turning defeat into victory or victory into defeat, each time he imposed himself on the course of events, he obscurely felt he was making amends to himself for his inadequate handling of the situation at the party. Obliging himself to act in a way that was unnatural to him, he brought the episode at the Dorchester Hotel to another and more fortunate conclusion. He could have said something to Colum, meaningless to the other guests, which would have made the film-star hasten from the room; he could have welcomed him like an old friend; he could have greeted him with casual civility. All those courses were open to him but they would have been against his nature, and it was his nature which had betrayed him and which must be brought under the discipline of his will.

It so happened that only a few weeks after Margaret's marriage a murder trial gave Nick his chance. Since he was a junior his name did not figure largely in the papers, but in his profession it was made.

After this success Nick practised his new methods with a difference. It was as if he had another self to call on – a harder and more cynical self, formidable and uncompromising in the law courts, assured and almost genial in private life. The rankling sense of inferiority left him. He had felt that he had had to knuckle under to Colum's celebrity; that, more than anything, had wounded his pride. Now he could dislike him on equal terms, for he was a star, too, not in the vulgar, newspaper sense that Colum was, but a star in a much more exclusive and respected firmament. He did not have to persuade himself of this: his colleagues told him, his briefs told him, his bank-book told him. He need not envy Colum any longer; he need not feel that Margaret had left him for a more successful man. His heart might hurt him but his pride was assuaged.

Stuart and Diana were quick to congratulate him on his success, and Diana was among the first to notice that his attitude to the world had become mellower. His face had relaxed and seemed to have grown broader; he smiled at things he once would not have smiled at; he was altogether more approachable and forthcoming. Diana did not hold with feuds. 'We must try to be civilized and grown up,' she told her husband. Stuart drew in his chin a little and did not answer, but Diana persisted. She could not let the situation go on festering: it was time to apply the knife.

Nick paid them a weekend visit at The Starting Point, and Diana broached the subject. 'Old Mr Pennefather was asking about you the other day,' she said. 'He wanted to write and congratulate you, but I said I'd do it for him.'

Stuart straightened his black tie and signalled with his eyebrows.

A neutral expression came into Nick's face. 'How is the old boy?' he asked politely.

'Getting along as well as can be expected,' said Diana briskly. 'Of course he's a good deal by himself now.'

Nick raised his eyebrows. 'Why "of course"?'

'How slow you are for a distinguished barrister! Because Margaret' – she let her voice dwell defiantly on the name – 'doesn't come here very much.'

'Who has he looking after him?' asked Nick.

'No one; he prefers to housekeep for himself.'

There was a silence and Stuart said, examining his cuff-links, 'Girl can't find time to get away, I suppose.'

'Does Colum McInnes take up all her time?' asked Nick. The way he said this would have warned off most people, but Diana was constitutionally unable to be afraid of men.

'No,' she said, as though replying to an eager question, 'he doesn't. He's out all day working terrifically hard, apparently. A film-star's life is not one long day-dream, like a film-goer's is.'

'Or like a film-star's wife's is,' said Nick suavely.

'Fellow's got to make his living like the rest of us,' interposed Stuart, fingering his blond moustache as though to make sure that it was there.

'Oh Stuart, what trite things you sometimes say. And Nick, how can you think that Margaret would spend her life day-dreaming? She could hardly tell you what a day-dream is.'

'She ought to know, she married one.'

'Yes, but she doesn't see him like that. What she wants, of course, is to help him in his work, but I gather he won't let her.'

'How could she, anyhow?'

'That's not for me to say. I suppose she could make him say his lines to her, and see he was word-perfect. Or she could go to the studio and give him her advice. I've no doubt there are all sorts of boring details connected with his work which she would love to take on – she always was a beast of burden.'

'Not my beast,' said Nick, shortly.

Diana stared at him. Recovering herself, she all but lost her temper. Really Nick was being impossible.

'Oh, I see,' she said. 'Perhaps I ought not to, but I always think of you as Nick, not Burden. No, she wasn't your beast, and it was all too sad, and no one minded more than Stuart and I did. And we take a great deal of the blame, for bringing you together. But how could we have known? Things do go wrong in life, Nick, that's how you make your living and it's just too bad that you should be the one to suffer. But there, it happened – and what's the good of crying over it? I'm sorry that I brought the subject up, if it still hurts you. If you don't want to hear about Margaret, let's talk of something else.'

Diana flushed. She didn't mind Nick seeing that she was upset and annoyed. Stuart looked at her expressionlessly, his elbow on the arm of his chair, two fingers propping up his chin. Nick leaned back, looked from one to the other, and said, ungraciously but with a glint of humour: 'I don't mind hearing a *little* more about her.'

'Well then, for goodness' sake,' Diana said, 'do *look* as if you didn't mind. You look as if I was reading the Burial Service to you. Now, where was I? Oh yes, Colum's new film. I'm told he wishes he was back in Hollywood. His new part doesn't suit him.'

'What sort of rogue is he portraying this time?'

'A well-bred, well-dressed gigolo type of man – Mayfair, Monte Carlo, Palm Beach and so forth – with a line of amusing patter and a propensity for blackmail.'

'I should have thought,' said Nick, 'that he had every qualification for playing such a part.'

'That's where you're wrong,' Diana said. 'He's used to doing rough stuff, and can't be himself in a lounge suit or a white tie. The film's to be called *The Devil is so Distinguished*, and they say he's not distinguished enough.'

'Did Margaret tell you so?' Nick asked.

'She did. She was most indignant about it.'

Stuart coughed and said,

'Always thought distinction meant something you couldn't put your finger on – the absence of certain things, like swank and so on. But on the films I suppose it has to be more positive – man's got to register distinction all the time. It must ooze out of him. Colum's figure isn't willowy enough – that's where he falls down.'

'Stuart would like the part himself,' Diana said. 'It's the sophistication, you know, the Adolphe Menjou stuff, that Colum can't get. Margaret said, rather pathetically, "It would be all right if he only had to be a *gentleman*!" But he can't walk the right way. Apparently nothing's harder to alter than the way you walk – it's much, much harder than the way you talk. He's quite lost the American accent he picked up in the States, but he can't cure his slouch.'

'He never could,' said Nick. He stopped and looked up; his slip had gone unnoticed. 'Well, what's to happen? Is the film to be abandoned?'

'No, more's the pity. I thought a man in Colum's position could more or less dictate what kind of film he acted in – but apparently he can't. He has to do what his employers want him to, or what his employers think the public wants him to. He's got to do this film and another rather like it before he can go back to his old stuff.'

'Meanwhile,' said Nick, 'I suppose the money's coming in?'

'Yes, but not enough,' began Diana, but Stuart interposed, 'Well, we don't really know that, Di. You just gathered from something Margaret said that they might be a bit short. We mustn't put that sort of thing about, Nick, must we?'

'Better not to, I suppose,' said Nick indifferently. 'But I imagine he's worried about the future.'

'Yes, and of course he's madly extravagant. That flat of his must cost the eyes out of the head. And then there's his country cottage, only it isn't a cottage, of course. They only use it for occasional weekends, and think of the money it must run away with! And his secretary and all the people he pays to do things for him! He's always sending people to run errands in taxis, when a postcard or a telephone call would do just as well.

Special messengers going in all directions – and they all get a rake-off, Margaret says. He's got a sort of Aladdin-complex – everything must be done as though by magic. The works must never show. Margaret would like to arrange the routine part of his life on business lines, which she's perfectly equipped to do, being very practical, but he won't hear of it. He wants her to be a houri, beautifully dressed and not lifting a finger.'

'I can't see Margaret like that,' said Nick, for the first time speaking of her as if he saw her.

'Nor I – she isn't used to it and it doesn't suit her. She tried to keep on some of her work here, in Dittingham; she tried to find some social work in London – there must be plenty to be had – but he didn't want her to. She says she would have insisted, for he always gives into her and never makes a fuss, but she doesn't like to be away from him, especially when he gets depressed about his work.'

'It's a pity that she married him,' Nick said, in a neutral voice, not at all as if he might have married her himself. 'She's a bread-and-butter woman, she doesn't want to be fed on éclairs . . . But perhaps I'm not a fair judge.'

He stifled a yawn, and for a moment looked so unhappy that Diana regretted having, for the sake of a smoother social surface, probed the wound again. That people should get on with each other on a plane of easy social intercourse was almost her religion; she believed in it much more than in the emotions. Those she enjoyed seeing on the films, or reading about, or gossiping about; but when she met them in the raw she shrank from them; they must be stifled somehow, like children's naughty tempers. She did not feel, as Stuart did, that they were bad form; she resented their effect on social relations. Like her mother before her she was a born hostess and hated to see her parties spoilt. But now her heart was touched and she regarded Nick not with impatience as a guest who had failed to pull his weight, but as a human being who was entitled to his grief.

'I wonder what her father thinks,' Nick said.

'Mr Pennefather? Oh he's too sweet, but what can he do? He never wanted the marriage, as you know; he made the best of it for Margaret's sake.'

'But you don't really think it's going badly?' Nick asked.

'Oh *no*. It's early to tell yet, but when one thinks how unsuited they are to each other, I think you could say it was going well. Not quite the way that one expected, though. I mean this slight hitch in Colum's career – he seemed Fortune's favourite, if ever there was one. Poor Margaret, she'll think it's her fault – she's always so anxious that men should get on in the world – for them, you know, entirely, not for herself. It's a relic of her Victorian upbringing. I never try to make you get on, do I, Stuart?'

Embarrassed by this personal appeal, Stuart was understood to say that at any rate Diana had not hindered him.

Nick was looking thoughtful.

'When you see Margaret . . .' he began.

'Yes?' said Diana, eagerly.

But Nick had already changed his mind. 'Oh nothing, nothing,' he said, and shook his head.

15

As magistrate and social worker Margaret was quick to take in the bearings of a situation. Where she had no personal stake she could objectify; her feelings might be engaged – they often were – but they did not cloud her judgment. Rather they clarified it; for few of the cases that came before her did not have some sort of emotional background.

But where she was herself concerned she saw much less clearly. Indeed she would scarcely have thought it fitting, or even possible, to be judge in her own case, any more than it would have been fitting or even possible for the men, women and children whose problems she pronounced on to settle them themselves. She was there for that, and she shouldered the responsibility without fear. If she did not actually think she knew what was best for them, she thought the system which empowered her to adjudicate was the right system. She was an agent of justice even if she was a faulty agent. She might make mistakes, but they were inseparable from the system and she did not worry about them overmuch.

But in the conduct of her own life she had no such assurance. Unconsciously she regarded herself as being in the same lowly position as the wrong-doers and messers-up-of-lives who came before her. As they erred and strayed, so did she. To have planned her life, even to have seen its issues clearly, would have seemed to her presumptuous almost. The moment her feelings were aroused, as they were aroused when she met Nick, she felt impelled to follow where they led. Her mind, her moral sense, must act as brakes, not motors. The joy of life was in its details, not in the pattern you imposed on them. Everything that turned up must be treated at its face value, piecemeal, as she felt about it and as her instinctive sense of proportion rated it, not graded accordingly to some worldly or convenient standard of importance. She had a standard to which she referred the miscellaneous happenings of her emotional life but it was a personal one, it was Colum. Everything she did must somehow benefit him.

Her efforts to find herself work and occupation were not a contradiction of this; she felt she would be happier if she had them, and if she were happier, so would Colum be. She was not so besotted that her idea of what was good for him always coincided with his; about her good works, as he called them, she argued and protested, but when she saw he didn't like it, she gave way. She enjoyed giving way very much.

A magistrate in other people's lives, what was she in her own? It never entered her head that she herself might be someone in search of a magistrate. Colum was there, and he was very unlike one.

That Colum was sometimes depressed about his work she realized; but he was not always depressed, and she treated his attacks of low-spirits as they came, not looking beyond the symptoms to the cause. She did not like what she knew of the new film, but she did not like any of Colum's films, she only liked him in them. That she ought to have tried to persuade him to take a stand and find something more suited to him did not occur to her. She could not externalize him or think of him as a 'case'. Her idea of helping him was to adapt herself to his needs as they arose – to be what she thought he wanted her to be.

But this was not easy, for Colum had or seemed to have a most fluid character. Watching him with his friends she could hardly count up all the Colums she saw. With Mrs Bel, who had now returned to her mansion in Queen's Gate he was wistful and pathetic and younger than his age, and he had a range of facial expressions to go with this. With Lauriol, who was also in London still looking for a part but never finding quite the right one, he was older than his years – casual, debonair, and man-of-the-worldly. Once when he told Margaret he could not hit off the kind of character they wanted for 'The Devil', Margaret said involuntarily 'Be as you are with Lauriol!' At that he shot her a quick look which did not come out of his repertory. Next day he was able to report that he had taken her advice and profited. Always anxious to help him in some practical way, Margaret got more happiness out of this one bull's eye than out of all the children whose delinquent feet she had turned on the right road or the married and unmarried couples whose tangled affairs she had helped to straighten out. But after a time he was again saying that he could not get the part right. 'If only I could have Lauriol acting with me!' he said, looking at Margaret with sad mischief in his eyes. 'But why don't you?' Margaret asked. 'Surely you could get her into the cast, and she's always looking for a part.' He shrugged his shoulders and she felt baffled; she always resented, and could hardly believe, that in his own sphere he was not omnipotent.

One evening he told her that the making of this film was going to be an even longer business than he thought. He reached forward and took the paper knife and tapped his knee. This, she knew, was a sign of real feeling; the expression of an inner need. 'I hope we shan't find ourselves in Short Street,' he said. His worried expression was deservedly famous; it had youth and helplessness and ferocity behind it; it was the scowl of a baby lion, and made one long to help him. Margaret was learning to read his looks bilingually, and could often make the necessary adjustment between what they said and what they meant. She enjoyed doing this and did not feel him to be insincere. 'But, darling, I have lots of money,' she said.

'You mean you'd give me some?' he said.

'Well, what do you think?' said Margaret, her heart beating as though it would burst her purse strings.

'I know, I know,' said he, 'but you didn't marry me to spend your own money. You may need it for yourself some day.'

The chill of fear crept into her heart: 'What do you mean?' she said.

'Oh,' said he, 'there wouldn't be much fun in sticking to a ham actor who can't support himself.' She kissed him and tried to make him see what she thought reason; but he shook his brown head dolefully and only when she was on the point of tears did he give her one of his best kisses.

Meanwhile their merry life went on apace. Colum gave and went to parties whenever he had time to, and Margaret usually went with him. Sometimes, indeed, she went without him, for though she had not quite got over her feeling of strangeness with his set she did not want them to think her shy or hostile. It was their glassy, non-adhesive surface that alarmed her, the fact that, as Colum himself said, 'A burr wouldn't stick on them.' Colum was fond of parties – had he not come to Margaret's? – they had a ritual value for him and he had an almost royal memory for acquaintances, however humble. He was extremely popular in his profession. Lauriol once said to Margaret, 'If Colum hadn't been the pet he is, you would have been torn to pieces.' Margaret was very proud of Colum's personal popularity and loved to hear him praised. Nor, as far as she could make out, was he losing ground with the public. Several of his films were still being given; the fan letters poured in; the newspaper cuttings were too many to read, almost too many to count. There was no reduction in their style of living, rather the opposite, for since his marriage Colum had replaced the daily woman with a resident house-parlour-maid. With Richards and the cook, that made a staff of three. Colum never had the smallest difficulty in getting servants, indeed he had difficulty in keeping them away, for nearly every day some beglamoured girl wrote offering him her services – sometimes free. Thus the servant problem, the modern housekeeper's supreme concern, did not exist for Margaret. If her staff did not always do things the Fair Haven way, Margaret had to admit that they did them with more style.

It did sometimes seem to her as though Colum was working to weaken her connexions with Fair Haven, but would any husband have done less? When she went home Colum sometimes went with her, but more often he excused himself, feeling, as was indeed the case, that Mr Pennefather chiefly welcomed him for Margaret's sake. Colum could not be expected to bestow charm where it was only half appreciated, and Mr Pennefather was too old to be permanently dazzled. It was not what he wanted out of life. He was settling down well without a housekeeper, who (he said) might boss, neglect or bully him. She did not feel anxious about him; she did not feel anxious about anyone or anything. That was just it.

Oh for a raison d'être! She would have one, she knew, in a few month's time, but meanwhile with so many things arranged for her, so many she could not touch, so many in which her co-operation would have seemed like interference, she often felt at a loose end; and then she would remember Venice, and the churches, and the tingle of excitement she had felt when Colum asked her to become a Catholic for his sake. That, she knew, would have given her a purpose. Remembering it, she was half-hearted in her search for other occupations.

*

The dark days of winter drew on and burglaries became more frequent. In their own block, several flats were visited. With four people in the house besides herself Margaret did not feel uneasy: Colum alone would be more than a match for any burglar.

So when it happened, when a frightened, excited parlour-maid bringing Margaret her breakfast announced that the flat had been broken into, she was as surprised and horrified as if it was the first time a burglary had taken place.

If only Colum had been there! But he had gone down to the country for the night on business and would not return till lunch-time. So all the morning she had to face their sitting-room, which looked as though a tornado had been through it, not daring to touch anything, but trying to find out exactly what was missing. Meanwhile she had to endure alone that sense of personal defilement – that creeping of the nerves and skin, as though some of the dirt and dust which burglars create had got into them – that curious sense of moral damage – which is so much more bearable when shared with someone else.

More practised in observation than herself, the parlour-maid detected what was missing: the Renaissance child's head that Colum was so fond of, the Tanagra figurine that he had given her, were two items out of a haul of ten – mostly small works of art.

The beefy gimlet-eyed detectives when they came were at once more polite and more intimidating than she expected. Accustomed though she was to interviewing the police she had not realized the difference between being interrogated on one's own account and someone else's. Their capacity for suspicion seemed unlimited; she was not sure that she herself escaped. At first she longed for Colum to come; then, as her self-confidence returned she almost hoped he wouldn't. She was, she told herself, likely to be just as good at this kind of thing as he was, perhaps better: and now at last she was able to take something off his shoulders, and help him in a practical way.

Where had the thief got in? That was the problem that preoccupied her and it was one that the detectives, for some time, ignored. The questions they asked did not tell her what was in their minds; she guessed that they were trying to find points of likeness between this and other burglaries. Presently, however, they asked if they might take a look round, and the method of entry was soon revealed. It was all too simple. The thief had got in through the lavatory window and he hadn't even had to force it open. Margaret had to confess that this special window wasn't always fastened at night. He had, however, left traces of his entrance, smudges and a scratch on the white paint of the window-sill.

When they had looked out, Margaret climbed on to the chair and looked out too. Next to the block of flats stood a house of ordinary height; the complicated relief map of its roof was spread out many feet below her, and a convenient pipe came up the wall. She felt a twinge of giddiness, and an unwilling respect for the thief mingled with the general distaste that the thought of him excited.

'The window-sill is rubbed on the outside,' she said.

'Yes,' said the Chief Inspector, 'we had noticed that.'

They left the little room, which, such was the transforming effect of crime, it had not seemed embarrassing to share with two strange men. To the last the policemen kept their own counsel; their departure was as unexpected and unheralded as everything else they did. She could not tell whether they had any clue as to who the burglar was or whether they had any hope of recovering the property.

She was still sitting in the room, gazing blankly at its disarray, when Colum came in. He threw his hands up and slowly turned his head from side to side.

'Good God, what's this?'

Margaret told him, adding that the police had asked her not to have the room put straight until they had seen him.

'When are they coming?' he asked.

'They wanted you to ring up and make an appointment.'

Colum went irresolutely to the telephone and came back again.

'When would it be most convenient, darling, for you to have them?' he asked.

She was touched, as always, by his thought for her.

'Anytime suits me. I hope you aren't too dreadfully miserable about it all,' she said.

He drew a long breath.

'It's your figurine I mind most about,' he said. 'That and the child's head.'

'Were they worth a lot?'

'Well, a few hundreds, I suppose.'

'Oh, that's not a great deal.'

He smiled at her, amused.

'Darling, I never know what you'll think a lot of money.'

'Were they insured?' she asked.

'Well, as a matter of fact they were.'

'Then we needn't worry any more, need we?'

All the same she was glad that she was present when the police came back. Colum was nervous, more nervous than she had been, and laid himself out to charm them. He was the glamorous, burgled film-star being interviewed by the police. She didn't think it would go down with them and she was right. Perhaps it didn't matter; he couldn't help putting on an act for every stranger; but she knew how literal policemen's minds were, and felt uneasy at his over-articulateness and anxiety to meet them half-way. By contrast their brief, business-like inquiries sounded almost unfriendly.

Could he with certainty identify all the pieces that had been stolen, if they were recovered? 'Yes, of course. You know how it is with works of art. You get to know and love every crack and blemish on them.'

The detectives, it was evident, did not know what it was to care for works of art in this intimate way.

And if descriptions of them were sent out, would antique dealers be able to recognize them from the descriptions?

Colum hunched his shoulders and looked appealingly at their unmoved faces.

'Possibly, but I don't think so. None of them was a masterpiece, of course. Just good sound specimens of their type and period.'

Had he the vendors' receipts, describing each article technically?

Colum let out an exasperated sigh.

'It's just what I haven't got. You know how it is, one can't keep all one's receipts, can one? The flat isn't big enough.' He glanced round the large luxuriously furnished room, as though expecting sympathy. But the police officers didn't respond: perhaps they thought the room quite big enough to keep receipts in. 'Several of the things were bought at sales,' Colum went on, 'and I haven't kept the catalogues either. You've no idea how they mount up. Or perhaps you have?' He gave the Inspector a smile, as one collector of antiques to another; but the Inspector showed no sign of knowing how catalogues mounted up, nor did his companion. 'You see,' said Colum, 'I never meant to sell the things, or I should have been more careful to keep proper records of them.'

The Inspector and the constable appreciated this. 'But you said they were insured,' said the Inspector. 'Won't the Insurance Company have a detailed description of each object?'

Colum shook his head.

'I'm afraid not. The things were separately listed – I did have the sense to see to that – but only in the most general terms. 'Tang Horse and rider' – well, there are thousands of those up and down the country, though mine was a specially nice one. You must often have seen them yourself, Inspector. Perhaps you've got one?'

The Inspector smiled rather grimly, then something in him seemed to soften.

'No, sir, I can't say I have, but I think I know what you refer to. A rather high-backed animal, of a cart-horse type, surmounted by a thinnish figure wearing a tall headdress, and generally a good deal chipped?'

'That's it! that's it!' cried Colum. 'You've got it exactly. Most of them, as I expect you know, came out of tombs. I don't suppose that any two are quite alike, but they all bear a general resemblance to each other. I shouldn't like to be called on to identify one, would you, Inspector?'

The Inspector admitted that he wouldn't.

'That's our headache,' Colum said. 'Probably none of the blasted things could be recognized from a description. Or do you think they could?' he added, his face brightening. 'You know so much more about these things than I do.'

'Well, sir,' said the Inspector, in a much less professional voice than he had used hitherto, 'in a way I suppose I do – that is to say I've had more experience in detecting crime than you have. But in committing it, if I may put it that way, and without offence, you've had more experience than I have, sir.'

Colum was sitting between the Inspector and the constable. They both gave him a look – the Inspector with middle-aged confidence that his joke would be taken in good part; the constable deprecating and apprehensive, wondering if his superior had not gone too far. Margaret saw Colum stiffen, just as he stiffened on the films when someone had said something to displease him. Then he began to laugh. His laugh was well-known. It seldom happened more than once or twice in any film, he was so sparing with it. It entailed a reversal of his whole film personality, the grimness and sadness of his usual aspect, the stern hang-dog lines, being erased to make way for a face all sickle curves and lateral fan-shaped wrinkles. Even Margaret, who had often seen the transformation take place on the screen, but never before in real life, could hardly believe that it was he. Both the policemen recognized the phenomenon and knew it was being put on for their benefit. Yet not only were they flattered by this, but the mimetic mirth was so infectious that they could not help joining in, and they were still laughing when Colum, his self-generated seizure over, had become grave again.

Appreciation of the art they both knew best had for the moment taken the detectives out of themselves and made them both forget their mission.

'That was a good one, sir, if I may say so,' the Inspector said admiringly, and the constable said fervently, 'Yes, it was.' 'We're all fans of yours in the police,' the Inspector said, with a sudden expansiveness as if he had wanted to say this all along, but had refrained from motives of professional decorum. 'You won't mind me saying so, but there are sometimes small slips in your films, mistakes of routine and procedure that the public wouldn't notice, though a policeman does. But you yourself, sir, well, I suppose I ought not to say it, but you're the only actor on the films who knows how to make crime attractive. It isn't very attractive in real life, not to us policemen, anyhow; of course we see it differently from the public. It isn't very attractive here when you've been robbed of so many valuable objects. But when you're on the movies, sir, well I wonder that everyone who sees you doesn't want to become a burglar.'

He ceased, and the constable who had been following the Inspector's tribute not only with his eyes but almost with his lips, murmured 'That's quite right.' Colum, who never received a compliment ungraciously, bent his head in diffident acknowledgement, at once of their plaudits and his power to please.

So it had come, the moment which Margaret had been longing for but which, from the rigour of their demeanour at the outset, she had quite ceased to expect. She had not yet learned to get over her disappointment if Colum's glory went unrecognized, or ceased to feel the stab of happiness when it was. Insensibly she had become a hero-worshipper. Hero-worship might be dying out of the world, but it still flourished wherever Colum was.

Now they were chatting together, naturally and without constraint; and Margaret noticed with amusement that Colum had taken on the appearance and almost, it seemed, the nature of the two detectives. His eyes were as bright and hard and restless as theirs were; his body had the same solid controlled strength, as of a bull that might at any moment become dangerous; and his clothes, despite their superior cut, had the same air of being 'plain clothes' masking some alien activity. For the time being he was one of them and they accepted him as such. Like many women, Margaret took pleasure in being present at masculine confabulations; she liked them to take themselves so seriously; she felt uplifted, not repelled, by their self-importance, and confirmed in the secret otherness of her own sex. She did not resent being left out, she did not feel impatient or lowered in her own esteem, as a man would have felt had he been forced to listen to the prattle of three women. It spelt glory to her, these male creatures conferring under her maternal eye.

Presently they rose and, excusing themselves, made a further tour of the premises, in which she did not join. She could hear their voices, suggesting, arguing, agreeing.

'Well, that's over,' said Colum when the detectives had been ushered out. He touched his forehead with his handkerchief.

'Those policemen have made the room feel stuffy. Quite nice fellows, though. They didn't hold out much hope of getting the things back. In future, my dear, I think you'd better give your valuables to me, and I'll put them in the safe with mine. We don't want this burgling business to become a habit.'

Margaret agreed. The jewellery that Colum and her father had given her was worth a good deal and she seldom wore it.

'But I think I'll keep my bracelet out,' she said. 'St. Anthony will look after that.'

'Ah, I had forgotten he was a pal of yours,' said Colum. 'You ought to get in touch with him. But don't forget he's a *farceur*. He doesn't always play fair, and may lead you up the garden path, especially if you promise him money.'

'Oh, I shouldn't do that,' said Margaret, shocked.

Next morning the sitting room presented something like its normal aspect. But there were the gaps to remind her of the burglary, the rifled chimneypiece, the pedestals and stands ending in nothing; and the strange feeling of defilement, like a bad smell, still persisted. Margaret had not quite lost the sense of violation; it had touched in her being nerves she knew nothing about and left her restless and ill-at-ease with herself. A kind of compulsion seized her to revisit the only place where the thief had left tangible traces of his visit; the fact that it was the lavatory emphasized the squalid feeling it aroused in her. The window-sill had been cleaned, but looking down she saw the pipe smeared and streaked with the marks of the burglar's body. It was a long drop to the roof below, that fascinating diagram of broken surfaces. She wondered which way he had come, and looked for footmarks on the sooty leads. But there were none, not even at the foot of the pipe.

Suddenly she heard Colum's voice behind her. 'Darling, what on earth are you doing?'

Guilty at being caught out, embarrassed at being discovered in the lavatory, she jumped down from the chair.

'I was looking for footmarks on the roof,' she said.

'But, darling, there wouldn't be any. He wore socks over his shoes, the Inspector said. They generally do when they're on a job. Sometimes they put on plimsolls, but not often, because they make a bulge in their pockets which the bobbies can see.'

'Yes,' said Margaret. 'But surely his stockinged feet would have left some traces on the roof – it is thick in dirt and dust, just as the pipe is. There should be tracks leading to the pipe and away from it, but there aren't.'

Colum climbed up and looked out.

'You're right,' he said. 'But he may have hugged the wall, in which case his footprints wouldn't be so easy to see. I believe I can see some marks. You have a look.'

Margaret saw what Colum meant, but she didn't think the marks were footprints.

'Ought we to tell the police?' she asked him, doubtfully.

'I shouldn't bother. For one thing, what has struck us is more than likely to have struck them; and if it hasn't they won't be pleased at having an obvious bloomer pointed out to them. In any case, they couldn't identify the burglar by his socks, any more than they could by his gloves.'

'Oh, he wore gloves?'

'So they say. You mustn't be a fusspot, Margaret darling.'

Margaret felt that she deserved this mild rebuke – one of the few that Colum, whose tongue on the screen was generally so rough – had handed out to her. She said no more.

All the same, when he had gone, she fetched her opera-glasses and not once but several times surveyed the roof-scape. Now she could see every ridge and scratch; but nothing corresponding to a sock-print. It didn't make sense. If the marks on the drain-pipe were a blind, the burglar must have got in another way. And how could he have got through the little window, carrying a sackful of highly fragile objects? But that, too, was a point that must have struck the police. In the afternoon a violent downpour came, and when she looked out again she saw, rather to her relief, that even the tell-tale smudges on the drain-pipe had been almost washed away.

16

In London St. Anthony did not show the same alacrity in answering Margaret's prayers that he had shown in Venice. Perhaps it was that among the heathen – in partibus infidelium – he could not do so much; he was handicapped by their unbelief.

Margaret persevered, however. She went from church to church – sometimes to Anglican, but more often to Roman Catholic churches, for there, she obscurely felt, his influence must be greatest. She did not like them as much as the Venetian churches; she missed the sense of agelong use and custom, she felt self-conscious in them, and as though she was a trespasser; yet she never failed to feel a welcome at the doorway, and was happier inside than she had been outside. Not that she was unhappy, but she still felt the need for a more definite focus to her life, a rallying-point for her spiritual forces. It was only a temporary need, she told herself; in a few months she would have plenty to occupy her, but meanwhile . . .

Colum laughed at what he called her church-lust; he told her that St. Anthony would give her just as much, or as little, of his attention, wherever she applied to him. 'He specially likes to be prayed to in a bar,' he teased her. 'People are always praying to him in churches, he gets quite bored with all their petitions, and often doesn't listen.' Margaret had misgivings of another kind. She felt that her behaviour might be superstitious and irrational; and if it wasn't, if it had its roots in some reality, that she was not going about it the right way, that she was cheating, trying to get something for nothing, travelling on the celestial railway without a ticket. When she came out of the church door she would look round nervously in case someone – who? – should touch her arm and ask for her credentials.

All the same she went; and as the days passed she sometimes forgot her errand, forgot St. Anthony and the stolen treasures and prayed for other things. One of the things she prayed for was a closer relationship with Colum – to be nearer to him, more necessary to his life: since their honeymoon, when they had so eagerly explored each other's minds, she felt she had drifted away from him, and that their love was becoming a matter of routine. The complete freedom she had vowed to give him – never to question anything he did – now seemed to her a counsel of indifference. She had come to terms, she thought, with all the men he was; her own character was not very pliable, but she had made unceasing efforts to adapt it to the versatility of his. She had fitted tolerably well into the society he frequented; she had never shamed him, she believed, by her bourgeois, not to say suburban ways of thought and speech; many of his friends had congratulated her on making him such a good wife. Only in one respect did she feel that she had conspicuously failed him – in her appreciation of his art. It was no use pretending, but art – certainly the art of the cinema – was not in her line. His feelings were subtle and sensitive: some crass remark she had dropped about his acting might well have made them curl up at the edges. Had her comments been more instructed or more intelligent he might not (she told herself) have put an embargo on her going to see him working at the studio. He explained it by the same superstition that made him unwilling to discuss his films with her while they were in the making; but from hints dropped she gathered that some of his friends did go, and this wounded her.

It distressed her all the more because she felt that at this critical, or at any rate important juncture in his career she might have helped him. She did not profess to know much about devils, nor did she wish to enquire into their habits; she was ready to leave the diabolic aspects of Colum's new role to him and the director. So little did she associate him with the Devil that it never occurred to her that he might be inadequate in that part. But to the matter of distinction she had given a good deal of thought; she had studied this quality in people who she believed possessed it (without *parti pris* she thought her father was one) and she had discussed it with people who might know. Though she had never seen Colum trying to be distinguished in his professional capacity, she had seen him in real life. It was in Lauriol's company that he came nearest to it, as she had told him. 'But I can't be thinking about Lauriol *all* the time,' said Colum plaintively. 'Sometimes I want to think of you!'

Margaret believed she knew where he missed the mark – where he fell short and where he exceeded. It was chiefly a matter of exceeding. Most of her advice would be 'don'ts.'

'Don't let your body or your face be too expressive . . . keep still . . . don't slouch or crouch . . . don't respond too actively to other people . . . don't let your personality slop over . . . keep it braced, as though you were wearing stays . . .' Some of these suggestions she had thought of for herself, some she had been told. She imagined herself trying to tell Colum. It would not be easy but she believed she had the moral courage to do it, if only he would give her an opening. The wounds are faithful of a friend; and how much more mortifying it must be in the studio, with the director shouting out to him 'Now Mr McInnes, do that all over again and try to be more distinguished!' – or whatever he did say. The thought of such scenes made Margaret's eyes smart; she could not bear to think of Colum struggling, subjected to the criticism of other people, not having

163

everything his own way. He talked to her very little about his work; but sometimes he told her that he had spent hours on a single episode or the mere fraction of an episode – for instance where he had to tell a wife, on whose honour he had designs, that he was in a position to ruin her husband's financial reputation – and in the end it had all had to be scrapped. On such occasions he would come home looking tired, almost with rings under his eyes, he whose health had always been so triumphant. If only she could help him in this, give him some practical expression to her sympathy, that might find its way into the current of his being, invigorating it, instead of vainly returning to her again!

She raised her face from the hard wood of the pew, and at the end of the dark neo-Gothic nave with its engine-turned arches she saw the candles shining on the altar. To whom should she pray? What saint would intercede for her? It was part of her diffidence and uncertainty in the face of religion that she felt uneasy about addressing its higher powers; with a saint, an intermediary, she felt more at home. A saint was still a person, and could be appealed to as such; the others, she knew, were Persons, but Persons so transcended, so august and awful, that they seemed to require from her not an expression of private feeling even in a matter that was of the utmost importance to her, but an abandonment of personality so complete that she could scarcely conceive it, and from which her being shrank, though she would sometimes feel its secret pull. Roman Catholics, she knew, had their special saints, of whom they asked favours too trivial, perhaps, to be included in that general offering up of the self, unattainable to her, known as prayer; it was more fitting to appeal to one of them than to the fount and source of all spiritual power.

But she knew little about them, or which of them would be most likely to take an interest in her case; she had not, so to speak, been introduced to any of them, except St. Anthony. She pictured them each as having a devoted crowd of postulants, among whom, perforce, they would give precedence to the older-established. But St. Anthony was an old and tried friend and though his speciality was the recovery of lost property he might also be a Saint-of-all-work. There was no question of recovering Colum, for she had not lost him; what she wanted was a feeling of closer identification with him.

Hardly had she formulated this thought and launched it on the aether, than an idea came to her: why not give Colum a present? Since their wedding, she had hardly given him one, and the chief reason was, not that she had lacked this natural impulse, but that Colum was such a difficult man to give a present to. He had everything! – and, besides, to make him a present was, unfortunately, the automatic reaction of many of his countless fans. Presents were always arriving and as they were seldom what he wanted they had become, for him, first a joke and then an embarrassment; there was no room for them in the flat or in their country cottage; they had to be secretly disposed of, quite how, she never knew. The only really welcome ones were the food parcels which poured in from many countries and helped to make the job of housekeeper a sinecure. To give Colum a present was to give a new meaning to the time-worn phrase of sending coals to Newcastle. He might well have put a notice in the Agony Column of the Times: 'No Presents by Request.' He was an utterly un-presentable man.

That was one of the difficulties of her relationship with him – the difficulty of giving him anything – not only in the material but in the emotional sphere, of which the material is but a symbol. The chief object of a present is to raise the recipient in his own esteem by the knowledge that someone cares for him to the point of making a sacrifice for him. Few men or women are proof against such demonstrations; after childhood a present that is more than a routine token of good-will is a rarity for most of us. But not for Colum. All the vast complex of hungry emotions connected with being loved, admired, flattered, preferred, idolized, with him had a surfeit every day. These things came to him as a matter of course. Whether he would have missed the chorus of adulation and the smell of incense had they not been there Margaret could not tell, for they always were there. He was compliment-proof, just as he was gift-proof. But alas, the converse did not hold. One word of disparagement set the chorus jangling, one breath of criticism blew away the incense; what he had suffered in his pride from *The Devil*, Margaret could only guess.

But though the intention behind a gift could not soothe the soreness of his spirit, a gift itself might. A gift had its own power to please, quite independent of the giver. It was a question of knowing what to give him, and now Margaret knew.

She left the church with her precautionary, propitiatory glance to left and right and turned her steps towards Bond Street. Only when the circulation began to return to her stiffened limbs did she realize how cold the church had been. A church in winter would be cold, of course; what was surprising was that she hadn't, at the time, felt cold. She went into two or three shops without seeing anything that remotely resembled what she sought. No matter; she had all the morning before her, she had many mornings. Here were some sale rooms; why not look in here?

She bought a catalogue and went up a staircase into a corridor that surprised her by its lightness and then into a fair-sized room with rugs and pictures hanging from the walls. They did not interest her and she passed them by. In an inner room porcelain objects and figures were set out in trays on tables, a miscellaneous collection before which her faculty of discrimination faltered. Then she realized that what she was looking for was staring her in the face.

She went up to it at once, and at once recoiled. For it was not only like the head, the Renaissance child's head, that had been stolen; it was the head itself.

Again she approached the dimpled, naughty, cherub's face that Colum had been so fond of, and that even here – in this atmosphere of solemn connoisseurship and decorously controlled desire, where money talked in whispers and with an Oxford accent – made its gaiety so infectious, so redolent of Southern joie-de-vivre, that Margaret could hardly stop herself from smiling back. For yes, it was the stolen head; bending over it – for the handful of spectators round her did not scruple to examine the exhibits closely and even to touch them – she saw the scratch below the ear which had come, the servants could not explain how, since it had been in her care.

Lot 223. She looked up the number in the catalogue. It was one of a dozen or more objects, collectively described as 'The Property of a Lady', all of which she now saw were displayed on the table round it. She began to study them with avid curiosity, piece by piece, wondering if anything else of Colum's was among them. She soon saw there was not; but as she stared with sharpened eyes at the porcelain figures – so white that the honey-coloured marble of the head looked dark beside them – she realized that she did know them, she had seen them before, many times, in Lauriol Sorensen's china cabinet.

Often at Lauriol's parties she had been at a loss for conversation, and from the position of near-recumbency which they all assumed, or, more restless, on her feet, she had gazed at Cupid with his bow and Diana with her crescent, at the four Walton Evangelists and the Five Senses (so fresh, so unjaded compared with one's own!), the Chelsea figures which were Lauriol's special pride, until she almost knew their colours and lines by heart. And Lauriol had had to sell them! She must be hard up, thought Margaret, to whom the idea of selling anything, however small, suggested bankruptcy; she had never got the job on the films or on the stage, which she was always on the point of getting but which she always in the end turned down – unless, as Margaret sometimes thought, it was she who was turned down.

Margaret liked Lauriol though she never quite knew how she stood with her; and she began to wonder if there was anything she could do to help her. Why, yes, there was! She could buy one of Lauriol's figures, and give it back to her. She chose a group, a woman with two children, that was not one of a set, and marked it on her catalogue.

Again her eyes fell on the child's head, a living laughing reality among these graceful eighteenth century trifles. How had it come to be there? Lauriol was a close friend of Colum's; was it conceivable that she was selling the head without his knowledge? A thought-proof curtain rattled down on Margaret's mind.

She took a turn round the room, half expecting to see something she recognized among the other lots, but there was nothing. When was the sale? To-morrow. Well, one thing was clear; to-morrow she would be there and buy the head back, cost what it might.

Yet walking home doubts started to assail her. Should she tell Colum that with St. Anthony's help she had found the head? No, she decided; if for no other reason than that the present must be a surprise. How would he take it? Almost for the first time there mingled with her thought of him an itch of curiosity – to know something about him that perhaps he did not mean her to know. Not to catch him out, of course. But to show herself, for once, as someone who could keep him guessing.

She bought the head for two hundred and twenty-four pounds, one figure higher than its number on the catalogue. At first the bidding had amused her by its unemotional tone, but when her turn came she began to grow excited, and could not help making her bids more emphatic than they need have been; her nods were quite portentous, compared with the casually raised eyebrows and negligently lifted forefingers around her. For a moment she sat on in a daze. Then, with a start, she remembered the piece she meant to buy for Lauriol, and threw her hand up just in time. It was knocked down to her for a trifling sum, almost disappointingly less, in terms of money, than the impulse that had prompted her to buy it. But Lauriol's other things were fetching more. Over the delicate heads of the Five Senses the figures soared like midges. Lauriol was doing well. Lauriol wouldn't have to take another job . . . Lauriol . . .

But the strangeness of her situation in the sale-room still enveloped her, she could not detach herself from its undeclared yet compelling tension, where art and money fought their loving battle, heedless of her; and instead of going out, as she had meant to, and whiling away the time until the sale was over and she could claim her prizes, she lingered on among the bidders, sometimes strolling about as they did, sometimes sitting, sometimes even bidding for a thing that took her fancy, though she let it go without a pang when the bidding went beyond her. It was the head she wanted; her second present scarcely seemed to count.

She had only a little way to go, but her purchases were heavier than she thought, and for fear of dropping them or having them snatched from her she took a taxi. Not till the lift gates closed on her did she feel safe. Now she had her treasure with her, in its rightful home, and her first impulse was to unpack it and replace it immediately on its ebony stand, which with the others had been put away. But she did not wish the servants to see it, she wanted the first eye that brightened at it to be Colum's. It was only four o'clock; he would not be back from the studio until eight; she must somehow control her excitement; and what better way than to spend the rest of the afternoon in thanking St. Anthony for his help? She had made it a rule not to indulge her secret church-going more than once a day. But this was a special occasion and it was not only excusable, it was a plain duty, to go a second time.

17

ON his way back from the studio Colum told his chauffeur to call at Lauriol Sorensen's. He found her, as he hoped he would, alone. He kissed her and sat down. They both found themselves staring at the dismantled china cabinet.

'Well, Lauriol, how did the sale go?'

'Not too badly, Colum. I rang them up and it was over seven hundred.'

'Pretty good going,' said Colum. 'But I wish you'd let me help you, Lauriol.'

'We've been into all that,' Lauriol said, 'and I don't want you to, not yet, at any rate. You've done enough for me in the past. And you're not too flush yourself, you know. But I'll help you to a drink. You look as though you needed one.'

'I won't say no, but I'm as fit as a fiddle.' Colum hated to be told he didn't look well.

They sipped their cocktails in silence, then Lauriol said, 'How is *The Devil* going?'

Colum shrugged his shoulders.

'A little better, I think, but, God, I'm tired of it. By the way, you didn't happen to hear what my piece fetched?'

'No, they didn't give me any details.'

'I wonder who bought it,' Colum said. 'I was fond of that thing, I hated parting with it. I suppose I could find out.'

'They publish a list, I think.'

'I might have a crack at getting it back if I knew where it was.'

'On its way to America, I dare say . . . Have you disposed of the whole lot now?'

'Yes.'

'And got the insurance money?'

'Yes. It's been a good haul. I might stop now.'

'You've said that before.'

'I might try just one more.'

'You've said that before, too.'

'I know,' said Colum. 'If it hadn't been for this blasted film. It's got me down a bit. I had to do something.'

'Just for the money?' Lauriol asked, with the minimum of question in her tone.

'Well, partly. But you know how it is with me . . . Nothing else gives me quite the same kick.'

'Not even getting married?'

Colum smiled. 'No, anyone can do that.'

Lauriol disagreed.

'Not everyone can marry a girl who's engaged to marry another man in a week's time. I suppose that's why you did it.'

Colum looked at her admiringly.

'It may have been. How clever you are, Lauriol.'

'Or did you marry her for her money?'

'I suppose the money was an inducement too.'

'But then why don't you let her give you any?'

'I may, I may, but I don't like taking what's offered me. There's no fun in it.'

Lauriol sighed.

'You are the vainest man I ever knew, and yet everyone thinks you're so modest. "Colum McInnes, most modest of film-stars." Doesn't it mean anything to you when everyone tells you how wonderful you are?'

'Of course it does,' said Colum, 'otherwise I shouldn't mind when Johnny Finkelbaum tells me I'm not. But the public are fools mostly. That's why I can give myself something that they can't. It's my good opinion of myself I want. They think I'm the hell of a fellow. Well, so I am.'

'But not quite in the way they think,' said Lauriol. 'They know you're a Roman Catholic, of course. Many of them think you are religious. Do you get an extra kick out of that?'

Colum frowned, and suddenly looked more tired.

'I've never tried to advertise my religion,' he answered shortly.

'If you mean you're not an advertisement for it! But what about all that religious stuff in Venice, getting married in the Salute and so on and making Margaret trail round churches?'

'She enjoyed it,' Colum said.

'Yes, but was that why you did it? – and not to get the good opinion of R.C.s all over the world? Colum, I very nearly hated you in Venice.'

'I know you did,' said Colum smiling.

'I nearly told Margaret that it was you who stole her bracelet.'

'I know you did,' repeated Colum, still smiling. 'But she wouldn't have believed you if you had.'

'Is she so stupid?'

'She doesn't see me as that kind of fellow.'

'Doesn't she know anything about you at all?'

'Darling, she knows how fond I am of you.'

'Does she?' said Lauriol.

There was a silence during which they stared at the two bars of the electric fire, stretched incongruously over the glowing half consumed stage coals.

Lauriol said at last:

'Colum, why didn't you marry me? I didn't offer myself. You could have pretended it was rape.'

'Darling, because you know too much about me.' He gave her his mischievous smile. 'Aren't we much happier as we are? If we were married, you might want to start reforming me.'

'I haven't in the past, have I?'

'No, you've been an angel to me.'

They were silent again for a moment, then Lauriol said: 'I don't see what you've got out of your marriage with Margaret. She hasn't much money according to your standards, and you won't touch what she has, she's nice-looking in a soft-cheeked, English way, but no one could call her really pretty, she's sweet and dependable and all that, but she's on the dull side; I can't see what you see in her.'

'Ah, am I a mystery to you?' he exclaimed in triumph.

'No, you're not,' snapped Lauriol, vexed with herself for having half admitted that he was. 'You're a little boy who's always play-acting. Some day you'll grow up, and then . . . Supposing I give you away?'

'That's a risk I take,' said Colum.

'And are you so in love with taking risks?'

She felt the tug of his attraction for her threatening to silence what she meant to say. Her tongue was always more candid than her mind; lack of funds, the necessity of parting with things she valued, had sharpened it. She wanted love and a stable relationship, and the thought of risks as an end in themselves, an end to be pursued regardless of a woman's love, exasperated her and made her want to wound him. 'It seems childish to get so much excitement out of deceiving people. It isn't really very clever. And what is there beneath it? It's like sitting on a bubble.'

'A bubble's a pretty thing,' said Colum.

'Yes, but are you happy? Is Margaret happy? What is to come of it all?'

'A baby.'

Lauriol stared at him incredulously.

'A baby? Are you serious, Colum?'

'Yes, why not?'

'I believe you're lying to me.'

'Time will show.'

There was no gainsaying that. Lauriol's heart sank. Somehow she had never regarded Colum's second marriage as other than a temporary arrangement, as short-lived as the first. There would be a few weeks of uncertainty and rumour, of questions that could scarcely be asked, and if they were, would not be answered; and then Margaret would slip down into an oubliette, to be absorbed in her own environment, the suburban background whence she came, hardly leaving a legend, perhaps not even a name. What had been the name of Colum's first wife? Lauriol couldn't remember. Jennifer, yes, that was it, she had been as pretty as a picture and as hard as nails, a precarious hanger-on of the smart world; but she had had her wits about her, she had made sure of her way out of the gilded cage before she entered it, and given little trouble, either to Colum or herself or to the Catholic Church. Lauriol had always liked Margaret, but it had been on the basis of her impermanence, the slight feeling of pity and protectiveness she evoked; the certainty they all felt that she didn't realize what was coming to her. And she was not much to be pitied really; she had money, a position of her own, and the man Colum had filched her from would no doubt be only too glad to marry her when she was free again.

But if Margaret was to be a fixture, if the child was to be a bond between them, what then? Colum was unpredictable; he always had a surprise up his sleeve; what if the unsatisfactory conditions of the last few months, the tedious contrivings, the uncertain tenure, were prolonged into years? With always at the back of her mind the suspicion that he did not really belong to her and depended for some of his happiness on another woman?

'You'll have to settle down into being a heavy father, you know,' she said. 'You won't like that.'

Colum laughed boyishly.

'Oh, well,' he said, 'Try anything once.'

Lauriol did not answer – a conversational technique that she frequently applied to most of her friends, but seldom to Colum. How, she was thinking, could she separate him from Margaret? An idea came to her, an idea she had before, but she had an almost overwhelming distaste for it.

'So you're thinking of giving up your operations on the side,' she said.

'Did I say so?' Colum asked. 'Be an angel, Lauriol, and give me another drink.'

'Isn't that against the rules?' she asked.

'It is,' he answered, 'but I feel I want one . . . Now, what you were saying. I might have a last little fling.'

'You always say that,' Lauriol reminded him, bending over the cocktail shaker.

'I know, but I'm serious this time. As soon as I'm through with this confounded film and all the damned depression it gives me – well, I shan't want to.'

'You'll be too busy rocking the baby, no doubt,' said Lauriol.

'Ah, my dear, we neither of us know what it is to be a parent.'

'You won't be cracking safes.'

'Except on the films,' said Colum.

'But aren't you pledged to do another gentleman before you go back to the rough stuff?'

Colum's face fell.

'Yes, but I shall get out of it. Margaret wants me to.'

The name slipped out; his face apologized for having uttered it; but it pierced Lauriol's feelings like a knife.

'What would she do if she knew about us, Colum?'

'She's a sensible girl, my darling, she wouldn't mind. She likes you almost as much as I do.'

There was something bitter-sweet in this remark which Lauriol didn't stop to analyse.

'And supposing she knew about your other little games?'

'Other little games?' repeated Colum. 'I haven't any. I'm not that sort of man, as you should know.'

'I mean on window-sills and roofs,' said Lauriol.

Colum's face became expressionless.

'She would leave me, I suppose.'

The words seemed to dissolve into the room, leaving it utterly empty and silent. Colum rose to his feet.

'Well, I must be off, Lauriol. A million thanks for being my saleswoman. Next month we'll give a terrific party, fancy dress, and you must come to it as a fence.'

'A fence?'

'Well, there's a Wall in Shakespeare.'

'I suppose you mean that I'm as thin as a rail?' said Lauriol, wilfully misunderstanding him.

He looked her up and down affectionately.

'You're as slender and precious as a meat-ration,' he said.

She did not scold him for his bad-taste joke: her heart was beating much too hard. 'Colum,' she said, trying to keep her voice steady, 'you don't have to rush away, do you? Stay and have another cocktail, since you're in the mood.'

'Another cocktail?' he said. 'Is that what you call it?'

Again she ignored his irony, and threw her pride to the winds.

'You're so late as it is,' she said. 'Surely it won't matter if you're a little later?'

Looking down at her he seemed to hesitate, but then he said, 'You're a dear girl, but don't you see that things are altered now?'

'Altered?' repeated Lauriol. 'Why? Because of the child?'

He nodded. 'It wouldn't be very pretty . . .'

'Do you really mean that?' Lauriol asked.

'Well, yes,' he said, 'I do.'

She stared at him and was still staring at him when he left the room.

*

The chiming clock struck nine and still Margaret had not untied her parcel. She sat with it in the chair next to her, like an anxious passenger in a railway-train, looking at it from time to time with a mixture of longing and distrust that she could not account for. Colum was often late, but seldom as late as this. She always worried about him when he was late, fearing he might have met with an accident, either in the streets or when he was acting. On the films he had to do such dangerous things. Not, she hoped, in *The Devil is so Distinguished*; there, she gathered, the risks he ran were not of the physical sort; but she could not be sure. She was never entirely comfortable about him when he was out of her sight.

Perhaps it was because she was filled with anxious thoughts about him that she did not hear the door open or his footfall on the thick soft carpet. She looked up and there he was.

'Colum!'

'Why,' he said, 'you look as if you had seen a ghost!'

Joy and relief at seeing him drove all other preoccupations from her mind; but just as they were sitting down she cried, 'Oh, mind the parcel!' and snatched it from under him only just in time.

'What have you got there?' he asked.

Already her fingers were busy with the string.

'You'll never guess!'

'Well, let's have dinner first and then I'll guess.'

Rather unwillingly Margaret gave way to him, for she thought him looking tired; and during the meal he talked but little, and, with Margaret's encouragement, drank a good deal. She was less concerned than she would have been at his low spirits, knowing that soon it would be in her power to raise them.

The moment they had finished dinner she went straight to the parcel, like a child.

'Colum, you never tried to guess!'

Usually he threw himself into any project of this sort but now he said, 'My guessing-box is empty. Put me out of my misery and tell me.'

'I'm not going to tell you – it's a present.'

'Shall I like it?'

'Yes, very much.'

'Well, show it to me.'

'No, it's your present, you must undo it.'

Margaret always enjoyed watching Colum open a parcel.

However tightly it was tied it seemed to fall apart in his hands. This time he was not so dexterous, but it only gave expectancy a longer lease.

'It can't be anything to eat,' he said, trying to meet her mood. 'It's too hard and too heavy.' He weighed it in his hands and looked at Margaret quizzically. 'More like something to bash you with,' he said. 'What *can* it be?' A portion of the marble surface appeared, dark brown against the tissue paper. His fingers clenched, then suddenly he tore the wrappings off, and the head lay in his lap, face downwards.

Margaret never forgot the look of terror that crossed his face. He recovered himself.

'Why, it's a head!' he exclaimed.

'Of course it is,' cried Margaret. 'But look at it, Colum, look at it properly! You can't see it like that!'

Slowly and most unwillingly he turned it over, and his face, drawn and narrowed with suffering, looked straight into the laughing face of the child.

He raised his eyes and said, halting over the words, 'But how extraordinary! It's almost the exact image of the one we had.'

This was Margaret's moment. Her voice rang out in triumph.

'But it *is* the one we had, the one that you were so fond of, the one that was stolen!'

He bent over it again as in a daze, and cautiously explored it with his fingers.

'But it can't be. The likeness is amazing, but it can't be. There are hundreds of heads like mine, of course. The same man probably turned out dozens.'

'But it *is* ours, Colum! If you look you'll see the scratch under its ear.'

Gingerly he turned it over.

'By God, you're right,' he said.

'But Colum,' cried Margaret, wild with disappointment, 'aren't you *glad*? I thought you'd be . . . so very glad.' she gasped.

'Of course I'm glad, my darling.' Colum's unsteady voice began to gather strength and naturalness. 'It's the most wonderful thing that ever happened. How did you find it?'

Margaret told him the whole story, and Colum listened with rapt attention.

'And we owe it all to St. Anthony,' she wound up.

'Yes, dear, we do, and I shall burn a candle to him, which you can't, being a heretic. But how on earth did Lauriol get hold of it? I have an idea, but I'm not sure. Shall we ring her up?'

'Yes, let's,' said Margaret.

Half way to the telephone he stopped. 'No, she'll be out, I expect. I'll ring her in the morning. Now let's do some gloating.'

He turned the head over and over, fondling it, and then put it on the table by his side.

'When I first saw it,' he said, 'I couldn't believe that it was ours. You can understand that, can't you? It seemed too good to be true.'

'I was a little disappointed,' Margaret confessed, 'that you didn't seem more pleased.'

'I was too flabbergasted, it was like a miracle.' He looked at the head again. 'Darling, we must put it back in its old place. Can you find the stand?'

Margaret went to fetch it. This was one of the moments, in the chain of happy moments, that she had most looked forward to.

'We've had to rearrange everything,' Colum said when she came back. 'I think we'll put it on the mantelpiece, for the time being, it will look better there.' Suiting the action to the word, he put the pedestal on the mantelpiece, and was going back to fetch the head when he called out to Margaret, quite loudly, though she was standing by him,

'Oh, Margaret, it's a bit dusty, can you bring a cloth or something?'

Hardly had she got outside the door when it struck Margaret that after all its adventures what the head really needed was a wash. She was re-entering the room to consult Colum on this point, when she saw his raised hand, which was putting the head into position, jerk forwards. 'Take care!' she cried, but the sound was lost in a splintering crash, and the next thing she beheld was the fragments, lying on the tiles of the fireplace, broken beyond repair.

Colum did all he could to comfort her and to turn the scene of calamity into a love-scene such as she had never known since her honeymoon. Between his kisses he almost, almost persuaded her that it had been his culpable, his most culpable, carelessness. But not quite. Something in her mind refused conviction, and something in her heart resisted his endearments, even when she was giving way to them; and when it was all over she lay tossing and turning beside his quiet body, still seeing in her mind's eye the unkind jerk of his hand on the child's head, and unable to persuade herself that it was accidental. And other things about him which had puzzled her, and which she had thrust out of her mind, but not out of memory, issued from their holes and corners, mouthing a message whose import grew plainer the more passionately she refused to recognize it.

18

NEITHER could Lauriol sleep that night. The news that Margaret was to have a child, combined with Colum's refusal to stay with her, magnified itself in her tired active mind into a conviction that Colum had ceased to care for her. He would settle down into domestic life and gradually slough her off. Everything pointed to it, and not least his assertion that he meant to give up his old ways. Only once more, he said, and then he would be an honest man. He had said this many times before, as she reminded him, but in reminding him she had not convinced herself; for on those previous occasions there had not been a child to consider, nor a wife, the mother of the child. She did not know how much Colum's religion meant to him; she believed it meant very little; but if he was not religious he was superstitious; he went to confession sometimes. This time the marriage was no mere civil tie, and if the Church succeeded in exerting its influence . . .

But Margaret was not of his faith and could not be expected to have any prejudice against divorce. It would not make her leave him, Colum had hinted, to be told that Lauriol was his mistress; she would condone it. But she would leave him if she knew he was a thief.

Lauriol had no moral principles but she had a certain amount of moral taste, and she shrank from the idea of telling Margaret about Colum's secret life. Nor was she sure that the disclosure would have the effect she wanted. It might turn Margaret away from him, but would it turn him to her, Lauriol? Nine people out of ten would probably say no, and until far into the small hours no was the answer that Lauriol gave herself. Colum would never forgive her for betraying him.

But she would not be betraying him to the police. He would not be in the slightest danger from Margaret, she felt sure; Margaret would never tell on him. She would have no difficulty in finding a plausible reason to give the world for leaving Colum; she, Lauriol, would willingly provide it. Indeed, in Lauriol's world divorce was so much more the rule than the exception that Margaret would find it harder to explain why she was sticking to him than why she had left him.

So what was the real danger? Only that Colum would be too angry with her to forgive her. But would he be? They had had many quarrels, and all had been made up. Colum was not the man to cherish a grievance; he hated hard feelings and could not understand them. It was utterly outside his nature to dislike anyone on moral grounds, because they had done something 'wrong'. He had no right to, being what he was. But even if he had been an honest man himself, he still would not have minded. And he would realize that she had not done it to injure him, or even to injure Margaret, but because she felt it was the only course left open to her, the only way to get him back. Consciously or not, he would sympathize with that. And the rest would come – come with the long habit of their love, their natural affinity to each other, which was so much stronger than anything that either of them could do or say.

Lauriol was not a creature of habit; long before the winter morning broke she was up and had made herself some coffee; and still feeling restless she walked down the tree-lined, five-tiered boulevard of Queen's Gate and out into the Park. And that was why, when the telephone bell rang (it rang many times, for Lauriol used the telephone a great deal), she was not there to answer it.

During the greater part of her long walk she could see the block of flats where Margaret and Colum lived towering above the sky-line; it seemed to beckon her and confirm her in her resolve, and presently at a time when she felt sure that Colum would be out and Margaret in she bent her steps towards it. Lauriol often dropped in at the flat and Margaret never stood on ceremony with her, so Lauriol was surprised when Richards, with an air even more reserved than usual, told her that he would go and find out whether Mrs McInnes was at home. After an interval he came back and said yes, but would she mind waiting, and she was ushered into the sitting-room from which all traces of last night's disaster had been cleared away.

At last Margaret came in, but a Margaret so different from her ordinary self that Lauriol was startled. She had evidently been crying, and in an effort to banish tear-stains and conceal swollen eyelids she had put on a great deal of make-up, so that she appeared almost bedizened. Gone was her customary gentle dignity of manner; she seemed nervous and preoccupied, her eyes were restless, and her voice showed signs of strain.

They soon began to speak of Colum, for Colum was their staple subject; and in normal circumstances Margaret was only too glad to do so, for she recognized the position Lauriol held in Colum's life, though she had not allowed herself to speculate on its furthest implications. And in a way she was glad to talk about him now, for he was the topic that was dearest to her and she had little small-talk, but her mind was in such confusion about him that she did not know what to say and kept starting and stopping like a defective motor-engine.

At last to excuse herself she said, 'Lauriol, dear, I'm afraid you must find me rather distrait, but such a sad thing happened last night and it upset me more than it should have. You remember our child's head, the one that Colum was so fond of, that was stolen? Well, I found it again in the strangest circumstances.' She started to tell Lauriol the story, and so absorbed was she in it herself that she did not notice the unnatural fixity of Lauriol's face. Nor did she mention that she had identified the lady whose property was being sold. She felt a delicacy about doing so, as Lauriol had preferred to be anonymous; it would look like prying; and she thought that Lauriol would herself refer to it afterwards, as a matter of course. She ended up, 'And when Colum was putting it back on the chimneypiece' – she pointed to the place – 'he knocked it off and broke it.'

'He knocked it off?' repeated Lauriol, her voice incredulous.

'Yes,' said Margaret, and suddenly, at the recollection, almost before she had time to get out her handkerchief she broke down and sobbed.

Lauriol knelt down beside her and put her arm round her, trying to soothe her. When at last Margaret grew calmer Lauriol said, 'But, Margaret darling, did it matter *so* much?'

This brought on a fresh outburst, which Margaret tried to stem by shaking her head vigorously from side to side. Between her sobs she gasped, 'I believe . . . he did it . . . on purpose.'

Lauriol was on her guard at once.

'Oh, but he couldn't have. You must be mistaken.'

The paroxysm over, Margaret said,

'You see, I saw him do it, and he didn't know I was looking.'

'But why should he want to break it?'

'That's what I want to know – that's what worries me.'

She sobbed afresh, but less convulsively. Lauriol's mind, as always, worked quickly – it darted in all directions, yet in the deeper sense, she no longer knew her own mind, or whither it was leading her.

'Lauriol,' said Margaret, suddenly, 'do *you* know why he broke it?'

'I haven't the faintest idea,' Lauriol said, 'and I don't believe he did. Have you asked him?'

'Oh no, how could I? How could I?' Margaret's agitation began to come back. 'It would, it would look as if . . . as if I . . . I suspected him of something.'

'Suspected him?'

In Margaret's misery the one thing she wanted, the life-line that her troubled mind was reaching for, was certainty. Lauriol was Colum's friend, his best friend. Where Colum was concerned, where his interests were concerned, talking to Lauriol was like talking to herself.

'I thought that . . . for some reason . . . he didn't want anyone to know we'd got the head back.'

'Didn't the servants see?'

'No . . . Colum did something with the pieces.'

'Perhaps he took them to be mended,' Lauriol said.

'Oh no, it was much too badly broken.'

There was an uneasy pause during which they looked away from each other and nothing seemed to pass between them.

'I think you're making a mountain out of . . . well, nothing,' Lauriol said. 'You're imagining things, Margaret, you really are. It sometimes happens to women, when—'

'How did you know?' asked Margaret.

'I guessed . . . You're mixing Colum on the films with Colum in real life. You're being frightfully unfair.'

'Do you imagine I haven't thought of that?' said Margaret. 'I thought of nothing else, all through the night. And there are other things I couldn't tell you about. They seem to point one way. Oh Lauriol, tell me that he isn't . . . promise me that he isn't . . .'

'What?'

'You know what. I couldn't bear it if he was. It's the one thing I couldn't bear. Surely, surely, he couldn't be? You see, for one thing, he's religious in a way, though he isn't what they call practising. And he has always been so good to me . . . he's good

186

to everyone. It isn't possible, is it? It would break my heart if it was. Tell me it isn't, Lauriol.'

'I don't know what you're talking about,' said Lauriol harshly.

'Oh yes, you do, you do, and that's what frightens me. Oh Lauriol, in some ways you know him so much better than I do – I don't mind that a bit, believe me I don't, he would tell you himself that I don't mind – if only it was something else, if you could say something to make me believe he wasn't . . .'

Lauriol still played for time.

'Wasn't what, Margaret?'

'A thief.'

The little word fell between them like a feather, yet it made a barrier that neither of them could cross. Lauriol had not believed that Margaret would bring herself to utter it, she thought that by daring her to say it she could stifle it, and it found her unprepared.

'Supposing he was a thief,' she temporized, 'what then?'

Margaret opened horrified eyes.

'Oh, I don't know, I don't know, I couldn't bear it. It would make him seem a different person, I could never feel the same with him, I couldn't think about him in the same way. It's something I've always had a horror of. He wouldn't even look the same to me . . . He doesn't now.'

'Would you leave him?'

'Don't ask me, don't ask me, I might, I think I should. What use could I be to him, with all my thoughts about him poisoned? What should we find to say to each other? How could we even look at each other without feeling ashamed?'

'Thieves have had wives before now,' Lauriol said, 'and their wives have stuck to them in spite of it. Or do you think all thieves are single men?'

Margaret passed her hand across her brow. 'I've thought of that. It sounds idiotic, but I've thought how in his films Colum has sometimes been married, and his wives haven't minded what he did. But I couldn't help minding, Lauriol. I couldn't stay with him. Could you?'

'Yes, I could,' said Lauriol, and a gleam came into her eyes. 'I could, but it's beside the point, because, you see,' she went on softly, 'he isn't a thief and when you come to yourself you'll realize what a hideous injustice you have done him. Colum a thief! Why, he's the most generous man in the world. Have you known him sponge on anybody? Has he ever sponged on you? And as for stealing – it's a monstrous suggestion, Margaret, and you know it is.' Lauriol spoke with mounting indignation, forgetting that she was saying the opposite of what she had come to say. Margaret was much more impressed by her anger than she had been by her sympathy. Already half ashamed of her suspicions, she timidly let her eyes seek Lauriol's. The cloud above her spirit lifted; she saw light under it, and had a glimpse of the Eden that was theirs before the serpent entered. But then another picture came – Colum with his hand on the child's head, jerking it outwards, willing its destruction; and her craving for certainty remained unappeased. Half doubting, half reassured, she said, 'But you do see why I was so worried, don't you? Finding the head in such odd circumstances, and then Colum . . .' she broke off, not trusting herself to speak.

'What one would like to know,' said Lauriol reflectively, 'is who the woman was who sold the thing, and how she came by it.'

Margaret stared at her.

'But it was you, Lauriol!' she gasped.

A tremor ran down Lauriol's back, and her chest and shoulders seemed to contract with fear.

'Me!' she exclaimed. 'Me! Margaret, you must be mad. What on earth makes you think I sold it?'

'Because all the other things were yours that were sold with it,' Margaret said. 'I recognized them – they used to be in your china cabinet, I'm sure they were – the Four Evangelists, and the Five Senses, and the other figures. Don't you believe me?' she went on wildly, feeling the ground crumble under her feet as it had never crumbled before. 'You must believe me, Lauriol! Stop, I bought one of them as a present for you, because I thought you'd like to have it back! I'll go and get it.'

Without looking at Lauriol, but feeling that she must get away from her, she went out, and lingered for a minute in her quiet bedroom, trying to adjust her mind to this last development. What would happen now? Had she really gone mad? Would Lauriol take the figure and smash it before her eyes?

Lauriol had slipped down in her chair, and was almost lying in it, when Margaret came in. She looked at Margaret as if she was a stranger.

Margaret began to fumble with the string of the parcel. 'I must be careful,' she reminded herself out loud, 'or I shall break it, and that would never do.' She shot a glance at the still figure on the chair. 'I'm sure you'll recognize it, Lauriol,' she rambled on, half pleading, half encouraging. 'It really is yours, you know, or it would be,' she added with a nervous titter, 'if I could get it out.' She thought of Colum's fingers and how deft they were. But at last her gift emerged, the tall lady in her red cloak and flowered gown. Her head was bound in a white scarf. One of her two children was kneeling at her feet; the other, caught up in a fold of her cloak, was perched upon her shoulder. It was whispering in her ear and she bent her head to listen. 'Widow and Orphans' ran the legend upon the green base, encrusted with moss and strewn with flowers; and perhaps to symbolize her widowhood, her lack of a man's support, she was leaning with elegiac grace against the stem of a dead sapling. How often had Margaret, in the long pauses that punctuated conversation in Lauriol's flat, studied this charming and by no means unfeeling representation of bereavement.

Getting up from her chair she proffered it to Lauriol, who mechanically held her hands out to receive it.

'You remember it now, don't you?' she pleaded. 'It is yours, isn't it?'

Lauriol examined, or seemed to examine, the figure without answering, and with no light of recognition in her eye. Suddenly she rose to her feet, and said rather formally and coldly,

'Thank you, Margaret. It was sweet of you to think of giving me a present, and I appreciate your kindness very much. But please believe me, I never set eyes on this before.' Shaking her head, she turned the figure over, and then, opening her bag with great deliberation, slipped it inside. 'I must go now,' she said. 'And, Margaret, you're not well, you need a rest. If you should want me at any time, if I can be of any use to you, please let me know.'

She gave Margaret the discreetly commiserating look one gives an invalid, and adding, 'Please don't bother, I can see myself out,' had reached the door with her long stride almost before Margaret realized she was going.

Margaret moved restlessly about the room, trying to take comfort from its familiarity; but it didn't seem familiar, it seemed strange, and the ridiculous but disturbing idea occurred to her that perhaps she was losing her faculty of recognition, and this way madness lies. But however much one's nerves may play one up, to use the current phrase, Reason is slow to renounce its sovereignty, its confidence in itself as arbiter of what is so and what is not so; and shaken as she had been at first by Lauriol's denials, she became more and more convinced that they were lies. And if they were, what followed? Another link in the chain of evidence whose chilly grip was tightening on her heart. If Lauriol had lied about the head, and lied about the figure, might she not have lied when she said that Colum was not a . . . How had she ever come to say that word? It was one thing to refute Lauriol in the matter of the figure; her desire, her pride, her sense of being a responsible person whose word must be accepted, urged her to. But Lauriol's defence of Colum, that was another matter. There is all the difference between a lie that suits one, and a lie that doesn't; and Margaret was still trying to tell herself that Lauriol might have been untruthful in the one case, and truthful in the other. Her thoughts switched. It hadn't been a breakage but a murder. When the head fell, a skull was cracked and brains were scattered. Whose? Why had she felt a pang go through her like a sword, as though something inside her was receiving its death wound? What was it that had died – her love for Colum? Or the symbol of her love for him, his child?

If it was one, she thought, it couldn't be the other. But couldn't it? Were they not both the same? How could one survive without the other?

Her body sagged. The living weight within it turned to lead, and what had warmed her life now chilled it. Terrified of moving, of receiving physical confirmation of her fears, she sat quite still, her eyes fixed on the empty chimneypiece. The laughing face was looking down at her, but it wasn't the face that she remembered; it was another child's face, perhaps her own child's. Who is it like? she wondered. And then quite suddenly it was effaced, it wasn't there, and Colum was.

'My darling,' he exclaimed, and came to her and kissed her; but tasting the salt tear on her cheek drew back.

'Why, you've been crying!' he said. 'Tell me what's the matter. You were sleeping so sweetly when I left I didn't like to wake you.'

Margaret's tears started afresh.

'Oh Colum, Lauriol has been here.'

Colum knit his brows.

'Has she, by Jove? I stopped at her place on my way, and she was out. But what did she say to you to make you cry? I'll have her on the mat for this.'

'She wasn't unkind – she didn't mean to be unkind. But she told me a lie – I know she did.'

'Well, has no one ever told you a lie before?'

'Yes, but this was so important. It was about – you know, the head. She said she hadn't sold it, and she said the group I bought her wasn't hers, and never had been.'

'What was it?'

Margaret told him.

Colum whistled.

'Whew! It sounds as if Lauriol had been fibbing. She never was a very truthful girl, you know, though she's a darling. You don't mind me calling her a darling, do you?'

'No . . . o . . . But Colum, I'm quite sure the group was hers.'

'If it was the widow with the children, it was hers all right. I used to think that was how you'd look, if I popped off.'

Margaret closed her eyes against the image, but she would not be deflected and went on,

'Then why did she deny it? I wasn't . . . accusing her of anything. And the head too. How did she come to have it?'

Colum's white teeth closed over his full, square lower lip. He shook his head meditatively and said, 'I've no idea. She must have picked it up somewhere.'

'But she *knew* it was one of the things that had been stolen from us. I told her, so did you. Why didn't she tell us she had it? Why didn't she offer it to us first? She must have *known* we wanted it.'

Colum suddenly looked very tired. 'My darling, I'm afraid I can't tell you. Lauriol's a law unto herself.'

Aware that she was being tiresome, Margaret went on, 'But she's your best friend, Colum. I don't mind that. I don't mind a bit, but I know she is. And she knew how fond you were of the head. It's incredible that she shouldn't have told you. I believe you're shielding her. Please, please, Colum tell me how it happened. It will make me . . . it will make me ill if you don't.'

Margaret's voice rose to a wail, and the tears poured helplessly from her eyes. She had lost her grip of the situation, and her being was concentrated into the one wish that Colum should say something that would clear him of her suspicions.

He began to kiss her, murmuring endearments, but she pushed him petulantly away as a child might have, sobbing, 'I'm sure it's something between you, it's something between you!'

Colum rose to his feet.

'Listen, my darling,' he said, 'and do be reasonable. I'll see Lauriol as soon as I can and no doubt she'll have an explanation. And anyhow, what *does* it matter? The head's broken, worse luck, that does matter, but we can't do anything about it. Come, darling, dry your eyes, and powder your nose, because I've got the day off, that's what I came to tell you. Would you believe it, the cameramen have staged a lightning strike. I'm free! We've heaps of petrol: let's take the car and go to Canterbury and have a look at the Cathedral. You've always wanted to see it, and it'll be a change from church-crawling in London.'

He put all the persuasiveness he could into his plea, and his face, which answered as promptly to his moods as to his health, suddenly regained its freshness. The countenance which had enchanted millions glowed for her alone. But she could not respond to it. The prospect of spending the day alone with him, once the greatest joy she could conceive, was now unbearable.

'I can't,' she said.

'You can't? Why not?'

'Because . . . because I promised Daddy I'd go down to Dittingham. He isn't well.' It was the first deliberate untruth she had told Colum; she blushed for herself and could not meet his eyes.

The happiness went out of Colum's face.

'All right, darling, but let me drive you down.'

'No, I'd rather go alone. I don't know how bad he is.'

'Well, then, let Phillips take you.'

'No, thanks, I'd rather go by train. I want to read.' Once started, lies seemed to pour off her, but the truth was that she wanted to free herself, as soon as possible, from every link with Colum.

It was partly self-protective; she had an instinct that as soon as she got away from him her old feeling for him might come back.

'Then shall I call you a taxi?'

'Yes, but I must pack first.'

'Pack?'

'You see I may be away for a day or two.'

She suddenly thought, How dry my eyes feel. Can I ever have cried?

Colum looked at her wonderingly.

'You don't know what mischief I may get into,' he said. 'Anyhow, let me help you to pack.'

She could not refuse him that; he was a much better packer than she was and enjoyed it. But when she saw his hands among her things, and turned away from him to get others from the chest of drawers, she found herself wondering whether anything would be missing when she got home.

19

DESTINY took Margaret at her word and would not have her a liar; she found her father laid up with a chill. It was nothing serious, she was certain; and childishly she felt relieved, when Colum rang up, to be able to tell him truthfully how matters stood.

Her father's indisposition recalled her to a sense of actuality. The sickroom, the medicine bottle, the thermometer, the need to think of someone other than herself, purged her mind of some of the accretions of unregulated emotion that had formed round her thoughts, and she was able to separate what she really thought from what she wished or feared to think. Two impulses had been behind her flight: the blind desire to get away from Colum, and the need to confide in somebody: her father. The first was satisfied; the second must wait.

With the natural egotism of a sick man Mr Pennefather did not seem surprized at Margaret's unheralded arrival. She had always tended him when he was ill and she was doing so now; it was all quite regular. He asked how she was getting on, of course, and if she found it easier than she feared to tell him she was getting on quite well, she did not reproach herself, for she had the unexceptionable excuse that an invalid must not be worried. To no one else did she feel accountable for her comings and goings, and as a matter of fact her absence from Fair Haven had been longer than usual: it was that that needed explaining, not her return.

To all appearance, then, her presence was normal and commendable, and this had its effect on Margaret's state of mind. She began to see herself not as having fled from a criminal husband but as having returned to a sick father, as having momentarily exchanged a conjugal for a filial duty. It was easy for her to slip back into the life of the place. Even to strangers Fair Haven had a peculiarly enfolding atmosphere, an air of being insulated from the outside world; it seemed as safe and solvent as the Bank of England. To-morrow, perhaps, or next day, she would ring up Diana. She rather dreaded that, for women are so perceptive; they can tell by the tone of a voice when things are not going well. But there was no hurry.

How long then, she asked herself, did she mean to stay? Was she in flight from Colum? Had she in the technical sense of the word, 'left' him? Of course not; she would only be away for a few days, at most the inside of a week. It was all quite simple. She would stay until her father was well enough to hear what she had to tell him, and on his answer would depend her future attitude to Colum. For she must have an attitude, an attitude founded on an objective view of the case. She could not allow her state of mind to be at the mercy of her hopes and fears.

She did not think her father would advise her to leave Colum. If she had thought so, she would not have made her mind up to consult him. He would give her the advice she had given herself: Colum must be weaned from his bad habits. Her life-work from now on must be to reclaim him. She must put from herself the horror that his misdeeds had given her, must snap out of all that, it could do no good to anyone. She must adopt the attitude that had come to her so easily on the Bench – of enlightened sympathy with wrong-doers. She must summon up her magisterial fact-facing self. On the Bench she reminded herself, she had had many cases of theft to deal with, and never had she felt the slightest touch of superstitious horror when the malefactor was brought before her. He was just a man, like other men; very often he was a child – a delinquent child, and it would be for her to help to decide whether or not he should be sent to an approved school. And when he was sent there, if he was, the officials of the school did not throw up their hands in horror and exclaim 'A thief! What *shall* we do?' They did not feel they must at once retire into private life – return to their parents' homes – to escape the contamination of such a monster; on the contrary they treated him with every kindness, and made him an appointment – a series of appointments – with a nerve-doctor. They did not feel that they must love him less because he had fallen into a very common form of human error. They would be ashamed to own such sentiments. Their job was to promote his moral welfare, to straighten him where he was warped, and send him back to the world a useful citizen.

A delinquent child! That was what Colum was, and she had always felt a special sympathy with delinquent children ... perhaps she had even thought them more interesting than other children, because more in need of pity. They symbolized humanity's fall from Grace – and many people, even religious people – especially, perhaps, religious people – believed that true goodness could only be found in the pit of moral degradation. Margaret did not like that idea, which seemed to belittle the moral exertions of conventional aspirants to salvation. Why try to be good, if it was more pleasing in the sight of God to be unashamedly bad? – but she saw now that there was something, in it, if it could be cited in Colum's defence.

But Fair Haven did not induce a religious mood in Margaret. She had never felt the need for support outside herself while she lived there: the assurance of material and moral security it gave her was too strong. On the other hand her home enabled her to consider with a quieter mind and a greater show of objectivity offences against the law which were committed outside it, in places such as London flats. It was a moral eminence, exempt from private passion, where if Colum himself were to appear, she could pronounce a judgment as cool as Solomon's.

But first the evidence must be given, the separate items with which she was so familiar but which until now, she had refused to add up into an indictment. What would she tell her father? First, the episode of the pin-cushion, that loving theft that had seemed so endearing when it happened. Next, the stealing of her bracelet in Venice. He thought she would never suspect him of stealing something he had given her. She would never have recovered it, but for St. Anthony's aid. Then the faked burglary which Colum had staged in London, and the drain-pipe clue which had somehow taken in the police. Of course he had not entered by the drain-pipe; he had let himself in through the flat door with his own key and later laid the drainpipe trail. While she was asleep in the next room he had tiptoed about, gathering the swag; what would he have done if she had wakened and discovered him? The Insurance Company had paid up without a murmur and Colum had been a gentleman – yes, despite her protests, he had insisted on her taking the money for the Tanagra figurine which he had given her. Then one by one the objects had been disposed of through convenient channels – or had they? Of that she could not be sure: perhaps the child's head was the first he had unloaded. Once again St. Anthony had answered her prayer and directed her feet to the sale room. Triumphantly she had brought the missing treasure home and then Colum had deliberately broken it – broken it to destroy the evidence. After that she could not remember very well, but Lauriol had come round to disarm her suspicions, and had only succeeded in confirming them. She had told Margaret two thumping lies – three, for she had said that Colum was not a thief. He was a thief and Lauriol was his accomplice.

If she was to be of any help to him, it was essential to forget the fact that she was his wife. The effort to tabulate chronologically the details of Colum's dishonesty had somehow worked her up. When she spoke to her father she would have to be briefer and more precise. Perhaps it would be better to make notes beforehand; otherwise she might leave out something vital.

When, her father might ask her, did you first suspect him? She tried to remember when, but the seed had grown as slowly and secretly as the seed inside her body; it had grown, moreover, as that other seed had not, against the wishes of her mind and heart; her whole being had shrunk from putting two and two together. Perhaps in Venice, when she had first formed her habit of secret church-going? Had that habit begun as a kind of compensation, an outlet for an inner unrest?

No, she told herself with relief: the habit had begun before that, it had begun with Colum's asking her to become a Roman Catholic. Yet would she have persisted in it, and found it such a solace, if she had been as happy with Colum as she believed herself to be?

Morning and evening Colum rang her up and his voice showed or seemed to show increasing uneasiness. 'But how are *you*, darling?' he said when she told him her father was on the mend; 'that's what I want to know.' Surprized, she assured him she was perfectly well; but he did not seem convinced. 'Well, take care of yourself,' he said. 'Good people are scarce.' 'And you take care of yourself,' Margaret said. 'Oh, I'm all right,' he answered, 'it's you I'm thinking of.'

The next day brought a letter from him, a most unnusual thing, for he almost never wrote.

'My darling,' the letter ran, 'I have been feeling so anxious about you: are you sure you are quite well? I don't want to say anything to alarm you, and I'm sure there's nothing to be alarmed about, but when we were last together you seemed so excited and unlike yourself. You said the oddest things – not only to me but to Lauriol too. She was quite frightened for you, and I was much more upset than I showed. I expect you have forgotten all about it now and I don't want to remind you, but you had some kind of little *crise-de-nerfs*; women in your state do, you know, and you said all kinds of things you didn't mean. The head was ours, of course – but Lauriol didn't sell it, and the figure you gave her wasn't hers, it was different in a dozen ways, as you'll realize when you see the two together. But no, you won't, because Lauriol has taken the hint and decided to part with some of her things, now she knows how much they fetch. But she's not going to sell yours. Groups of widows and orphans abound – they were a favourite subject with the Staffordshire potters. So do, my darling, put all that out of your mind, and have a happy holiday with your dear old father, to whom my best respects, and my love too, if I may. It worries me that you should be a hospital nurse, when what you really need is nursing yourself. Thanks to my blasted job you've been left alone too much, and you get to brooding – anyone less level-headed than you are would have gone clean off their rocker! I'm sure it was just a temporary nerve-storm, but if you still believe that Lauriol and I were hatching some dire plot between us I shall really have to take you to a psychiatrist!!!

I shall come down to lunch on Sunday to see that you are following my instructions – bringing with me something that you'll *both like*.

Ever your devoted
C.

P.S. Nerve-storms are common form in *my* profession – but I never thought *you'd* have one.

It was Thursday – plenty of time to stop Colum from coming And she would stop him, of course.

The impudence of it!

Lauriol and Colum had laid their heads together and concocted this preposterous story which they expected her to believe. Because they were two to one, they thought they could put it over, bounce her into believing it, by a kind of hypnotism. Because Colum was such a successful illusionist on the screen, because he could make a foolish and improbable story so real to people's imaginations that their own lives seemed colourless and unreal by contrast, he believed, no doubt, that he could perform this miracle on her, make her mistrust the evidence of her mind and senses, and accept his version of what had happened. And just as on the screen he was used to falsifying values, and presenting crime as something glamorous and romantic, so he thought he would woo her from her incredulity by clothing the episode and all that had preceded it in the charms and graces of his personality. She would cease to wonder whether his story was true; she would take it from him as unquestioningly as she took his other gifts, his looks, his kindness, his love. It would cease to be a question of right and wrong – it would be just an attribute of Colum, to be swallowed whole, as he was.

Well, she would show him.

Not otherwise had the dictators of totalitarian countries bemused their devotees, inflaming their love and loyalty to such a pitch that any statement they made, however preposterous, however demonstrably untrue, had the appearance and authority of truth because they uttered it, and because their personal prestige gave the lie an attractiveness, a plausibility to the minds of their worshippers that mere abstract truth could never have. It aroused in them the will to believe, which was more than half-way to believing. Truth does not exist, they cynically said; truth is what you can persuade people to believe.

But she, Margaret, was made of sterner stuff: she would not go back to Colum and live a lie with him.

She read the letter again. How ingenuous it was. Had he really written it to deceive her? Was it really a conspiracy between him and Lauriol to browbeat her into believing something that was not true?

It was unlike him to do that, he was not that kind of character. Deceitful, yes, she had to admit he was deceitful. But the kind of brazenness implied by a frontal attack on another person's mind – that, in private life at any rate, he was incapable of. Even Nick admitted that he had never been a bully. He had always respected her independence; he had no power-complex or itch to impose his will on other people. He might throw dust in her eyes but he would never try to blind her.

For the first time since she had left him she found herself thinking of his good qualities, for, she told herself, they existed still, even if they had been blotted out by the name of thief. He had been so imaginatively considerate to her. How tenderly he had steered her through the deeps and shoals and rapids of their short married life! What mortifications he had spared her! How gentle and unhurting he had made the contact between her world and his! She was set in her ways, very conscious of what ought and ought not to be done; whereas they followed the opposite convention: to be conspicuously natural, never to deny an emotion its expression, even when perhaps, it would have been less trouble to. They lived by exhibiting their temperaments, she by curbing hers. But for his tact and *savoir-faire*, what a target they might have been for her priggishness, and she for their derision – and being in a minority of one she would have been the sufferer. But it had not turned out so: by making a little comedy of their differences, Colum had kept their strangeness to each other free from hostility; it had become almost a bond. She had been the foreigner in their midst, entitled to a foreigner's privileges, one of which was to be regarded in a kindly way as rather queer; and on that footing their relationship had prospered, and though it had never developed into real intimacy and had left her fundamentally lonely, it had given her a sense of comradeship.

And this she owed entirely to Colum and his sleepless but unobtrusive activity as a solvent.

Must she be condemned to think him a bad man, a crook (horrible word), somebody she could not associate with on terms of trust, without which there is no love?

It was long past getting-up time but she read the letter again, and in the light of her softened feeling for Colum a new interpretation came to her. Perhaps it was not what it seemed – an attempt to persuade her that, in a fit of hysteria, she had put a totally false construction on an innocent, commonplace transaction, perhaps it was not meant to bamboozle her at all. Perhaps it was – well, a tacit admission of guilt, so framed as to leave the way open to understanding and forgiveness; a face-saving letter, both for Colum and her. She had caught him out, yes; but the letter took it for granted that she still loved him; and the charges of hysteria and loss of mental balance, the false account of what had happened – they were not impudent attempts to confute an enemy, a prosecuting counsel, they were offered to her as to someone who loved him, and who would grasp eagerly at the opportunity – not to think better of him, but to preserve his good name in the eyes of the world. She could not, how could she? expect him to confess in so many words that he was a wrong 'un; but he could provide her with a loophole large enough to admit both her knowledge and her love.

'Do this for me,' the letter now seemed to say. 'Pretend for my sake that you have made a mistake.'

Was it a great deal to ask of love – a mere act of forgiveness for an offence committed against the law, not her? The stealing of her things, she realized, had only been a trick to put her off the scent. He had not meant to injure her. If he had trodden on her toe it would have been a greater personal injury. Ought she to withhold forgiveness from him? *Could* she withhold it, if she loved him?

Forgiveness meant accepting the letter, tacitly admitting that she had been wrong, and going back to Colum as if nothing had happened. Could she?

Forgiveness is one of the strongest impulses of the heart, and for a time it seemed to Margaret that she could. Indeed, the returning impulses of her love made her feel guilty towards Colum. Perfect love casteth out fear: she thought of this and many other noble utterances about love, and felt that she had failed him. What right had she to judge him? How would she have felt if he had suddenly taken exception to something she had done that transgressed his code – or even his codelessnes – and decided that for him it put her outside the pale of love? Film-stars were notoriously capricious: they might take offence at an eyelash out of place and make it grounds for divorce. Colum had never pleaded his artistic temperament to find fault with her; yet she, who had been brought up to believe that marriage is sacred and love eternal, had not hesitated to condemn him.

It was not easy for Margaret to acknowledge herself in the wrong but when she did she did it thoroughly. She almost felt grateful to Colum for testing her love for him by his crooked ways. But later in the day her mood underwent another change. Not to anger – she felt she never could be angry with him again – but to another view of what their future relationship must be. Colum was once more the delinquent child, but a child to be petted and adored, and never to be called naughty. No doctors need be called in; all she would have to do would be to wrap him in a love so vigilant that evil impulses would never get by it. Love is an antiseptic; in the moral sphere it is what sunshine and fresh air are in the physical, a natural germicide.

No other disinfectant would be needed. Colum's letter amounted to a confession; and in the circumstances, confession must also mean repentance and the determination to amend.

What else could it mean? It would not be easy for him, at first, to live with her, knowing that she knew about him; it would be a daily mortification and she would have to lighten the burden of it. She would be the most considerate of policewomen, but a policewoman she would be, her presence and her knowledge his safeguard against further lapses. That would be his punishment – if she could think of punishment in connection with him – to be always within sight of the one person who knew his secret but would never tell it, not even to her father, least of all to him.

Unconsciously, but not unwillingly, Margaret began to think of herself as a kind of celestial blackmailer, levying on Colum a perpetual tribute of good behaviour, perhaps, more positively, of good works, a servitude he would gladly undergo since it would be sweetened on both sides by love.

But would love be enough? Ought Colum to go through some decontamination process? He had written (no doubt facetiously) of a psychiatrist for her: why not a psychiatrist for him? She couldn't imagine him submitting to it. Love would find out a way; but how? What would she do? Season her daily behaviour with a sprinkling of moral precepts, nudges and reminders – don't look, don't touch, don't covet – whenever she thought temptation was passing through his mind? Recommend him books of a lightly tendencious character, in which stealing was deprecated or held up to ridicule? Such expedients were unthinkable. Be a general example to him, a living proof that honesty was the best policy? But what more odious than to imply his wrong by her right?

It would be an almost superhuman task to try to reform him by direct action, but she would have attempted it, for where Colum was concerned, her responsibility had made her think of herself as superhuman; and thanks to the influence of Fair Haven, where the Victorian belief in moral progress was reinforced by more up-to-date theories of counteracting anti-social tendencies, she had no dread of failure.

But all such precautions and provisions were unnecessary. She herself by her mere loving presence at his side, and her fatal, blessed knowledge of his weakness, would be sufficient to keep him on the straight path. Knowing that she knew, he would never dare to stray again.

Before the day was over she wrote Colum a letter brimming with love. She had too much delicacy to refer directly to any of the points at issue between them. She made admissions. She said that she had been very much upset, and perhaps even hysterical, at the time of leaving him, but she did not say why – it might have been inferred that the pain of parting from him was the cause, for she added – what was indeed the truth – that thinking about him had made her feel much better. She said – which was also true – that she thought she loved him more than she ever had, and understood him better, and that in the future she hoped to be more of a help to him than she had been in the past. She said she had been thinking of her own faults, and thanked him for being so patient with them – but she did not say, or even suggest, that it was a consideration of his faults that had reminded her of hers. She said that though it was lonely for her seeing so little of him, it was much worse for him to have to work so hard and such long hours, day after day; she understood now how irksome it must be for him, what a strain, and how he must pine for any kind of excitement and relaxation; she looked forward to sharing them with him when the film was made. How was it going? she asked; and she ventured to suggest one or two points which might add to the *Devil's* distinction. 'Don't, don't be discouraged,' she said. 'I thought your letter sounded a little discouraged. I shouldn't mind so much – I shouldn't mind at all – if it was for the same reason that I have been feeling depressed – because we are separated from each other. But perhaps it is. And don't lose faith in your-self, my darling. Nothing that you could do, or not do, would make me lose my faith in you. I thought, from your letter, that perhaps you did think I was losing faith in you – but I never, never should. We are too close to each other for that, aren't we? You may be sure that I should always back you up, whatever happened.'

This was the nearest Margaret got to saying what was upper-most in her mind. She concluded by telling him her father was better and that they were both longing to see him on Sunday.

It was an ambiguous and misleading letter, but to Margaret it did not seem so, for it expressed what she wanted to express, her love for Colum and her faith in him.

20

EARLIER than usual next morning Colum rang her up. He sounded excited, trembling with pleasure. He blessed her for her letter; he said it was wonderful how she understood him; his language was emotional and almost poetic. More than once he thanked Heaven for having given her to him and for restoring her to health. Many times he professed his love for her, but not more often than she was prepared to hear. His speech became a little incoherent, he could not find words – yet his meaning was clear to Margaret beyond verbal articulateness. Presently through the broken sentences came tidings of more definite import – he was going away for the night or two on business, and might not be able to get down to Fair Haven on Sunday.

Margaret scarcely minded, for she felt more closely in touch with him at this moment than she had ever done.

Still in her mood of rapture she went to see her father. He was not so well. His temperature had gone up and he was coughing a good deal. She did not feel seriously anxious about him, for his illnesses were subject to these sudden relapses. Her happiness was not diminished by having her thoughts diverted from it, for happiness, unlike misery, is self-supporting. It makes no demands on one's thoughts, it does not drag the mind into the argument, for happiness does not argue. It is a companion that neither speaks nor needs to be spoken to, except in the most general terms.

To Margaret service was a blessed word. Anything done in its name acquired a sanction; it created a standard of importance beside which other things assumed their right proportions. And the service of the sick-room had pre-eminently this effect. It created a simplified world in which she felt at home. So absorbed was she that she did not notice how the time was passing, and when bedtime came without Colum having rung her up she did not feel surprised.

He rang her up next morning, however. He was in the country, he said, and just off to the studio. He missed her terribly and could hardly wait for Sunday. When was she coming back?

Margaret told him that her father's slight relapse made the date of her return uncertain. Colum showed much concern for her father, and disappointment at her delayed return. She tried to reassure him and could hardly understand his distress at their separation; she could not tell him that what she had missed even more than him was her love for him, and that she could bear his absence for a few more days, now that this had returned; but she did tell him how much she loved him. All over England, no doubt, telephone wires were humming with such messages, yet she felt that hers was the only one.

Mr Pennefather proved to be a little better; he asked for a cigarette, he questioned some of her arrangements, and showed other welcome signs of fractiousness which go with returning health. She did not altogether trust them, for she had suffered many disappointments when the disease, having exhausted itself in one part of his system, suddenly broke out in another; but towards evening, with his temperature hardly more than a degree up, she felt her responsibilities grow lighter and her mind reach out for other contacts. Diana was the obvious one, since Colum would not have reached home yet.

Diana was indignant: Margaret had been at Fair Haven all the time without ever making her a sign. Margaret explained as best she could; but although her excuses were all swept aside in a torrent of affectionate abuse, she noticed that Diana did not make the expected demand for an immediate reunion, and it was Margaret who first said, 'When can we meet?'

'Yes, when *can* we?' Diana echoed despairingly. 'How long did you say you were going to be there?'

'Until Daddy's better.'

'I hope that will be a long time – oh dear, you know what I mean, I hope he'll soon be better, but that you will stay a long time.'

'Anyhow I shall be here over the weekend,' said Margaret.

'Yes, yes, of course. The weekend, *well*, the weekend isn't too good, as a matter of fact.'

'Oh,' Margaret's voice betrayed her disappointment.

'Well, the thing is – it's no good beating about the bush – Nick's coming down, in fact I expect him with Stuart almost any minute.'

'Oh, I see,' said Margaret.

'You wouldn't want to meet him, would you?'

'Would he want to meet me?' asked Margaret doubtfully.

'Of course he would . . . Oh, here they are. Hold on.'

Margaret held on for what seemed an interminable time. She could hear their voices, animated, tinkling, metallic, but not what they said. They seemed to be arguing about something. She thought she could distinguish Nick's voice, although its level tones were unlike his. Did she want to see him? She could hardly say. The meeting would be embarassing to them both. Would it be anything more? Would anything be gained from it except the fact that they had met, the ice had been broken, and they could meet again without having to be warned?

Margaret thought about Nick. She had long ago ceased to feel unkindly towards him. The fault had been at least as much hers as his. She could not remember what it had been like to be in love with him; she could not think herself back into that position. Yet she could remember liking him; and his voice, every time she heard it, reminded her that she liked him still.

Could she have him as a friend? Suddenly she realized how few friends she had. The realization was not painful, for while she had the sun she did not need the stars. But it was a fact; she could hear in Nick's voice, far off and distorted as it was, something that she missed whenever Colum was not there, or her mind was emptied of the thought of him. The easy, friendly presence of someone who spoke her language and to whom she did not have to adapt herself, yet who extended her vision and made her value herself in a way that Stuart and Diana could not. They took her for granted; she had always felt she was being discovered when she talked to Nick. All this time she had missed him without knowing it.

Other women had men friends, why not she? Would Colum mind? Sure of her love for him and his for her, she felt she could ask him anything and he would not refuse; but Nick might. Nick might not want to meet Colum's wife, not even in Colum's absence. Was it that they were debating, all this long time?

She thought it must be, and her cheeks began to burn. She guessed their quandary; how unlucky it was that Nick and Stuart should have caught Diana in the act of telephoning to her! Even Diana's well-known aplomb would be unequal to such a situation. Now she was waiting for their verdict: would it be yes or no? Mortified as Margaret was, she hoped it would be yes; in her relaxed, expansive mood, all the sap rising, she could not bear to have a tendril nipped.

She tried to recollect Nick's face and fit it to his voice. She had his photograph here at Fair Haven, put away carefully with other mementoes of him; but since her marriage she had not once looked at it. Yet she had better success in trying to evoke it than in trying to recall its subject, for it is easier to remember a photograph than a face. But the likeness eluded her; all she could see was the look of gravity he sometimes wore and this she construed to mean that he was still unfriendly to her. 'No, no,' he was saying; 'I don't want to see her, she treated me badly and married a bounder and a cad.' She heard the words almost as distinctly as if he had uttered them; they wounded her, they were so unfair to Colum. She felt she would like to explain things to Nick, tell him exactly how everything had happened. He had been fond of Colum once: why could not they again be friends?

Suddenly the voices ceased and other sounds succeeded, shuffling of feet and the rattle of the receiver being taken up. Her heart began to beat uncomfortably.

'Darling, are you still there?' Diana asked.

Margaret muttered something.

'I thought you'd certainly have gone away. I didn't mean to keep you holding on such hours – but Nick and Stuart brought back the evening paper. Perhaps you've seen it?'

'The evening paper?' repeated Margaret. 'No.'

'Then perhaps you've heard?'

'Heard what?' said Margaret, her voice trembling.

'Oh darling, don't be alarmed, it's nothing serious, only we didn't know whether you had heard, and we didn't like to break it to you, as you had your hands full already with your father – if I can put it so. But of course it is always rather a shock – so lucky that you weren't at home.'

'Has there been a fire?' asked Margaret.

'No, darling, nothing as bad as that. Just another burglary. There! I hope you're not terribly upset. Nick didn't think we ought to tell you, but I thought you would have heard already.'

'Another burglary?' gasped Margaret.

'Yes, it looks as though the thieves must have known something, for you were away from home and so apparently was Colum.'

'Did they take much?' asked Margaret.

'They broke open the safe and took some jewellery of yours and some other rather valuable things – silver and so on. More than a thousand pounds' worth, I'm afraid.'

Margaret said nothing.

'The servants found out in the morning and telephoned to Colum at the studio – hullo, darling?'

'Yes, I'm here,' said Margaret.

'Darling, I'm afraid it *is* a shock to you, but you're insured all right, aren't you?'

'I . . . I think so,' Margaret said.

'Well, then, it doesn't matter so much. But you are unlucky. How long is it since the last one?'

'Oh, several months.'

'I thought it wasn't so long. Well, darling, cheer up. It all comes of marrying a film-star, The burglars would think you must be frightfully rich. I must say they have a nerve, knowing that Colum is better at their own game than they are.'

'Their own game?'

'Safe-breaking and so on. I mean, he's one of the leading cracksmen of the films.'

'Yes, of course he is.'

'Darling, don't hate me for telling you. You sound so depressed. But you had to know sometime, hadn't you?'

'Yes.'

'Nick thinks they may catch him this time.'

'Oh, why?'

'Because every burglar has his special method, it's his style, like a writer's or an actor's. He can't help imitating himself, and they get to recognize it.'

'But it might not be the same burglar . . . How is Nick?'

'He looks a bit tired. He's getting on very well, you know. He's working most frightfully hard. If they catch your burglar, you must ask Nick to prosecute him, or whatever they do to burglars.'

'Oh, I don't suppose they will catch him . . . Besides, Nick wouldn't bother with a police-court case, he must be much too grand.'

'Perhaps you're right . . . Margaret?'

'Yes?'

'He spoke of you – how shall I say? with affection, as one speaks of an old friend . . . It's all right, they've gone upstairs to change. You know Stuart insists on that, he's so old-fashioned. Margaret?'

'Yes?'

'I haven't had time to sound him yet, but I can't help *thinking* he's still fond of you. There isn't any talk of anyone else. Perhaps he still has hopes.'

'Hopes?'

'Well, you know what I mean. It's rather touching, isn't it? To be so faithful when he's so successful, and girls must be tumbling over each other to marry him. Hullo?'

'You don't know that he is,' said Margaret.

'No, but I rather feel it. I believe Stuart does too, but of course he wouldn't breathe a word, it wouldn't be cricket. What I should like would be for us all four to meet here, when I've done a preliminary reconnaissance. What do you say to that?'

'Diana,' said Margaret desperately. 'I would like to, but I really don't know what to say. And Daddy isn't quite so well to-night.'

'Oh, I am sorry. I thought you said he was better.'

'Well, he isn't really.' Margaret's conscience pricked her: even in the turmoil of her feelings she wondered how she had fallen into this habit of telling fibs. Would fate again take her at her word and make her father have a sudden relapse?

'Ring me up again, please do, Diana. And Diana . . .'

'Yes?'

'I was thinking if there was any message I could send to Nick.'

'I'm sure there is.'

'Tell him I . . . I wish him well.'

'Oh, I couldn't. That sounds as if you hated him.'

'Well, say I often think of him . . . That is, if you think he'd like it.'

'Of course he would. Darling, I must fly. And don't let the burglary get you down. I hope those diamond clips that we gave you were stolen. I never liked them. I'm sure you'll get something much nicer with the money.'

Left to themselves, all Margaret's thoughts rushed to one point. It never crossed her mind that the burglary might be genuine. Colum, she felt sure, had done it; and he had done it directly after receiving her letter.

That meant, could only mean, one thing. He had misread, misunderstood the letter; he thought he had convinced her that her suspicions were unfounded, born of her own brain, the outcome of her hysterical imaginings. He believed he had managed to put all this across.

A burglar, like a conjuror, tries to take his victim off his guard. He does what one would least expect, when one would least expect. He contrives that one's attention shall be turned another way, and then he strikes. Margaret's letter showed that she was off her guard and that her attention was turned another way. She had suspected him once, and repented of so doing: now her suspicions would be slumbering. Burglars, she knew, were often neurotic men; and just as a thrown horseman jumps back on to his horse to keep his nerve from going, so, for the same reason, a burglar may quickly follow one job with another.

Job! Margaret had never liked the word, and she liked it much less in connection with Colum.

Burglars were also said to be conceited. They overvalued their own cleverness. Was Colum conceited? He had never seemed so to her, but he must be, he must be utterly bemused and taken in by himself if he thought that he had put her off the scent. He was not treating her as an intelligent human being. He was treating her, how? As one of the vast audience of his fans, who could never think anything evil of him – the besotted audience, whom Margaret had once despised, and whose spines tingled whenever Colum McInnes escaped his just deserts – the willing dupes of the illusion he knew so well how to create. Among them, doubtless, were thousands and thousands of women who doted on him, who would boast, if asked, that they loved him.

And who, among these myriads, loved him the most? Who would be the least likely to suspect him? Who would be the first to leap to his defence if he was accused, however plausible the accusation? Whose love could he rely on to see him through? Hers, Margaret's. She had told him as much in her letter.

She saw what a mistake the letter had been, but it was too late to recall it, the mischief was done.

She dreaded speaking to him on the telephone, but happily when he rang her up he assumed she would have already heard the news and made no comment on her jerky and unnatural manner. He made light of the whole thing but said what a mercy it was that she had been out of the flat. Above all she must not worry; he was very emphatic about that. She told him she could not help being anxious about her father; perhaps in the circumstances it would be better for Colum not to come on Sunday; she would let him know how things went on.

Emotion wears channels in the mind and when there is a single exciting cause it soon ceases to seek new outlets and confines itself to whichever of those old channels suits its immediate orientation. Emotionally Margaret was back again at the point where she left Colum in London; he was a thief now and she could not bear the thought of seeing him. Moreover, to keep his secret was too heavy a burden; she must consult her father.

She went up to his room, half fearing to find him as ill as she had made him out to be; but he was contentedly playing patience and made several jokes at her expense. After supper she sat with him until it was time for him to go to sleep. This was contrary to her custom for it tired him to talk and as long as she was there he would talk; also she had a superstition that the unwatched patient gets well quicker. But she felt she could not face an evening of solitary clock-gazing and while she was with him she could try to imagine what it would be like to tell him about Colum.

She tried to think of Colum as she had thought of him only a few hours before: with tenderness and love. But it was no use: that way was barred.

Such sober Sunday papers as her father took made only brief allusion to the theft: they did remark, however, that it was the second robbery there within four months, and one of them said that the police believed they had a clue.

Margaret's first impulse was to ring Colum up and warn him. Discarding that as dangerous and unnecessary, since Colum would know what the police had to go on far better than the papers, she still wanted to get in touch with him – she hardly knew why, for talking to him had become a torment: she thought she heard the falseness in his voice and thought he must detect it too in hers. But would it be safe to ring him up? Would there be snoopers listening in? Might Colum say something rash?

She realized, with a shock, that she was trying to protect him from justice – justice that she herself had once helped to administer.

Telephone in hand, she was debating with herself when she suddenly remembered that she had not been to see her father, or taken him the morning papers. But when she was half way across the room she stopped. Should she tell him about the burglary? If she didn't, he would almost certainly read about it in the papers, and would think it very odd of her not to have told him.

She shrank from telling him. She felt she couldn't break the news without betraying to him that she believed the burglary was a fake. Her face, her voice would give her away. But if she did not take him the papers he would certainly ask for them.

To her surprise she found herself toying with the idea of telling him they had not come. Newspapers did fail to turn up sometimes. But he would be sure to ask her to go out and get some, for he was a great reader of the papers, especially when he was ill.

When he was ill! His illness was one of the few facts, the few patches of firm ground, in the morass of uncertainty in which she floundered. She would take him the papers straightaway: if he read about the burglary, and asked her why she hadn't told him, she would say she had not wanted to worry him. In any case it would be far easier to answer his questions than to volunteer information. And as to that she was armed with ignorance; she could truthfully say that Colum had given her only the barest details.

Mr Pennefather greeted her with a challenge in his eye. He was much better, he told her: his temperature was down to normal. He had got out of bed to wash and shave, which was against the rules, but this small act of disobedience had evidently been a tonic to him; he looked guiltily pleased with himself. He was wearing the old golfing jacket which he always put on to mark his convalescence; its pockets and leather buttons gave him the jaunty air of some old fashion-plate. His hands were thin and his face was pale and papery; but Margaret welcomed that, after the flush she had been used to seeing.

She gave him his morning kiss, asked him what sort of night he had had, and tenderly rebuked him for his premature escape from sick-room discipline.

'We don't want to have you ill again,' she said.

'We, who is we?' he retorted. 'You talk like a hospital nurse. You don't want to make an old man of me, do you?'

Margaret disclaimed any such intention. 'Then give me those papers, will you? Is there anything cheerful in them?'

'I haven't really had time to look,' said Margaret, and after tidying his bedside table she left the room.

But she could not leave herself. Her mind was more confused than it had ever been. The impulse to protect Colum was irresistible; but whom was she protecting? Someone she loved? She did not think she loved him; how could she love him if she thought of him as a criminal? The loss of her love for him was her greatest misery, just as her concern for his safety was her sharpest anxiety. She strove to fuse the two into one predominate feeling, but in vain.

She was trying to occupy herself with household tasks when the telephone-bell rang.

She started, and for a moment thought she would not answer it. Subterfuges seemed to be growing on her, but she managed to repel this one.

'Yes?'

But it was Diana's voice that answered her, not Colum's. 'Hullo, darling, how are you? You haven't been burgled in the night, I hope?'

Margaret made a suitable rejoinder, and answered, or parried as well as she could Diana's further inquiries. Yes, it was odd that Colum hadn't told her more. How was her father? Her father was rather better, but one never knew with him; she did not know whether she ought to leave him or not. She realized that she was temporizing in view of a possible invitation from Diana to join them at The Starting Point, perhaps fishing for one. Diana said,

'Oh, my dear, I'm longing to see you here – we all are (it's all right, the men have gone out to play golf). But I'm not sure if this is quite the moment – I'll tell you why. We talked a lot about you last night, and Nick knows that you are here; but though he joined in the conversation and spoke of you . . . well . . . very *nicely*, he didn't actually *say* he wanted to see you, which he easily could have, and oh dear, where was I? What I mean is, if he had felt well . . . indifferent to you he would have jumped at the opportunity – the fact that he didn't shows that he cares too much.'

'Do you think so?' Margaret said, surprised that she could still feel disappointed.

'I'm sure of it,' said Diana. 'Nick isn't the sort of man to wear his heart on his sleeve – he's one of the people – how unlike me! – who have slow, *painful* feelings. Stuart of course said I oughtn't to have said *anything*. It's the public school code to damp down all emotion. And what happens? They just atrophy, like Stuart's have.'

'Oh no,' said Margaret, mechanically.

'Well, very nearly. But I wouldn't have him different from what he is. I expect you feel just the same about Colum.'

As Margaret did not answer, Diana answered for her.

'Of course you do! All the same, I often think you were wonderfully brave to marry him. I suppose I should have, if he'd asked me, but I'm not sure. I'm afraid this safe, cosy, suburban life is what I'm suited for. I was always much more of a gad-about than you are; yet it's you who have gone out into the world. Such exciting things happen to you! No one would ever dream of burgling us.'

'Still, you have compensations for not being burgled.' said Margaret, trying to be jocular.

'Yes, of course we have, we do sleep sound at nights, and Margaret, I have something I want to tell you. I wanted to tell you before, but I wasn't sure . . .'

The conversation suddenly became elliptical and allusive. Snatches of important, intimate news flashed back and forth. No other news had the urgency and interest of this, that could hardly declare itself above a whisper. And while the exchange of confidences went on, expressing the closest approximation that the spirit and the flesh ever attain to, Margaret felt her burden lifted; she had something in her more important than her thoughts, she could appeal from the phantoms in her mind to the child in her body.

Whatever happened to her she would have the child, and in the child her own lost innocence would be re-born, and perhaps, who could tell? Colum's too. She lost herself in an idyllic picture of him playing with it, making fun for it. He was, she thought, his truest self with children. Something came through to him from them, something he hadn't put there. Nature, through her, would work for him, work for them both, in ways they could not guess.

But a shadow crept across the picture, a hand, a cruel hand, Colum's hand behind the child's head, jerking it forward, willing its destruction; and all was dark again.

Yet the conversation, with its affirmation of an innocent, happy life outside her own did somehow strengthen and tranquillize her spirit. Though nothing bearing on her own problem had been said – or very little, and that little far from reassuring – she had felt the immediate comfort that comes from contact with another's mind. And though nothing could lessen the gravity of the situation she was faced by, she instinctively felt that her attitude towards it could be altered, if only she could bring herself to talk about it to someone. To objectify it – that was the thing; to rid it of the fearsome and shameful associations that clustered round it and prevented her from seeing it as it was – something that might have happened to anybody. By allowing it to become a matter of feeling, rather than of action or even of thought, she was making herself incapable of dealing with it.

Her father was quite well enough now to be told her troubles and besides, she reflected with unconscious cynicism, there is something almost life-giving in another person's tale of woe. She set out with a firm mind, closed against second thoughts.

'My dear child!' Her father paused and looked at Margaret keenly. 'Did you say you hadn't read the papers?'

'I just glanced at them,' said Margaret.

'But did you miss the main item of news?'

She felt wretchedly unlike herself, fencing with him. 'What was that, Daddy dear?'

'Well, to put it bluntly there's been a burglary at your flat.'

Margaret drew a long breath.

'Oh yes, I did know about that,' she said as airily as she could.

'Then why didn't you tell me?'

Margaret said her piece explaining why.

'But I'm not as ill as all that,' her father exclaimed. 'I think I feel much better since I read about it. And after all a burglary's nothing to be ashamed of.'

'It's nothing to be proud of, either,' Margaret said.

'Oh I don't know.' Returning health made her father argumentative. 'It shows you are worth burgling, I suppose. But have you lost anything valuable?' he went on, almost accusingly. 'Hasn't Colum given you the details?'

Here was a chance.

'Colum's a bit curious in those ways.'

'Curious? I should have thought he wasn't half curious enough. Oh, I see, you mean curious in the other sense. Well, I suppose he's got so much money he doesn't bother.'

'It isn't quite that.'

But Margaret's tongue would not obey her.

'As a matter of fact, he is a bit worried about money.'

'But doesn't he get paid all the time he's working? This new film – I never can remember its title – the Devil something – he's been working at it for months.'

'Yes,' said Margaret. 'It's nearly finished now, but it hasn't been altogether a success, and he isn't happy about the next one either.'

'I'm sorry,' said Mr Pennefather. 'I suppose a film actor has his ups and downs like other people. Anyhow, he'll get the insurance money. That should be a tidy bit.'

Here was another chance. Margaret could feel her heart thumping. She looked round for a chair.

'I think I'll sit down,' she said.

'Of course, my dear. How thoughtless of me. You mustn't stand on ceremony with me.' He smiled at his unintentional joke and Margaret drew the chair up to his bed.

'You were insured, of course?' her father said. Inattention to business matters sometimes made him impatient.

'Oh yes, we were.'

'Well, then.'

Margaret made a great effort.

'It's one of the things I feel uneasy about.'

'Because the Insurance Company will have had to pay up twice? My dear, they're sheltered by a big umbrella. They didn't make a fuss the first time, did they?'

'Oh no.'

'Well, then, I don't see what you have to worry about. And besides, the paper says the police have found a clue – they may catch the chap, and get the things back, so you won't have to trouble the Insurance Company.'

Here was a third chance. Although she was sitting down, Margaret thought she might be going to faint. She had her back to the light, or surely her father would have seen how ill she looked. Yet she persisted.

'I almost hope they won't catch him.'

'But why not? Is it because you'd rather have the money? Or do you feel half sorry for the fellow? I've heard of people with a soft spot for thieves. I can't say I have.'

'If it was somebody you knew—' Margaret began.

'Well, that might make a difference, I grant you. But it isn't. Or do you boast a burglar among your acquaintance?'

'It's my—' Margaret said, but the word 'husband' refused to be uttered. Wave upon wave of nausea, spiritual as well as physical, began to beat against her. 'It's . . . it's this horrid sickness,' she had the presence of mind to say. 'Excuse me a moment.' With lurching steps she reached the door and, once outside, leaned up against the wall. Soon, with the release of her mind from the strain she had imposed on it, she began to feel better. But she knew now that she would never be able to tell her father that Colum was a thief; and if she could not tell him, whom could she tell?

21

1st April

I'VE come back. What else could I do? I couldn't stay any longer, Daddy was quite well and had told Colum so when he wrote to condole with him on the burglary. Besides, my place is here. But I still feel like a sleep-walker and shall, until I've had it out with Colum. He speaks of the time I was away as my 'eclipse'. Such and such a thing 'happened during your eclipse', he says.

This morning he made me an April Fool. I was in bed, as I usually am when he goes to the studio, and he came in, as he always does, to say goodbye, and said so innocently, 'Darling, where is the gold musical box I gave you for a Christmas present?' I said, 'In its usual place, of course,' and I jumped out of bed to go and find it, as he must have guessed I should. But it wasn't there and I came back crestfallen. 'Didn't you find it?' he said. 'I didn't think you would. It was in the safe with the other things. Darling, does it feel nice to be an April Fool?' 'It wasn't very clever of you,' I said, trying to laugh, but I felt much nearer crying.

I'm quite sure it wasn't in the safe when I went away.

A lot of people have written to sympathize with us. Not Lauriol – she's gone for a holiday to the South of France, on the money she made out of the sale, I imagine. I haven't had the heart yet to ask Colum exactly what we lost. He's bought a whole lot of new things. Some of them are very pretty, but I don't feel I shall ever get fond of them, as I was of the old ones. I have a ridiculous feeling that somehow they don't belong to us – as if nothing in the flat does – and someone might walk in and claim them.

I could not tell anybody this – I couldn't tell anybody even a tenth of the thoughts I have every day. I believe that if I write them down I shall get rid of them and forget them. Funny, – when I tried to keep a diary in Venice it was because I wanted to remember them. How things change. I shall take good care that Colum doesn't read this one. Each time I write in it I'm going to put it in a despatch case, and lock it, and take it downstairs to the porter, for safe keeping. I shall only have it with me while I'm writing it. I suppose it shows the state of mind I've got into, but the porter won't think it odd, after what has happened in our flat.

I was at Fair Haven for nearly a fortnight. It didn't seem long at the time but now that I'm back here I feel I've been away for years. I suppose it's the burglary coming in between. It's like a great hill in time which blots out the past.

Colum says that while I was away he made some new friends. He doesn't think I shall like them but he's going to try them on me. They are going to give a party before long, I gather. I believe they are hangers-on of Mrs Bel's. She's been abroad the whole winter, but she's coming back, or come back.

Colum said he warned me he would get into mischief if I went away. I don't know what he meant and I didn't ask him. Perhaps he meant the burglary. It worries me to think that if I'd stayed he might not have done it. But I couldn't have stayed just then. I'm not sure that I can stay now, but now it won't be so easy to get away. I want to ask Colum about the clue the police found, but I can't.

5th April

We went down to Withycote for Sunday. It may be my bad taste, but I can't like it. 'Eyebrow-deep in creepers', someone called it, and that describes it. The thatch is so thick you can hardly see out of the windows: it hangs down over them like hair over the eyes of an Exmoor pony. And all the flowers look self-conscious. Colum is very proud of the daffodils, as well he may be, they are like the cover of a bulb grower's catalogue. He has had one named after him – very pale, almost white – and it costs £25 a bulb. He calls it the white flower of a blameless life. Two people from the cast of *The Devil* were there – quite nice – and they teased Colum about his lack of vices. 'You don't smoke, you don't drink, you don't gamble, you don't get divorced – we can understand that' (they looked at me) – 'but what do you do? – what *does* he do, Margaret, that he shouldn't?' I didn't answer, but Colum said, 'Oh, I'm only a plaster saint. We're all sinners, thank God,' he added devoutly, but it seemed to me an odd thing to thank God for.

I wasn't a good hostess, I didn't feel up to it, but they made every allowance for me; I didn't even have to say I had a head-ache. One of the nice things about film people is that you never have to explain anything to them: they take whatever you do for granted.

Low spirits make you seem complaining, and as if it was other people's fault that you aren't happier. I have an alibi because I'm going to have a baby; but I wonder if Colum minds me being so dull. I never could be amusing, but sometimes I could make him laugh, because I wanted to. Now I don't want to, or not often. Sometimes I should like to make him cry, some-times I should like to make him jump, but most of the time, I suppose, I want to reform him, to make him *better*.

How hopelessly priggish and Victorian that sounds, even to me.

Whenever I speak to him there are at least three things that I *could* say; but I don't want – I have no impulse – to say any of them, and I have a morbid feeling that, whichever of the three I chose, he would put on a different face to suit it. So we have no communication, except between feigned versions of ourselves. That is one reason why I'm so dull. For me, the main pleasure of conversation is the click one sometimes feels when one's mind is joined to someone else's: one almost hears it, and it gives one joy. Even the tedious business of making conversation, even talking about the weather, may lead to it. But to deal out insincerities, like cards, and have them dealt one back – what fun is there in that? And yet I know people who are insincere and would admit they were and still are most amusing talkers. At least I used to find them amusing, I'm not sure that I should now. Insincerity is only amusing against a background of sincerity that makes the contrast: *two* people talking for effect are just boring.

I don't know what makes me think of all these things, I never did before, but then I was never in this situation before.

Colum and Arturo motored up to London on Sunday night – they had to start work early. Eunice stayed with me, as she wasn't on the set. We come back by train to-day (Monday). There is a limit to the extra petrol that even Colum can get.

8th April

Three blank days, and always at the back of my mind this gnawing dread about the *clue*. I hoped I should forget about it but it seems to burrow into me. There are several reasons why I don't want to discuss it with Colum. One, and I suppose the chief, is, lest it should turn out to be a real danger. Then I have an instinct, learned from my small acquaintance with legal proceedings, that in certain cases it *is safest not to know*. The third is that it might, and probably would, open the whole question of my relation with Colum, which is now buried under ambiguity and surmise. Since I came back we have hardly said a word about *why* I went to Fair Haven. Colum has said many times how glad he is that I look so much better; I think he believes that I believe I had a breakdown. And of course if I let him go on believing that, we could perhaps settle down and jog along somehow, and keep up appearances to ourselves, and to the world.

But it would be a false life, false in almost every particular, and I don't think I could bear it – especially when I remember the complete trust in each other that we had, or seemed to have. I should always be wondering about him and he would be wondering about me – perhaps he doesn't *mind* that; I remember Nick saying that he was a 'cabotin' character – the word stuck in my mind. I didn't know it, but it seems to mean someone who enjoys playing a part, a rather second-rate part, who has no core of personality and is somehow hollow, a creature of appearances: all things to all men. Of course Nick disliked Colum, in spite of, or because of their schoolboy friendship, when he said that, and now he must positively hate him – but I can see what he meant. Of course Nick is utterly sincere, too much so, some people would think – he can't act against, or even disguise, his feelings. I didn't realize that at the time, it just seemed that he was being unreasonable. He wouldn't see me the other day, even after this long time, even to get over a social awkwardness, because his feelings wouldn't let him. I wonder if Diana was right and it was because he still cares for me. I don't think so, I hope not, for his sake. What good would it do either of us? It's true I did want him for a friend, but that was while I still loved Colum: I haven't enough happiness now to make a friend, and I couldn't bear him to know what a mockery my life with Colum has become.

I think Colum must believe he succeeded in humbugging me, or else why did he at once stage another burglary? In my letter I meant to tell him that I understood everything, that I forgave it, if forgave is the word. It isn't for me to forgive, of course, God forgives, and Colum has done nothing to injure *me – I* have nothing to forgive – I tell myself that over and over again. I wasn't angry with him for trying to steal my bracelet. But why be so crafty and underhand? Why not have asked me for the money – if he wanted it, which I don't think he did. I should have loved to give it him.

No, it isn't that he's done me any harm, it's the fact of his dishonesty that I can't get over. It's like a bad smell all round me, and even his name rings in my mind like a false coin.

I thought my letter would prevent him doing anything of that sort again. I thought he would be *obliged* to turn over a new leaf when he knew that I knew.

But he hasn't, – which means one of two things: either he means to carry on as before in spite of all that I can do to stop him, or – but the other I can't put down.

I must do something to end this uncertainty.

9th April

Last night for the first time Colum seemed to notice how depressed I was. When he asked me what was the matter I couldn't help crying – the kind way he did it brought our old times back, and made the past weeks seem like an evil dream, and for a moment I was able to think of him as I used to. When I cried he became still sweeter to me (some men hate tears, I believe), and said how it suited me to look pale and transparent, and how proud he would be of me when I was a mother. Mothers are quite a rarity in my profession, he said, fathers are much more common. I couldn't help laughing through my tears: he can be so funny! Then he suggested that we should dine early and see a film. I was astonished, because he hardly ever sees a film unless he has to, – for business reasons or to please a friend. I asked him what film, and he wouldn't tell me at first. I made myself look as nice as I could, – it isn't very easy just now – and put on most of the jewels I have left, and we went to Colum's pet restaurant, where they always keep a special table for us, in a corner where he can't be too much stared at. All the same, I noticed that several of the other diners began to nudge each other and look furtively in our direction – with admiration at him and a kind of veiled curiosity at me – I expect they noticed I was pregnant, though they wouldn't know that I was Colum's wife. But the pride I used to take in the happiness that the mere sight of him could bring to strangers was half spoilt: what would they do, I thought, if they *knew*! Some of them might even get up and walk out, and telephone to the police. But Colum didn't seem to feel any of that; he put on the air of demure wickedness, just as if he *was* some sort of criminal, that he often wears in public, and they seemed to love it. And presently I too seemed to forget what he really was, and I began to look at him for himself and not as if he was some dreadful problem that had somehow got into my life, and I saw, to my secret amusement, that the work he has been doing all these months in *The Devil*, as they call it, *has* left a mark on him. He insisted on dressing for dinner, for one thing, which he never used to; and his movements have become restrained, as though he was putting an invisible check on himself – I noticed it when he pushed the pepper pot towards me, and when he paid the bill (not with a flourish, like he used to) and when the cloak-room attendant helped him on with his coat. Somehow he *has* become more distinguished!

When we got to the cinema I looked up while he was paying the taxi and saw the electric sign: COLUM MCINNES IN THE SECRET THIEF. I jumped, and all my soreness of heart came back. I couldn't help giving him a reproachful look, but he said impishly, 'Don't you like the title? It's an old film of mine, it belongs to my remote past, I thought it would amuse you to see how I behaved in those days, before I had the benefit of your influence' – or something like that. I didn't know what to say and we went in.

It wasn't very different from his other films. It was about a boy, the child of wealthy people, who is kidnapped by some gangsters while he is a baby walking with his nurse in the Park. Of course it wasn't Colum, but I couldn't help wondering if he looked like that when he was a little boy. The parents are quite distracted but they can't find him and give him up for lost – he is their only child. The gangsters hold the parents up to ransom and it is all arranged by people meeting at street corners and under archways, but the gangsters suspect that one of them is double-crossing them, and they lose their nerve and decide not to give the boy up to his parents after all. He is too young to remember where they lived or even what their name was; he only remembers his own Christian name, which was Marmaduke: the gangsters think this a sissy name and they call him Duke for short, and afterwards the Duke because his manners are more refined than theirs, and he always wears smart clothes when he is off duty – I was going to say – but as they say, not on a job.

When he next appears he *is* Colum, who has been brought up by the gangsters as one of themselves and taught to steal. He is dour, and unsmiling, and unshaven, and very desperate. I had to shut my eyes several times, it seemed dreadful that anyone so young could be so wicked: but of course they are, I know that, it isn't just an invention of the films. And when I opened my eyes, there was Colum, looking so like the young man on the screen, and yet so unlike – I couldn't tell *what* I felt. Then he finds a girl who has been knocked down by a motor-car which drives on without stopping; and he tends her and takes her to hospital, without of course telling her who he is (indeed he doesn't know) or anything about himself, except that his name is Marmaduke. She is called Clarissa, which he thinks a very beautiful name, and often says it over to himself, in tones of love and wonder. He sends her flowers every day and goes to ask about her; and when she has left the hospital they meet in secret – he wearing a cheap ready-made suit and a very flashy tie. But I could see why she was so much in love with him, and so could the audience.

But all the time he goes on being a burglar, – and I suppose in case the other part of the story might seem too sentimental he is made to do some very horrible things. I couldn't look at the screen but I looked at Colum looking at it and tried to imagine – or rather tried not to imagine – him doing such things. His face, Colum's real face, didn't alter even when in the film he shoots one of his pursuers in the stomach (he falls down and writhes in the most dreadful way but doesn't actually die, because when I looked again he was up and walking about). I suppose a man wouldn't be affected, yet it gave me a cold feeling to see Colum taking it so calmly, and I thought how little I knew about him *really*, and that he *might* be capable of such acts. His voice is blood-curdling in those parts – a low, menacing growl like an animal's, devoid of pity, utterly unlike his ordinary voice, and yet if you know his speaking voice as well as I do you can hear some of the same intonations in it.

There was a moment when I should have been glad to go out, not so much because of the film itself as because of the thoughts it aroused in me. It was a little panic, rather like claustrophobia, I suppose, but I got over it.

The next thing I saw was the big house in Park Lane, quite near our own flat, where the Duke's parents live; they are expecting someone to stay with them, their niece, she is an orphan, and so much beloved by them that they have practically adopted her as their daughter; she is also an heiress in her own right. They talk a lot about her and at last she arrives. I'm not a great film-goer but even I was not surprised to find that she was Clarissa. She arrives in full evening dress, looking very lovely and they sit down to dinner. After dinner Mr Tudor

Fleming, for that is the parents' name, goes off to play billards, and his wife asks Clarissa various womanly questions and whether she is in love with anyone; but Clarissa says no.

Then Clarissa goes to her bedroom and begins to undress; then you see her reading in bed, with her hair loose on the pillow, then she shuts the book with a sigh and turns out her bedside lamp and the room is quite dark except for a glimmer coming through the curtains. Then you hear a scratching and the sound of the sash being raised and the curtains begin to sway and part, and between them you see the Duke crouching on the window-sill. He comes into the room without making a sound but as he is tiptoeing towards the door he trips over something and there is a crash. Clarissa wakes up and switches on the light, and seeing the burglar, she screams. He recognizes her but she doesn't recognize him, because he is wearing a mask.

Then he says her name and she recognizes his voice and he pulls the mask off and they cling together in an embrace; and she urges him to go, but it is too late – there are steps at the door, it opens, and Mr Tudor Fleming enters carrying a revolver. He points it at the Duke, and the Duke snatches at his hand, but Clarissa flings herself between them crying, 'Don't shoot, don't shoot, he is my lover!' 'He is not your lover,' her uncle says; 'he is a common burglar and you're trying to shield him. But it's no use, the servants are already astir, and the police will be here in a moment.'

You hear the sound of voices and shuffling feet outside, and Colum's – the Duke's – features become absolutely devilish. He just says, 'You've had it, pa,' in a sort of deadly sing-song, but before he can shoot Clarissa catches hold of his arm, crying 'Marmaduke! Marmaduke!'

The uncle – the father, I should call him – staggers back, and passes his hand over his brow. 'Is your name Marmaduke?' he asks in a bewildered voice. Colum – the Duke – still with his hand on the revolver, grunts, 'It was'. Trembling the uncle says, 'Marmaduke is the name of the son I lost. He would be about your age. I cannot wish harm to anyone who bears that name.'

Then the audience tittered – I suppose they are more hard-boiled than they used to be, though Marmaduke has always been thought a funny name. I was sorry, because until that moment the film had held me, silly and preposterous as it was. I suppose it was because I couldn't help identifying the Duke with Colum. But anyhow it was nearly over and I didn't expect to be excited again. Clarissa goes out crying. The father sends the servants back to bed, calls upstairs to his wife that everything is all right, and offers to lead the Duke downstairs to let him out. Then the Duke stops at the door and says, 'This room used to be my room.' 'Your room? – it was my son's room, his night-nursery.' 'But the bed isn't in the same place – it used to be there.' 'My son's bed was there.' 'And the room had another wall-paper – not this plain one, but one with roses tied up in ribbons.' 'Have you been here before?' the father asks. Then comes the recognition scene, which moved me almost unbearably because it seemed he was recognizing the real under the false Colum, whereas they are both the same, both false. I hardly took in anything more, though I did just see the police arriving, and being told it was a false alarm: 'Mr Marmaduke Tudor Fleming has arrived unexpectedly after a long absence.'

We walked down the gangway in silence, nobody apparently recognizing us. But when we were in the foyer a little girl who had been sitting on the other side of Colum came up to him shyly with an autograph book. While he stopped to sign it some more people recognized him and a small group collected, just a handful of people, and all at once they started clapping. It has happened before, and I have felt embarrassed and awkward, though proud of course; this time I was quite overcome by feeling that so many people loved him. They showed it in their faces as well as with their hands, – and they had smiles for me too, half envious, I could see, but I liked them none the less for that. Tears came into my eyes, but they only clapped the harder. Colum took a step forward and they stopped clapping and you could have heard a pin drop. Though he was only a yard away from me he seemed to be in another world – there is nothing that sets people apart from their fellows so much as applause. Sometimes one is tempted to think that it is only luck that puts men into the front rank – that hundreds of other people could have done as well if they had been given the chance. But I had only to look at Colum to realize that it wasn't so. Even without his admirers' gaze fixed on him you could tell that he wasn't an ordinary man, that he had that indefinable extra bit of something, even if it's only a gift for facial expression, which distinguished him from the rest.

If that is what distinction means, then Colum has it.

He said: 'Thank you very much. I can't tell you how touched I am, and how grateful for your appreciation. I could stay here all night lapping it up, if you would stay to give it me. But—' and then he stepped back and put his arm round me – 'we shall have to go now, because you see what an effect it is having on my wife. She always cries when she's happy. I can't imagine what she would do if you were less indulgent and started pelting me with rotten eggs. Perhaps she'd laugh then.'

I heard the clapping start again, and through a blur saw kind and sympathetic faces turned on me, and then we were out in the street, with the commissionaire looking for a taxi for us.

As we were driving home Colum said, 'Well, are you glad she didn't hand the Duke over to justice?' I couldn't think of anything to say, and he went on, 'I don't believe you are. I believe you think Clarissa should have denounced me to the police.'

'Oh darling, how could you think so?' I said.

'Well, at heart you are very severe, a magistrate and all that.'

For a moment I wished I'd never been a magistrate; it seemed a dreadful thing to be. I longed to be able to say, 'But the question couldn't ever arise,' or something of that sort – but I couldn't, and began to cry again.

'Was it true what I told them?' he asked, 'that you only cry when you're happy?'

'Yes, it was,' I said, and with his arms round me forgot that I had told a lie.

13th April, morning

It hadn't lasted – the love I felt for him again that evening. Perhaps if he could have been with me throughout the day it would have; but he has had to be away more than ever, putting the final finishing touches on *The Devil*, for it is really to be finished in a week, they say. I can hardly believe it, they've said it so often before: but this time Colum thinks it's definite. In fact he's having a party to celebrate it with some of the new friends he told me of – I haven't seen them yet.

I still can't realize that it will soon be over – these months and months of uphill work – and then we're to have a real holiday, he says, and go abroad, perhaps to Venice! 'Then you'll be able to church-crawl to your heart's content,' he said. 'You've been neglecting that side of your duties lately.'

It's true, I have. I haven't felt like it. While I was at Fair Haven I didn't feel the need for it – well, perhaps I don't quite mean that: it sounds presumptuous and perhaps it *is*. I told Colum once that I didn't feel religious at Dittingham and he said something about 'You don't need a Heavenly Father when you have a Pennefather.' I suppose my life there was rather materialistic; it was so secure and we were so much looked up to that there seemed no reason for us to look up! Even when I was so wretched there I didn't think that anyone could help me, except Daddy. We have helped a good many people in Dittingham but no one has ever helped us. If anyone saw me praying in church by myself they'd think I was mad. My father is a firm supporter of the Church but it would never occur to him to look for support from the Church.

But in London it's different and I should have gone long ago if I'd known what to pray for. Surely you must pray for something? I can't bring myself to pray for what I believe to be impossibilities – why should a miracle be performed for my sake? There was only one thing I wanted to pray for, and after the second burglary I felt that it would be useless. Besides, I have always been chary of praying for him, for his spiritual life is in other keeping than mine. Yet that was my great desire, the only one I had that mattered. All the smaller ones were offshoots of it. If that could be put right, everything would be right. Failing that, nothing would be right. Perhaps I was mistaken, but after the second burglary I didn't believe that anything could change Colum's nature. If his confessor cannot change it – and I believe he goes to confession – how can I? So I didn't pray for him, and there was no one else, and nothing else, to pray for.

But the evening he took me to the film my love for him came back with all its sweetness. I knew he was all those things he shouldn't be, and yet I loved him in spite of them, and I wanted nothing more: I didn't even want him different. There was no mingling of pain in my thoughts of him, none. I didn't have to say 'I love him though I know he is a thief', or 'I must love him but hate the bad in him' – Christian teaching says you should, but for me it's impossible. I couldn't love anyone with such a reservation. No, I loved him with all his faults, and more than before I was aware of then, I think.

That lasted for a day and a half and then, quite suddenly, I felt dry and cold towards him. While he was away at the studio

I longed to see him, but when he came back I couldn't feel happy with him and I wished he was not there. Again I felt he was a thief and saw him doing all those awful things he did do in the film, and they were part of him, and I had had a glimpse of his true nature when I saw him breaking the child's head.

But all the time I could remember the sweetness of my reconciliation, my reunion with him; that wasn't an hallucination, it was a fact; and if I have loved him once, knowing what I know, surely I can love him again, and not for a day and a half but forever. Then it won't matter whether he is a thief or not. I shall pray to St. Anthony to find me my lost love. That is all I ask for now.

Later

I have come back. The church was very quiet, but two or three people came in when I was there – I like it better so, it gives me a sense of unlonely intimacy which I don't get in formal collective worship. I feel these people have come because they want to – not because it's customary or the thing to do. They have problems like mine – perhaps more difficult ones. If I had come to praise, that would be different – a congregation swells the sense of praise. But perhaps I shall, one day.

I knelt a long time before I tried to pray – to let myself feel whether I should be permitted to, for there are so many influences, almost like currents in the air, acting sometimes with and sometimes against one's intention, modifying it, transforming it, putting it in accord. For other people one can ask many things, but for oneself what can one ask but the ability – the grace – to love God? And I hadn't come to ask that – I had come to ask something quite different, and the longer I knelt the more I realized how different it was. So much so, that for a long time Colum's name wouldn't come to my lips or even into my mind. It was as if an invisible shutter kept him out, and I even wondered whether the idea of him was hateful to this holy place, and almost a desecration, considering what he was. And perhaps, I thought, all that I ought to do is to pray for us both and go away: and if from the conjunction of our two names, which means much, all, to me, there could emerge the smallest blessing that belonged to both of us, – that we could share – well, that should be enough.

I felt myself dwindling and my heart being emptied of desire except for the least thing possible that could be offered – and though I knew, in a way, that this was right, I couldn't reconcile myself to it and felt horribly disappointed; and before I could be taken further out of myself I made a great effort, like the effort one makes to keep awake, and said St. Anthony's name over many times, and begged for the return of my love for Colum. 'Find it for me, find it for me!' I besought him and gradually my mind began to clear like a looking-glass that has been steamed over and I recovered the confidence of my desire and felt that it might be granted. So I knelt for a time with my whole heart fixed on that, until it tired, as the eye does when fixed too long on a single object. And just as the eye relieves itself by seeking other sights and suddenly sees them with intense distinctness, so I seemed to see our flat. It was dark and somebody was moving about, and I knew that it was Colum, but he looked much more like the Duke in the film we went to. Then he knelt down by the safe and did something to it and presently it opened and he took the things out one by one and put them in a bag. He had an electric torch in his hand and suddenly I saw one of the things quite plainly – it was the gold musical box that he had made me an April Fool with. And then it was dark again and all the light I could see was the colours that come before one's eyes when one has been pressing them.

I got up to go, for I felt it could not be right to see such things in a church. But then something told me that the vision had come without my seeking it, and it was a sign that I should pray to St. Anthony for the return of the things that Colum had taken. I had not meant to think of him as a thief, for that is what divides me from him; if only I could regard it as a mystery how much happier I should be. I didn't want to admit he was a thief, even to St. Anthony, so I prayed a light, quick prayer, half hoping he wouldn't hear it.

There is the telephone-bell. I must go.

Shutting the note-book, and holding it in her hand for she did not dare to leave it about, Margaret went to the telephone.

'Hullo!' a man's voice said. 'Is that Mr Colum McInnes's flat?'

'Yes.'

'This is Inspector Attenborough of Scotland Yard. Is Mr McInnes at home?'

Margaret's heart turned over.

'No, I'm afraid he isn't. He's working at the studio. Can I help? I'm his wife.'

'I'm speaking to Mrs McInnes?'

'Yes.'

'Well, Madam, there is a little matter I wanted to see him about in connexion with the recent burglary at your flat.'

'Oh yes. Could I perhaps give him a message?'

'When do you expect him back?' the Inspector asked.

'Oh, not till late, eight at the earliest. They work such long hours.' Margaret felt obliged to defend Colum from the popular misconception that film actors led an easy life.

'That's a pity,' said the Inspector. 'It was rather urgent.'

'He's generally very tired when he gets home,' said Margaret. 'Is it anything that I could do?'

'Well, Madam, I really think you could, probably just as well as he. It's only a routine matter, but you will appreciate that we are anxious to lose no time.'

'Of course. What would you like me to do?'

'If you could find it convenient to come round here, we could settle this small point very quickly.'

'Has it . . . has it an important bearing on the case?' asked Margaret in a trembling voice.

'We think it might have.'

'I'll come at once.'

22

THE next entry in Margaret's diary had no date.

I still don't know what made me do it. Colum came back later than usual, and I didn't tell him until after dinner. It wasn't only to spare his feelings; I was just as anxious to spare my own. He was in very good spirits because the film is coming to an end, and he believes he hasn't done so badly after all. 'They tell me I've made a pretty good Devil,' he said. 'I thought you had taken all the devil out of me. But I wonder what the public will think.'

I tried to share his excitement, and listened with half an ear while he told me about the party there was going to be: it would have some novel features, he said, but I can't remember what they were – if I ever heard. The idea of a party was very far from my mind.

But when he saw I wasn't eating anything he changed his mood at once – how much easier it is to make someone sad than happy! He pretended to think of all sorts of things that might have gone wrong with my day, and invented remedies for them, but I shook my head. When shall I be able to give him some good news? Only when the baby is born, and I begin to wonder if it ever will be.

I was frightened of the servants hearing, and suggested that we should go out for a walk, but it was raining. 'Shall we take a taxi to a church?' he said. 'But I'm afraid they're all shut now.'

I couldn't tell him about the church (it seems there is always *something* one can't tell) though I'm sure it had a good deal, perhaps everything, to do with what came next. So I started with the telephone call and at once he became as agitated as I was. When I saw this, I grew calmer; my chief dread was that he might think I had gone mad. Either that, or that he would be extremely angry with me. I almost hoped he would be.

But I was quite calm at the time, I told him. I felt prepared for anything, though I was sure that it would turn out to be the clue the police had spoken of. The Inspector couldn't have done more to put me at my ease, and yet I felt there was a catch in it. Dissimulation comes naturally to many people – it is a kind of game to them – and from my own experience I know how difficult it is to tell, from a policeman's manner, whether he believes a person guilty. There was just a hint of menace in the Inspector's voice when he said, 'If you will sit down here, Madam, I will bring the article in question to you.'

Colum sat quite still but his fingers fidgeted with the arm of his chair.

It was wrapped up in creased brown paper, but I knew from the shape what it was going to be.

'Do you recognize this musical box, Madam?' he said. 'We thought it might be one of the objects stolen from your premises.'

'We had a musical box,' I said.

'Yes, a gold musical box was among the items listed in the inventory,' said the Inspector. 'Would this be yours?'

Colum was lighting a cigarette. I generally notice when he does, it happens so seldom. He looked at me through eyes narrowed against the smoke, and said,

'You said "yes", of course.'

'No, I didn't. I said I didn't think it was.'

Colum leaned forward and stared at me in amazement. 'You said you didn't think it was?'

'Yes. Then the Inspector said, "Do you remember the tunes that your musical box played?"'

'You said "yes", of course,' repeated Colum, in the same tone he had used before.

'I said it played two tunes, a lively tune called "Good-humoured and merry" and a slow sad tune called "When that bosom".'

'What made you think of them?' asked Colum.

'We have a musical box at home that plays those tunes,' I said.

'What did the Inspector say?' asked Colum.

'He said, "Then, Madam, I'm very sorry, but I'm afraid the musical box isn't yours".'

'He said that?' asked Colum jumping to his feet.

'Yes. But as he was wrapping it up again I said, "I shall tell my husband, of course. He might like to see it".'

'The devil he would!' cried Colum.

He sat in silence for a long time, and then said, 'What made you say the musical box wasn't ours?'

'I thought they were laying a trap for you,' I said. 'I don't know why.'

'You were right,' said Colum. 'They were. I gave the musical box to a new man. I knew it was a risk. I oughtn't to have trusted him. There aren't many people you can trust.' He lit another cigarette from the one he was smoking, and said, rather harshly, 'How much can I tell you?'

I couldn't answer him.

'How much do you want me to tell you?' he said, in a softer voice.

Still I couldn't speak.

'Would you rather I told you nothing?'

I nodded, and he looked a way and puffed at the cigarette.

'In that case,' he said at last, 'you needn't know anything about it.'

'But,' I burst out, 'I *do* know. How can I not know? I believe it's the *only* thing I know.'

He opened and closed his hands.

'Well, then,' he said, 'what are you going to do about it?'

'That's one of the things I don't know.'

He rose from the chair and walked softly to and fro, every now and then looking down at me.

'Do you think you ought to give me away?'

'Of course not, Colum.'

If he felt relieved, he didn't show it.

'I thought you might,' he muttered.

'But I told them the musical box wasn't ours.'

'Yes, you did,' he admitted, 'I'd forgotten that. I haven't thanked you for that, have I? Do you want me to thank you?'

I couldn't answer.

'You saved me,' he said, 'you saved me from justice. Do you know what else you did?'

I stared at him stupidly, and suddenly he said,

'Darling, must we be unhappy?'

I began to cry, I suppose it was the word 'darling' coming so unexpectedly.

'Has it made you unhappy?' he asked. 'Are you regretting you told the Inspector what you did?'

'No,' I said. 'I believe it was the happiest and proudest moment of my life.' That was quite true. I was beside myself with joy at having deceived the police for Colum's sake. Even now I tingle at the memory of it and try to imagine myself in other situations like it.

'Look here,' said Colum. 'We were quite happy, weren't we? I know I left you to yourself a lot, which a husband shouldn't, but I couldn't help that. Have I done anything else to hurt you?'

I shook my head, without trying to think of anything else he'd done.

'Then why must we be unhappy?' he repeated. 'We aren't any different, are we? Am I different? I feel just the same. Are you different?'

I still couldn't answer, and he went on,

'I've often wondered about hospitals – I mean why women take on that awful job of nursing – they don't so much now, but still a few do, and they're not paid much. I couldn't stand it, being with sick people, and broken limbs and operating tables – I hate all that, the sick would have a thin time if everyone was like me. But women are found to do it, and they don't suffer from disgust, I'm told. I should, in their place, I suppose they think it's worth it, when the fellows get better.'

'There are women patients, too,' I said. 'Hospitals aren't only for men.'

'Yes, but women look after them. They needn't, they can have heaps of other professions.'

'Are you comparing me to a hospital nurse?' I said.

'Good Lord, no, Margaret. I was only thinking how different women are to men. I mean, a woman is never a man's job—'

'What is she, then?'

He thought, and said, 'How can you ask me, when you know so well? What I meant was, sometimes the patients get better, sometimes they get quite well.'

'Some cases are incurable,' I said.

'Only a few . . . I don't see why I shouldn't get *quite* well.'

His voice was tinged with wistfulness.

'What would my job be?' I asked.

'Your job, Margaret?' he echoed in surprise. 'Why should your job be different from what it has been?'

'I shall have a baby to look after, for one thing,' I said.

'I know, I know, you'll have two babies to look after, and you won't have so much time for me. But you will always be *there*, won't you, and that's all that matters.'

'Has it mattered much so far?' I said. 'I don't think it has. If I were tempted to regard myself as your good angel, Colum, as you seem to want me to, I shouldn't be able to give a very satisfactory account of my guardianship.'

'Why not?' he retorted. 'Have I gone down hill so much?. Am I a social outcast? Am I in gaol? You don't know what my difficulties are, Margaret, or how much you have helped me, especially in these last months when I've been half mad with depression about my film. Yes, you've been my guardian angel, all right. I shouldn't be sitting pretty as I am if it weren't for you.'

'That's only because you haven't been found out,' I said.

'Perhaps, perhaps, but isn't that something? Does it mean nothing to you that I haven't been found out? I don't think it can, for but for you I should have been found out about the musical box. Why did you say it wasn't ours, if you didn't care whether I was found out?'

'I had a sudden impulse,' I said. 'I can't explain it.'

'But if you had really known what hung on it, wouldn't you still have said it wasn't ours?'

I said nothing.

'I believe you would,' said Colum. 'I believe you love me much more than you think. And if you love me surely you can see how badly I should have fared without your love? And should fare if you took it away? Oh, Margaret, Margaret, don't be hard on me.'

'I'm not being hard on you,' I said.

'Yes, in your heart you are, and it's because you don't realize what you have done and can do for me – even without becoming a Catholic, as I asked you to. You only look at the present, which might have been so much darker, or at the future, which might be so much brighter, if you chose to make it so.'

'You mean—?' I said.

'Oh yes, yes, of course. How can you doubt it? – That I should ever want – that I should be ever as they say tempted – well, to feel that way again? – after the proof you've given that you love me? Why, it was almost a miracle—' He broke off and his face became remote and stern, as if he were thinking about

248

the miracle. 'But of course that's nothing to you,' he went on almost roughly. 'How can I expect it would be? If I could perform a miracle for you, that would be another matter. I can, I could if you would trust me. But you won't, why should you? You don't believe in miracles, and perhaps you don't think I'm worth one.'

I saw the picture he was building up of me, of the Pharisee who passed by on the other side, and felt my heart harden against myself while it softened towards him. 'I can tell you one thing,' he said, 'it sounds like blackmail but it's just the truth. If you were to fail me, I should give myself up. You stand between me and that. But perhaps you don't mind – you've finished with rescue-work.'

When he spoke of giving himself up I stared at him in terror, and hated myself for making him plead with me, when he was so much more important to the world than I was. Suddenly I felt shy and humble, in the presence of his abasement.

'Why do you suppose I married you?' he said. I couldn't answer, being near to tears, even if I could have thought of a reply. 'It isn't a fair question,' he went on penitently, 'there were a hundred reasons. But answer me this, and you will also answer my first question. Why did you marry me?'

I reddened miserably and painfully, and hid my face in my hands. He came over to me and took my hands away and made me look him in the face.

'Is it so hard to say why?' he asked.

I gulped but couldn't speak.

'I'll make it easier for you,' he said, 'and spare you the injustices you are inflicting on yourself. Whom did you marry? Was it Colum McInnes the film-star?'

I turned away from him again.

'Whom thousands of women admire and talk about and are in love with?' he said, harshly. I couldn't hide my shame and wretchedness, and looked at him imploringly; but he went on, as it seemed to me, without remorse.

'The man who was at the top of his profession and could give a woman everything she wants?'

'Oh please Colum,' I implored him, 'I may have deserved it but don't, don't torture me.'

'Then I'll answer for you,' he said in a much gentler voice. 'It wasn't that man at all you married.' He sat down by my side and took my hand. 'You married somebody quite different, someone you were sorry for and thought you could help – the Duke, the bad boy of the films, that's who you married. And you have helped him, Margaret.'

Then I turned to him and we said no more for a long time, but suddenly I remembered something and said to Colum,

'When you told me I had saved you from justice—'

'Yes?' he said. 'But you wouldn't do it again.'

'No, of course not,' I rebuked him tenderly. 'Once is quite enough. But you said I had done something else as well.'

'Well, so you had.'

'What was it?'

'You made yourself an accessory after the fact. As a magistrate you know what that means. Darling accessory, do you mind?'

I answered him with a kiss.

'And would you do it again?'

'Of course I would. Oh *yes*.'

'As often as I asked you to?'

'You wouldn't have to ask me.'

I said it and I meant it, and that's what our new life together is going to be – a real partnership.

23

But Margaret's dream of partnership was shattered by a dream. It was dark and all she could see at first was a shadowed archway like the entrance to a brick-kiln, through which came the glow of fire. People were going through the door, one after another; they did not want to go and scuttled to and fro like sheep at a gate, but they could not escape because the man in front of her was pricking their bare legs with a pitch-fork. 'Why are you doing that?' Margaret asked him. 'Don't you know it is a gas-oven?' 'Yes,' he answered, without turning round. 'But these people are enemies and must be incinerated.' 'You are a wicked man' said Margaret, 'and will burn in hell for this.' He leaned forward to prod another victim and then said, 'No, I'm not wicked, I'm following my impulses. You should be sorry for me.' 'Sorry for you?' echoed Margaret. 'Why should I be sorry?' 'Because I am a human being like yourself,' the man said, 'and I am so terribly afraid.' 'Afraid?' said Margaret. 'Who are you afraid of?' 'Of you, for one,' the man said, 'because you don't like me and I can't bear that. With all my faults I am extremely lovable.' 'I shouldn't call you lovable,' said Margaret. 'Oh, wouldn't you? We'll see,' the man said. 'Supposing I was someone you were fond of?' 'Then I should hate you all the more for what you are doing,' said Margaret. 'But you wouldn't give me away?' the man said anxiously. 'I should get into serious trouble if they caught me.' 'Indeed I should,' cried Margaret. 'Stop doing that! Stop it, I say!' The man turned to her slowly and when she saw that it was Colum she threw her arms round him and kissed him.

Then the dream faltered and seemed to be fading out, but it re-formed and now she was alone with Colum and she knew she had been helping him to put people in the gas-oven for she too held a pitch fork. But the battle had gone against them and the night was full of their pursuers. 'We must run,' said Colum. 'If they catch us you know where they will put us.' 'Run if you like,' said Margaret. 'I shall stay. They can't do anything to me, I am a magistrate.' 'Oh yes they can,' said Colum, and Margaret saw that their pursuers were closing in on them, silently, like Red Indians. 'They can, because, you see, you're an accessory. Darling accessory, do you mind?'

The oven-door swung open and the red gas tongues darted out at them. She screamed and woke, but she must have dreamed the scream for Colum was lying beside her and he did not stir. She turned away from him and tried to sleep, but the glare of the gas-oven seemed painted on her eyeballs.

Father McBane came to the telephone himself. Yes, he remembered her, he said. Could she see him? Margaret asked. He hesitated before answering. Was it anything urgent? because he was very busy. Well, it was rather urgent. Could she give him any idea of what her business was? Well, no she was afraid she couldn't. There were other priests, he said, who might be able to help her more than he could: should he give her their names? No, no, she said, frightened and almost piqued by his unwillingness to see her; no one else would do: it was very private and she begged him to see her. Well, when? he said, almost ungraciously. Could it be to-day? she asked. At half-past three to-day, he said and put down the receiver. Margaret was chilled: the people with whom she made engagements usually said how much they were looking forward to seeing her and what fun it would be.

*

Happily for her she had no time to dwell on this interview as she had had when she tried to consult her father; she arrived at the presbytery with twanging but not disordered nerves. And as she waited in the high room with its lancet windows, whose narrow, pointed sashes almost touched the ceiling, in that special twilight produced by book-lined walls, in a silence augmented by the gas-fire's steady hiss, she was aware of an awakening defensiveness, as if the priest were to be her accuser, and not she herself.

He came in and shook hands with her hurriedly. He was paler than she remembered and his eyes, though they met hers, seemed filled with the memories of other presences and other problems.

'I forget,' he said, almost at once and as if it mattered to him, 'at whose suggestion you first came to me.'

Margaret explained how it had happened.

'Ah yes,' he said, 'through some friends of a friend of yours. You don't remember their names?'

Margaret said no, and he seemed relieved.

'And now?' he said, with a slight interrogative smile, ready to be sad, indeed sad already.

Margaret plunged; and her heart, which had pounded unbearably at the first few words, gradually quietened down. At last they were out, the things that she believed could never be uttered; they were out like the poison from an ulcer; it was a physical sensation too: she felt light and free, almost bodiless with relief. And she felt that by telling her troubles she had disposed of them, and the guilt and terror that went with them. All she had to do now was to go. Had she been eligible to receive absolution she would scarcely have waited for it, so completely did she feel herself absolved. All the greater was her disappointment when she saw that the shadow had deepened on her confessor's face. He turned to her, very grave, and said,

'As I see it, you have only one course open to you.'

'What is that?' asked Margaret.

'You must leave him.'

'Leave him?' echoed Margaret.

'Yes.'

The words had no sooner left his mouth than Margaret realized that she had never faced the possibility of leaving Colum. She thought she had, when she fled from him to Fair Haven; but it had never been real to her. The difference was as great as that between fancying one is ill and hearing it confirmed from a doctor's lips. In a muddled way she felt the priest should have admired her for opening her heart to him, and her first reaction, as it often is after a shock, was anger.

'But I thought—' she began.

'I know what you are going to tell me,' said the priest. 'You are going to tell me that we Catholics believe above all things in the binding force of the marriage tie. We do, but there are exceptions.'

'Then would you advise any woman whose husband is dishonest to leave him?' Margaret asked.

'I should not,' said the priest, and the warmth in his voice showed she had ruffled him. 'To most of them I should certainly say No.'

'But not to me?'

'No, not to you.'

'Why?' asked Margaret.

'Because your own soul is in peril, as well as his.'

Spoken in a quite ordinary voice, in keeping with what for him was a quite ordinary idea, the words sank deeply into Margaret's mind. But she rebelled against them. Was she not armed with love? And did not love cover a multitude of sins? She told the priest so.

'Your love is of little value to him,' said the priest, 'if it comes from a heart as perverted as his own. Do not imagine that love is a substitute for behaving well. You are his accomplice in crime; you are also his accomplice in sin, and from what you say you mean to go on being.'

Margaret could not tell him she had made this promise in a moment of physical abandonment, only half meaning it; but the memory of the embrace was sweet to her and she cried,

'Oh, what do *I* matter? Why must I be so careful about my soul? And is not love the best thing for my soul? We are all sinners; if I am not to love a sinner, whom can I love?'

'You matter to God,' the priest said. 'And I didn't say you weren't to love your husband: how could I? But you asked my advice, and my advice would be to leave him.'

'How can I leave him? Do you mean divorce him?'

'I didn't say divorce him,' the priest answered. 'If you did, he, of course, would not be free to re-marry.'

A thought struck Margaret.

'Was that why you advised me not to become a Catholic,' she asked, 'when Colum wished me to?'

'It was not only that,' said Father McBane. 'I did not wish you to enter the Church as a thief might, and learn its holy ways from someone who is not fit to teach you. What would you have thought of us? You would have been offended; you would have left us. And I don't want you to leave us,' he said, 'when you become a Catholic.'

Margaret thought she discerned a gentle Jesuitry in this, and it annoyed her. And she thought it was unfair of Father McBane to use the information she had given him about Colum against him.

'A *Roman* Catholic,' she corrected him, hoping the phrase would hurt, for until now she had been careful to say Catholic. 'I don't think I shall, Father. My experience of Roman Catholics hasn't been very encouraging so far, as you say. What has his religion done for Colum? What has his confessor done for him? All they have done is to make him a man who, according to you, no ordinary decent woman ought to live with.'

Her indignation seemed to thrive on lack of opposition, and express itself, as anger will, in a vulgarity of utterance that made her still more angry. The priest said quietly:

'It was original sin that made him want to steal, and Holy Church is not to blame for that. What we can do to keep him from straying we have done and shall do. You must measure our success not by what he is, but by what he might have been.'

'You mean he might have been much worse?'

The priest shrugged his shoulders.

'You seem to know a great deal about him,' Margaret said.

'You have told me a great deal. And don't forget, I advised you not to marry him.'

Margaret thought this over.

'You are trying to kill my love for him,' she said, 'but let me tell you this, if I had the chance I'd marry him again a hundred times.'

'Then why did you come to me,' the priest said, 'if you feel that way about it, and have no care for the welfare of your soul?'

Margaret pondered. Side-tracked by defending Colum, she had almost forgotten why she had come. Was she so indifferent to the welfare of her soul and would she still be, when the interview was over?

'My soul is in God's keeping,' she said, speaking with difficulty. 'My conscience, I suppose, is in my own.' A sense of theological inadequacy oppressed her: she looked at the priest for confirmation.

'Or is it in your husband's?' he said.

'Oh no,' cried Margaret. 'I am a much, much, stronger character than he is. He relies on me – he told me so. That is why I thought – why I felt sure—'

'That you could influence him for his good?' the priest said. 'But it has been the other way about; he has made you an accessory.'

That was it, that was the word, and the need to get away from it and whatever it implied, that had brought her to this consultation. Accessory! Darling accessory! She remembered now; much as she loved Colum, she did not want to be an accessory. Wife, helpmeet, slave; but not accessory.

'You told me you were a magistrate?' Father McBane said.

'I was once, Father,' Margaret said. 'I'm not now. I gave it up soon after I married.'

The priest sighed, and his sigh was eloquent of everything he did not say.

'Does sin matter so much?' asked Margaret naively. 'I should have thought love mattered more – God's love, perhaps even my love.'

'If you persist in sin,' the priest said, 'it separates you from God. You may say "I have done this and that, but fundamentally I have not altered: I am what I was, my sins and I are quite detachable." They are but they leave their mark. By drinking you become a drunkard. The reward of virtue is to be virtuous, the punishment of vice is to be vicious. With your permission I will read you something.' He went to a bookshelf. He did not have to look for the book, he did not have to find the place; the well-worn volume opened at it.

'This is the meaning of a statement of mine which has furnished matter for one of those special accusations to which I am at present replying. I have, however, no fault at all to confess in regard to it; I have nothing to withdraw and in consequence I here deliberately repeat it.'

Father McBane's voice dropped. He raised his eyes from the book and fixing them on Margaret's went on without looking at the text, speaking so distinctly that the words seemed to be carved out of solid sound.

'I said, "The Catholic Church holds it better for the sun and moon to drop from heaven, for the earth to fail, and for all the many millions on it to die of starvation in extremest agony, so far as temporal affliction goes, than that one soul, I will not say, should be lost, but should commit one single venial sin, should tell one wilful untruth, or should steal one poor farthing without excuse." '

Releasing Margaret's eyes he closed the book and said,

'You know who wrote that?'

Margaret shook her head.

'Cardinal Newman, and he spoke for the whole Church.'

Margaret responded to the awe in his voice. Womanlike she did not feel the instinctive reverence for a great name that many men do; she thought all men were fallible, and that life was more important than any man's pronouncement on it. But the sins that had been singled out for censure, lying and stealing, were precisely those which had been worrying her.

Father McBane went on: 'My advice sounds harsh, I know, and I don't suppose you will care to follow it. It was meant for you, Mrs McInnes – I know you will appreciate that – and not for X or Y or anyone else who comes to me with a burdened conscience. You have been very truthful with me, perhaps more truthful than some of my co-religionists would have been: and for that very reason, unconsciously perhaps, I have been led to meet your veracity with a more naked truth than I might otherwise have done. It offended you because it seemed to question your right to love your husband: it does not do that, for love cannot be controlled. If I say you must choose between your husband and your conscience – not as things to love but things to follow – I am only saying what you have been saying to yourself. From the aesthetic standpoint you were quite right to say "What does it matter about my soul as long as I love my husband?" – it sounds well, most ordinary folk would applaud you, and some moralists. You came to me on your own behalf, but you spoke on his: yes, you were his envoy, pleading for him. What you really wanted me to say was, "Your husband is a perfectly good fellow, with one little weakness. Love him, keep an eye on him, and all will be well with you—", something like that. That was all right for you; but I had to consider you apart from him, not as his adjunct, not as his accomplice, but as a separate unique and immortal soul, seeking counsel, and that was why I advised you as I did. And I had another reason, almost as strong, perhaps you would think stronger. Can you guess what it is?'

Margaret shook her head.

'There is a third soul at stake. You are soon to become a mother. Have you thought of what your child's life will be, brought up by parents (I must not mince my words) who have compromised with dishonesty? – who are hardly ashamed to own themselves thieves? You know from your own experience, perhaps better than I do, what sort of life such a child is likely to have, and how he will turn out. A little dishonesty – how intriguing, how attractive, how innocent it sounds! – why, we could almost dine out on it! But I needn't remind you what it leads to – you will have seen its effect in many homes.'

Margaret was unprepared for this attack. The child was to be a bond between her and Colum, a fount at which they would renew their innocence, a pledge of good behaviour. That the dishonesty of the parents might be handed on, that their punishment might be to watch their child grow up in dishonesty, had not occurred to her. She tried to adjust herself to it; and as she did so there slid into her harassed, undefended mind the image that still terrified her; Colum's hand on the smiling alabaster head, and his face as he jerked it off the mantelpiece: and it seemed to her this might not mean what she once thought it might, that she would have a miscarriage, or that the child would be born dead, but that its spiritual life would be destroyed, that it would grow up a criminal as its father was – as both its parents were.

'The child will be brought up a Catholic. I promised that,' she said.

'He may be, so was his father.'

'You know that!' exclaimed Margaret.

For a moment Father McBane, whose voice had settled down into a post-crisis tranquillity, almost sonority of utterance, seemed taken aback.

'I . . . I have every reason to suppose so. And though I am a Christian and believe in miracles, I do not underrate the effect that heredity and environment may have on a child's mind.'

Something prompted Margaret to say:

'Would you tell Colum this, if he were here?'

Again he looked away from her, and then said, almost with heat,

'In truth, I should.'

'Do you then think so badly of him?' said Margaret sadly.

'I don't think he would make a good father,' the priest said.

'But isn't any father better than none?'

'We have our Heavenly Father,' the priest answered.

It was over; there was nothing more to say. Margaret felt the ebb tide in her heart, could almost feel its motionlessness, almost see its freight of hopes and fears, joys and sorrows, drifting aimlessly, waiting for the tide to turn.

'Do you think I shall become a Catholic?' she asked, detachedly, almost as if she were speaking of someone else.

'I shall pray for that,' said the priest.

'To whom will you pray?' asked Margaret.

'To God,' said the priest, surprised, 'to Jesus Christ, and to the saints.' He looked at her almost slyly. 'I have my favourite saints.'

'My favourite saint,' said Margaret, 'is Saint Anthony.'

'Ah, you told me so,' Father McBane exclaimed in a tone more homely and confidential than he had used to her before, and almost as one Catholic to another. 'A blessed, holy saint, a saint of power.'

'I know,' said Margaret, warming to his mood, 'and in a way he has never failed me. Except once, except once, I only asked him for, well . . . for unimportant things – the return of things that I – that we – had . . . lost. They all came back. But—', and this was a thought that had vexed her for some time – 'I should have been so much happier if they hadn't. They brought misfortune with them.'

'Happier?' the priest said, puzzled.

'Yes, happier . . . Because I shouldn't have known . . . oh . . . everything that I know now.'

'And do you think St. Anthony wasn't aware of that?'

'You mean it was a way of showing me?' asked Margaret doubtfully.

'I do. He found you more than you asked for, and more than you bargained for – the truth. The truth is more precious when it comes by a hard way. Did you think he was playing a trick on you, like Fate in a Greek legend?'

'I had wondered,' Margaret said. 'And now it doesn't matter. I have nothing left to ask him for.'

'You will have, you will have,' said the priest. 'Life doesn't let us alone, and God doesn't either. St. Anthony has helped you on the way. It was a fool's paradise you lived in, the real one is much better,' he said briskly. 'And do not think the seeking is all on your part. You are being sought for, too.'

The conviction in his voice made Margaret believe him. She had no excuse to stay on in this room which the love of God made seem much less bleak than the world outside without the love of Colum. She said:

'You really think I ought to leave him?'

'That is my advice,' said the priest. 'I don't expect you to follow it – indeed I hope you won't, unless your conscience consents.'

'But if I leave him,' Margaret said, 'what will he do?'

'What did he do before?' said Father McBane with a cheerfulness that sounded almost callous. 'He managed without you once; he will again. When the world's smile is brightest, there he turns his face. He can take care of himself. You need have no fear for him.'

'Yet you fear for me with him.'

'Yes, he would destroy your life. You have no defence against his weapons, for he will always use your love to serve his ends.'

'Aren't you too hard on him?' said Margaret.

'I wish I was. But I see him as he is, the worser self of anyone who is with him, for he has no self of his own.'

'Where have you seen him?' asked Margaret. 'On the films?'

'I certainly have seen him there,' the priest replied. 'Perhaps that is where he is most real. Our hearts have a screen too, and shadows move across it. If the audience could bare their breasts when he is playing to them, what kind of shape would you expect to see?'

Margaret was startled by the intensity of his voice.

'I don't know,' she said.

'Nor do I,' said the priest, 'but I can guess. What is the name of his new film to be?' he asked inconsequently.

'Oh,' said Margaret. 'Such a silly name. I hardly like to tell you. It's called *The Devil is so Distinguished*.'

'Ah,' said the priest. 'He must have a talent for that rôle.'

'Do you know,' said Margaret, glad to be able to score a point at last, 'he hasn't. He's been worried all along because he doesn't do it well. He blamed me – he said I'd taken the devil out of him.'

Suddenly Father McBane burst out laughing, and laughed a long time, quite uncontrollably. The sound was almost shocking in the austere little room, with its air of sanctity and its pious reminders. 'Forgive me, forgive me,' he said, when he had regained possession of himself. 'That was quite inexcusable. If you have taken the devil out of him, so much the better, but it still doesn't alter my opinion.' He smiled apologetically and began to rise. Margaret noticed how tired he looked and her heart smote her; she begged him not to get up. 'No, no, I'll see you out,' he said. On the mat, in the hall, lay a scattering of letters, the afternoon's post. Father McBane stooped down to pick them up and clear the way for her. They were in his left hand as he held out his right to say goodbye, and she saw – she could not help seeing – the topmost envelope. Its shape and colour were familiar; the brown ink, like dried blood, was familiar, and the handwriting was more familiar still, for it was Colum's.

Across the envelope their eyes met. 'Yes,' said Father McBane, 'I know him. It is an accident of a priest's life, and I count on you to keep it to yourself. But we must not meet again.'

Margaret left him in confusion, almost forgetting to say goodbye. But halfway down the street she remembered her offering and ran back and slipped it in his letter-box.

24

'But what do we want the masks for?' Margaret asked.

'Oh, I don't know, it's some idea they have.'

'I don't feel comfortable about this party,' Margaret said. 'Lauriol rang me up, and said she wasn't going.'

'Oh, is she back? Bad girl, she didn't tell me.'

'She got back last night and found the invitation.'

'Dear Lauriol, did she say why she wasn't going?'

'She said she didn't think that she'd enjoy it, nor should I.'

'That was considerate of her, wasn't it? I think you will enjoy it, all the same. But I'm so glad that you two girls are pals.'

Yes, I suppose we are pals, Margaret thought, as they drove onwards to the party. But how astonishing that we should be! The telephone call was the first communication she had had with Lauriol since their momentous interview in which Lauriol had told her so many lies. She had thought that they could never meet again; yet she had felt no embarrassment when she heard Lauriol's husky voice, she had even welcomed it, and they prolonged their talk, as women will, for upwards of twenty minutes. Not a single reference to their last meeting, except a laconic, but by no means perfunctory, inquiry from Lauriol as to how she was. The rest was chatter, and such animated chatter, about the South of France, about Colum's film (of which, mortifyingly, Margaret could tell her little, except that it was finished), and their projected holiday in Venice. Just at the end, Lauriol had said casually, 'Are you going to the Sindons' party to-night?' And when Margaret had said she was, Lauriol said, 'Well, I'm not, I'm tired and I don't think I should enjoy it, and I don't think you will either. It's not your sort of party at all. Why not say you have a headache, and stay at home, and make Colum stay with you?' 'Oh, I couldn't do that,' said Margaret, still automatically truthful and promise-keeping. 'You see, it's a party *for* Colum.' 'I know. Don't think me interfering – I just thought you would be a fish out of water.'

And there it ended, and it was only now that Margaret felt surprised. Was she the same Margaret who, that afternoon, had listened to Father McBane's warnings against sin, and the danger to the soul of keeping bad company? Who had come out of his presbytery half convinced that it was her duty to leave her husband? Could it be, she asked herself, that the mere act of confiding her secret to another person had so relieved her mind that the very motive for her confession no longer weighed with her? Did she think everything was all right because she had told somebody, made a clean breast of it? Would it have done just as well if she had confided in a passing taxi-driver or a railway porter? Had Father McBane's recommendations been completely without effect?

She told herself that she had had no time to consider them, she would consider them to-morrow. She glanced at Colum's unsuspecting profile and remembered what the priest had said about him. Roman Catholics were reputed to be tender towards sinners. Father McBane was not, but even he had not denied that sin could be wiped out by a last-minute repentance. Margaret felt sure it could be: God would not refuse anything to Colum.

The episode which seemed so vital then had now become external to her, she could not think herself back into the state of mind from which it sprung. Instead, her mind went running ahead of her to the party, where for the first time she was to meet these new friends of Colum's. Why had Lauriol advised her not to go? Lauriol liked gay parties: did it means that this would be a dull one? Somehow Margaret did not think so. She thought of Lauriol sitting alone when she might have been at the party – bored, her feet up, perhaps wishing she had gone. Margaret would tell her all about it afterwards, tell her what she had missed. She found herself looking forward to going to Lauriol's flat again. At one time the prospect had embarrassed her; confronted by the empty china cabinet she would not know which way to look. Now she felt she could even join in a joke about it. Was this what it meant to be Colum's accomplice? Never mind if it was.

The party would be much more fun if Lauriol was going. To think that she should be more dashing than Lauriol! That she should go where Lauriol wouldn't go! What a change that was.

'Did you remember to bring your mask?' asked Colum.

Margaret felt in her bag.

'Yes. Shall I put it on?'

'We shan't need them yet, but we might try them on.'

'Won't they frighten the driver?'

'Oh no, it would take more than that to frighten him.'

A moment later the driver put the light on and Margaret cried, 'Oh Colum, is it really you? I shouldn't recognize you!'

'Well, come to that you don't look altogether like yourself,' said Colum.

Laughing, they took their masks off.

A waiter was handing drinks round on a tray. Margaret remembered him, she had seen him at other parties, but except for Colum he was the only person in the room she did know. Dinner was over; other guests had come in. Some walked about, some sat. Margaret was among those who sat. She would much rather have stood, for then she could have circulated; as it was she was stuck with a man she did not care for. But she wasn't feeling well; she had a headache. At last she heard a woman saying to their host:

'I'm afraid we must go, it's been a lovely party.'

It hasn't, Margaret thought; it's been decorous and dull, Lauriol was quite right. Shall I get up? she thought, and signalled to Colum. But he disregarded her.

Soon another couple rose and then by fits and starts the guests began to go. Margaret noticed that of those who remained the men considerably outnumbered the women.

Another tray of drinks went round, and the man sitting next to Margaret said, in a thick, confidential undertone, 'Are you going on to the party?'

'I didn't know there was another party,' Margaret said. 'I'd better ask my husband.' Not sorry to leave her unprepossessing neighbour, she went to Colum's side.

'Darling, isn't it time we were leaving? It's getting on for twelve.'

'Oh, but we're going on to Mrs Bel's,' said Colum. He too spoke in a thick voice, and had a glass of whiskey at his side. A very little alcohol affected him. 'We mustn't miss the fun.'

'Darling, I am a little tired,' said Margaret, and suddenly felt weighed down by fatigue and by the thought of meeting Mrs Bel. 'Do let's go home.'

He shook his head and raised his eyebrows, to indicate that they might be overheard. Disappointed and surprised – for it was not like Colum to thwart her – she turned away, looking for another partner than the one she had left. But the rest of the remaining guests were all paired off; so unwillingly she went back to her place.

'Well, what did he say?' her companion asked her.

Margaret disliked the familiarity of his tone.

'He wants us to go on to Mrs Belmore's,' she answered shortly.

'I thought he would,' her neighbour remarked, his voice implying satisfaction that he knew her husband's intentions when she did not. 'And you don't want to go?'

'I'm feeling a bit tired, that's all,' Margaret said.

'Wait till you get there,' the man advised her; 'it'll be quite a show.'

Margaret didn't answer.

More guests went out, reducing the company to about a dozen, of whom only two, besides Margaret, were women.

'They're beginning to thin off now,' her neighbour said. 'I expect we shall soon be moving, too.'

'What time does Mrs Bel expect us?' Margaret asked.

'She isn't expecting us, that's part of the fun.'

'Not expecting us?'

'No, it's a surprise visit. Didn't you know?'

'But if she isn't expecting us will she still be up?'

'Oh yes, Mrs Bel goes to bed very late.'

'I know nothing,' said Margaret. She glanced again at the man at her side, and her distaste for him and his appearance – she wondered that anyone dared to look as sinister as he did – deepened into fear. A suspicion slid into her mind.

'Is our host' – she tried to remember his name and found she had forgotten it – 'waiting for some of the guests to leave before he starts?'

'That's the idea. We're to be a picked bunch. Sort of commando stuff, you know.'

Uneasy though Margaret now was, she felt that if she humoured him she might find out more.

'A kind of raid?'

'That's right.'

Margaret tried to raise a smile.

'Shall you abduct her?'

'It's we – you're coming too, you know. Well, that depends. Of course it's all a joke.'

268

A joke! Margaret did not feel reassured. Suddenly the room seemed to become unreal to her and at the same time profoundly hostile. She longed to get away from it. But how could she escape? Dotted around her were the remaining guests, talking to each other with the exaggerated animation that precedes departure. The woman with Colum was showing herself almost extravagantly sensible of the honour: she was actively grimacing. Often as Margaret had seen it happen before, she was again surprised that he was not utterly spoilt. Ah, but there was an excuse for it. She was saying good-bye to him. Another guest was leaving.

'Zero hour at any minute now,' said her companion with a smile.

Without answering or looking back at him Margaret jumped up and made her way to the vacant seat by Colum. She drew a long breath.

'Colum,' she entreated, 'please, please come away. I don't like—' she tried to lower her voice still more – 'I don't like the idea of this party that we're going to. There's something queer about it – I know there is.'

Colum gave her his most bewitching smile.

'Darling, what are you getting worked up about?'

Margaret glanced round; their host was lighting a cigarette and looking at her with speculation in his half-closed eyes. Despairingly she tried another tack. 'And besides I have a headache and I don't feel well. It's bad for me, you know, especially now. Please, please, Colum, I beg you.'

'It's only going to be a little frolic, darling,' Colum said. 'You'll enjoy it as much as anyone. We understand each other, don't we? We're together, aren't we? You won't let me down?'

She turned away from him and all unknowing flashed a signal of protest and despair at her fellow guests. But if they saw it they paid no attention; they were not going to aggravate her breach of manners by recognizing it. 'Oh!' she exclaimed. But even that appeal slid off the glassy social surface; it had no more effect than a yawn or a sneeze, less, for it was even more deliberately disregarded. Irresolutely she took a step towards her vacant chair; the man beside it patted it invitingly. That decided her: she could not go back to him, could not stay another moment in this room that was stifling her.

The realization that she not only must but could go steadied her, and the routine act of taking leave restored her mental poise. She even managed to put some plausibility and dignity into her farewell and found an ironic satisfaction, almost a sense of achieved revenge, in saying how much she had enjoyed herself and how sorry she was to go. She even mustered courage to glance at Colum; he was watching her with intent and disbelieving eyes and as she went towards the door he rose and caught her up.

'Darling,' he said, loud enough to be heard by the whole room, 'I am sorry you're not feeling well. Let me go down with you and help you find a taxi.'

'No, no,' said Margaret, woundingly. 'I couldn't think of it. You must stay here with your friends.' But the moment they were outside the door she had another change of feeling and begged him to come with her. 'I can't explain,' she said, shaking her head, 'but they aren't the right sort of people for you.' She was at a loss to put what she felt into civilized, unsensational language; and he began to smile, and said, 'Darling, you're making a great fuss about nothing. I'll see you later.' He kissed her in his swift, practised way, which always took her by surprise, and was gone before her lips had lost the feel of his.

In a daze she crossed the silent, white painted vestibule and let herself out into the corridor. She paused, wondering which way the lift was: and at the same moment the door she had come out by opened, and Colum appeared, with her fur coat in his arms. A shiver of delight passed through her, as if he had returned to her after many years. 'I guessed you'd go out without your cloak,' he said with tender mockery as he helped her into it. 'You should think more of your own good, and less of mine.' She tried to catch his hand but he eluded her and vanished through the doorway. The door closed after him without a sound, and became like all the other doors in the long corridor: she could not even remember which it was.

The commissionaire was standing on the steps. She asked him to get her a taxi and he responded with so much good will that when he came back, perched precariously on the foot-board of the taxi, she said, 'Would you do something else for me?' He asked her what it was. She looked at her watch. 'It's now two minutes to twelve,' she said. 'Would you wait a quarter of an hour and then go to Flat 22 and tell Mr McInnes that his wife isn't well and would like him to come home? Say you've had a message.'

'I'm not supposed to leave the door, Madam,' he said. 'Well, perhaps this once? It's so important.' He took the note she gave him and saluted.

During the drive back Margaret's spirits rose. She felt certain that her ruse would be a success. She even began to think of the excuses she would make to Colum for having taken him in. She blessed the flat for being so empty and silent. Still full of confidence she began to undress.

But when a quarter of an hour passed and he did not come, her uneasiness returned. She felt too restless to go to bed and wandered about miserably, half-dressed. The sitting-room became filled with the ghosts of missing objects; it was a scene of crime and she could not stay in it. She went back to her bedroom and began to dress again. The process brought a painful sense of anti-climax; it was like a reversal of the natural order. But at last it was complete: she found herself putting on her coat and taking up her bag. What now? Where now? She glanced at her watch: it said a quarter to one.

He would not come now. If he did not come at once in answer to her message, he would not come. He would go on to the party – perhaps he had already gone. He had not heeded her last appeal.

She was seized by a sudden impulse to know what she looked like. Like someone with a train to catch, the mirror told her. Begone, the whole room seemed to say; you have finished here, your place is elsewhere. The thought of the sleeping servants increased her loneliness. If she stayed, what might not happen? Get out of this, the room urged her; this is no place for you, you will be sorry if you stay, you may be burgled. You may even be murdered. She went back to her bedroom, and found herself mechanically putting her night things into a suit-case. I am packing, she told herself, I am packing. She even tried to pack carefully, so that the things shouldn't get crushed. Now she had her suit-case in her hand and looked more like a traveller than ever. Am I turning myself out? she thought confusedly, or am I being turned out? It was nearly one o'clock; a sense of urgency, an acute journey-fever, began to possess her. But there was still something to be done. Like an automaton she went to the telephone book, found what she sought and dialled a number. The bell rang and rang, but there was no answer. Mr Sindon's flat was empty; they had gone on to the party at Mrs Bel's.

She thought a moment and then dialled another number, this time without consulting the book. Yes, the night-porter answered, yes, he remembered Miss Pennefather perfectly well, of course he did. He remembered her the last twenty years, but he hadn't seen her for some time. Well, she was now Mrs Colum McInnes. Was she really? Why of course she was, now he

272

remembered. Well, she wanted a room for the night. The porter would see what could be done. The instrument made vague gulping noises, as if it was inhaling silence. Then the porter came back. Did she want a single room, because there, wasn't one. There was a double room, would that do? Margaret said it would do.

She went to the writing-table and wrote a note. 'Colum, I feel I can't stay. We must try to get on without each other. Love, Margaret.' She put the envelope on his pillow. Still she could not bring herself to go. She kept looking at her watch, giving herself one time-limit after another. Only when it showed one-thirty did she feel empowered to act.

The rest was easy. The night-porter was at the other side of the building, as he often was, having two entrances to watch; but a taxi answered her raised hand at once. During the short drive she thought very little and it never crossed her mind that she was following Father McBane's advice. Nor did she look out of the window or she might have seen, a minute after she started, Colum's trim figure hurrying towards the flat. And had she seen she might not have believed, for she had ceased to connect him with truth, or even with reality.

25

DRIVING back next morning Margaret thought a great deal but to no purpose.

The newspaper paragraph had had a big headline, but it gave few details. All it said was that a band of masked men had entered Mrs Belmore's mansion in Queen's Gate shortly before 1 a.m. and that Mrs Belmore had died, presumably of shock. The police had been called in and were making investigations. All this was a blur in her mind, but the last sentence stood out clearly. 'It is alleged that one of the masked men was a well-known film actor.'

One state of mind so quickly overlays another that she could scarcely remember what she meant to do before she read the announcement. She had slept late – that she remembered; she had dressed and come downstairs wondering if breakfast was still being served. While it was being brought she went out and asked the porter if he still had a newspaper. He was not the night-porter of course, but he remembered her from old days. Was there something peculiar in his manner as he said, 'No, Mrs McInnes, I haven't. I'm afraid they're all gone.'? But in one of the lounges she came on a stray paper and stifling the scruple that its owner might return for it she took it with her, partly because she always read a newspaper at breakfast but more because reading it would give her a few minutes respite from the problem that was thundering at the gates of her mind. She could not now remember even what she thought her answer was going to be; for she opened the paper and at once saw the paragraph – as the night editor had intended that she, along with the rest of the world, should see it.

She remembered to tell the waiter she would not want any breakfast after all and took the lift back to her bedroom, and lay down on the unmade bed, for she believed that the crisis she had been dreading was upon her. She took the sedative she had taken the night before, and lay quite still, with her arms by her sides, trying to think of nothing; and gradually the tremors, which she had taken for signs of something more serious, began to abate, and the warmth stealing through her limbs told her that she had nothing to fear.

Nothing to fear! And for a moment, with the removal of that strongest and most instinctive dread, her whole being gratefully saluted her reprieve. Only for a moment; then the other fear rushed in, flooding her heart and mind. But her nerves stood up to it, inoculated as they had just been by deliverance from a greater peril.

'I must thank God for this,' she thought, and did so, marvelling at the strength she found to pack her things and wondering where it came from. But when she paid the cashier and asked the porter to call her a taxi, she realized, though nothing in their bearing gave her cause, that she was turning a defiant face to the world, the face of some one who must meet its disapproval.

26

WHEN Colum saw her he rushed up to her. 'My darling,' he exclaimed, 'thank God you've come back.' She tasted the salt tears on his cheek and saw how white and haggard he looked and her heart smote her. Then he gently disengaged himself and began to walk up and down again. 'Poor old girl! Poor old girl!' he kept repeating. Margaret thought that he meant her, and her tears began to flow, blinding her thoughts as well as her eyes. She thought of what she could say to him that would not be completely untrue, not a complete climb-down from her position of last night, but that would assure him of her love and trust. But when she heard him say, 'Poor old soul, she wouldn't have hurt a fly,' she realized that he meant Mrs Belmore, and was chilled. She did not like to interrupt his grief but she felt increasingly that his feelings were not the only or the most important aspect of the situation, and at last she said,

'Please tell me what happened, Colum.'

He stopped short in his walk and stared down at her. 'What happened?' he repeated. 'I know no more than you do. I wasn't there. I only know what the papers say.'

'The papers suggest you were there,' Margaret said. She tried to make her voice sound loving, but she wasn't sure if it sounded even friendly.

'Well, I wasn't,' he said shortly. And then, as if that was settled, he went on,

'Poor old girl, the whole thing was a joke. I'll tell you all about it,' he said with a sudden rush of animation. 'Not long ago – I can't remember when, but it was while you were staying at Fair Haven – we were at Mrs Bel's one evening, and one of them, I think it was Sindon, said what fun it would be to stage a hold-up, wearing masks and so on, like burglars do in books, like I do, on the films. And we should pinch a few things and of course return them afterwards. The police would be called in and take everything very seriously – finger-prints and all the rest of it, and the papers would be full of it, and then, after things had gone a certain way, we should return the stuff we'd taken and explain it was a hoax, and the owner and the public and the papers and the police would be left looking silly, specially the police.

'Well, Mrs Bel quite took to the idea. I know you never much liked her, Margaret, but she was a good old girl. And she made suggestions, and we worked out some of the details and thought out the kind of things we'd say to the prospective victim.

'And there it rested, and I for one forgot all about it. But one day one of the gang – Ripman I think – you were still away, Margaret, it was during your eclipse – said what a good idea it would be to try out the joke on Mrs Bel herself. It would give it a sort of extra twist, d'you see? The only snag was that we thought she'd be sure to spot us, but we were ready to risk that, for the sake of amusing her; you know how much she's always done to entertain us, and there isn't a great deal one can do for Americans in this benighted country, to return their hospitality. So we arranged it for last night and had the other party first, to warm ourselves up a bit – it's dreary going to a late party when you've had nothing to cheer you up first.'

'Why didn't you tell me what was going to happen?' asked Margaret.

'Well, I wasn't sure you'd like the idea to start with, but I thought you'd fall in with it when you got into the swing and saw what fun it was going to be.'

'Lauriol was in the secret, I suppose,' Margaret said.

'Well no, but she rumbled something and didn't cotton to it – I can't think why. Lucky for her she didn't, as things turned out. Oh Lord, why did it have to happen? Poor old soul, she never did anyone any harm in her life.' He made a gesture of helplessness and brushed away a tear. Suddenly his face cleared. 'Well, what will be, will be. I shall have a mass said for her – that is, I'll have it said for my intention. It will be another joke on her, for she wasn't a Catholic. She used to say I only pretended to be one,' he added reminiscently. 'Cheer up, darling, don't look so glum. She'd had a good life, she'd had everything she wanted, and she always used to say she hoped she'd pop off quickly, at a party, and that's what she did. Perhaps you might pray for her, when you're on one of your church-crawls.'

Margaret could not share Colum's sorrow at Mrs Belmore's death, but neither could she share his levity. To Roman Catholics, she supposed, the idea of death was less grievous than it was to Protestants. For a moment, amid her multitudinous concern for the affair, she thought of its religious aspect.

'I suppose there'll be a memorial service for her,' she said.

'Yes, darling, and a funeral, and we shall all have to turn up – at least I shall. The others may decide to keep away, they're not church-goers.'

'I'm not sure I shall go,' said Margaret.

'Darling, why not? Because you didn't like her?'

'I don't think it would look well, somehow.'

'Don't you? Then I'll represent you. I wonder when it'll be. In a few days, I expect.'

'There'll have to be an inquest first,' said Margaret.

'An *inquest*?' Colum's voice dropped at the word. 'Why should there be an inquest? It was only a joke.'

'All the same, there'll have to be one,' Margaret said, astonished at Colum's ignorance.

He drew a long breath.

'Oh well, the inquest will be purely formal.'

'We may be called as witnesses,' said Margaret.

'Darling, you *are* a ray of sunshine. How can we be? I wasn't there, and you – you were too upstage to think of going.' He looked at her speculatively; a tentative twinkle came into his eye, and faded out. 'Darling, I haven't asked you till now, we've had so many other things to talk of, but what *did* you mean by your note?'

As Margaret was trying to find an answer which should not, immediately, open up the whole extent of their relationship – for she felt utterly incapable of such an undertaking – the telephone bell rang.

She rose at once.

'Darling, don't run away. It may be for you.'

He went over to the instrument.

'It's Sindon,' he said, flatly.

'I'll come back when you've finished,' said Margaret, her hand on the door.

Colum put a wealth of meaning into his reply.

'Mind you do, darling, mind you do! I'll come and call you. I'm not taking any risks.' The last she saw of him was a mischievously lifted eyebrow and a gay wave of the hand.

Margaret's first impulse was to make her face up. As Margaret Pennefather she had sometimes been slack about it; to Margaret McInnes it had become a No. 1 priority and first as well as second nature. She did it for Colum. But she could not do it now because she had left her bag – her powder-magazine, as Colum called it – which contained the requisites, in the sitting-room. She was divided from him by more than a wall – by an *unsoigné* face. Well, there was nothing to be done about it.

But as she sat in the brocaded easy chair, wearing an ill-fitting face, her eyes on the stripped dressing-table, which had held so many mementoes of her marriage, the ties of married life seemed to loosen their hold, and she began to remember what it had felt like to be single. Not to have one's happiness bound up with someone else's! To be free to make one's own decisions! To be among events which meant what they appeared to, and people who could be counted on!

It lasted only a minute or two, this recovery of her old, unencumbered self, and then the present claimed her. But it gave her the increase of strength that even the memory of happiness sometimes gives. Not strength to follow the right path, or even to see where it lay; but strength to ask herself whether she must continue to let her moods wait upon events, changing as they changed. In the past her moods had been under her control; they scarcely affected the conduct of her life. But now she was one person one moment and another the next. Last night she had fully made up her mind, she believed, to leave Colum for good. This morning she had returned to him, and why? Because she believed him to be in serious trouble. Perhaps it was not so serious after all; in spite of her misgivings his sanguine mood had affected hers. She had come, as she thought, to comfort and support him; but she had come on a false errand, for apparently he needed neither.

Why then was she staying? Not to share his grief at 'Mrs Belmore's death, for that she could not share, nor his subsequent elation, for that she thought ill-timed. What reason had she to be here that she had not had the night before? None; the circumstances were just the same, the same arguments held good.

Was she always to be his mirror, faithfully giving back whatever reflection he chose to evoke? No, she must take a stand at some point, and cling to her integrity whatever demands for sympathy he made. She must find some mood that was pity-proof and stick to it or he would wear her out. Loving him she could not live with him, living with him she could not love him: that was her quandary.

She tried to keep out of her deliberations any question of whether he was a good man or a bad man, but to base her conclusions simply on her experience of living with him. She tried not to see the problem in terms of its extreme instances. Even a little while ago when he took her to see the 'Duke', she had enjoyed such rapture with him as she had not known before. Twice she had left him, the first time on impulse, because she could not bear to be with him a moment longer; the second time, as she believed, in good earnest, because she had made up her mind. She had written to tell him so; she had meant him to take that pillow-message for a farewell.

Why had she written it? Because he wanted to take her to a party that she didn't want to go to? Surely of all reasons for breaking up a marriage that was the most trivial. Was it because, almost for the first time, there had been a naked clash between their wills and she hadn't wanted to give way? That explanation reflected hardly more credit on her than the other.

But credit implied self-justification and she was not trying to justify herself, or him, but only trying to find a solution, a new pattern of behaviour that would make their marriage work. What made her feel as she had felt last night, and how could she take precautions against feeling it again?

Was it all a matter of temperament, of chemical reactions which neither of them could control? No, for when they were first married, to fit her mood to Colum's, to be what he wanted her to be, was the greatest happiness she was capable of. It must be something else.

Her thoughts went back to her interview with Father McBane. She could hardly believe that it happened only yesterday. Events had followed each other so quickly that she had had no time to think about it. She could not even remember exactly in what state of mind it had left her.

But she remembered his advice. His advice had been to leave Colum, because to stay with him would imperil her soul. Against that she had protested, 'What does my soul matter?' But when he told her that the soul of her unborn child would be in peril too, she had had no answer ready. She could take responsibility for her own soul, but not for her child's. The priest had told her that the children of dishonest parents did not have a very good chance and she knew that that was true. Her anger against him had cooled; she realized that from his point of view he was only saying what he had to say.

With some distaste she forced herself to think of herself as a dishonest parent, Colum's accomplice, 'Darling accessory', he had called her. The phrase had an unpleasant ring, it was not the description of herself she would have chosen, but she must not be afraid of it: as a magistrate she had seen a great many dishonest parents, and could honestly say, if a dishonest parent could speak honestly, that she had not shuddered at them. She had regarded them at worst as social misfits, who should and probably could be re-educated and readjusted and received back into the community as properly integrated social units.

Again she tried, again with some distaste, to think of herself as a social misfit, and again told herself she did not mind; but when she thought of her son (for she was convinced her child would be a son) under that appellation she did not like it.

Crime (to use an old-fashioned word) was something she knew about. It was something that other people did; but she had enough imagination to see herself as a criminal and accept the implications. The world at large, the non-criminal world, thought thus and thus about criminals, its disapproval being proportioned to the nature of the crime. Or was it? Was it not also proportioned to the nature of the criminal, and his place in society? But she did not pursue this inquiry, not knowing where it led to. Sufficient for her self-review that she was, in the eyes of the law, a criminal, and should its eyes ever be opened, she might be known for such. Well, she knew what it meant and for herself she could bear it. But whether she could bear it for her child, her son, she was not so sure.

On the one hand a loving and devoted, but criminal wife and mother – mother possibly of a criminal son; on the other a woman who has divorced her husband and broken up his life.

So much for crime. But what about sin, what about the soul? To Father McBane crime meant sin; and his objection to it was not so much that it might land her in prison as that it might separate her soul from God. Crime was an act against society, sin was an act against God. And as to that Margaret knew nothing; she hardly knew how it affected her thoughts, or if it affected them. In her laborious summing up, which she had tried to keep as impartial as if she was sitting on the Bench, considering the case of someone else, it had no place. In courts of law the soul was not referred to. But yes, she remembered, it was referred to once, in the death-sentence when the judge said, 'And may God have mercy on your soul'.

The thought that He might not have mercy made her shudder a little, and she realized that if one believed in it, sin was a much more serious matter than crime. What had made her a church-fiend, as Colum called her? Why did she find so much happiness – almost guilty happiness – in praying by herself in a church? What was it that impelled her to go? Not duty, not conscience; the impulse sometimes came from without and she almost felt she ought to resist it, as if it was an indulgence, a temptation, a voice calling to her that she ought not to answer.

The habit, if habit it was, had begun with Colum's telling her that he was a bad Catholic, and that if she became a Catholic he might become a better one. It was her effort to meet him on the religious plane – to do and be what he wanted, one of her many efforts to please him. It all went back to him.

At the thought of him her eyes filled with tears, and she was no longer able to go on thinking of herself as a case, a case that only she could deal with. She felt the oncoming of another mood, almost another personality, but she fought it off.

The habit had outlasted her wish to please Colum. It had indeed survived his ridicule and acquired an independent existence, an authority and prerogative of its own. It wanted to be obeyed for its own sake, not for his.

She remembered the conclusion of her visit to Father McBane and the sense of peace and homecoming she had then, though it was associated with no decision that she had taken. No doubt her mind had been relieved by making him her confidant: but she had not decided to follow his advice. It was just a state of mind that was utterly congenial and restful to her, brought about, or rather signalized, by that unimportant (and in a Protestant perhaps, rather unbecoming) gossip about saints. She was cut off from herself, that was what was so blissful: she could enjoy her mind without having to make it up.

Yet that very night she had found the resolution to tell Colum she must leave him; and where else could the seed have taken root, if not in those few minutes of passiveness and receptivity?

If human life were eternal, she told herself, no direct action would be needed; one's destiny would fulfil itself by minute modifications as gradual as those of evolution. But it was not; Time pressed; and if it was true, as the priest said, that Colum would always make her love for him serve his own ends she must cut herself adrift from him. Not, he had said, unless your conscience consents. Well, it consented. 'What did you mean by your note?' Colum had asked her. She would go into the sitting-room now and tell him.

But why had he not come to call her, as he promised? She looked at her watch: more than twenty minutes had gone by since she had left him. Could he have been telephoning all that time? She rose from her chair and again looked round instinctively for her compact. This was not the moment to offend his fastidiousness. If he was still telephoning perhaps she could creep into the room and fetch her handbag without his noticing.

With her hand on the door she stopped and listened. No sound came from within. Making as little movement as she could she turned the handle.

27

COLUM was sitting on the sofa, staring straight in front of him. His expression did not change when she came in: she thought he had not seen her.

'Oh Colum, what is it?' she cried, running to him.

'I've been speaking to Sindon,' he answered without turning his head.

'Yes, I know, but –', she stopped, awed and frightened by his lifeless voice and vacant face. 'Can't you tell me what he said?'

'Why did you go away?' he asked in the same lifeless tone. 'It would have been all right if you'd been here.'

She did not answer his question – the question she had come primed to answer; she felt she could never answer it. But she had to say something.

'Tell me what happened,' she implored him.

'How can I tell you? I don't know anything. I wasn't there.'

'But didn't Mr Sindon tell you?'

'Oh yes, Sindon told me.'

He seemed to be sinking back into apathy and speechlessness. Margaret felt she must rally him. She had not got him into this trouble, whatever it was, but she must try to get him out. The invigorating hand of responsibility touched her. But he seemed very far away from her, as far away as the prisoner from the magistrate.

'What did Mr Sindon say?'

Colum seemed to make a great effort to pull himself together.

'He thought I was one of the people who broke into Mrs

Bel's house. But I wasn't – I wasn't there.' He seemed unable to get away from that.

'Where were you?'

'I was on my way back here.'

But he must be made to tell her what happened, he must be made to face his position in all its bearings. He would have to, later on.

'Try to remember exactly what he told you,' she said, and added, with an effort, 'my darling.'

'What he told me?' said Colum indifferently. 'Let's see. He told me that shortly before one – that's in the newspapers – they all went into Mrs Bel's house.'

'How did they get in?'

'With a key.'

'With a key?'

'One of them – it was Ripman – had a key. The man you talked to. He'd been staying with her a few days before.'

'I see,' said Margaret. 'And then what happened?'

'They put their masks on in the hall, and then went up into the drawing-room.'

'Was Mrs Bel there?'

'Yes, she was sitting reading. She always goes to bed very late.'

'And what did she do when she saw them?'

'She screamed and tried to ring up the police.'

'Why couldn't she?'

'Because one of them stopped her. He had his work cut out – she's a tough old girl. I mean she was.'

'But I always understood she had a weak heart.'

'Oh yes, but she'd had that for a long time. She was tough all right – all American women are.'

Margaret said:

'Were they . . . were they very rough with her?'

'How do I know?' said Colum listlessly. 'I wasn't there. The police seemed to think they were. There were some marks, they said.'

Margaret sat silent, divided between her feelings as a magistrate and a wife.

'Who called the police up?' she asked.

'Sindon did. But that was later, after the maid had come in – Mrs Bel's French maid, her personal maid. She was the only servant in the house. All the others had left. Mrs Bel was looking for a new staff. We knew that, of course, I mean, they did. 'By the time the maid appeared Mrs Bel was . . . well . . . she was passing out. She actually died in the maid's arms.'

'What were the others doing?' Margaret asked. 'Didn't they try to help?'

'No, that's just it, they didn't. Like fools they lost their heads. Doll Funkhorn began to have hysterics as soon as she saw what was happening to Mrs Bel, and screamed to Rudy to take her away. Then the others panicked, all except Sindon. As soon as they saw the maid come in they bolted.'

'Leaving Mr Sindon?'

'Yes, he stayed until the police came. If the others had stayed, it would have been all right.'

'How do you mean it would have been all right, Colum?' asked Margaret, astonished at such a phrase in connexion with the affair.

'The maid swore there were six people in the room,' said Colum. 'But there weren't, there were only five. I wasn't there.'

'Where were you?' Margaret asked.

'On my way home, as I told you. – You don't believe me?' he said, giving Margaret a reproachful, pleading look which wrung her heart. 'You needn't tell me, I can see you don't.'

'Of course I believe you,' Margaret said, mechanically, only wishing that she did.

Colum put his hands on his thighs, and drew a long breath and looked away from her.

'But didn't the others know whether you were there or not?' asked Margaret.

'Apparently they didn't. They were all of them pretty well bottled, you see. They put their masks on in the dark, in the hall – and a hell of a time it took them, from what Sindon said – and then crept upstairs. As soon as they got into the drawing-room the fun began, I mean, the balloon went up, and I don't suppose they had much time to count each other, even if they'd been in a condition to.'

'Colum, darling,' said Margaret suddenly, 'please, please don't think I'm questioning your word, but how do you *know* about them putting on their masks, and so on?'

'Sindon told me on the telephone,' Colum said.

Margaret heard the evasiveness in his voice.

'But if they can't say you weren't there,' she said, arguing with herself aloud, 'they can't say you *were* there, can they? How do they know?'

Colum didn't answer. At last he said, 'It isn't any use trying to hide it from you, Margaret. They know because I *was* there.'

'You were there?' cried Margaret.

Colum put his head in his hands. All at once he dropped them, and looking at the mantelpiece began to talk very fast.

'I was and I wasn't. I got your message, Margaret, the porter brought it up, about your not being well and so on. Well, I didn't believe it. I knew why you'd done it, but I felt sure it was a trick. If I hadn't taken so much whiskey I believe I might have left them then . . . I wish to God I had. But in the state I was it just annoyed me – you won't understand that. I thought it was just your suburban upbringing – heavens, I've never mentioned it before, have I? – and at that moment it made me see red. I won't try to excuse myself. And it did me a bad turn in a way – not that it makes any difference – but the porter saw me and knew who I was, and of course he'll tell the police, if he hasn't already. Then at last when all the stool pigeons had gone we came downstairs and there the porter was, and he saluted me, damn the fellow. And we asked him to get us two taxis and he heard us give Mrs Bel's address, and saw me get into one of the taxis. Of course it doesn't make any difference really, but except for Sindon I was the only one he knew by name. The taxis kept close to each other, and all the way I was thinking how you didn't want me to go, and I began to think perhaps you weren't well after all – whiskey always does that to me – it depresses me as soon as I stop drinking it. That's one reason why I never touch it. And then I began to wonder whether the whole idea was a good one, and whether Mrs Bel would see the joke – you can't tell with Americans, they haven't got the same sense of humour as we have. Well, to cut a long story short, the two taxis drew up almost together and we all tumbled out – Ripman literally tumbled out, he lay flat on the pavement and I thought we should never get him up. We were afraid he'd give everything away and spoil the plan, but as soon as he was on his feet he was all right, and he let us in with the latch-key Mrs Bel had lent him when he was staying with her. She knew it was missing but he swore he hadn't got it. I went in last and began to feel about for my mask like the others. I saw it was going to be a long business, for some of them hardly knew where their pockets were, much less which pocket to feel in; some of them had taken off their overcoats and dropped them somewhere in the dark and couldn't find them again. And all at once I got fed up, and it seemed a sort of fool thing to do and not so specially funny, and I thought about you and wondered if you were all right. The street door was open – I'd forgotten to shut it – and I just walked out. Nobody could see me and anyhow they were too busy looking for their masks. I couldn't see a taxi and my head was going round – I haven't had such swirlers since I was a boy –

and so I thought I'd try to walk it off. I came straight back through the Park. Our porter didn't see me – he was at the other entrance, as he so often is. So I took myself up in the lift and let myself in, and then I found your note and I thought to myself, 'What the hell?' – you wouldn't believe it, but I was stone sober in a moment.'

For the first time since he had begun his story he let his eyes stray in Margaret's direction.

To Margaret the letter and all the feelings of which it had been the outcome seemed infinitely far away. The person to whom they belonged seemed to have no connexion with her present self. She felt curiously calm, but it was not the calm of a taut mind but of one limp from many tensions. Little spurts of interest started up in her, – what were their plans for the day, had they many engagements? – and leading nowhere, flickered out. She was confusedly aware that all standards of relative importance had broken down. But the letter – irrelevant as it now seemed, she must try to explain the letter.

'You must forget about my letter, darling,' she said, and again the endearment seemed a stranger to her lips. She could not understand her coldness; she did not realize that it came from an instinctive disbelief in Colum's story, a deep-down conviction that it was just another of his many lies. 'It was only that I got so lonely and upset – about the party and everything. I didn't really know what I was doing. You mustn't give another thought to it. I . . . I was a bit mad, I believe.'

He looked at her gratefully and shyly and for the first time something like a smile came into his eyes. The sight of it brought a sort of reflex of love which struggled along her nerves but did not reach her heart.

'How good you are,' he said. 'How . . . how generous. If only I'd followed your advice at once. I did follow it in the end, you know. I . . . I could kick myself.'

Again she felt the tremor of dread which the idea of any hurt to him – above all a self-inflicted hurt – had always caused her; but it came up against her numbness towards him as against a wall.

'I am so sorry,' she forced herself to say. 'It must have been awful for you coming back, in . . . in the state you were, and finding that letter.'

He smiled at her again, with more assurance this time.

Oh, she thought, suddenly seeing the thing in its wider aspect, as it should have been between hearts that truly trusted each other; if only I could tell him, if only I could *want* to tell him, exactly how I felt – what made me do it! I owe it to him, I owe it to our love, the uttermost, fullest explanation worked out in every detail, with not a single point left out! If only this barrier of hardness would melt!

Her eyes sought his, and she must have seen the relenting in them, for suddenly he said,

'It's the first time I've given you a really bad break, isn't it?'

'It is, it is,' she murmured, and stopped, for it was not – it was only the worst of many bad breaks.

But he did not notice her change of feeling, for he said,

'That was the ghastly moment, coming back to find you gone. Then I did feel I'd had it. You could have done so much for me, just by being there.'

'Darling, what could I have done?'

He did not answer for a moment, and then said, 'You look so far away in that chair.' She came and sat by him on the sofa and he took her hand.

'You could have done this,' he said. She let her hand rest in his. Her heart beat wildly but it did not give her the messages she used to know.

'You could have done this,' he went on, his hand tightening on hers, 'and perhaps you could have done something else.'

'What else could I have done?'

'You could have given me an alibi.'

Toppling on the edge of emotion, seeing the table spread and aware of her own hunger, Margaret felt herself jerked back into the region of hard fact. She tried to remember the hours and minutes of the night and to realize that they were all-important: from now onward how much might depend upon the clock! Emotion fled before such calculations. She tried to concentrate as if she were doing a sum and as if her consciousness and range of feeling were bounded by that sum.

'Do you remember what the time was when you left Mrs Bel's?' she said.

'Five minutes to one. I always time myself when I go for a walk – it's an old habit. Don't you remember?'

She didn't remember.

'And what time did you get here?'

'At one thirty-three.'

'And no one recognized you on the way?' She noticed an impersonal, official note creeping into her voice, as if she was cross-examining him.

'Nobody, worse luck. How could they, in the dark?'

'If only one of them had seen you leave!'

Colum sighed.

'I took good care they shouldn't. They would have made a God-awful row.'

'If only we knew how long they took to put their masks on. I mean, exactly what time they went upstairs. But it couldn't have been very long – not more than ten minutes. Say five past one. And you weren't here until one thirty-three?'

'Who's to know that? I might have taken a taxi.'

How quickly, Margaret thought, he slides from one story to another.

'If you had,' she said, 'the police would be able to find out. There can't be many taxis dropping fares here at half-past-one.'

'But the fact they couldn't trace the driver wouldn't prove that I *hadn't* taken a taxi. It would only be negative evidence.'

Margaret agreed. But she couldn't see what this was leading up to, and she found that it was tiring her mind and exhausting her nervous vitality to discuss what might have been.

'If I'd come by taxi, darling,' he began. He said the word 'darling' experimentally, as though testing his right to say it; and she suddenly realized that it was the first time that he had used this commonplace of their conversation. She had called him 'darling', darling with a difference, perhaps making him feel the difference, several times. He, from diffidence, from a fear perhaps that he had dropped in her esteem, would not use it, would not debase the currency of affection, had voluntarily relinquished his right to it. He was more sensitive than she was. She was touched and humbled, and wondered if she ought to say 'You may call me darling if you like.' But all she did was to pat the ball back to him.

'Yes, darling?'

'If I'd come by taxi, darling,' he repeated, using the sweet word more confidently this time, 'you could have said I was here by ten minutes past one, or even five past. Taxis go more quickly at night.'

His voice dropped, but it throbbed with a passionate appeal, an innuendo so powerful that the very air seemed to re-echo it. Margaret turned to him.

'Do you mean you want me to say that?' she said.

'Darling, would it be too great a sacrifice?'

Margaret withdrew her hand from his. How strange her hand felt, how lonely, missing the companionship of his. Then she raised it to her face, her other hand joined it, and she said,

'I couldn't Colum, I couldn't.'

'Couldn't you even say,' he asked her, as if this was much less of an untruth, 'that you saw me here at one thirty-three?'

Hardly had she said no, and felt the downward drag of his disappointment, that sounded to her inward ear like a spent wave sucking back the shingle, than her refusal horrified her: it seemed unpardonable that she should value her integrity above his safety.

'You see, darling,' she began, 'it wouldn't work, because . . .'

Here the door opened and Richards, his usually impassive voice suggesting that this was once too often, announced, 'Two officers from Scotland Yard to see you, sir. Shall I ask them to come in?'

Colum nodded and Margaret, rising to go, hissed at him, 'Stick to your original story, darling, and don't try to be too clever with the police.'

Outside the door she wished she had made her warning sound less offensive. And she wished – how she wished – that she could persuade herself of the truth of Colum's story. If she did not believe it, why should the police?

28

THE days that followed the inquest were the worst. Before the inquest Colum was in alternate moods of elation and dejection – elation when he did not believe he would be called, dejection when he did. Elation predominated for his solicitor did not think he would be. His solicitor, who was fond of practical jokes, thought that the Coroner's Court would be lenient with this one; he did not anticipate serious trouble for anyone.

It was unlucky for Colum that Sindon had telephoned to him before the police came. If he had not already known some of the facts he could more easily have convinced the police that he was not present when the tragedy occurred. He told them how it came about that he knew so much; and they made full allowance for this. Yet they were handicapped in putting their questions to him and he, in answering, was unwilling to admit the extent of his knowledge; and more than once he contradicted himself over some point, first denying that he knew it and then showing that he had known it all along. 'I don't know, I wasn't there!' was still his cry; but for the police the trouble was that whether he was there or not, he did know. Ignorance is harder to simulate than knowledge. The police were perfectly polite to him and showed no signs of disbelieving his story, but the interview was inconclusive and he felt he had not made a good impression.

So he told Margaret; and she, with far more wish and far less reason to believe him than the police had, was in the same quandary as they were – with this difference, that she was tormented by it. The harder she tried to force her will to credit Colum's story the less she felt able to. Instances of his past untruthfulness kept coming back to her, unbidden, whereas the love with which she would have silenced them had to be dragged into action, like an old, tired war-horse. In the circumstances Colum's egoism and self-concern were excusable enough; but they did not make him the more lovable.

Margaret, too, had her interview with the police. Hedged about with alibis as she was – the porter at Sindon's flat, the porter at her own – she thought it would be all plain sailing, but it was not. The Inspector did not even ask her whether she had been at Mrs Belmore's, but he did ask her why she hadn't been. 'Because I wasn't feeling well,' said Margaret. 'It was not because you knew about the hoax and disliked the idea of it?' asked the Inspector. Margaret said no, and they accepted her reply without demur, but it was not true, and this shook her confidence in herself. She dreaded lest they might ask her what her movements had been when she got back. This they forebore to do, but the interview put Margaret out of conceit with herself and increased her sense of grievance against Colum. So despite her efforts to keep his flag flying she felt she only gave him cold comfort when he was down, and little support when he was up – when, for instance, he came back from his solicitors in high feather and told her the solicitor's latest witticism about practical jokes. 'You wouldn't get much sympathy from a jury if you broke your leg getting into an apple-pie bed,' he had remarked.

The inquest was still two days away and Colum still did not know whether he would be called when another blow fell that shook them both. This was the announcement, in the Press, that in her will Mrs Belmore had left Colum ten thousand pounds. 'To my dear friend, Colum McInnes, £10,000 or the equivalent sum in dollars.'

Ten thousand pounds was not a large sum for Mrs Belmore to give or for Colum to receive; she had much more money than that, and so, presumably, had he. But seldom could the news of a legacy have caused the beneficiaries so much disquiet. Margaret felt as if the dead woman's hand had reached out to strike them. Characteristically Colum was at first more cast down than she was. His grief renewed itself and again found an outlet in the exclamation, so wearing to Margaret's nerves, of 'Poor old girl! Poor old girl!' – whereas she was chiefly concerned for the effect the bequest might have on public opinion. And characteristically he was the first to recover his spirits. His solicitor, ringing up to congratulate him, said 'It's an ill wind that blows nobody any good', but he admitted that the announcement came inopportunely. Yet a windfall has a tonic quality that few griefs can altogether resist, and before the evening was out Colum was asking Margaret how they should spend the money. Some of it, he suggested, should be put aside for their child's education but not much, because a girl's education cost less than a boy's. Colum had made up his mind that Margaret would have a daughter and they wrangled affectionately about this till bedtime.

But a worse blow fell next morning: Colum's notice to attend the inquest. At first he seemed stunned; but on the telephone his solicitor again assured him that he had nothing to fear. 'The jury are human beings like yourself,' he said; 'they can see a joke as well as anyone else.' Colum repeated this to Margaret, who had her doubts. Colum, as far as she knew, had never seen the inside of a law-court, though more than once he had figured in one on the films, and he didn't realize that the kind of joke permitted there is generally at the accused's expense. Not that Colum had been officially accused, but her thoughts accused him.

On the morrow he rose early, and Margaret heard him moving about in his dressing room and was surprised, for as a rule it took him a short time to dress. Presently he knocked on her door and asked what suit he ought to wear; she thought he only wanted company, for he knew what to wear much better than she did. 'And now my tie,' he said. 'Had it better be plain black?' She thought he might allow himself a white spot or two. Her heart ached as it had never ached before.

But soon it was to ache much more.

In spite of Margaret's insistence on an early start the court was full when they arrived. A seat had been reserved for Colum with the other witnesses; Margaret thought she would be separated from him or might have to stand, but finally a place was found for her next to him. She did not feel as nervous as she expected to; the atmosphere of a court was familiar to her. Colum was miserably nervous. He kept crossing and uncrossing his knees, folding and unfolding his arms; his face was pale and drawn and he could not keep his eyes still. Yet she noticed with sad pride that he was as handsome as ever; his were the kind of looks that seemed to take an added grace from every state of health or spirits. She was glad that he was not asked to identify the body. She could not help feeling protective towards him and hoping that when the time came for him to give evidence he would do credit to her coaching.

Afterwards she found it hard to disentangle what had happened before her eyes from the accounts given by the Press. In the cases she had been concerned with the actual Court proceedings had always seemed more important and impressive than the newspaper reports of them. Now it was the other way round; she could scarcely believe that the scene she read about was the one she had been present at. For until the final stages there was very little drama; everything went forward in an orderly, unemotional way. She would scarcely have recognized the witnesses, her fellow-guests at Sindon's party, so subdued was their demeanour when they went up to take the oath. They were smart people and they looked smart, for black clothes often bring out smartness; and the one woman was dressed in black so unrelieved that it would have seemed like mourning had it not also been so fashionable. But according to the newspapers they might have been birds of Paradise alighting on a railway siding. It was true that a rustle of movement followed by a silence greeted Colum when he went up; but not true, Margaret felt sure, that necks were craned and you could have heard a pin drop. Her heart was beating so hard, however, that she could scarcely take in what happened; the chief thing that struck her was how small Colum looked and she remembered, rather absurdly, his gift of looking large or small, short or tall, according as the occasion seemed to call for. If now he wanted to look small, what was there wrong in that? – yet some of the reporters, who had also noticed the phenomenon, seemed to hold it against him, as if he looked small figuratively too. The Coroner asked him what he knew about the circumstances of Mrs Belmore's death, and he replied quite simply that he wasn't there, he only knew what he had been told. There was nothing jaunty in his bearing, as some of the papers alleged, or crushed, as others said. Those came nearest who said that he looked manly and composed. The Coroner asked him no more questions and he came back to his place. He did not remember where it was, that was the only sign of agitation he showed; he stood looking round him at the serried faces until Margaret, half rising, caught his eye.

She breathed more freely after that, she even allowed her attention to wander when Mlle Laplace's name was called and a small figure sitting in the same row as herself but hitherto unnoticed by her – there were so many more noticeable persons in between – disengaged itself and waddled rather quickly towards the Coroner. Then she did look up, for something in the woman's bearing caught her attention, something that set her apart from the other witnesses. It was not that she was weeping, as the reporters said; she did not weep till afterwards; but her figure was bowed and the rusty black she wore seemed both habitual and a mark of the deepest mourning. Her grief was not put on for the occasion. She held her hands clasped in front of her, and unlike the others she seemed unconscious of herself, enclosed in sorrow. This evidence of feeling immediately won the sympathy of the spectators, including Margaret, and the thrill of genuine emotion made itself felt in the court for the first time.

It was true that she made the sign of the Cross before she took the oath, and that this gesture, rapid as it was, did have an effect on the spectators. But she held them by her grief, by the emotion which she made no effort or pretence to hide. Only at the last minute did she give vent to Bernhardt-like ravings, as the Press described them. These took the Coroner, as they took everyone else, by surprise. Under cover of surprise she was able to say a great many things she might not otherwise have said. She was protected, too, by being a foreigner; she did not, or affected not to, understand some of the questions put to her and brushed them aside: she was determined to have her say. She would not heed the Coroner when he tried to call her to order. She was not in the least awed by the court.

'But I know there were six persons!' she exclaimed. 'I have seen them with my own eyes: how could I be mistaken? And he was there!' she went on, pointing an accusing finger at Colum. 'You say I should not recognize him because of the mask, yes? I tell you I should recognize him anywhere. Have I not known him for ten, fifteen years? Has he not always been in and out of Madame's house, *un ami de la maison*, as we French call it? Has she not paid for his telephone calls, and his washing when he made the long stay in her house? And has she not left him in her will ten thousand pounds, him on whom she has spent so much money while she was alive? Oh, yes, *M. le Président*, he was incontestably there! And he knew she had a feeble heart, he has known it very well!'

It was true that while she was speaking the Coroner made one or two ineffectual attempts to interrupt her; but she did not heed him, indeed she did not see him, for, carried away by her own eloquence, she turned round and faced the spectators. Mrs Belmore was, as Margaret afterwards learned, the one person she cared for in the world; she loved her with a fanatical devotion. She spoke with the passionate conviction, intellectual and moral, of a Frenchwoman to whom other people's testimonies were merely voices to be silenced.

She put all the venom she could into her parting shot. But it was not true that she was hustled from the dais. The Coroner's officer and a policeman came one on each side of her and as soon as they could attract her attention escorted her back to her place. It was then that she burst into tears.

If her outburst did not electrify the spectators it certainly impressed them deeply. Heads turned to see how Colum was taking it. Margaret's heart sank; for what suspicions might not start up in the public mind? The Coroner looked about him and casually moved the papers on his table; the foreman of the jury came up and conferred with him. The Coroner nodded and said,

'Mr McInnes, I should like to ask you another question.'

Margaret guessed what he was going to ask, and in an agony lest Colum should not speak the truth she hissed in his ear, 'Say yes'.

Colum gave her a look, whether of gratitude or reproach, she could not tell; he walked as if twenty years had been added to his age.

'Did you know that Mrs Belmore had a weak heart?' asked the Coroner.

'Yes.'

It was not true that this admission caused a sensation, but a sound like a sigh went up from the spectators.

'If you knew that,' said the Coroner, dropping his thin, lined face and looking at Colum over the rims of his spectacles, 'don't you think it was culpably imprudent of you to expose her to a violent shock?'

'I didn't,' Colum said. 'I wasn't there.'

The Coroner made no comment and Colum came back to his place without looking at Margaret.

One after another the remaining five members of the party were asked the same question, to which they returned the same answer: none of them knew that Mrs Belmore had a weak heart.

The foreman of the jury again conferred with the Coroner, who said,

'There seems to be a difference of opinion as to whether or not Mr McInnes was present at the actual moment of Mrs Belmore's death. Mr McInnes says he was not, Mlle Laplace thinks he was. It is no part of your duty to inquire into this matter but I should like it to be cleared up. Will you, Mr Sindon, tell me whether you believe Mr McInnes to have been present?'

Sindon said he could not be certain but he thought so, and the others said the same. More than one repeated what they had said earlier in the inquest, that they could not remember clearly what had happened after Mrs Belmore screamed.

So it was Colum's word against Mlle Laplace's; and Margaret, still impressed by the woman's grief for her dead mistress and by the way she had given her evidence, felt her heart harden against Colum.

The Coroner, addressing the jury, said some very severe things about the masked visitors. They were educated people, and they had rewarded Mrs Belmore's hospitality after this fashion. They had entered her house, frighteened her and manhandled her, with the result that she had died of shock. They had behaved in the most irresponsible and disgraceful manner, and were an example, if example were needed, of the way our moral standards had gone downhill. He had been especially shocked to find a woman amongst them. Men less to blame than they were had been charged with manslaughter. But, he reminded the jury, there was no evidence that they had intended Mrs Belmore any harm, and this was the most important fact they had to consider in arriving at their verdict.

The jury filed out in a silence broken only by the French maid's sobbing. Margaret took Colum's hand, without speaking; without speaking the five culprits looked straight ahead of them, as if they could see the Coroner's strictures written on the air. The spectators close to them scarcely spoke above a whisper; further away they talked in ordinary tones, and it seemed to Margaret that every word they said was 'Colum'. She dared not look at her watch for fear of seeing how slowly the time went, and although her mind and her legal experience reassured her, she caught the tension from the whispering round her and from the trembling of Colum's hand.

The door through which the jury had retired stayed obstinately shut; it seemed more immovable than the wall in which it was embedded; she fixed her eyes on it in an agony of hope and fear. Yet something distracted her for she did not see it open; she only saw the solemn, inscrutable faces of the jury-men as they came back into the Court. When she heard the foreman's verdict, 'Death by misadventure', the physical pang of relief was slightly muffled. Why had she been such a fool as to allow herself to doubt? Dazed she was turning to her neighbour, wondering if this radiant stranger could be Colum, when Mlle Laplace's voice rang out:

'But it is not true what he has just said! It is a lie! I tell you they killed her, all the six, just as surely as if they had struck her with a hatchet!'

The newspapers did not exaggerate the sensation that this outburst caused.

29

NEXT day began the avalanche of letters. Afterwards Margaret reproached herself that she had ever allowed Colum even to glance at one. But how could she have stopped him? And how could she have known that hundreds of total strangers would feel impelled to write and tell him what they thought of him?

She might have guessed, because after the breaking-off of her engagement she had received many letters from people unknown to her. But they had been almost invariably sympathetic and her chief trouble was to know how to answer them. Nick had received many disagreeable letters but he had never shown them to her; they had been part of his experience, not hers, and she had associated them, perhaps unfairly, with the chilly reserve in which he wrapped himself. Now she felt for him . . . but she did not suppose he had received in all one tenth of the letters that came by every post for Colum – letters that called him blackguard and scoundrel and names she had never seen before in writing.

Soon he was only too thankful to hand over his post to her – she could not bear his secretary to see it – but by that time the damage had been done. Colum's morale gave way. Margaret had not realized, nor perhaps had he, to what extent his self-esteem was nourished by the world's good opinion. Perhaps good opinion is an understatement. He had been idolized, adored; for years the incense of popular acclaim had streamed up to him, an offering so unstinted and so constant that he had come to take it for granted. His popularity had come upon him gradually without his noticing it; he did not realize that the air he breathed contained a draught of oxygen denied to other men. Soon he ceased to be grateful for the elixir, its taste became insipid, he was bored by it; it did him no credit in his own eyes; it seemed mechanical, as much a property of him as his own good looks; so that, as he had confessed to Lauriol, he had bolstered up his sense of his importance, that self-esteem without which the humblest cannot live, with practices of which the world knew nothing.

Now, at one blow his popularity was taken from him and universal execration substituted; and he was like a fish on a bank, gasping for breath.

He believed the execration to be universal because the few letters he had seen all happened to be hostile. But in fact it was not. Quite a large proportion of the letters were sympathetic, some passionately so, and accompanied by protestations of undying devotion. Margaret had always known but never quite realized how many women were in love with Colum. Ninety per cent of the correspondents, and almost all who wrote in a sympathetic spirit, were women; most of the male correspondents said that they had always believed Colum was a cad and now they knew. Not a few of both sexes called him a murderer and said that hanging was too good for him. Margaret began to divine, almost by instinct, which of the letters would be comforting; a word on a page, even the look of the handwriting, was enough to tell her. Sometimes she could scarcely bring herself to read them, they were like a blow between the eyes; but she was conscientious and by now inured to mental suffering and she plodded through them, partly from an innate conviction that any letter ought to be read, partly because she hoped her careful editing would bring practical results. All the letters that she thought would put heart into Colum she read aloud to him, as he sat huddled in a corner of the sofa.

'Now you'll like this one,' she would say, ashamed of herself for talking to him like a child, and trying not to be ashamed of him for submitting to be talked to like one; 'she says – Miss Fallowfield of Surbiton, this is – "My blood boils whenever I think of what that dreadful Coroner person said. Men of that sort ought to be shut up. Of course he didn't mean you – nobody could be such a fool as to think you were present when it happened – why, you said you weren't, and that should be good enough for them. I should like to know why they allowed that frightful Frenchwoman to give evidence. What is a foreigner's word worth, anyhow? I know she was jealous of you – she wanted the old lady to herself, servants get like that. Well, I for one should never lose my faith in you, whatever you did or were supposed to have done, and I only wish I had been with you instead of your wife, who seems to have left you properly in the lurch." ' Margaret hurried over this bit and would have skipped it if she hadn't felt that it might make Colum laugh. ' "I should have told them where they got off, and the Coroner too. I wish I could meet you in Piccadilly or some public place and give you a good hug, just to show the world there's someone who hasn't lost faith in you! I've always longed to meet you, but it seemed hopeless, you were always up in the skies, but now you've been unlucky perhaps you would consent to – I'm free any weekday after five o'clock, after one o'clock on Saturdays and all day Sundays. I was only joking about Piccadilly. I should prefer a quiet place, of course, but I don't a bit mind where I'm seen with you. From one of the millions who still trust in you and offer you their love, DORIS FALLOWFIELD." '

'God!' said Colum, idly burying his fist in the sofa-cushion, 'what a ghastly woman!'

'Well,' said Margaret, thinking how different letters sounded when they were read aloud, and wishing she had put this one in the 'doubtful' pile, instead of with those marked 'yes', 'it isn't very well expressed, but it's the spirit behind it that matters, isn't it? I mean, the feeling that people still . . . trust in you and love you.'

'You don't trust in me,' said Colum, 'and I'm not sure that you love me, either.'

This was one of the worst things she had to fight against – her failure to convince Colum, or herself, that she believed his story.

'Of course I love you, darling,' she protested, and felt she did, if pity is akin to love. Leaving the other charge unanswered she hurried on. 'Here's another – quite a short one:

' "Darling, what is all this fuss about an old woman? I think it was very bad taste of her to die on you. If you had come into my room, masked or unmasked, I shouldn't have died, I promise you!" '

'That's more the spirit,' said Colum listlessly. 'But if you're writing to her, you might tell her that I wasn't there.'

'The letter isn't signed,' said Margaret. Nearly all the abusive letters were anonymous, and a good many of those that were kindly meant were anonymous too. This lightened Margaret's task in answering them. But even so the task took far more time than she had to give, and after a few days the three piles overflowed her writing table. Soon she began to doubt the wisdom of reading Colum even the most sympathetic letters. Their writers nearly always showed, in one way or another, that they were sorry for him; implicitly or explicitly they contrasted his present state, wretched, misunderstood, down-trodden, with the pinnacle of glory he had once occupied. She could see how these expressions of pity relaxed and weakened him; the damning letters might have braced him.

She came to dread the post almost as much as he did. Letters from their real friends had to be answered carefully; she had to put something of herself into them, try to say exactly how

308

matters stood. 'Colum isn't very well or he would be writing to you himself', was one of her stock conclusions.

But by no means all the letters were addressed to Colum; Margaret had her share, and on the whole they did not make pleasant reading. She did not like it when the writers condoled with her on having such a husband; she liked it even less when, writing to her, they condoled with Colum on having such a wife. 'It is a judgment on you,' one woman said. 'You threw over a good man to marry a rotter, because he was rich and famous, and now you are punished. I don't pity you in the least, nor does anyone that I know of.'

Margaret pondered over this letter; it kept recalling her to herself even when she was most occupied with the thought of Colum. Had she treated Nick so badly? She hadn't thought so at the time nor had the strangers who then wrote to her. They had warmly taken her side. If she had married Nick she would never have got into this mess. She would have had the kind of life that she was suited to. She caught herself thinking about it, wistfully.

One of the most disquieting things about the letters was the suggestion that they represented a great body of feeling behind them. In vain to tell herself, and Colum, that only the more worthless kind of people, spiteful people who had nothing better to do, would write such letters; that writers of anonymous letters were held in universal contempt, and so on. For every one who wrote, there must be scores who thought the same, but were deterred by indolence or good manners from saying what they thought. Everywhere tongues were wagging like the clappers of innumerable bells, ringing down the curtain on Colum McInnes.

At first, the reports of Colum's publicity agents were quite optimistic. It will all be an advertisement, in effect they said. It will make his name known in sections of the community which have not hitherto been Colum-conscious. Old Mrs Belmore was not the sort of person to make a martyr of; no one will put out flags for her. On the other hand, the public was taking the five, or six (it scarcely mattered which) masked gangsters to their hearts; they were already known affectionately as the 'Queen's Gate Rangers'. 'I spied two of the Queen's Gate Rangers dining unmasked at Lucullus's the other night,' wrote a gossip-column writer; 'but I didn't ask them whether they had any new practical jokes in view.' Latterly, however, the bulletins had not been so encouraging. 'Colum's reputation will take no ultimate harm,' they said, 'but we are frankly disappointed by the public's unhelpful reaction to the inquest. This may not be the moment to launch *The Devil*.'

Meanwhile Colum sank still further into apathy. He would not leave the house even to take a walk. He would hardly leave the sofa, and even on the sofa, spacious as it was, he sat only in one place – at the far end, nearest the window. The sofa was at right angles to the window but Colum never looked out. One side of his face was always in shadow and Margaret seldom saw the other side. When he turned towards her – which rarely happened, for he generally stared straight in front of him – the light travelled across his pale forehead. Occasionally he would get up and go into his study. What he did there Margaret did not know, for she never followed him. Sadly she would go over to the place where he had sat, which was as forlorn and untidy as an abandoned bird's nest, and plump out the cushion and pull the cover straight: she came to know the creases he would leave.

He would not answer the telephone which buzzed all day until at last they had to make a sound-proof box for it in the hall. (Colum's name still carried enough weight to get this difficult feat done promptly.) He would see nobody except two or three cronies of whom Lauriol was one. Margaret welcomed Lauriol with a quick rush of delight, kissing her almost before she was in the room; and she was slightly dismayed, though not at all chilled, by the gravity of Lauriol's demeanour. Lauriol in her turn was bewildered to see Margaret looking so radiant, for she could not guess, and perhaps would not have believed, that she came to Margaret like an angel of light. 'Hullo, Lauriol,' said Colum from the corner of the sofa; 'good of you to come, old girl.' 'Can I go into your room and tidy myself?' Lauriol asked Margaret, after a salutation to Colum as laconic as his own. Margaret was surprised, for Lauriol never needed tidying; she seemed always to have stepped out of a beauty-parlour.

When they were alone together Lauriol said, 'My dear, this is a wretched business. How are you bearing up?' Lauriol had never spoken to her in that tone before, and Margaret had difficulty in keeping back her tears. 'Oh, I'm all right,' she said, 'but Colum is taking it rather badly.' 'He was a fool to go to that party,' said Lauriol. 'He's knocked about the world a lot, but he knows no more about it than an unborn baby. I wish I had warned him, but I thought it would have more effect if you did.' Margaret couldn't help feeling touched and almost pleased. She told Lauriol about her efforts to make Colum come away. 'It's the French maid,' she said, 'saying that she saw six of them that's done Colum so much harm. That and his not being able to prove that he never went upstairs.' 'Do *you* think he didn't?' asked Lauriol bluntly. Margaret writhed at the question, and turning away, she said, to avoid answering it, 'Oh, if he had only called in at your flat, instead of coming home! It's almost next door to Mrs Belmore's, and he so easily might have. And you would have been at home wouldn't you, you didn't go out?' Confident that she had concealed her disbelief in Colum's story she turned to Lauriol, who said rather slowly, 'No, I didn't go out. I had every reason for staying in.' She looked interrogatively at Margaret, and added, 'But it would have been rather late for a call, wouldn't it?' 'Oh, I don't know, I don't know!' cried Margaret, her mind occupied exclusively by the thought of Colum's alibi. 'It would have seemed more natural, somehow.' 'More natural?' Lauriol asked. 'Don't ask me what I mean,' said Margaret, 'I suppose I mean more natural than his walking home – I mean, they would have thought so. But I mustn't keep you from him, Lauriol dear. I know he's longing to see you.' Easy to say; but when they went into the sitting-room together, wearing bright smiles and betraying by feigned unconcern their concern for Colum's welfare, he did not even turn his head.

Before her father came the situation had deteriorated.

Margaret had assumed, and had persuaded Colum, that the verdict of the Coroner's jury would be final; Mrs Belmore had met her death by misadventure, and that was that. The case was closed, they had nothing more to fear, all they had to do was to live down, as best they could, the inevitable talk and scandal. And they were living it down. Already the dreaded letters were becoming fewer – one post brought only five. Public opinion, Margaret learned, was swinging round; the audiences at Colum's current films, which had fallen off, were picking up again. Perhaps they would not have to postpone the trade show after all. They must be grateful, she was told, to whoever coined the phrase 'Queen's Gate Rangers'; it had confounded the censorious and put the whole thing in a comic light. Margaret began to see daylight at the end of the tunnel and persuaded Colum to see it too. Slightly disguised, he even took a walk with her in the Park. Margaret was surprised that no one recognized him, for he wore no make-up except a pair of spectacles and a bowler hat, but she herself kept looking at him to make sure it was he. It was his walk that made the difference, she decided, she was walking with the Devil of Colum's new film. But what a pathetic devil, who hardly dared to be seen in public!

Next morning Colum's solicitor rang up and asked to speak to him. Colum was still unwell, said Margaret: would she do instead? Yes, said the solicitor, but he was afraid that Mr McInnes could not be kept in ignorance. The police were not satisfied with the evidence that had come out at the inquest and were making further investigations. On what lines? she forced herself to ask. In connexion with the disappearance of several articles of value from Mrs Belmore's flat, the solicitor said. If they obtained sufficient evidence the consequences might be serious. But not for Colum? Margaret exclaimed. The solicitor said he would rather speak of it between four walls.

She found him graver than she had seen him yet. 'If only your husband had an alibi!' he said. 'The weakest, flimsiest alibi would clear him.'

'You think he will be implicated with the others?' Margaret said.

'He started out with them.'

'But it was part of the . . . the joke to take something and then return it to Mrs Belmore.'

'Yes, but the things haven't been returned.'

Margaret turned cold. 'You think I ought to tell Colum, in the state he's in?'

'Better prepare him now than give him the shock of hearing officially.'

'He would have to appear in Court of course,' said Margaret.

'Yes. Whether they could convict him is another matter.'

'But it would do him . . . and his career . . . great harm even to appear.'

'It certainly wouldn't do him any good,' the lawyer said. 'That's why it's important he should be up and doing now. Fresh evidence might come to light.'

'You can't suggest anything?' asked Margaret.

'I'm afraid not, but one never knows. What a pity she was an American, and a well-known American at that! I won't say that the law is influenced by extraneous causes, but the American Press has been following the case closely – you know how outspoken they are – and they don't seem to think that a joke which ends in the death of one of their respected nationals is a harmless prank. You can't altogether blame them. It takes an Englishman to see the fun of a rag. And the Americans, if you will forgive my saying so, attach an importance to your sex which we think exaggerated. They would have liked the verdict to be manslaughter.'

'But it couldn't be!' cried Margaret. 'The Coroner's jury—'

'Yes,' said the solicitor, 'but taking into account the thefts, and the fact that Mrs Belmore was forcibly prevented from ringing up the police, it might be made to look like robbery with violence.'

Mr Pennyfather arrived betimes; for ten o'clock had hardly struck when he came in. She was overwhelmingly glad to see him. Spare and keen-eyed and a little bowed in his town suit of old-fashioned cut and good material, he looked fitter than she had seen him look for some time; and at last after many days of paying out, a credit instead of a debit feeling momentarily possessed her. She had never quite lost a sense of guilt that she had not stayed at home to look after him; the fact that he was getting on so well without her, that she was not so indispensable as she imagined, lightened her burden of responsibility. Actually, though she did not know it, his heightened colour was partly due to excitement: recent events had fanned his love for his daughter into a flame, and he came in a fighting mood, as she soon discovered.

'It's all a lot of fuss about nothing,' he declared, 'I don't know what this generation's coming to. It's a tea-cup storm, blown up by the Press to gratify the sensation-loving public. Where's Colum?'

'He's in his room.'

'Well, isn't he coming in?'

'We'll call him later,' Margaret said. 'I've so much to tell you that I couldn't say on the telephone.'

'But he knows about the latest developments?' Mr Penne-father asked.

Margaret shook her head. 'No, not yet.'

Her father clicked his tongue, and Margaret, who had a raw nerve for any criticism of Colum, at once embarked upon her story. So much was dammed up, she felt it would come pouring out; but soon she found that the necessity for editing it made it come haltingly. She could put Colum's quandary in a favourable light and enlarge on the injustice with which he was being treated; but she could not even hint at her own, and at the private know-ledge that compelled her to distrust his story. 'You see, I can't believe a word he says!' – that phrase, the theme song of her thoughts, kept starting up, and tripping up the words before they left her tongue. If only she could have uttered it! She thought her father must notice her hesitations, but he was too intent on following the facts, the misleading facts, as she felt them to be, that she was serving up to him. Besides, he came with a closed mind; hard-headed in business, where his daughter was concerned he did not look at the other side. Only when Margaret was telling him of Colum's state of apathy and despair which she saw no reason to disguise, did he begin to show signs of impatience.

'But I can't understand it in the fellow!' he exclaimed. 'Forgive me, Margaret, but on the films he always seemed the toughest of tough guys, and to look at him you wouldn't think he had a nerve in his body. I don't like it, his putting all the burden on you – it looks as if he'd got no – well, guts, I suppose I should say.'

Margaret tried to explain that the kind of nerve required for dangerous physical feats was quite different from the kind of nerve required to confront unpopularity and possibly disgrace. 'All good film actors are highly strung,' she said. 'They wouldn't be good film actors if they weren't. Nearly all artists are, Daddy. You and I wouldn't understand.'

'But I do understand,' he insisted, and she saw he was working himself up into the state of irritation which opposition, even from her, sometimes excited in him. 'I understand quite well it's trying for him. But you talk about his state – what about your own? When do you expect the baby to be born?'

'In about four weeks,' said Margaret. She realized that since the inquest she had hardly given a thought to this.

'Four weeks, and you knocking about, attending inquests, interviewing lawyers, and so on. Why, you ought to be resting, you ought to be at the sea, you ought to be—'

'I know, I know,' said Margaret. The tears came into her eyes; it seemed that she could not find sympathy, or sympathy of the right kind, anywhere. It was natural and generous of her father to feel annoyed with Colum, but what good did it do her?

'I rang up Diana last night,' her father went on. 'I knew you wouldn't mind, she's such a great friend of yours, and told her something of what you were going through. I thought you would have told her yourself, and she seemed surprised you hadn't.'

'She's just been having her baby,' Margaret said. Diana and her affairs seemed infinitely remote. 'I didn't want to bother her.'

'Bother her?' Mr Pennefather said. 'She seemed quite hurt you hadn't told her.'

'She would have read about it in the newspapers, of course,' said Margaret.

'Yes, indeed. That was why she wanted to hear from you. She said she would have written, only she didn't quite know how things stood.'

'I'm sorry, Daddy,' said Margaret, 'but I've had so much to do.'

'Of course you have, of course you have,' her father said, instantly mollified. 'I told her that, and she quite understood. But she was surprised to hear that Colum wasn't, well . . . playing up, and she'd have been horrified if I'd told her what I know now. However, I've made it all right with her, and she's coming to see you sometime this morning. She asked me to tell you. She didn't want to ring you up, she said you must be pestered by the telephone. She's bringing Stuart with her.'

'Oh, is she?' Margaret said.

'Yes. He's taking the morning off on purpose.'

'Do you know how they feel about it all?' asked Margaret.

Her father's eyebrows came together.

'Well, my dear, they sympathize enormously with you, of course.' His voice dwelt lightly on the 'you'. 'They think you've had a very rough deal. They're a *little* critical of Colum – you couldn't expect them not to be, being such great friends of Nick's.' He glanced at her from under his brows; Margaret shifted in her chair. 'I daresay they still feel disappointed. And Stuart is old-fashioned and conventional, you know – more than I am,' added Mr Pennefather, suddenly struck and pleased by his own up-to-dateness. 'Of course Colum isn't quite our sort, but I've always got on well with him, haven't I?' he appealed to her. 'Stuart's so public school – he thinks Colum must have got into a bad set, and all that. He judges people by the company they keep – and those Queen's Gate Rangers or whatever they are called must be outsiders, don't you think? The public seem to want to make pets of them, I can't think why. Well, Stuart sort of feels that Colum shouldn't have got mixed up with them or let you. Of course he won't say so to you.'

'No, I expect not,' Margaret said.

Her father detected a shade of tartness in her tone.

'Well, my dear, you asked me what he thought . . . Now the thing is, what are we to do? Who shall we get to help you?'

'I suppose the solicitor will see to that,' said Margaret.

'Yes, but we want the best man possible. I don't know how Colum's off for funds – this film-acting is a precarious business – but you know you can call on me for anything you want.'

'How good of you,' Margaret said mechanically.

'But solicitors are apt to be a bit slow,' Mr Pennefather said. 'I think we ought to start at once. Why not call Colum in and have a conference?'

'I haven't prepared him at all,' said Margaret.

'Well, wouldn't this be a good moment to? It might be easier with me here.'

Irresolutely Margaret went to the door of Colum's room, listened and turned the handle.

To Mr Pennefather it seemed that she was away a very long time. The room with its low ceiling, its grey upholstery, its expensive and slightly arrogant combination of the very old and the very new, was unsympathetic to him, and his thoughts turned inwards. He remembered Margaret with her mother, as a baby; he watched her growing up in the shelter of Fair Haven. His feeling about her then came back to him. She was to be respected, distinguished, a Portia among women. His fantasy fixed her at a certain age, about twenty-eight. She was to be always twenty-eight, but she was not to be married. He saw her through all the stages of infancy, childhood, girlhood, young-womanhood, progressing decorously, usefully, admired by all the district, towards the age of twenty-eight. After that, he saw her no more. His imagination would not contemplate her as the wife of Colum McInnes.

As Nick's wife, yes. Strangely enough, as Nick's wife she still belonged to him. Searching the lumber-rooms of his memory, he came across a long discarded vision of her as Nick's wife. That vision of her had been acceptable to his wishful-thinking. It did not quite embrace children – it quivered and grew indistinct when confronted with them – but it included a home, a home that was not his home but hers, and even provided for her growing older. Yes, as Nick's wife he could see her with grey hair – even with white hair, though he would not be there to see it. But she was not Nick's wife . . .

At last the door opened.

'I'm sorry, Daddy,' Margaret said, in the careful voice of someone choosing her words, 'but Colum doesn't feel that he can see you.'

'Not see me?' Mr Pennefather cried, as if such a thing was inconceivable.

'He doesn't feel up to seeing anyone,' said Margaret flatly.

She saw her father struggling against a rising tide of irritation. His tongue, that unruly member, made sounds of disapproval, which his lips would not let pass. At last he said,

'Poor fellow! Poor fellow! I suppose you told him what he might be in for.'

'No,' said Margaret, 'I couldn't.'

Her father shook his head. For a moment it seemed that they had lost their tongues and were reduced to communicating by dumbshow. Then,

'Poor fellow! Poor fellow!' Mr Pennefather repeated. 'And poor *you*!' he added. 'It's you I feel most sorry for.' Margaret did not cry; she was too much stricken to feel sorry for herself. Her father rubbed his chin in the palm of his hand, bringing his fingers hard against his lower lip, a way he had when he was at a loss. 'Well, I suppose there's nothing for me to stay for?' he said, his eyes searching her face. Margaret shook her head, and Mr Pennefather rose with a kind of shaky briskness. 'You mustn't let it get you down, you know,' he told her. 'Worse things happen at sea. I suppose you wouldn't lunch with me at my club?'

'I don't think I'd better,' Margaret said. 'To tell you the truth' – she stopped. She had taken to using this locution lately, as if her unsupported word was not enough. Like crossing a cheque, it was a safeguard: it made the truth truer. 'To tell you the truth I should be a little anxious leaving him alone.'

Her father sighed. 'And he seemed such a stout-hearted chap! Well, when you want me you know where to find me. And remember this – get hold of the best man possible, and don't count the cost.'

They embraced, and Margaret went out with him and saw him into the lift.

Back in the sitting-room, she tried hard to compose herself. She felt utterly deserted. While her father was in it, the room had given her some support; he had brought something of Fair Haven into it; now she felt it to be as alien as he had. She fixed her eyes on the tall mantelpiece, so distressingly close to the low ceiling, and for a moment thought she saw the child's head on it, and Colum's hand coming round to pull it off. 'Don't! Don't!' she almost cried. 'You don't know what you're breaking! You're breaking our child!' He hadn't broken that; the child was still alive, but he had broken something the child stood for, their mutual love.

She knew she ought to go into the room where Colum sat and beseech him to rouse himself, but she could not bring herself to. Not because she was afraid of his bent head and averted face, and queer unnatural stillness. She was afraid of them; she was in terror lest he should lose his reason; but she would have faced them, she would have faced any manifestation of his sick mind. What she dreaded was the part of him that still clung to normality and said, 'You don't believe me! You don't believe me! You still think that I was there!'

Yet she had never said she didn't believe him; she had proclaimed her faith in his word a thousand times.

Dimly she heard the door-bell ring and a moment later Richards appeared and said, 'Mr and Mrs Tufton to see you, Madam.' Her hunted gaze swept the confining cornice, then rested on the man's dispassionate face appealingly. 'Tell them I'm out, Richards,' she said.

'Very well, Madam.'

She heard the murmurs of explanation and regret.

What have I done? thought Margaret. She had a rush of panic. Why did I send them away – my best friends, even if Stuart wasn't very understanding about Colum? Was there no one she could turn to, was she allowing this to cut her off from everyone, as Colum was, letting go the life-line which bound her to her fellow-creatures?

She had been so much absorbed by marriage that she had neglected friendship. At first she had felt no need of it. She was determined to get on with Colum's friends and approached them in the spirit of making herself acceptable to them; but friendship is not made that way, it is kept at bay. Only with Lauriol had she come to feel intimate, and her friendship with Lauriol was an enmity in reverse; she could not tell at what moment the suspicion and jealousy she had felt of Lauriol had turned to liking. But she could not confide in Lauriol, because Lauriol would not tell her, or let her tell, the truth about Colum.

Her quandary was that she could not tell anybody. And not only because it would be betraying Colum. Loyalty to him sealed her lips but in her heart she knew that even if she could force that barrier it would bring her little lasting comfort. Her estrangement from him could only be referred to a higher Power. She wanted the assurance of forgiveness for him – that was it. If a voice of sufficient authority could have told her, 'It doesn't matter that he steals, it doesn't matter that he lies; you may, you can, you must, love him as he is,' she would have accepted it, for she still wanted to love Colum. But no voice qualified to speak them uttered the words; the heavens were silent; and the only voice she trusted had spoken in a different fashion.

And yet, though his counsel was so little to her liking, she had felt with Father McBane a peace of mind that satisfied her because it was like an answer to all questions. It was not a final answer because her will was in the way and as soon as she got outside his study it began to operate. But while she was with him it had ceased to be *her* question, *her* problem; she had freed herself of it, almost as if it was something she held in her hand, by offering it to the will of God.

Now it had returned to her, but if only she could recapture that feeling, she might get an infusion of strength that would carry her and Colum through. She snapped a shutter over her mind and went to the telephone. But before she reached it the shutter went back and she heard the priest's voice saying, 'Yes, I know him . . . and we must not meet again.'

That was final. She had accepted it then and must accept it now. Even the spiritual sphere was not immune from the blight of earthly circumstance. But there were other priests, scores of them in presbyteries all round her, waiting to minister to sick souls. Why not go to them? Margaret considered it; but when she thought of the mere physical effort of the recital, of making its points plain to someone who knew nothing of it, of putting up yet again the complex scaffolding of the story, all the accumulated details without which the meaning could not be understood, and yet with which it was perhaps still more obscure, she quailed. She could not pull herself up by the roots again; she lacked, she knew, the nervous strength, and above all she lacked the time.

The clock was nearing twelve. Yes, she had no time. She had no time to answer letters; no time to see to her household duties; no time to make up her face; no time to comfort Colum, no time to rest before her baby came, no time to have it, no time, perhaps, to die of having it. No time to die! She had never realized before what a luxury time was.

'Get the best man possible,' her father had told her, 'and don't count the cost.' She had almost smiled at that, for her troubles were so far from being money troubles. And yet she knew, she had known for days, who was the best man possible, and she *had* counted the cost. What would she have to pay? Not very much in money, perhaps, for there must be many barristers who commanded higher fees. The price would be in pride; not only in her pride, but in Colum's too. It might be quickly paid, for Nick would almost certainly refuse to take the case up; he might refuse to see her; but it would have to be paid.

It had seemed too high a price: but was it? Might it not pay for something else, as well as for the best chance of saving Colum? – something which, she now believed, had always haunted her, and which she had been so sharply reminded of in more than one anonymous letter? To lay her pride at Nick's feet would be a sort of expiation, an expiation for having treated him so shabbily. Perhaps her unknown correspondent was right, and all her troubles came from that; they were a judgment on her. Trying to recall the circumstances – it seemed incredible that they should have happened only a year ago – it seemed to her she had behaved atrociously. None of the arguments with which she had made a case out for herself held water. They were – what was the word? – rationalizations of a motive much less avowable. She had preferred an infatuation to love and thrown over a good man for a bad one. Her punishment was just.

So it was not too high a price – if anything it was too low; for how could a mere gesture restore to Nick the happiness he had lost and heal the hurt which, so they said, prevented him from marrying? He had prospered in his career and at the thought of that she felt a quick flush of pride, which she as quickly stifled; for what right had she to feel proud of him? How lonely the months must have been, lonely and embittered, the feelings crushed, the mind mastering the heart. What might be an expiation for her would certainly be an embarrassment to him, – perhaps it would be nothing more than an embarrassment.

And Colum, what right had she, in his forlorn, pitiable state, to bring him into contact with a man who she knew disliked him – the falling with the rising star? If any man could bring home to him his present wretchedness more sharply than another that man was Nick; and though Nick would not openly triumph over him, his rather reserved, cold manner – which was not likely to be less cold or less reserved – would turn the knife in Colum's wound. She had had no idea of how sensitive Colum was, as sensitive in his way as Nick, and with far less inner stamina for resisting a reverse. Who could foretell what would happen when they met? Colum might break down and cry, he might have a brain-storm and come to blows with Nick. Anything was more likely to happen than what she wished to happen – that Nick should take up Colum's case and somehow find a way out for him that none of them could see, a North-West Passage out of his predicament.

It was in short an unpromising idea, risky and unlikely to succeed. Margaret knew this, and yet in her present mood, which was very near despair, the mere fact of its being unpromising somehow recommended it. Desperate diseases need desperate remedies; a crisis can be best be countered by a crisis. So she told herself; but the fact was her feelings were so much worked up that she could no more have adopted a reasonable, sensible line of action than a wind-lashed sea can subside into a calm.

It did not take her long to bridge the gap between intention and action – a distance no further physically than the newly installed telephone box in the hall. She got through very quickly, but even then she did not like to give her name.

'Is it very urgent?' a voice asked, not Nick's. 'Mr Burden is engaged at the moment.'

'It is rather urgent.'

'What name shall I say?'

'Say I'm a friend of his.'

The clerk came back and said coldly:

'Mr Burden would like to know the name.'

'Mrs Colum McInnes.'

She drew a long breath and it seemed to her she held it till the clerk returned.

'Mr Burden will see you at any time.'

'Tell him I'll come now.'

Before she went she opened the door of Colum's room. He was sitting at his writing table. His hand made movements on the paper without writing anything, as far as she could see; yet every now and then he screwed his face up as though passing judgment on something he had written.

'Darling,' she said, 'I'm going out for a breath of air but I shall be back in time for lunch.'

'Enjoy yourself,' he said.

The hint of mockery in his tone made her shiver, and she closed the door without a word; nor did it occur to her that just as once she had sought out Colum without getting Nick's leave, now she was seeking Nick without getting Colum's.

30

NICK did not need to rise; he was standing when Margaret came in. He did not smile when he shook hands with her; his gaze wandered about her in broken arcs of circles.

'Please sit down,' he said, and moved a chair an inch or two. When she was seated he too sat down and said, 'What did you come to see me about?'

'About Colum,' said Margaret with an effort.

Nick's eyes showed no sign of recognizing the name, but a new austerity sharpened the lines of his face. His hair was grey at the temples; he looked as though the law, like a sculptor, had worked on his living flesh. No wonder people are afraid of him, she thought.

'Is it to do with Mrs Belmore's death?' he asked.

She nodded. She wished she did not have to face the window which, even in this shadowed court, glowed with the late May sunshine and gave her the feeling that she was grimacing at it.

'I only know what I've read in the papers,' Nick said. He raised his eyebrows and added 'And what Stuart and Diana have told me.'

Margaret was not glad to hear this, but she was glad that he had said it; it was only a trifle but it was a signpost and helped her to know where she stood.

'They may have heard a little from my father,' she said, 'but not much and Stuart is prejudiced against Colum.'

Nick's eyes became if possible still more expressionless. 'Can I help you in any way?' he asked politely.

Strung up as she was, Margaret nearly tittered at the well-worn phrase, but she mastered that and other emotions too and said in the most matter-of-fact voice she could command,

'I wondered if you would act for him if the case ever comes into Court.'

Nick rose from his revolving chair and walked to the window, turning his back on her.

'I couldn't do that, Margaret,' he said. 'I am afraid I must say no.'

Margaret's heart sank at the finality in his voice, but he had called her by her name for the first time, and his face, which she could see reflected in the window, betrayed an indecision that was at variance with his words.

'Oh Nick,' she said.

At that he turned towards her, his head bent as though of its own weight, and his expression inscrutable.

'Oh Nick,' she repeated, 'Couldn't you?'

He sat down again and breathed with heavy, noisy sighs, showing as little restraint as if he had been alone.

'I would do anything for you,' he said at last. 'You know that.'

'But not for him?'

Nick did not answer, but she thought he shook his head.

'Oh Nick,' she pleaded, 'can't we forget the past? Not all the past, I don't want to forget it all,' she said, and saw a new expression dawn in his eyes – 'but all that it has meant of sorrow and suffering and anger? I won't press you, I won't ask you again, I know that it is asking you too much. But it isn't the only reason I came to see you – I mean, to ask you to do me this impossible favour. I want to tell you – I've wanted to tell you for a long time – how sorry I am for everything that happened. I never said so, did I? I never told you I was sorry?' She looked at him for confirmation, but his eyes were fixed on the oblong of pink blotting-paper. 'I see it now,' she went on, almost as if the past was being unwound before her on a scroll, 'and I realize

327

what a . . . what a mistake I made. I won't try to defend myself, and I won't try to explain. I can't explain even to myself why I acted as I did.' She stopped, paradoxically trying to think of explanations, or of words to fit the explanations, for she did not want to spare herself, indeed she was terrified of doing so. But Nick, looking at her with his eyes wide open, said,

'My dear, I can think of any number of explanations. You don't have to tell me.'

'Oh no, no,' she said, scarcely noticing his change of tone and dreading lest she should somehow be robbed of her repentance, 'it was all my fault. I don't know how, but I was carried away by him.'

Nick got up from his chair and stood beside her. 'My dear,' he said again, 'it was at least as much my fault as yours.'

'Oh *no*,' she said waving her hand, as if to disclaim anything that might be said on her behalf, and beginning to cry from a feeling that even the kindest opposition was unbearable; 'it wasn't, it wasn't, and even if it had been the least bit your fault, who could expect a man to apologize?'

She looked up at him as though inviting him to agree that a man was somehow exempt from apology, and went on inconsequently, 'and you had your career too, I might have ruined that. I'm glad I didn't.'

Nick knelt down beside her and took her hand. 'Margaret,' he said, and then as she still continued to cry, and move her head unhappily about, 'Margaret, darling.'

She stared at him; her tears stopped; she fumbled in her bag for her handkerchief, and began to struggle to her feet.

He held her hand to prevent her from getting up. 'Margaret,' he said urgently, 'don't go. I'll . . . I'll do what you want me to do. I wish I could do more.'

She still stared at Nick in wonderment, for in the emotion of the last few minutes the real reason for her mission had faded from her mind. And a new element had entered which she dared not acknowledge.

'I must go,' she repeated.

'No, please don't go,' he said. 'I'll do what you asked me, Margaret. I shouldn't have let you say what you have said, I should have stopped you.'

'Why?' Margaret asked, not understanding him.

'Because I ought to have said it first. I ought to have said it long ago, on the day when it all happened. If you have reproached yourself, Margaret, so have I, and with how much more reason. I shouldn't have waited for you to . . . to take the first step.'

She smiled at him, distressed and almost embarrassed, for what she had said was true: she didn't like to hear a man apologize, or see him kneel.

'I'll do what I can,' he said, 'I'm afraid it won't be much, but at any rate it will be . . .' An expiation, he meant to say, or some such word, but dismissed them all as having the wrong emotional overtones and substituted, 'something. Something to show . . .' he stopped, wondering how far he dared trust himself, 'what you still mean to me. You will stay?'

Margaret said she would.

Awkwardly Nick rose from his knees. Returning to his swivel chair, he looked at Margaret more professionally.

'But first,' he said, 'you must tell me all about it.'

Margaret told him the same story she had told her father. And the inevitable cuts, instead of taxing her brain and tripping up her tongue, seemed to fall into place quite naturally. But being word-perfect she was better able to realize how much she was concealing. She could not tell Nick that it was the fact of things being stolen from Mrs Belmore's flat that made her morally convinced of Colum's participation. She couldn't tell him, or felt she couldn't, that Lauriol had warned them against going to the party. She made as little as possible of her efforts

329

to get Colum away from Sindon's flat. She did tell him – what she had not told her father – of her flight to the hotel, but put it down to a sudden horror of being alone. She did not tell him that Colum had tried to make her perjure herself to give him an alibi. As far as she could, she told the story as Colum would have told it. But two contradictory pictures dominated her mind and gradually imprinted themselves on Nick's: Colum's lonely figure striding through the night on his way home, and the French maid's, squat and dumpy in her worn black clothes, passionately assuring the Coroner's court that he had been present at Mrs Belmore's death.

'And which of them do you believe?' asked Nick when she had finished.

He had caught her off her guard; she hesitated, and by hesitating knew that she had given herself away. She closed her eyes against the realization and opened them upon a fresher world, a world in which she had been surprised into telling one lie less. All through her story she had felt that each suppression of truth was cutting her off from Nick, erecting a new barrier between them, so that by the end he meant scarcely more to her than a stranger whose support she was trying to enlist; in a cause in which she did not believe. Now at one bound she was back with him again in an intimacy the more precious because of its brief interruption. Now it did not much matter what she said; for decency's sake she would rebury the truth, but in an open grave.

'To tell you the truth, Nick,' she said – crossing the cheque – 'I don't know which to believe.'

'I oughtn't to have asked you,' he said. 'It was most unprofessional. But somehow I felt I had to. It won't make any difference, of course, to what we say later on.' His eyes clouded with reminiscence and he suddenly broke out vindictively,

'He was always a liar, and at school he was light-fingered as well. At any rate you haven't had that to cope with.'

Margaret was silent; distress worked in her face; she had an impulse to break her self-imposed reserve and tell Nick the whole story of Colum's dishonesty.

But Nick was already apologizing.

'My dear, I shouldn't have said that. That was unforgivable. But you'll forgive me, won't you? To-day is our forgiving day.'

He smiled at her and she smiled back through unshed tears.

For a time they talked of practical matters – what could be done and what could not be done. It appeared that very little could be done; the field of inaction was much wider than the other. Margaret must ask Colum's solicitor to get in touch with Nick and then they must await developments. They had nothing definite to go on yet; it might be all a mare's nest.

'In that case I shall have troubled you for nothing,' Margaret said.

'For nothing?' he repeated. 'Yes, I suppose it is for nothing – not even for a kiss?' His chair swung round, he clasped his hands together and darted a glance at her, winged with urgency.

Margaret did not stir, but it was the stillness of acceptance, not rejection, and though no kiss was exchanged the electric thrill passed through them almost as searingly as if it had been.

Nick's hands fell apart. 'Then it isn't for nothing,' he said quietly. 'But if I had known beforehand you were coming . . .'

'You did know,' Margaret said.

'I mean days, weeks, months beforehand – do you suppose I would have sat still in these chambers and waited till you came?'

'I didn't know until this morning, either,' said Margaret. 'Perhaps it was better that we didn't know.'

They were both silent for a moment, then Nick said,

'Tell me one thing – has he made you very unhappy?'

How could she answer this with truth?

'Well, latterly he has,' she said.

'Not all the time?'

Grudgingly, unwillingly, she remembered days of ecstasy with Colum and said,

'No, I couldn't really say he has, no, no.'

If only she could have said 'He used to beat me!' She wondered if her answer disappointed Nick as much as it disappointed her. But apparently it didn't, for he said,

'Because if he had, I couldn't . . . I really couldn't, even for your sake, lift a finger' – unconsciously he lifted his right forefinger and let it fall.

'No,' said Margaret again. 'In his way he has been good to me . . .'

'Yes,' Nick broke in. 'I know what his way is.'

Margaret hardly noticed the interruption. She was anxious to clear something up and did not quite know how.

'This that has happened,' she said, 'isn't something between him and me. I mean it's nothing that he has done to me – against me – to hurt me. He has done things to hurt me – little things – not meaning to. It's something that I ought not to mind at all, something between him and . . .' God, she would have liked to say, but deeply moved as she was, in touch, as she believed, with her strongest feelings, she could not utter the word and substituted 'his religion'.

'His religion?' Nick repeated, evidently not understanding. 'He's a Roman Catholic, isn't he? He used to be, as far as he was anything.'

'He still is,' Margaret said.

'But you're not, are you?' Nick almost snapped at her.

'No,' she said. His sudden vehemence surprised her. 'I sometimes feel that if I had been I could have helped him. I know it sounds presumptuous.'

Warmly Nick took her up.

'It doesn't sound presumptuous in the least. If anyone could have, you could. But it wasn't a matter for you, was it,

Margaret? It wasn't your pigeon, if I may put it so. I mean, how Colum lived up to his religion. It's for the priests to see to that, his confessor, if he has one. I don't see why you should mind. You aren't responsible. You're not the keeper of his conscience.'

'No,' said Margaret, 'I suppose I'm not.'

If she told Nick why she minded, she would have to tell him everything.

'I should think you're glad you're not,' cried Nick, for try as he would he could not always speak of Colum with the forbearance due to Margaret's husband. 'From what I remember, it would be no sinecure.' He coughed uncomfortably and looked away. 'Besides, if you were a Roman Catholic you would be . . . you would be . . .' He stopped.

'Yes?' said Margaret.

'I was going to say, you would be tied to him for life.'

They gazed at each other across the corner of the table over which so many private thoughts had been given utterance, but possibly never this one, until now, and for the first time since their interview began the thought of Colum stung her with a sense of shame. She lowered her eyes, but Nick was unrepentant. The magnetic needle of his being turned to Margaret and quivered there, but in spite of what he had said about forgiveness, he had not forgiven Colum or himself.

'Margaret,' he said, 'I told you I'd do anything for you and it's true. It's less than the truth, much less. But I must ask you one thing – I won't call it a condition, for of course there are no conditions.'

'What is it?' Margaret said.

'I'll do anything I can, but don't, don't ask me to see him.'

Margaret went back, revitalized and recharged, a different creature. The paralysing conviction that she had caught from Colum of being cut off from the world's purposes, as if its

333

activities were going on without her, and were in a sense directed against her, had been replaced by an active confidence. And the reason was, she freely told herself, that she had taken her father's advice and found the best man possible. With Nick beside her she could face anything. She had found security at last. Whatever surprises the future might hold, he would know how to meet them. Even the thought of the police 'making further investigations', burrowing, – undermining, as she some-times felt, the very building where she and Colum sat – no longer haunted her.

What she did not tell herself, for she did not realize it, was that she had once more fallen in love with Nick. But her nature exulted in the consciousness of it, nor had she felt, except at the moment when she tacitly refused his kiss, guilty of disloyalty to Colum. There were many reasons for this, – his apathy and helplessness which she couldn't help secretly despising, and the slow erosion of her feeling for him not only by his own offences against her sense of fitness but by the allowances and excuses she had had to make for him. She had wanted to look up to him and been forced to look down on him; instead of the pride she had hoped to feel, the elixir of feeding on the thought of him, she had been condemned to a diet of unpalatable truths which she had to consume in secrecy. She was very English in that she could forgive offences against herself far more easily than she could condone offences against her moral standards. Had Colum wounded her, she could have made it up with him; she could not make it up with him over the third-party quarrel in which she believed him to be in the wrong.

Who the third party was, and why she felt she must side with it, was something that Father McBane had understood; certainly Nick hadn't.

And another reason why she felt such an excess of confi-dence was hidden from her. It was her nature to love, it was her

334

vocation, for which her devotion to good works was only a substitute. As long as she was in love with Colum, and as long as she felt free to love him, she hardly asked herself whether he loved her. When the opportunity for loving was taken from her she suffered as any creature does that is denied the exercise of its function. She did not expect to be loved in return, or thought she did not; all that mattered to her was what went out of her; she did not rely on anything coming in. But this did not mean that she was unable to benefit from such an influx, any more than a constitution unaware of its need of a tonic is unable to benefit from taking one.

Margaret did not realize that one reason she felt so much better for her reunion with Nick was the assurance, outside the cognizance of her conscious mind, that he loved her. She only knew that something was pouring into her and strengthening her. Had she become aware of it suddenly, she might not have known what to do with it, and felt embarrassed and guilty, as those who are accustomed to conferring favours are apt to feel when a favour is conferred on them. She did not realize that by humbling herself to Nick she had made a gap in her being which his love had filled. She felt the poignant happiness of reconciliation, and did not guess at the more powerful emotions that it was letting loose. The egotism of humility blinded her and made her deaf. But love has a thousand tongues and they were beginning to whisper a message she would have to listen to.

She soon needed all her new-found fortitude. When she got back she found Colum as altered as herself. He was in a state of great excitement, walking up and down the room, unable to stay still a minute. For a few minutes her heart leapt with joy at the difference in him, at the kindling eye and vigorous movements that had replaced his lethargy. 'Do sit down,' she begged him, forgetting how for days past her one concern had been to get him to leave his chair, 'and tell me what's happened to make you so happy.' She wasn't sure that he was happy but she felt it would be best to pretend he was. Her memory flashed back to the time when he had spoken of the miracles that hospital nurses could perform for sick and broken men. Well, she would treat him unemotionally as a patient. 'Please tell me, Colum.' But he couldn't or wouldn't; he kept staring at her with a nakedness of expression that was almost unbearable, and then looking away. She wondered whether he could somehow have divined her mission to Nick, and if this was the result: an access of fury which might be dangerous to them both. 'Now do sit down,' she besought him, and suddenly feeling nerved for strong measures she took him by both hands and almost forced him into a chair. To her surprise he offered no resistance but looked at her half-puzzled, as if he did not know how he came to be sitting down. She mixed him a strong whiskey and soda and said with all the authority she could muster, 'Colum, I think you ought to see a doctor.'

He seized the glass and drained it at one go.

'It isn't a doctor I need,' he said, 'The p-p—.'

She was so relieved to hear the sound of his voice that she scarcely registered the fact that never before had she known him stammer.

'The p-p-?' she prompted fatuously, beginning to catch his stammer from him. Her sinking heart released the tension in her mind, and the missing word swam into it.

'The police?' she said.

He nodded. 'Yes, the p-police. They t-told me something.' The effort of speaking had exhausted him, and he lay back with his head on the rim of the chair.

Margaret thought: How can I find out what has happened with the minimum of questioning? The police had evidently been here in her absence, and their interrogation must have left

Colum in this state. What had they asked him? Perhaps that did not matter much; the important thing was that they had told him something. The police had always been considerate to Colum – in a sense he half belonged to them; they had chased him so often on the films, they had come to have a tender feeling for him in real life. But why was he so frightened? Did it mean they had pinned something on him, as the phrase went? Did it mean . . .

She turned to Colum again. His head was still lolling on the chairback, and in the line of his jaw and throat, the line that had captivated millions, she could see a muscle twitching. He was shivering too.

'It's because I haven't an alibi,' he said, his chattering teeth letting the words through more easily than his dumb panic had. 'They d-don't believe I left the house and w-walked home. You d-don't either.'

'What nonsense, Colum,' she said. 'Of course I do.'

He shook his head. 'And they said s-something about the musical-box. Was I s-sure it wasn't mine? They said they thought you might have been mistaken. C-could I think of anyone's name in connexion with it?'

Margaret began to feel cold, too.

'I don't quite understand,' she said.

'It was the n-name of a receiver, d'you see? Perhaps whoever took those things of Mrs Bel's went to him, too.'

'Do you know who the man was, Colum?' Margaret asked. She realized that she spoke his name half threateningly, as one might address a criminal.

'Which one?' Colum asked. 'I don't know who t-took the things from Mrs Bel's, of course.'

He suspected her of laying a trap for him.

'No, the receiver,' Margaret said.

'I t-told them I didn't,' Colum said. 'Then they mentioned

several names and asked me if I knew them. I said n—' – his stammer became acute again.

'You said no,' said Margaret, wondering if she ought to help him out.

Colum nodded.

'Then they asked me about the legacy, whether I knew Mrs Bel was going to leave it to me. I said n—' His voice sputtered and died out.

'And then a lot about Aurélie, the maid. Did I think she d-disliked me. I said she h-hated my g-guts.' He spoke with a great effort.

'That would be in your favour,' Margaret said.

'I s-suppose so. And they asked me a lot more things. I c-can't remember now. And then said they were s-sorry but they'd have to ch—'

He couldn't get the word out, and Margaret listened patiently, as one does to stammerers long after their meaning is plain. The unuttered syllable was still chuffing in the air when there was a knock at the door. It was Richards. Margaret had never known him knock before.

'Luncheon is served, Madam.'

'Thank you, Richards.'

'Ch-charge me,' Colum suddenly exploded, and drew a long gasping breath, like a swimmer coming to the surface.

31

PUNCTUALLY at two o'clock an Inspector and a sergeant called for Colum. They would not sit down but stood holding their hats across their tunics, their faces wooden, as though they were dissociating themselves from what they had to do. It was a moment of acute distress for Margaret, she sank into a chair, feeling that the life they had made for themselves was dissolving round them. But Colum, though he had eaten nothing, was more composed than she had seen him yet. He looked round for his hat, and Richards who, contrary to his custom, had not left the room, produced it as though by magic together with his master's stick and gloves. Colum looked at these a little doubtfully, as though not sure whether the occasion called for them, or indeed, allowed them; then with a permission-seeking glance at the two policemen he took them, and for a moment looked as if he was off to a smart party. But only for a moment. Then something in his aspect crumbled; the shine and confidence went out of it, he looked up at his two captors, both exceptionally tall men whose heads seemed to scrape the ceiling and said, 'I am quite ready if you are.'

The swiftness of it all took Margaret by surprise. She had imagined that a happening so momentous for them both must needs take longer. She struggled out of the chair and said to the Inspector,

'Can I go with him?'

'I'm afraid not, Madam,' the Inspector said. 'You can come and wait for him at the station, if you so wish.'

Uncertain what to do she followed them through the door, through the hall, and out into the corridor. She had not given Colum a parting kiss or said any of the things she meant to say to him. Now, as they waited for the lift, he was cut off from her, not only by the presence of the policemen but by the fact of captivity. Perhaps it was his instinctive histrionic gift – in the films he had often been haled off to prison – but he looked more like a malefactor than it seemed possible to look. They belonged to different worlds. He was a prisoner and she was free.

The lift came rumbling up; the sergeant opened the gates and Colum stepped smartly in. She looked at him to avoid the appearance of not looking at him, until his downcast face, intersected by the bars of the lift grille, sank out of sight.

Then she telephoned – first to the solicitor to tell him what had happened and ask him to get in touch with Nick, and then to Nick himself. On the telephone his voice sounded cold. Was it cold, or was it only his business voice? She remembered him telling her, long ago, when she used to ring him up in office hours, that he put on a gruff voice to impress his clients. They would have less confidence in a man who cooed at them, he said.

His voice did not change much when she told him of the charge. It did not seem to him, as it had seemed to her, almost the most terrible thing that could happen. She took comfort from this. And yes, he could see her later in the afternoon when the business at the police-station was over.

A little braced, she put the receiver back. Then she remembered that she would be leaving Colum alone. If he consented to see anyone it would be Lauriol Sorensen. She begged Lauriol to come round at once. 'I've got to go out, unfortunately,' she said, 'and if you're here, he won't send you away.' Lauriol promised to come, and Margaret took a taxi to the police station.

She walked up and down outside. An indoor policeman, whose spectacles gave him a homely look, had invited her to sit in the waiting-room; but after a glance at it she preferred to remain outside, in the thin sunshine, among the passers-by who did not know her or her errand.

She remembered that charges did not usually take long: Colum would be out in a few minutes. She did not want him to stand lonely on the steps and limited her beat to about fifty yards. Moth-like, her thoughts battered at the bars of the future, and fell back, bruised into the past. It was a pre-Colum past. She saw herself in many situations – travelling abroad with her father, receiving delegates at home, and still more delegates; opening bazaars, organizing flag-days, judging at children's fancy dress competitions. She even contrived to see herself on the Bench without connecting it with her present plight. They were all honorific occasions, the crests of small safe waves, with the sun shining on them. She had only to move forward a step or two – smiling, gracious, for an answering smile to break out on all the faces round her. What security she felt then, and what security she imparted! The weather was always warm and clear, the colours were as soft and friendly as those of the drawing-room at Fair Haven. Scene after scene rose up before her, all with the same quality of decent, civilized, useful life, of esteem, unending esteem, enjoyed and conferred. Everything was all right, because Miss Pennefather was there. If only we can get Miss Pennefather, it's sure to be a success. 'We are lucky to have Miss Pennefather with us to-day.' How often had she heard these words – and though each time they were uttered they seemed conventional and flat, when they were added up they stood for something: legions of people, as far as the eye could see, counted themselves lucky because they had Miss Pennefather with them.

And now Miss Pennefather would bring no one luck, least of all herself. At any gathering she appeared at faces would turn away, scarlet with embarrassment. Meetings would dissolve, marquees would be left empty. Clouds would gather, rain descend, people in their best clothes would run for shelter. No confidence, no esteem, no smile of security reflected from face to face. No paragraphs in the paper thanking all the helpers; no photographs of distinguished visitors shaking hands with her; no prize-givings, no songs, no votes of thanks. The cream has curdled, the butter will not come. We are unlucky to have Miss Pennefather with us to-day.

What is the reason of this? Why has such a blight fallen on the proceedings? Why don't people come as willingly as they did to the meetings, the functions, the genial gatherings of every sort that Miss Pennefather used to preside over? Why do her letters suggesting this or that date for this or that rally lie so long unanswered? Why do people avoid her in the street, or hurry by with a brief nod? Why do the Tuftons, Stuart and Diana, who used to be so thick with her, now see so little of her? And her father, that nice old gentleman, a pillar of the place and a typical representative of the old school, fast dying out, why do we never see him at the Club? Why does he spend most of his time indoors? Is he ill? He easily might be, he's never been strong, and we hear his daughter neglects him. Why, she's hardly been to see him at all during the last ten months. They say the place doesn't suit him, Dittingham doesn't suit him, after all these years! – and he may sell Fair Haven and go and live somewhere else. What a shame, at his time of life! Why has all this happened? Why is there such a slump among our voluntary workers? Why all this unwelcome publicity in the papers? Why do people snigger when Dittingham is mentioned, Dittingham which used to hold its head so high, Dittingham the model suburb? I'll tell you why. Miss Pennefather is the wife of a gaol-bird, and that's why we are unlucky to have her with us to-day.

Oh it's not altogether her fault. She married him without knowing he was a crook. At least we suppose she did – we can't be sure. We do know that to marry him she threw over a steady, hard-working young man at a moment's notice, and broke his heart. Yes, he's done very well since but that's no thanks to her. He's dried up inside – his emotional life is quite dead. He's put all his energy into his work and doesn't think of love – sublimation, they call it. And in spite of that he tried to save her precious husband. But he couldn't – the evidence was too strong. It was all about a musical-box which she told the police had never belonged to her, but it had. That's how they caught her. She was his accomplice, an accessory after the fact. 'Darling accessory' he used to call her. Oh yes, she'd been in league with him for a long time. He got seven years. They let her off because she was a woman and because she hadn't been to the party, as he had. But she was just as guilty really. She aided and abetted him. That's why we're lucky not to have her with us to-day.

Each time she turned at the end of her sentry-go Margaret's thoughts took a slightly different direction, though always closing with the same refrain, – the theme-song of her coming ostracism. Without noticing, she had succeeded in projecting herself into the future, but the future disguised as the past: she was not looking forward to it, she was looking back on it, and by this device she found it more endurable. Suddenly she bumped into somebody; apologies followed; her chain-thinking was broken and a new pattern emerged. The skies were bright and blue again, and the streets were thronged with people. Who is this that everybody knows so well and seems so glad to see? A little boy walks and trots beside her, tugging at her hand: the welcomes are for him as much as her. Everyone has a word for him. And where are they off to? They are off to the local flower-show where Miss Pennefather is going to give away the prizes.

Of course she isn't Miss Pennefather any longer, didn't you know? She's Mrs Burden now, and her husband dotes on her. But she's still Miss Pennefather to us. Yes, the boy's name is McInnes, but all that happened a long time ago – nobody remembers it now. They live with her old father – it's just like old times. The place was quite dead while she was away – she was always the life and soul of it – the only one with any public spirit. Yes, her husband's a most distinguished man, most distinguished – the kind of distinction one can't acquire, one must be born with it. He's a lucky man and so are we – very lucky to have Miss Pennefather with us to-day.

Tears came into Margaret's eyes as the auditor within heard what was being told it. She looked up, she had reached the police-station again – the middle of her beat. The bespectacled policeman was standing on the steps looking about him. I wonder who he's looking for, she thought; and then he saw her and came down the steps to meet her, with a grave, unsmiling face.

'I'm afraid Mr McInnes will have to spend the night here,' he said, 'taking into account the seriousness of the charge. We thought he wouldn't have to, but it's the regulations. We've told him he can go home, Madam, in the company of a policeman, to get anything he needs for the night; but he seems all hazy about it, Madam. Perhaps you would speak to him.'

'What time in the morning is the court?' asked Margaret.

'At ten,' the policeman said.

Margaret followed him up the steps into the lobby, which now had all the attributes of a prison. Colum was sitting on a shiny yellowish wood-seated chair, with his left elbow propped in his right hand, an attitude that had become second-nature to him the last few days. He looked up when he saw her and then looked down again.

'He's taking it hard, Madam,' the constable said, lowering

his voice, 'but we've told him it's only a matter of routine. The room's clean and tidy, it's fit for anyone to sleep in, it really is.'

'Would you like to go back to the flat, Colum?' Margaret asked him. 'We can go all three together, can't we?' she appealed to the policeman.

'Certainly, Madam,' the policeman answered, eager to do what he could for her within the regulations.

Colum raised his head. 'I don't want to go. I see some people out there, w-watching for me.' His stammer gave the impression that he was always cold.

Margaret's eye followed his. The knot of loiterers at the door did seem to have thickened.

'Don't pay any attention to them,' the policeman said. 'You'll always find people with nothing better to do than stare at a police-station.'

'I don't want to go,' repeated Colum, shaking his head. 'They'll sh-shout out something at me. Don't st-stay, Margaret; they won't re-recognize you.'

'I don't mind if they do,' Margaret said. Her heart was full of pity for Colum, but she could not bear to see him look so cowed and abject. 'I'll go back to the flat and bring back anything you want.' Suddenly she felt at a loss, for she had never packed for him before. 'Let me see,' she said, trying to make her voice sound brisk and lively, 'you'll want your tooth-brush, and your sponge.' She paused for him to help her out, not knowing what a man's requirements might be. Colum guarded the privacy of his dressing-room most carefully: he had a horror of being discovered in an intermediate stage of dressing.

'Well, my comb and brushes,' Colum said, obviously making a great effort to remember, 'and my p-pyjamas.'

With instinctive delicacy of feeling the policeman moved away out of earshot.

'And my sh-shaving tackle,' went on Colum.

'Yes,' said Margaret. 'I can remember those. And would you like a shirt and a handkerchief or two?'

'Yes, p-please,' said Colum, like a child.

'And your dressing-gown and bedroom slippers?'

They looked at each other inquiringly, wondering if these would be allowed. After all, Colum was not going to a weekend party.

'Yes, I th-think so.'

'And your hot-water bottle?' Colum always used a hot-water bottle, except in the warmest weather; and he looked so miserably cold now.

'N-no,' he said, shaking his head. 'They'd laugh at me.'

'They needn't see,' said Margaret, but immediately reflected that they would see, and the same idea had evidently occurred to Colum, for he said,

'Yes, because they'll unp-p-pack for me.'

Margaret's thoughts again flashed to weekend visits, where guests were still sometimes given the luxury of having their things unpacked.

'Is there anything else?' she said, looking Colum's figure up and down, as though by studying him she might remember what he needed for the night.

'Oh, and my sleeping t-t-tablets.'

'Yes,' said Margaret, making a mental note to forget those.

'And anything else?' she said, hating to badger him.

He made a gesture of weariness. 'If there is, R-Richards will know. A few things that I u-use.' Evidently he didn't want to particularize. Then he said, 'Oh yes, there is one thing more.'

'What is that?' asked Margaret. Fearful of forgetting something, she opened her bag and found a note-book and pencil. She held the pencil poised.

'Your fo . .' He couldn't complete the word.

'My fo . .?' Mechanically she imitated the sound that had left his lips. What could he want of hers?

'Yes, your fo . .' He made a longer effort this time, and when it failed Margaret could almost see his energy flowing out like a spent wave. Yet the puff of sound still parted the air, a kind of rhythmical panting as of someone trying softly to blow out a candle.

'Is it very important?' asked Margaret helplessly.

He nodded. 'It's your fo . .' he began again. Then he got up from his chair and came over to her and stretched his hands round her face, framing it. 'It's . . y . . you,' he gasped.

Margaret turned away and the tears she had been trying to keep at bay started into her eyes.

'Yes,' she said. 'I'll bring it. I know the one you mean. The one we had taken in Venice.'

Her photograph.

The next morning, at the magistrates' court, Colum and the others were remanded to appear at the Old Bailey on a charge of robbery with violence. Bail was allowed and Margaret brought him back, more dead, it seemed to her, than alive.

32

DESPERATE as Margaret was, hardly able to take in what was going on round her, still less to respond to nuances of atmosphere, she could not enter the precincts of the Temple without a sense of awe. It summed up for her everything in a man's career that she most respected and admired. It was calm, dignified, impersonal. It was in the world and yet not of the world; dependent on the world for its livelihood, it still kept the world at arm's length. Every day the money of the world poured into it; yet who could think of money, the grubby, raw material for which men strive, in connexion with these quiet courts, their struggling grass, and shabby staircases. The bomb-damage, the trenches, the navvies handling drills and pushing barrows, did not destroy its magic: she remembered it as it was. Every day the world's miseries poured into it; it was as sad a place in its way as Bedlam or Harley Street or Pentonville; yet those miseries somehow became transmuted; disciplined, ordered, filed, docketed and pigeon-holed, they seemed to lose their cutting edge. Written out in copper-plate handwriting on shiny paper and bound in red tape their mischief was localized and confined and made to wait its turn; it could not overflow the world, for age-old convention, stronger than life or death, had appointed it bounds beyond which it might not pass.

Above all, the Temple was not to be hurried. It went at its own pace, which was emphatically not the pace of the emotions. Outside, the emotions would race at fever speed; a thought was enough to set them off. Inside, they had to wait in a queue and take their turn.

The sense of urgency was one of the most superficial of Margaret's troubles, but it was also one of the most uncontrollable. Alone, she could hardly sit down, she was almost as restless as Colum was himself. With him, she forced upon her limbs at any rate the appearance of rest she was so far from feeling. Only in the Temple did her thoughts relax. More and more it seemed to her a haven, and her visits to Nick the one thing to look forward to in a future where there was nothing to look forward to.

Oddly enough the mere fact that she was being a nuisance, that she ought not to come so often, that she was taking up the time of a busy man and must apologize for that before she said anything else, acted as a tonic to her, for it confirmed her in her sense of her identity, it was an assurance that she had an existence of her own apart from Colum's plight.

There were three doors to pass through: the staircase door, the door of the clerk's room, and Nick's. At each successive assault, the resistance within seemed to stiffen. Nick's clerk never seemed to recognize her; he spoke to her, and announced her name to Nick, in the same impersonal voice, and it was far from friendly. At first she thought that it was just his way, she remembered that in the past he had never been forthcoming. But now she wondered whether he was not cherishing a grudge against her for having treated his employer so badly: she knew that barristers' clerks sometimes identified themselves so closely with their masters as to refer to them as 'we'. Sodden and rudderless as her emotions were, unavowable and forbidden as some of them had now become, she felt a twinge of happiness that Nick's clerk regarded her as a menace.

So almost deliberately she refrained from reckoning how often in the past few days she had stood, a suppliant, outside

Nick's door. Each time she came it was with a special plea which seemed imperative, and which she broached to him the moment they were alone; she concealed from herself, indeed she scarcely realized, that it was always the same plea under a new guise. She approached it differently and tried to make it sound different. But this time – was it the fifth or sixth? – she detached her plea from its camouflage of suggestion and innuendo and presented it nakedly, as the last hope for Colum.

'But, my dear Margaret,' said Nick with a touch of impatience for which unconsciously she blessed him, 'what good could it possibly do for me and Colum to meet? It would only be well . . . exceedingly embarrassing and even painful to us both. Besides, as I've told you more than once, it isn't usual for barristers to meet their clients. It isn't unheard of, but it isn't usual. The solicitors are our real clients. I'm in constant touch with your solicitor, in fact I was talking to him on the telephone the moment before you came in. I assure you that everything that can be done is being done. We have made a little progress. I'll tell you this although I ought not to. We have evidence that the French maid had not been with Mrs Belmore anything like as long as she told the Coroner's Court she had. It's only a small point, but it slightly shakes her value as a witness. After all, she's the main plank in the prosecution's platform. It's her word against Colum's. If only one of the five would as much as say they *thought* he wasn't there! I don't believe they have such scrupulous consciences. They all swore they didn't know that Mrs Belmore had a weak heart; but we have evidence that it was common knowledge – it was the reason why she had a lift put in the house – so it's rather odd they shouldn't.'

'Colum said he did know,' Margaret said.

'Yes, and it will count in his favour. I own I'm surprised he did – I shouldn't have expected him to.'

Margaret was silent.

'It almost looks,' – Nick's voice was meditative – 'as if the others had a grievance against Colum for leaving them in the lurch. They might have – they're a pretty nasty crew, from what I hear.'

He shot a glance at Margaret, who did not meet his eye, for she had never really doubted the good faith of the five, in this particular instance.

To change the subject she said,

'Do the police know about the French maid telling a lie?'

'If we do,' said Nick, 'you may be sure they do. And they knew something that we don't know, something, I gather, that only they know – the exact moment when Mrs Belmore tried to telephone.'

'They asked Colum if he knew,' said Margaret.

'He couldn't know if he wasn't there.' As always, the familiar phrase set every nerve in Margaret's body twanging. 'But the others didn't know – Sindon himself didn't know. They were much too occupied with what was happening to think about the time.'

'How do the police know, then?' asked Margaret.

'Because, in the struggle for the telephone, a little clock that stood on the table fell to the floor and broke. It lay face downwards and nobody thought of looking at it. The police took it away with them.'

'How do we know that?' asked Margaret.

'Sindon saw them do it. So they know the exact time. If Colum could establish even the shadow of an alibi they would withdraw the charge, I'm certain. That is, unless they have something else against him.'

There was no concealed question in Nick's tone, nothing for Margaret to affirm or deny, yet she felt the weight of the *suppressio veri* and the sense of pain and isolation it gives to have to withhold the truth from a friend. She wondered, too, if it was the best policy. Might not Nick afterwards say, 'If only you had told me?' I should not want to tell him the truth so much, she thought, if I did not love him.

Nick was saying:

'So you see, Margaret, there's nothing to be gained by my seeing Colum. I can't find him an alibi; I wish I could, for your sake, and if we met, well, something might happen to make it impossible for me to go on with the case.'

A tired mind is soon turned from its purpose. While Nick was talking, Margaret had forgotten the chief object of her visit. Now it came back to her on a wave of almost unbearable disappointment, pure, unmixed with any other emotion, for she had long ago lost the balance of her feelings.

'It wasn't only for the sake of the case I wanted you to see him,' she said. 'It was for his own.'

'For his own?' said Nick, and his white starched collar seemed to contract and stiffen round his neck. 'How would it help him to see me?'

'Oh, it would help him in so many ways,' said Margaret. 'Nick, it isn't only about the case that I'm afraid for him. It's his health, his morale, his mind – everything. He's gone to pieces. Why, he can't even talk properly any more. I don't know what he'll do when he has to go into the witness-box.'

'Can't talk properly – what do you mean?' Nick asked. 'He never found any difficulty in talking, as far as I remember.' He did not try to keep the bitterness out of his voice.

Margaret told him about the stammer, and added, 'Since he appeared in Court it's been much worse. I've tried to get him to see a doctor but he won't. To-day I've been keeping him in bed, but he won't stay there. He keeps coming into the room where I am, looking so pale and weak. It's only a little thing, but after he spent the night at the police-station, in the cells I suppose you'd call it, he took a dislike to everything he had with him – the things he needed for the night, except . . . except my photograph. I've had to get him a new outfit.'

'I remember now he used to stammer at school sometimes,' Nick said, in a voice appreciably less hard. 'He was always highly strung.'

'I know – but Nick, this is more serious. I'm afraid to leave him alone, and yet he won't see anyone except Lauriol Sorensen – she's an old friend of ours, she's with him now. I'm afraid he might do something dreadful to himself.'

'Oh no,' said Nick, permitting himself a smile of reminiscence. 'He wouldn't, Margaret, he wouldn't. He's not that sort of man. He might want you to think he would, but he wouldn't do it. He never was good at being in a tight place, up a tree, unless it was a real tree. He flouted popular opinion always, but he was miserable if it turned against him. I remember once . . .'

'Yes?' said Margaret.

'Oh, nothing. But then he threatened to kill himself, and nothing came of it. He's only leading you up the garden path, to get your sympathy.'

'Nick,' said Margaret, 'I know he did you a bad turn.' She stopped, moistened her lips, and then said humbly, 'but that was my fault as well as his.' She did not add, as she well might have added, it was also your fault; for she had convinced herself that she and Colum were alone to blame for the breaking-off of her engagement. She went on earnestly: 'But I'm sure he isn't shamming now. You wouldn't say so if you saw him. Couldn't you, couldn't you find it in your heart to forgive him? Or if that's too much to ask, to see him, well, as impersonally as a doctor might? I have a feeling, I can't tell you how strong it is, that it would help him. He would get the same sort of benefit from it . . . that I have.'

Nick's eyes narrowed.

'What did he say when you told him I was acting for him?'

'I . . . haven't told him.'

353

'You haven't told him?' echoed Nick.

'No, you see that's one of my chief difficulties. He doesn't want to hear about the case, and he can't talk about it, it brings on his stammer. His solicitor came to see him, and I was there; I warned him not to tell Colum about you, but he couldn't get anything out of him.'

'Margaret,' Nick burst out suddenly, 'you can't go on living with a man of that sort. It's quite impossible. What good is he to you? He'll use you and infect you and throw you aside like an old bandage. He can't help it, it's his nature. He needs the cushion of someone else's feelings, and the more bruised and swollen they are, the better. He can't give you anything, he can only take. You mustn't stay with him. Leave him, Margaret, leave him!'

'But how can I leave him,' Margaret said, 'in the state he is?'

'He wouldn't be in that state,' Nick answered, 'if you weren't there to sympathize.'

Margaret's tired brain struggled desperately against Nick's logic. And not only against his logic, but against the urgency of his tone, the weight of personality behind him, and the respect for him and his superior wisdom which had grown rather than shrunk during their separation. She had no arguments to oppose to his and her feelings were traitors, they trusted what he said because he said it.

'I couldn't possibly leave him now,' she said. 'You see that, don't you? It would be too cruel. Afterwards, perhaps, if he gets off, if he gets off . . .'

'If he gets off?' Nick prompted.

His fresh, unused vitality, unimpaired by sleepless nights and divided counsels, bored into her.

'Well, then I might,' she said.

'And supposing we don't get him off,' said Nick, remorselessly pursuing his advantage, 'supposing he has to spend a spell in gaol, what then?' His voice was almost brutal.

354

'Then I couldn't,' Margaret said, but the words did not carry much meaning for her; she had begun to feel sceptical of the connexion between events and words; things would be what they would be, regardless of what she said about them. But Nick, to whom the spoken word was power, and who had used it and heard it used to alter people's destinies, said grimly:

'That's the best reason I know for trying to get him off. Will you promise to leave him, Margaret, if we do?'

He shot the question at her with extraordinary intensity and a compulsion in his voice so strong that it seemed to resolve all questions into this one. His face, it seemed, was waiting for her answer and for nothing else in the world. She felt a little faint beneath the fixedness of his single-minded gaze, and suddenly she thought, 'if I say "no" he'll drop the case.' She dared not put it to the test, the risk was much too great, and she did not realize that professional training had enabled him to make it very hard for people to say what he did not want them to say.

'Yes,' she said, breathing quickly. 'Yes, I promise.'

Could she have looked into his mind, she would have seen how the energy poured out of it at that moment, to be replenished almost instantaneously by another electric charge. For he gave her no time to recover herself, no time to seek evasion or organize resistance, no time to construct another world outside the two of them, before he said:

'And then will you marry me?'

One result of mental fatigue is that the sufferer cannot see ahead; the immediate problem is the only problem, he is enclosed by it, and cannot see over it. Nick's question took Margaret completely by surprise.

'Marry you?' she murmured, doubtfully. 'I hadn't thought of that.'

Nick laughed briefly and rather harshly.

'No, perhaps not,' he said, 'but I had, and for quite a long time. I admit that you've had other things to think about, but will you please think about it now?'

With head thrown back and folded arms he looked like a coiled steel spring in his spareness and slenderness and strength. He was on his own ground with all the authority of the law behind him, with all that imposing record, emblazoned almost visibly behind his head, of judges impressed, juries convinced and cases won.

'Can you think of anything you'd rather do?' he demanded.

It was a shrewd question, for not only did it light up for Margaret the utter barrenness of her future without Nick, but it awoke in her the beginnings of desire. For weeks, it seemed, her only choice had been between things she did not want, the choice of the lesser evil; things she might want were as unattainable, as unthinkable, as a shop full of goods to a man with an empty pocket. Between gusts of exasperated tenderness for Colum she knew that she loved Nick; something in her was aware that he loved her; but these also were things to disavow, items on the debit side of her account; and only the force of Nick's personality could have transferred them to the other page.

'Can you think of anything you'd rather do?' he repeated. 'If you can, tell me. I'm listening.'

Her mind went blank; then every kind of sweetness began to steal into it of smell, sight, touch and hearing. She could almost taste the bliss upon her tongue, and her intense weariness, which a moment since would not let her contemplate anything that did not irk her, now banished all but joy.

'You haven't told me of anything yet,' insisted Nick, and triumph travelled shining down his voice, 'that you would prefer to being married to me. I suggest the reason is, you can't.'

As though she was engaged in a parlour game Margaret obediently tried to think. The evident impossibility of finding

356

an alternative superior to the prospect Nick held out was like a longed-for invitation to give it up.

'No,' she confessed. 'I can't.'

The kiss they had denied themselves before they now indulged in. It was a short and overshadowed kiss but it restored them to each other and unsealed the tender feelings and the tender words. Lost to everything but herself and Nick in this one room, Margaret cried and laughed and laughed and cried; and Nick relaxed his grimness, only to resume it when he detected in her some faint sign of harbouring a thought that was not his, or that was not sanctioned by him. But when they had left off this – not from any pressure of the clock, but from the instinctive sense of their duration that such emotions have, she suddenly recollected something, and said, not at all humbly, as a suppliant should, but as if she were reminding him of an appointment:

'Only you *must* see Colum.'

'Is that an order?' he demanded, fiercely tender.

'Of course it is,' she told him almost gaily.

'Then,' said Nick, 'I will.'

33

FOR the first time since she had left Colum at the police-station, Margaret was sitting in the flat without him. She had offered to accompany him to Nick's and hang about till he came out: obviously she couldn't be present at their meeting; but he had preferred to go alone. Divided between hope and dread she sat, wondering what would be the outcome.

Nick had triumphed over her, carrying by storm the fortifications she had raised against him. How solid they had looked to her during these last days, when the thought of him had begun to prowl around the citadel of her heart; how flimsy they had proved, crumbling like a Maginot Line at his assault. Yet in the moment of defeat she had snatched a victory; she had persuaded Nick to lift his ban on Colum. They were quits. He had demonstrated his power over her, with noise and clamour, but it was a hollow victory really, for he already had the garrison on his side. Whereas she had surprised out of him a boon that he had never meant to give: it was a reflex action of his love for her, by-passing his will; in that lay all its sweetness. He had bludgeoned and brow-beaten her, treating her like a hostile witness; she had only slipped a question to him. If she had made it a condition of her yielding he would have refused it; by yielding she had gained it.

She wondered if Nick was regretting his decision. When she rang him up to say that Colum was coming his voice did not sound eager. And besides the unwillingness she thought she heard a hint of fear. 'Do be nice to him,' she said, at which Nick grunted. Colum would not telephone himself. When she broke the news to him he became literally speechless, so that she could not tell how he was taking it. Then he scuttled away into his own room, like a rabbit into its burrow. What a pitiable object he was: the mere travesty of a man. Looking back she wondered how she could ever have been taken in by him, or by the edifice of glamour raised on this tottering foundation; for when she reviewed the past she realized how jerry-built his pedestal had been, even at the moments of his greatest glory.

As objects of admiration – for Margaret's deepest instinct was to admire, and even to adore, and she could not adore without admiring first – how could a cinema reputation compare with a reputation at the Bar? All that was glittering and gimcrack in the one, all that was glowing and genuine in the other, were typified to her by Colum and Nick.

Colum was now only an object of kindness. She had never felt more kindly towards him in her life. He was like a servant under notice; she had dismissed him; and by dismissing him she also rid herself of her resentment towards him. The faults for which she had been obliged to sack him no longer counted; the act of dismissal had cancelled them, and she was free to dwell with some nostalgia on his virtues – perhaps one should say his graces, for virtues he had few. Her thoughts of him were sweetened by her thoughts of Nick; she did not find them incompatible, for she had brought them in the most literal sense together, thereby putting right an ancient wrong, healing a rift that she, Margaret, had only intensified, for it had happened long before her time.

But supposing that the meeting was a failure? Supposing she had asked of Nick something that he could promise in the floodtide of his love, but not perform? She remembered the vindictiveness of his references to Colum, the way that his very physical envelope seemed to shrink and crinkle at the mention of his name. What if there had been a few sharp, understated words, such as angry men exchange, and Colum was now on his way home, bleeding from another wound?

Certainly the rebuff would not have come from him, for when he came back from his room she saw a light on his face she hadn't seen before. It was a reconstituted Colum, a new version that she couldn't place among the dozens that she knew, because for once his expression seemed to come through his face, instead of being stamped on it. He said, not stammering, 'But do you mean he really wants to see me?' And she replied untruthfully, 'Oh yes, of course he does,' to which Colum replied obliquely, 'There's no one like you, Margaret.' A charming tribute, and how, in other days, she would have thrilled to it! But alas, one's appreciation of a compliment depends on the esteem in which one holds the speaker; and if she now felt pleased by it, it was because of Colum's implied compliment to Nick, by Colum's touching wish to see him. It was a comment on the shallowness of Colum's nature that he should feel no shame, or even delicacy, at the prospect of meeting Nick again – as though he had no criterion but the emotion of the moment, no sense of the dependence of the present on the past! But wouldn't that make things easier when the time for the break with Colum came? Wouldn't she feel much less guilty if she felt that his distress would hardly outlast the sentence, the few words, that inflicted it?

So she reasoned, and was comforted. But soon the future came at her from another quarter. Supposing it all went wrong – supposing Nick and Colum didn't hit it off and Nick threw up the case? Or, by-passing that peril, supposing he didn't get Colum off, and she was tied for life to a ruined man whom she no longer loved, a decomposing albatross round her neck, while Nick pined away on the periphery of her life, unable to come closer?

Not the least of her troubles was that she couldn't follow her thoughts far in any direction without being brought up short; if she abandoned the dubious shelter of the present, and its ambiguous garrison of untried hopes, she must leap the middle distance into the far future, where she and Nick were safely married, before she could enjoy that first condition of reliable happiness – the ability to see one's pathway straight before one.

'I shan't be long away,' Colum had said, and kissed her. Margaret nearly jumped, for though she had kissed him often during these last days, and been kissed back, the initiative had never come from him. In fact no initiative had; and to see him striding to the door, as if the outside world contained no terrors for him, as if he had not been shunning it for days, was like a miracle.

Nick was not the man to respond to easy approaches of good fellowship; she had seen him wince before a hearty greeting, even with no previous cause to make it unacceptable. How warily she herself had had to tread, almost visibly wearing a white sheet! Half in a panic, she tried to picture the scene: Colum entering Nick's room clad in one of his many mantles of self-assurance, or perhaps a false air of diffidence (and diffidence is less easy to assume), stretching his hand out, and Nick fumbling with his, not quite withholding it, but stiffening and becoming all chin and neck and collar, his face contracting with distaste. 'I hope, old boy, that all's forgiven and forgotten?' 'I'm sorry, Colum, but I'm afraid your wife over-persuaded me. I'm too old for experiments, I suppose. I shall have to drop the case.'

The telephone bell rang and she went out to the box to answer it. Colum's voice: she hardly recognized it, but then it was so long since she had telephoned to him. He was all right, he said, but would be out to lunch. She mustn't worry about him. 'Oh, but, Colum, Lauriol's coming for lunch.'

'I know, I'm sorry, but you'll have lots to talk about.'

*

Colum came in just before Lauriol left. He adopted at once a slightly party manner and Margaret saw that he did not mean to tell Lauriol of his visit to Nick. She was so curious to hear about it that she could pay little attention to what was being said, but she noticed that Colum was ready to talk about the case, that he stammered much less and that his whole manner was more natural. Encouraged by this, Lauriol re-told some of the gossip she had heard, the most interesting item of which was that one of the masked men had been in trouble with the police before, and served a term of imprisonment for some kind of swindling. Margaret knew what was coming so she was able to watch Colum's face to see if this was news to him – she thought she could sometimes detect when he was pretending ignorance; but this time she could not – he was being the perfect listener. But that he could listen intelligently was a great step forward.

'Tell me how you got on,' said Margaret, the moment Lauriol was gone.

Colum bethought himself a moment, during which her anxiety climbed to fever pitch. 'Oh,' he said, with a sly smile, 'it wasn't exactly like old times, of course.'

Margaret felt disappointed: she had hoped for something more sensational.

'What did you do – you knocked, you went in, and how did he behave?'

'You ought to say how did I behave,' said Colum, and she suddenly realized that it was Nick, not Colum, she wanted to hear about. But she must not let Colum suspect this. He must be kept in complete ignorance, until . . . until . . .

'Well, how did you behave?' she asked, to humour him.

'Quite nicely,' Colum said, 'rather as I behaved at your cock-tail party. You didn't find any fault with my behaviour then, did you, Margaret darling?'

Margaret turned scarlet.

'But of course you weren't there for me to rescue,' Colum went on. 'I was the victim this time. He looks much older, don't you think?'

'Yes, I suppose he does,' said Margaret carelessly, thinking how well Nick's grizzled hair became him.

'I didn't tell him so, of course,' said Colum. 'I thought it would be in bad taste for me to seem sorry for him.'

'Sorry for him?' queried Margaret.

'Well, darling, that you of all people should say that! I may have fallen low but I have you. He hasn't.'

Margaret's 'no' was scarcely audible.

'Had you forgotten, when you went to see him? I hadn't, nor had he. It gave me a sort of advantage, so to speak. But mostly we talked business.'

Business was not what Margaret wanted most to hear about, but she said,

'Had he heard anything new?'

'Nothing of importance, but he didn't think my prospects were too bad. He said I'd been in some worse scrapes at school.'

'Oh did he?' Margaret wondered if he had.

'Yes, and I said, "If I'm convicted, ought I to ask Margaret to divorce me?"'

'I'm sure you didn't say that!' cried Margaret.

'Why shouldn't I, he's my legal adviser. Darling, you never believe me now, or hardly ever. But Nick did: I'm sure he believes I wasn't there when Mrs Belmore died.'

'Of course I believe it, Colum,' Margaret said, and never had it cost her more pain to say.

'Not really. But that's nothing – we love each other just the same, don't we? Only it was nice that Nick believed it. He used to be such a great friend of mine.'

Margaret's mind was now awhirl with questions. Yet could she trust Colum to answer them truthfully? The fact that he lied sometimes did not mean he always lied.

'What did he say?' she began.

'What did he say, darling? He said so many things.'

'When you asked him whether you should divorce me?'

'When I asked him whether I should ask you to divorce me.' Colum corrected her. 'Darling, it sounds so funny, we've never contemplated such a thing, have we? At least I haven't. I don't know why it came into my mind.'

'What did he say?' repeated Margaret.

'Darling, I was only teasing. You don't suppose I really asked him. He might have said yes. But would you?'

'No,' said Margaret.

Colum drew a long breath, and it would have taken a harder heart than Margaret's to resist the look of relief that flickered like summer lightning across the curves and hollows of his face.

'Then I haven't so much to worry about, have I?' he said. 'What a beano we'll have if I'm acquitted.'

They were both silent, listening to the rumbling of the wheels of their ordeal as like the car of Juggernaut it lumbered nearer. What would be left of them when it passed by? For a moment, and for the first time, Margaret almost welcomed this irruption into her life of a fate she could not control. It would settle many things for her out of hand. She hated the deception she was practising on Colum, and felt that a calamity that flattened all her hopes would in some ways be preferable to it. Yet her confidence in Nick as her ultimate haven persisted; the thought of him was sweet to her; longing to have his image brought before her, she said suddenly,

'Was he nice to you?'

'Who, Nick?' asked Colum.

She nodded. Whom did he think she meant?

'Oh yes,' said Colum. 'Pretty nice, considering. Of course it wasn't as it used to be.'

Margaret felt she would have to be content with that. But she could not suppress a final spurt of curiosity.

'And then you went out to lunch?'

'Yes,' said Colum, 'I ran into an old friend and he suggested it. I couldn't very well refuse, I hadn't seen him for such a long time. Naturally I didn't want to eat in public, so he took me to his flat.' He kissed her and went out.

Margaret realized that by bringing Nick and Colum together she had robbed herself of herself of her best excuse for visiting Nick's chambers. She had gone there on Colum's behalf, to give Nick any information that might help the case; now that he was in touch with the principal, and could get his evidence from the horse's mouth, her role of go-between was finished. She knew how busy he was and felt that from now on he must be left alone. She had been far too importunate, hysterically importunate, a nuisance. She would show him that she could control her feelings and behave as a busy barrister's wife should behave.

His career, his career, she must not jeopardise it. Apart from the waste of time, it would do him no good for her to haunt his chambers. He might get talked about. If she was to marry Nick their names must not be coupled together. If they were, it might endanger her divorce. Colum she thought, might bring a counter-charge and cite Nick as co-respondent. She could not trust him not to. And divorce was a luxury that barristers must fight shy of. No, she must not see Nick again for the present.

The telephone bell interrupted her reflections.

'A Mr Burden would like to speak to you,' said Richards.

Margaret jumped. It was the first time since their reconciliation that Nick had rung her up. Now that he had seen Colum he might think precaution was no longer necessary, but it was, it was . . .

Nick's voice sounded nervous and distressed; it plunged about as it used to in the old days, instead of keeping to the level tones he had imposed on it.

When she had poured out her thanks she said,

'And did it go all right, Nick, I mean, better than you expected?

'Oh yes, not too badly,' said Nick, seeming to push the subject from him. 'I expect Colum told you.'

'He didn't tell me much.'

'No? Well, there wasn't much to tell . . . I say, Margaret?'

'Yes?'

'Could you come round to see me?'

'I'd love to, Nick, but you must be frightfully busy and I am, rather.'

He didn't answer for a moment, then he said,

'I do rather want to see you. Are you sure you couldn't come?'

Margaret could not tell him, on the telephone, her chief reason for not wanting to see him, but she could prove that she was not a clinging woman, who would always sacrifice his convenience to her whims. Humility strengthened her resolve; she instinctively believed herself to be more loving than loved, she could not have persuaded herself that his need of her was greater than her need of him.

'Darling, I couldn't come *just* now,' she said, as to a child who must be humoured. 'Wouldn't tomorrow do?'

'I've got to go away tomorrow for the weekend.' he said. 'I'd like you to come now, and stay a long time.'

Strangely enough his urgency, by convincing her of his love for her, helped her to disregard his plea.

'I shall have to teach you patience, darling, I can see,' she said.

His answer astonished her.

'Oh, don't talk like that! It really is important that I should see you.'

She hesitated. 'Is it to do with Colum?'

He answered irritably:

'Yes, it is in a way.'

'Oh, but he's so much better,' said Margaret cheerfully. 'You've had a miraculous effect on him. He's like another person.'

Nick's voice sounded still more exasperated.

'Oh, nonsense, Margaret, he isn't. He's just the same. That's partly why I want to see you . . . Hullo?'

It was sweet to Margaret to be able to resist him; it gave her a sense of power.

'My darling,' she said, 'you couldn't tell me anything about him I don't know. That's our bond, isn't it? He can't spring any surprises on us now.'

'Don't be too sure,' said Nick. He tried a last appeal. 'If I said it would be *good* for me and *help* me – would you come?'

'Darling,' said Margaret, almost laughing, so happy was she in this last proof of his love, 'I know what's good for you. I'll come on Monday.'

But long before Monday came their lives were altered. On the same evening notice was sent to Colum that the police had withdrawn the charge against him. No reason was given.

34

In the wild and whirling days that followed this announcement, Margaret was tossed up and down by waves of emotion like a cork. The event was much too big for her to realize except in its most immediate aspect. Stupendous relief possessed her.

And had she felt able to entertain other thoughts she was given no time. The slow, broken-backed rhythm of the past weeks was suddenly accelerated. Their door that had been kept shut was now thrown open; friends, acquaintances, everyone it seemed that they had ever known, poured in. Colum throve on this. Wherever he moved a knot of people followed; they jostled each other to get near him, half off their heads with joy. Margaret began to forget what the human countenance without a smile looked like, and when she went out into the streets, which she scarcely ever found time to do, she wondered why the people looked so glum. Case after case of champagne was brought up to the flat by men whose smiles were broad as those of Bacchus; towards evening, popping of corks was almost as continuous as the sound of water gurgling in a gutter. To find new looks, new words, new forms of thanks became an impossibility, and their guests did not require it; what they wanted was to demonstrate their own gladness, their inexpressible relief.

Hurried along beyond her natural rhythm Margaret could not co-ordinate her thoughts and feelings with the thing that she was doing; her time-table outstripped her, all her remaining energies were bent on catching up. She found herself answering the question before last, mixing up the hours of the day and the days of the week, feeling ready for bed at breakfast-time and at bed-time inconveniently wakeful. Her whole time-scheme was dislocated, her sense of stationariness deserted her, the very furniture seemed to come at her, riding on waves of joy. What had been for a few hours a tremendous tonic soon acted on her tired nerves like poison, and on Monday – the day she had promised to see Nick, but even this she had forgotten – between a receding chair and an advancing sofa she fainted.

Colum was deeply concerned. Unlike hers, his nerves had taken no harm from the time of stress and trial. He had instinctively protected them under layer upon layer of apathy, as a bruised or broken limb is protected by a tight shell of plaster. He had not tried to control them, he had given way to them, and now he reaped the benefit: they responded to every call he made on them. He knew exactly what he wanted to do and did it, without letting any time-lag intervene. The throng of visitors was dismissed, the murmur of congratulation ceased, the door was again closed to the outside world, and before Margaret really knew what was happening she found herself in an ambulance, being whirled away to Withycote.

Colum went with her and made all the arrangements. To assist the resident couple, servants were conjured up out of nowhere; a day nurse and a night nurse were installed; the local doctor was called in and a specialist brought down from London. Never had the slave of the lamp worked so magically for Colum, and never had she been so conscious of the power of the enchanter's wand.

For a few days she was kept in bed and all mental effort was discouraged. Books, newspapers, even letters were at first forbidden and then doled out sparingly. She lay in her white bed in her white room looking at the banksia roses which clustered round the casement window, lapped in peace and isolated from the world.

She would have been happier, she told herself, at Fair Haven. There she would have had the friendly feeling of a life she knew going on outside her door; here she was conscious only of smoothness, softness, luxury, and ease; the nurses were so expensive, so good-looking, so well-trained, so tactful, that she felt scarcely any contact with them. The place was unreal, and she felt unreal in it. She had murmured something about Fair Haven but Colum swept it aside. Never before had he assumed so absolutely or engagingly the air and authority of a husband. Indeed, all his faculties and attributes, like himself, seemed to be enlarged and emphasized. He moved with so much vigour that the very air seemed sluggish round him.

He spent his days in London and every evening motored down for dinner, which he ate with Margaret in her room. At first the nurse protested, but Colum paid no attention and he did not have to assert himself; his will was freedom as well as law. He behaved like a king, unfettered by the restrictions of a constitutional monarch.

She should be read aloud to, he announced, and took from his despatch-case a thick wad of letters. They were a selection of the letters of congratulation he was receiving by every post. How different they were from those earlier ones, and how different was his attitude to them. Then, he could not bear to touch them; now, he fondled them, and read them in an ascending order of merit, keeping those which were most obviously love-letters to the last. They had many a good laugh over these. Yet Margaret felt that he was not reading her these tributes solely or even chiefly out of vanity, or to confirm him in the recovery of his self-esteem. He was watching their effect on her.

He had engaged another secretary solely to answer them.

But his life in London was not all letter-reading, he told Margaret. His days were packed. There was so much to see to – so much that was coming on, so much that had accumulated in the past. And most pressing and important of all was the première of his film.

Should it be held, with the banquet that was to follow it, before or after the trial at the Old Bailey? Colum, so his publicity agents reported, was now at a new peak of popularity. The public regarded the withdrawal of the charge against him as something more honourable than an acquittal; to them it also meant an apology, an acknowledgment that he had been unjustly accused. He was not only reinstated, he was advanced in favour; he was not only whitewashed, he was glorified; a martyr's crown was added to his laurels. Those who had suspected him were anxious to make amends. He would get the best reception now that he had ever had; whereas if they waited till the trial was over, even if the five were all acquitted, it would recall to the public mind his association with them, tarnishing his halo. And if they were convicted it would cast a longer, darker shadow; the show might have to be postponed for weeks. Far better, his advisers told him, to cash in on the golden moment than risk unpredictable developments by delay.

But would Margaret be well enough to attend? That was the question. For the celebration would not be held, Colum was clear on that point, unless she was there to grace it.

Yes, the doctor said, or was persuaded to say, for doctors are human and in Colum's presence it was almost impossible to say what he did not want to hear; she would be well enough, if she was careful. 'Your wife is a very strong woman, Mr McInnes,' the doctor told him; 'she is suffering from exhaustion and perhaps a little from shock; but her heart is sound.'

*

The date was fixed. Margaret was to keep as quiet as she could until the final moment. All the organization would be done by others: she would only have to slip into one chair at the cinema and another at the banquet.

With her returning strength the days seemed to pass more slowly. The overmastering sense of relief which had carried her over the beginning of her illness began to ebb away and become a talisman she must evoke rather than a fountain of happiness springing up in her. She was now allowed to receive and answer letters, with the added advantage that she needn't answer them unless she liked: for many days to come she could plead ill-health. There were masses of them, nearly all with the same tone of glad congratulation. An entirely different set of people seemed to have written from those who wrote before. Evidently misfortune inspired one group of pens, good luck another. The burdened posts came in, but the letter she always looked for was not there.

Could it have miscarried? she wondered, and imagined many sets of circumstances in which it might have eluded the postman's vigilance. Nick must know she had been ill. Had he taken offence at her refusal to see him? Had it made a difference to his feelings? Why didn't he write? The uncertainty began to torture her.

'Your wife's heart is sound,' the doctor had said. Little of a hypochondriac as Margaret was, the phrase had had a reassuring ring and she liked to think of it. But now it pleased her less. Gradually the part of her that concerned itself with Colum's welfare grew less vocal, and her heart, her unsound heart, took up its tale. If Nick had written to her she could have borne her divided allegiance without too much discomfort. But a conspiracy of one is difficult to keep up; and though she minded much less than she would have done a year ago, she disliked the deception she was forced to practise. It seemed so ungenerous for one

372

thing; thousands of people were giving their hearts to Colum: only she held hers back.

One evening she asked him if he had seen Nick since the withdrawal of the police charge, and Colum said 'Oh yes, once or twice. We used to be quite buddies, you know.' Margaret could not tell whether she was pleased or sorry to hear this; any news of Nick was good news, yet she felt wounded that he had not written to her. 'I suppose he's very busy,' she said lightly, and Colum replied, 'Those barrister boys don't know what real work is.'

The next day she wrote Nick what she meant to be a guarded, non-committal letter. She owed him a Collins, she declared, for everything that he had done for Colum. She didn't quite know what it was, for Colum hadn't told her, but her gratitude was inexpressible. Then she tried to explain why she hadn't gone to see Nick when he asked her to. She regretted it now bitterly, she said, but at the time she hadn't thought it would be wise. She hoped he hadn't taken it amiss. But the subject was too delicate for her to dwell on. Instead, she dilated on the happiness it gave her to see Colum happy; 'he is now on the crest of the wave,' she said, 'I've never seen him in such high spirits, and I don't think that anything that happened now would seriously disturb him, anything whatever. Only unpopularity could do that. I believe, Nick, that his happiness depends entirely on other people's good opinion of him: as long as he has that, he is invulnerable. He has been most kind to me, I've nothing to complain of: but I'm sure I only count to him as just another member of the crowd singing his praises. He doesn't need me in any special sense – and I, I don't need him, except as the crowd needs him, to make us feel wonderful and tearful. He isn't anyone's possession, certainly not mine. I thought I'd tell you this in case you should think . . . well, that this change in our circumstances, for which we have to thank you, has changed me too. I suppose it might have, but it hasn't. I don't pretend I'm

373

not much happier than I was, I couldn't be otherwise, and he can make anybody happy, can't he, when he wants to? I'm so glad you have been seeing something of him. I didn't like to think I had somehow come between you – though I believe it wasn't altogether my fault, it happened earlier. And now I've been the means of bringing you together, and what a joy that is. But what I meant to say was, my real happiness doesn't come from the fact that we can both look the world in the face again, or even from the sight of Colum's happiness, but from the thought of you – which I believe I have cherished, so unworthily, through all these months. Oh, my darling . . .'

This was the first letter she wrote and it was not an answer to any of the dozens that lay piled around her. Had she re-read it in the mood in which she began to write it, she would have torn it up; but as her heart warmed so her judgment weakened, and the Nick whose image she evoked was not the barrister or the discarded suitor but the lover who had so imperiously commanded her to marry him. To him she was entitled to write in such a strain, indeed it would have been a betrayal of their love to write in any other.

Taking several letters at random from the pile she quickly scribbled answers to them. 'How kind of you to have thought about us – yes, we are devoutly thankful – it is wonderful to see Colum looking so much better – he is quite himself again. I've been laid up in bed – so maddening at a time like this – but letters like yours make me feel how lucky I am.'

When half a dozen of such notes were finished she slipped Nick's letter in between and put them, guarding their secret – yet why should she have troubled to guard it? She had every right to communicate with her husband's Counsel – on the table in the hall.

Now she must tackle the remaining letters in good earnest, and she began to sort them, putting into one batch those that could be dictated to a secretary, into another those that she must answer in her own hand, and into a third those that need not be answered – the unpleasant ones. The third batch was gratifyingly small, and some of the letters that composed it could be dismissed as the work of lunatics, but one immediately caught her eyes, and in the moment of being read branded itself on her memory.

'How did your husband get off?' it began. 'I suppose you know that he's a murderer.' Correspondents had told her this a dozen times; there was nothing new in it; but the letter went on: 'That Frenchwoman knew what she was talking about, only she's had her mouth stopped. Why did the police withdraw the charge? That's what some of us would like to know.'

Margaret pondered over the letter. The sprawling, ill-formed capitals breathed the very breath of enmity. To that she was accustomed, almost hardened; but the question remained unanswered: why had the police withdrawn their charge against Colum?

In her relief at being out of danger Margaret had not troubled to ask herself why. If she had thought about the matter at all, she had taken it for granted that they thought the existing evidence was insufficient. But it had not seemed so when they made the charge. Perhaps something else had come to light. What was it? Colum would know, of course. The question began to gnaw at her, and she could hardly wait for his return.

But she was disappointed. 'My dear, I know no more than you do,' Colum said, as if their joint ignorance was yet another blessing; 'and I confess it never occurred to me to ask. They just took my word for it, I suppose.' One eyebrow lifted in humorous raillery, but his mouth did not quite smile. 'We mustn't question the workings of justice, must we? And talking of that, I've sent the Inspector and the sergeant tickets for the show, but I was going to ask you as a one-time magistrate, should we invite them to the party too? Or might that seem a bit . . . well . . . ?'

'Of course we owe them a great deal,' said Margaret doubtfully. She always felt indebted to the law.

'My darling, we owe them nothing but a kick in the pants,' said Colum. 'All the same, it would be nice to see them cringe.'

'Have you invited . . . Nick?' asked Margaret with an effort.

Colum opened his grey eyes wide. 'My dear, of course I have. What *do* you think? You wouldn't want us not to ask him, would you?'

'No,' said Margaret, adding – for the notion for some reason offended her – 'that is, if he wants to come.'

'Oh, he'll come all right.' said Colum. 'I told him that he'd better wear a mask.'

'You *didn't*, Colum!'

Colum laughed. 'Darling, you're always so *serious*! I shall have to talk to you seriously about it!'

A thought struck Margaret and she said, almost accusingly, 'Talking of masks, what did you do with yours?'

'Oh, I've got it somewhere,' Colum said. 'And talking of masks, what did you do with yours?'

'I suppose I've got mine somewhere,' Margaret owned.

'There you are, you see.'

Margaret pondered. Yes, there she was: like Colum, still the possessor of a mask. Her thoughts could be excused, or defended, or condemned, or endured, but they could not be enjoyed, or not for long, because each trailed after it its *arriére pensée*, a guilty shadow, longer than itself. 'False! False!' her heart cried when she thought of Colum: 'False! False!' it echoed, when she thought of herself. Must this go on forever? No; as soon as she had Nick's answer, his reassurance, she would break her fetters, come out into the open, and let them all know where she stood.

*

But the days passed, and no answer came. Other letters poured in, but not his. Bitterly she reproached herself for not having gone to see Nick when he asked her. Could he be angry with her? She did not think so. She had done it for his good, his and Colum's; his time was precious, she did not want him to squander it on her, not at that juncture; afterwards there would be so many moments . . . She believed she had done what was best for everybody; but he had asked her to come, and he was so sensitive.

Meanwhile, her intercourse with Colum had something provisional about it; it was like a conversation on the railway platform, with this difference that she knew, and Colum did not, that their parting was at hand.

Wandering out into the June sunshine, as she was now allowed to, she took little walks about the countryside. It was the real country, not the tame and subjugated country of Dittingham, where every field seemed to be offering a last resistance to the invader; it was unruly and self-sufficient and free to go its own way – as soon that is, as it was free from the restraining influences, the expensive tailored smartness, of Withycote. Margaret, too, went her own way, and at times her mind was privileged to enjoy the freedom of her footsteps, to be as wayward as the little lanes were, imposing no restrictions on her, acknowledging no law save the principle of growth. How luxuriantly the dog-roses flourished! Touch them, try to pick them, and their petals fluttered to the ground. They would not lend themselves to any scheme of indoor decoration, they would not admit that they would look better, tactfully arranged, in a bowl; they would not tolerate any interference; they must be enjoyed where they grew, and as Nature intended them to be. If they got dusty from the traffic, if honeysuckle or hawthorn cramped them, giving them no fair chance, well, it was just too bad, but no good would come of trying to help them, they would only prick your finger and then fall to pieces.

And this little church, which Margaret hadn't seen before – for on their infrequent weekend visits to Withycote they made expeditions to distant places, a castle or a cathedral, overlooking what lay at their door – seemed to be almost as much an offspring of Nature as the fields it nestled in. Its village had receded from it, at any rate no houses were in sight; the very gravestones seemed to have grown out of the mown grass, and to exist more by their own right than as memorials to the dead whose names they so imperfectly preserved. Perhaps the church was derelict even though the churchyard was well kept.

But she would not go in, for if she went in she would have to review her position in all its bearings. It was weeks, perhaps months, since she had been inside a church: her church-crawling days were over. They had not been without influence on her life – far from it. It needed no great exercise of faith, perhaps the minimum of faith demanded of a Christian, to believe that the powers she appealed to then had intervened in her life and that without their interference her present situation would be very different. She might never have found out that Colum was a crook. She would never have consulted Father McBane a second time and been told she ought to leave him. She would have faced *l'affaire* Belmore convinced of Colum's innocence; Colum would have had no stauncher champion than herself. Most important of all, she would not have turned her thoughts towards another man, be living in the hope of a sign from him and miserable because she had not got one. She would be Mrs Colum McInnes in the full meaning of the words, prouder of him than ever, longing to bear his child, looking forward to new happiness in their relationship. Instead . . . She was waiting for a letter from Nick.

The Prayer-Book said for better for worse, for richer for poorer, in sickness and in health, and until death us do part. It did not say in sin and crime, in lying and prevarication, in robbery and stealing, in prison and out of prison, as an accomplice and an accessory, – a darling accessory: but perhaps they were all included in for better for worse.

What good (she tried to find a meaning for the word good in this context, but could not) what good would she get, what good – leaving herself out of it, and putting the question in its most general terms – would be born into the world that hadn't been there before, if she went into the church and invoked the Power that had brought so much suffering on her, that might even . . . ?

She was tired of herself as a penitent, and how much more tired must the Power be of someone whose contrition was so short-lived, who slipped out of one sin merely to fall into another? Who even now was contemplating? . . .

Father McBane had said that she had come by a hard way to a knowledge of the truth. But what good had it done her? What good had it done anyone, – putting the widest possible human interpretation on the word, allowing it to mean almost anything except harm? Who was the better for it? She could not think of anyone. And even if truth was good – a good, the good – what further truth was there for her to discover, by this hard way? The truth for her, the only truth that mattered, was that she loved Nick and he loved her, and as soon as possible they would be married. An unedifying truth, perhaps, but truth, and no revelation from on high could alter it. No, she would not go into the church.

She lifted the latch of the flimsy wire-work gates, turned the heavy round handle of the iron-studded door, and went in.

It was not disused, she saw at once; it was wide and low and light and empty, and so silent that its silence was like the presence of a third person; there was herself, the church and someone else. But it was clean and tidy; the emblems of devotion were there; the church dozed in a religious dream.

I won't pray, Margaret thought, I'll just glance at the monuments and inscriptions – sometimes one sees such touching epitaphs – and go out again. She tried to close her mind to any message that the church might bring, looked about her with a bold, appraising, tourist's eye, and did not allow any diminution of her critical regard when she passed by the altar. That's that, she thought, almost as if she had crossed some rubicon; then, feeling she had forgotten something she retraced her steps and interrupted them with a genuflexion. Why? Only for good manners, she told herself, and resumed her tour. Soon it brought her to the church door, which, seeing that this was to be the briefest visit, she had left open. Absent-mindedly she shut it, but again to her surprise, found she had shut herself in, not out.

All at once she felt very tired but she did not want to sit, she had not come for that purpose and besides the chairs had the air of being occupied; a service was in progress which she must not join. But her fatigue was more real to her than her fantasy; she sank into a chair, but only to rest, not to pray.

She went down on her knees but not to pray, only to recover the atmosphere of prayer, for if she prayed she would be carried in some direction in which she did not want to go. She fought against prayer but it took hold of her and her lips began to move against her will. What am I saying, she thought, what am I praying for? – and she tried to make a barrier between her intention and her lips, so that she might not be held accountable for what she said. She listened to herself – it was something about a letter: could the letter come, might it be brought, would St. Anthony find the missing letter for her?

Presently the part of her that fought against the prayer gave up and joined in with the other, doubling the flow of supplication. Rapt and abstracted from herself she sat, the tears running down her cheeks, for she felt that the meaning of her whole life was in jeopardy, and that if the prayer failed she would never find it again. But she did not think the prayer was failing; for though the reiterated words drained her emotions, they never became meaningless and the power to utter them and feel them was continually renewed. Nor when she ceased was it from a sense of emptiness or frustration, but because her need of praying was fulfilled.

She rose and went again to the church door. It was not a prison door, not a trap door in any sense of the word, she could open it at will; but she found she did not want to, and the metaphor of prison, taking hold of her mind, made her feel that the world outside was prison, and that here, in the little church, she breathed the air of freedom. An unaccountable reluctance to go out seized her; she felt the lethargy, the unwillingness to change her present state, that overtakes the lie-a-bed or the hot-bath addict. She went back into the body of the church and sat there without praying and almost without thinking, unconscious of desire. When she finally came out it was past tea-time; she must have been in the church the best part of an hour.

When Colum arrived she saw at once that something had gone wrong. His eyes were restless, his movements jerky, and he had lost control of his voice. He didn't stammer, but the intonations were wavering and uncertain and didn't follow the meaning of his words.

Margaret was alarmed. Her fears were so used to running in one channel that she could think only of one thing: the police must have made some new discovery threatening Colum's safety. His immunity, she was convinced, rested entirely on a precarious foundation of falsehood which might at any moment crumble. That accepted facts build up their own security, almost as certainly as if they were real ones, did not occur to her. She had been so much concerned with truth in the abstract she had forgotten that in real life it is to some extent what usage makes it.

She did not want to hear the worst but equally she could not bear to see him suffer; one must behave properly even if one has ceased to love; and at last she said,

'What is it, Colum? Has anything gone wrong?'

In mid-stride he stopped his tiger-prowl and said, 'You mustn't pay any attention. It's happened to me before. How long have we been married, Margaret?'

She thought a moment and said

'It's a little more than nine months, isn't it?'

His face softened.

'To think you should have to remind me of that!' he said. 'Have I been very selfish? I'm afraid I have.'

'Oh no,' said Margaret, mechanically, but she was touched, all the same. And it wasn't true that he had always been selfish.

Looking at her with a new appreciation on his face he said,

'You're so much braver than I am. I'm an awful funk. I'm only brave on the screen, really. And you have so much more reason to be in a funk than I have.'

'Have I?' said Margaret. She had never been able to discuss the reasons for his terrors with him and didn't feel she could begin now.

'Oh yes,' said he. 'Nine months. That's a time-honoured period, isn't it? It rings a bell. Well, it's been nine months for me, too. We began, you might say, together.'

She reddened at the allusion, and blushed the more deeply, remembering that she was now in love with another man. But she still didn't understand what he was driving at, and thought he meant their recent ordeal.

'I'll swear you've made a better job of it than I have,' he went on, 'in spite of all you've been through.'

'We went through it together,' said Margaret with an effort.

'Did we?' he said doubtfully. 'Did we?'

He looked at her appealingly. She knew what the look meant and could not meet his eye. 'I'm not so sure we did, you know,' he said, and gave a sigh. The sigh was a perfect one, the quint-essence of all sighs; even his insteps and his finger-tips took part in it. 'But we will in future, won't we?' he said brightening. 'When you've got your business over, and I've got mine.'

The distress returned to his face and Margaret said,

'What is it, Colum? Please tell me.'

He gave her his moodiest look.

'It's this damned film,' he said. 'I didn't tell you, but the Trade Show last week wasn't any too hot, and the Press Show last night was a flop.'

So great was Margaret's relief that she couldn't conceal it, though she knew that it must wound him.

'I'm sure it wasn't,' she said mechanically, and added with an effort, 'darling.'

He noticed the time-lag before the endearment, his face fell further, and he burst out, 'Oh, you don't know what it means to me – what it will mean to both of us. Have you thought what it means to be past your prime, a ham actor that everybody's sorry for? To see the change in people's faces, when you come into a room, even when your name is mentioned? To have to keep pretending you're the same as you used to be, and other people pretending too, and everybody knowing it isn't so? I've seen it happen scores of times – you wouldn't know, Margaret, you've only been among us like a visitor – but I don't exaggerate, by God I don't. The other thing was bad but we have got through it somehow, for people's memories are short and they want the sort of thing that I can give them – they want it like hell, and they come back for more. But when I *can't* give it to them . . .'

He stopped and shot at Margaret a quick despairing look.

'I'm sure that you're mistaken, Colum,' she soothed him. She tried to put herself into the state of mind in which her happiness depended on the success or failure of his film. It all seemed to belong to the remote past. 'Everybody told you you were doing better at the end, you said so yourself, you remember.'

But Colum wasn't to be comforted.

'I made an absolute — of it,' he said, using a word he had never used in Margaret's presence before, for he was anything but foul-mouthed, indeed almost squeamishly careful of what he said in front of her. The gross word startled Margaret but didn't shock her; it gave her an uneasy, unwelcome, guilty feeling that he was being sincere. 'I made a perfect — of it,' he repeated, lashing himself. 'Well, the reviewers will get a good laugh out of me this time. You know what they're like: they have to be damn careful what they say about an actor on the legitimate stage, or else they're for it, libel and all that – but they don't care what they say about a film-actor. At least they do care: they hot it up to boiling-point. And it's no good saying the public don't pay any attention to reviews, because they do. I know what they'll say: "Mr McInnes shouldn't try to be a devil, he isn't distinguished enough . . ." that kind of thing, only with more pep to it. And it'll be repeated everywhere. And you'll see, I shall go downhill, not quite at once, perhaps, but gradually. And I shall try to make a come-back, and that will be a worse flop still. And then I shall have to go about asking producers if they can't find a part for me, and they'll say, "Sorry, but we haven't got the kind of thing that would suit you. You're too 1939, you know." And I shall drift round, knocking at doors and finding that people are too busy. The not-at-home signal will be raised everywhere and I shall know I've had it.' He stopped, and then said rather harshly – 'And you'll want to leave me, Margaret, you know you will.'

'Leave you?' Margaret echoed.

'You'll get a divorce and marry some chap who can keep you properly.'

'Why do you think I should divorce you?'

He looked at her sombrely and said, 'I don't know – most women would, and I should, in your place. But' – his face changed – 'you're not like me, are you?'

'Aren't I?' Margaret said, half hypnotized by him.

'No, you're a truthful Protestant and I'm a lying Catholic. You believe in being truthful, don't you? I've never known you tell a lie.'

Margaret said nothing. Suddenly Colum rose to his feet and stood over her. He was trembling and she thought he might be going to faint.

'P-p-promise me,' he said, stammering uncontrollably. P-promise me.'

'What shall I promise?' Margaret asked.

'That you won't l – - -' His hands clasped in front of him, he struggled with the word. Margaret did not help him out, but when he gave up trying, she promised. What else could she do?

Colum went away betimes next morning. His parting kiss didn't wake Margaret, for he had made sure she was awake, but it was the first thing she woke to, and she hardly knew that she was being kissed or who had kissed her.

She lay still, trying to collect herself and feeling the kiss gradually becoming real, like a pain that has taken time to reach the nerve centres. Then the maid came in with her breakfast and a pile of letters.

Nick's letter lay topmost on the pile. She wondered if Colum had seen it or if he had put it there. She even wondered if he had steamed it open and read it. She did not open it at once but began looking the letters through, in case there should be two from Nick, for she still believed that one had gone astray. But there was not. Then she examined the postmark to see whether the letter had been a long time on its journey; but no, it was dated the day before. Obeying one of several contrary impulses she opened it, and as sometimes happens with a letter that means much to the recipient, she had taken in its contents before she had read the words.

My darling,

I didn't want to write, for words without faces are misleading, as I have cause to know. I would much rather have spoken to you. But until to-day, until this minute, I didn't know what I should say. Now I know, and it seems unfair and even cruel not to tell you.

But I think you will have guessed the reason of my silence. Dear, dearest Margaret, I cannot marry you. I needn't tell you what it costs me to say this. You remember that I begged you not to ask me to meet Colum, and afterwards when I had met him and we lunched together I begged you to come to me. I was beside myself, my feelings were all at sea. And if you had, perhaps we should still be as we were then. It was no pretence that I didn't want to see him, I didn't think I could be civil to him, but seeing him down and out brought back old times. There had always been misunderstandings between us, and it was on one of those we parted, but I suppose we never quite ceased to be friends.

He wanted to talk about you, but I wouldn't, not at our first meeting nor our second. Then I couldn't refuse, and I realized how much you meant to him. He said he could never have got through the time after Mrs Belmore's death without the help you gave him – it was most touching, Margaret, the way he spoke of you. He couldn't pretend to be a saint with me, of course – I wouldn't have stood for that – but he said that no one could be with you without feeling that the world was a better place – a banal remark, but it meant something, coming from him. The only thing he felt sad about – and it wasn't a criticism,

Margaret dear – was that he wasn't sure you believed him when he said he hadn't been with Mrs Belmore the night she died. Well, he wasn't always truthful in his young days and perhaps he isn't always now, but I've had a good deal of experience of witnesses, and I can assure you that I believe him.

You wouldn't want to divorce him just for doubting his word? I'm sure he'd let you, he'd do anything for you: but is it sufficient grounds? Margaret, I don't think it is. I know you've always had high standards – but human nature is human nature, and would you wreck a man's happiness because you suspect him of a lie? And your own happiness too – for the more we talked of you the more I realized that you had both been very, very happy before this came about. Couldn't you make it up and forgive whatever it is you feel you have to forgive?

It's odd I should be pleading for him, and I wouldn't now – it would be unbearably insulting to you – if I hadn't suffered on his account even more perhaps than you have. And am still suffering – choosing between my oldest and my dearest friend. You can't mind more than I do – I hope you will mind less, much less. You haven't had so long to mind, and won't have, once you have taken Colum back. I don't think you ever really ceased to care for him: certainly he doesn't suspect that your feelings have changed towards him. Mine haven't changed to you, how could they? I love you as much as ever, but I'm older now and these months have disciplined me. It was hard to lose you for what seemed a bad reason, it won't be so hard to lose you for a good one – that is, for the preservation of two people's happiness, for I'm sure that yours is bound up with his. Believe me, Margaret, at heart he is a good fellow. He may not have always been, I didn't think he was; but he says himself that he has changed. And what has changed him? Well, you have. It isn't a miracle – it would have been a miracle if he hadn't, after you have been together for so long. This is a fresh start for him, a new leaf, if you like. If you were to leave him now, all the good you've done him would be wasted.

It's not because I'm afraid of seeming a cad, robbing an old friend of his wife – you understand that, don't you? It weighs with me, I own, but I'm not afraid of a word. It's because I feel you were made for each other, and all this that you have been through together would be stultified and meaningless if it didn't bear fruit in deeper love.

Let me end with your name, not mine, Margaret darling.

So he had denied her even his name, even his name on the writing-paper. The 'he' in the letter was always Colum; Colum might have written it, perhaps, in a way, he had written it. He had stolen Margaret from Nick and now he had stolen Nick from Margaret.

She passed the morning in a daze of uneasy feelings, reading and re-reading the letter. Its arguments meant nothing to her. The plea that if she stayed with Colum it would be for the happiness of them both had as little effect on her as the idea that Colum had undergone a change of heart. Only she knew how untrue that was. To her the letter said just one thing: that Nick had been taken in by Colum once again and that he no longer loved her. She stood, like a figure in an allegory, between a man she did not care for and a man who no longer cared for her. If hands and hearts were joined in the picture, they were Nick's and Colum's.

She found the contemplation of the group unbearable, but though she could keep her mind from looking at it, its meaning coloured her whole consciousness and crushed her.

Later in the morning a telegram arrived from Colum. It was unlike him to telegraph; he hated the formalities and the effort of composing telegraphese. If telegrams had to be sent, his secretary sent them. But she did not think his secretary had sent this, for it was of letter-length and written like a letter; besides, he had a strong feeling about privacy and would not have entrusted it to his secretary – for although the message was not specially private, the manner of it was. He was most frightfully disappointed, he said (the whole missive offended Margaret's sense of fitness, it seemed a deliberate challenge to economy) but he wouldn't be able to come down to Withycote this evening and bring her back with him next day as he had meant to: he was terribly busy with last-minute preparations and couldn't get away. He would be out all day. Would she mind motoring up to London by herself to-morrow afternoon, arriving about tea-time? He hoped to join her then, but if he couldn't, all the arrangements had been made, Richards had her ticket, she could motor straight to the cinema where he would be waiting for her. 'Are you happy, are you hopeful, are you absolutely fit darling. Stop. If you aren't you mustn't try to come. Stop. I'm less miserable than I was yesterday but longing so to see you. Stop. Omens are more favourable but without you nothing can go right. Darling, dearest treasure, please don't fail me. Never mind about being a Protestant but pray for me to St. Anthony. Stop. Don't forget me for a single moment. Stop. You are my public really and it doesn't matter what the others say. Stop. Don't try to count the kisses and the blessings but love me always as I love you. Stop. Your own Colum, Colum, Colum.'

The last two Colum's seemed to have been queried and veri-fied by the operator: there was a tick against them. Could Colum have telephoned the message and stammered when he came to his own name? Or was the repetition deliberate? Colum, Colum, thrice-Colum? Nick's letter had been anonymous.

All day long and most of the night Margaret tried to correl-ate the telegram with her feelings, but they wouldn't mix. Her feelings wouldn't accept it, wouldn't admit that in the least degree it modified the situation. She only knew that the telegram was a blind, just as Nick's letter had been: they were both manifestations of the conspiracy against her. While the cat was away the mice had played; they had put their heads together and used the language of love to banish her to a barren place where no love was. Mortification brought tears to her eyes; indignation dried them; she would fight for her rights, her rights as a person to be valued for herself, not made the target for unmeaning endearments. While she had been away Colum had cast a spell on Nick, but the spell could be broken – it had been broken before and it could be broken again. One word would break it and that word should be uttered. Nick should be told that Colum was a thief. The part of Nick that succumbed to Colum's charm was no true part of him; it was a survival left over from childhood. Colum had reduced a million people to infantilism, but he had not reduced her and he should not again reduce Nick. She would not let herself be treated so – dropped, slighted, fobbed off with empty phrases of devotion, like a dethroned royalty. Odious as it was for a woman to have to remind one man, let alone two, of what was due to her, – odious, pitiful, undignified, she would do it, and see whether shame would not bring them to a sense of reality, even if it was only the reality of herself and her child. They should not so easily turn their late idol into a laughing-stock.

The night abated her pride and her anger. She felt the strength of the forces arrayed against her; dimly she realized that she drew her meaning from them. It was isolation that she dreaded, and she would be more than ever isolated if she stiffened in an attitude of defiance. Each gentler thought was also a happier thought, uniting her to the lost self she was seeking. But though the night abated her pride it did not impair her resolution; she was convinced that her only hope of happiness lay in Nick and that somehow she must win him back.

For several hours she watched the June morning brightening on the ceiling above her window-curtains. Then she got up and began to put her plans in motion. Although they did not include informing Colum that it was her intention to return that morning, they took much longer than she expected, and it was nearly one o'clock by the time she reached the flat.

35

As soon as she entered the room she saw Nick sitting there. He jumped up and came towards her, a question in his eye.

'Oh, Nick,' she said, and it was all she could say.

He raised his hand to his forehead as if shading his eyes from hers.

'So you got my letter?' he said in a dull voice.

'Yes.' But she knew she must not leave it on a note of acceptance, and added, 'That was why I came.'

Nick did not take up the challenge. 'It was a wretched letter,' he said, not dissociating himself from it.

'No, it wasn't.' Beginning to breathe quickly, Margaret hastily sat down. After all, it was her room. 'But did you mean it, Nick?'

He too, sat down, not facing her, and said,

'Yes, I meant it, Margaret.'

'Every word?'

'Well, certainly the substance of it.' He twisted about uneasily and added, 'I would much rather have spoken to you than written.'

'You're speaking to me now. Do you still say the same?' she almost pressed him.

'Yes, I think so. Yes.'

Margaret moved her head round jerkily in a semi-circle, as if her neck was too short to give it play.

'I'm not asking you to take back what you said,' she told him with an effort. 'At least . . . if I am . . . asking you to reconsider it . . . it's . . . not because of what you said, but what you didn't say.'

'What I didn't say?' repeated Nick. 'Oh God, Margaret, I thought I'd said everything. I thought I'd said too much. What more could I have said?'

Margaret tried in vain to make him look her way.

'It was about Colum.'

'About Colum?' Nick's pale cheek flushed. 'Surely you don't expect me . . . ?'

'Of course not,' said Margaret, not knowing what he thought she expected him to say. 'It's this. When you asked me to go back to Colum – well, I suppose I haven't left him – you didn't say what sort of man I should be going back to.'

'But I did, Margaret,' Nick protested. 'I said . . . he was a much better fellow than he used to be. That you had, well . . . that you had improved him a lot.'

'You're wrong, Nick,' Margaret said. 'You're quite wrong. He's a . . .' Suddenly she looked up; her visual sense became detached from her labouring mind and will, and she saw that the room was full of flowers. On every ledge and resting-place they stood – roses for the most part, with orchids and hot-house blooms among them. At every level little white cards like stars shone at her. Her wandering, wondering eyes rested on a bowl of deep red roses at her elbow. The card beside it read: 'To darling Colum and Margaret with love from Lauriol.' Love, love, did every card say love? It might, for love was the climate of Colum's existence, the key-word in the Colum language. Not the great lover, but the greatly loved.

'He's a what?' She heard Nick saying. 'What is he, Margaret?'

Now the perfume of the flowers, of which she had hitherto been unconscious, began to steal over her, mingling with the word love, embodying it, voicing its message, until the two were indistinguishable. Among all these love-offerings to Colum was hers to be a dagger, or a snake? But her will was not quite faithless to its trust and made her say:

'I meant, he isn't a satisfactory man to live with.'

'You mean,' said Nick, and the confidence of the successful advocate began to creep into his voice, 'because he isn't always strictly truthful. Is that it?'

'It's more than that,' said Margaret. 'He's a . . .'

For the last time she tried to say what Colum was, and failing realized that she could never say it. She realized, too, that by not saying it she was letting her case go by default and probably losing Nick forever. Still, she could not say it, could not give Colum away, above all not at the moment of his come-back; it would be too cruel.

'A pathological liar, perhaps you were going to say?' suggested Nick. 'I can assure you, Margaret, that he isn't. He lies like a child, to get himself out of a tight place and because it's the line of least resistance. But he's quite capable of telling the truth; he told the Coroner's jury he knew that Mrs Belmore had a weak heart, whereas the others all denied it. That made a very favourable impression.'

Margaret struggled with herself. She would not throw her whole hand in; she would play one card, feeble as it was.

'I told him to,' she said.

Nick raised his eyebrows; then, seeing at once how the point could be turned to his advantage, said,

'Really? But doesn't that exactly prove my point, that you are well . . . making a better man of him, Margaret dear?' He tried to smile at her unsmiling face and crushed a rising sense of irritation at her lack of humour. 'He'll soon be a George Washington, at this rate! But seriously, Margaret, the police aren't a particularly credulous body of men, nor am I credulous, for that matter, but they don't doubt Colum's word, in fact they think he's been more truthful in this business than most men would have been;

and so do I. So why can't you?' And as Margaret still said nothing, but continued to look at Nick with an expression of pained obstinacy and reproach he let his irritation get the upper hand, and said 'I suggest the real reason is that you don't *want* to believe him.'

His eyes bored into hers, as they had into those of many a witness at a cross-examination. The lover of a few days ago was completely lost sight of in the barrister, making his point at the expense of a stupid and refractory witness.

Tears came into Margaret's eyes blurring the sharpness of his, and almost for the first time a doubt assailed her.

What if Colum's story really had been true? What if she disbelieved it because, deep down, she wanted to disbelieve it? Because she was somehow tired of Colum, and wanted Nick instead? Uncertain of herself she took refuge in resentment.

'I don't think you ought to say that to me, Nick. Remember it was you who always told me that Colum had a bad character.'

'Had? Yes, of course, he had,' Nick took her up. 'But my contention is that now he hasn't – you've been a godsend to him, Margaret! And I do appeal to you if you ever loved him, to put your petty prejudices aside and take him back, as . . . as I have.' He considered the last sentence and disliked it. Angry with himself, and therefore less careful to spare Margaret, he hurried on. 'Really, your attitude isn't worthy of you and all the experience you've had of human nature. Untruthful, you say. But if he were, which of us is truthful? Are you quite truthful yourself? And then, Margaret, Colum isn't an ordinary man. He's a genius, in his way. We, you and I, haven't had much experience of geniuses, perhaps. But they're not like other men. They have to pay for their gifts in all sorts of ways – in nerves, in mental instability, in eccentricity – in lying perhaps. But my point is, they are a special race, and should have special allowances made for them, and very special allowances made for them by those who love them. It wouldn't surprise me . . .' he looked round the room '. . . if every single donor of these flowers would be prepared to tell a thumping lie for Colum's sake if they were given the chance, and be proud of it, and can you blame them? And they aren't his wives. I honour you for your high principles, dear Margaret, but we must all bow to life, of which high principles are only one part; and I think in this instance you would – how shall I say? show yourself in a more human light, and be happier with yourself, if you relaxed them and withdrew your charge, as the police did. After all, the police haven't the same reasons you have to feel tender towards Colum.'

With her hands clasped in front of her Margaret listened. Nick's eloquence sank in: she began to see herself as a strait-laced Puritan, intolerant and loveless, divided from her kind by lack of the genial current of sympathy with its frailties, a sour-puss, a spoil-sport, a kill-joy. Yes, even the police had withdrawn their charge: why shouldn't she? But she couldn't strike her colours then and there; the surrender was too great, the interior revolution required too absolute; and to gain time she said,

'What made the police withdraw the charge, Nick?'

To her surprise he didn't answer. His mouth opened, but no sound came. Puzzled, she looked up and there, just inside the door, Colum was standing. He had been so much in her mind that he seemed like a materialization; and it was only after-wards that she sought an explanation for his presence, and found it in the expert noiselessness of all his movements. It scarcely crossed her mind to wonder how much he had heard.

He came into the middle of the room and said, in his deep-est, deadliest screen-growl, 'Aha! The guilty pair!'

To Margaret he was not the Colum of yesterday, he was a new strange figure, divested of the associations of crime and guilt that had been gathering round him. New but not new; he was Colum as she had first met him, exuding that indescribable freshness of something recently washed and scrubbed, super-naturally clean, the pristine, unblurred Colum, whose outlines had a sharpness denied to other mortals. But she could find no answer to his pleasantry nor anything to say that did not seem inadequate, so she repeated her question.

'I was asking Nick why the police withdrew the charge against you, Colum.'

Again Nick didn't answer, but Colum said,

'Why, do you want them to put me back on it?'

She smiled, but her eyes were on Nick's face and caught the look he flashed at Colum.

All her mistrust returned.

'Oh, you're hiding something from me!' she exclaimed. 'I know you are! But I'll find out! I'll go to the police!'

'The police don't have to give a reason for withdrawing a charge,' Nick said. 'They found the French maid's evidence most unsatisfactory: they were convinced that she was speaking from vindictiveness.'

'But you told me that before,' cried Margaret, 'before the police withdrew the charge. They must have had something else to go on. I want to know what it was. Don't you know, Colum?'

'They had the exact time, hadn't they, Nick?' said Colum. 'The broken clock, and all that. Well, it gave me an alibi.'

'But how could it, when no one saw you?'

'What would you say if someone had seen me?' said Colum, slowly.

Margaret turned ice-cold.

'I shouldn't know what to say.'

'Well, someone says they did.' His whole expression changed; he came and sat down on the arm of her chair. 'Should we leave it at that, Margaret darling?'

'Leave it?' cried Margaret. 'Leave it? Haven't I a right to

know?' Colum looked at Nick but Nick had turned away, and was rubbing the hearth-rug with his foot.

Colum took her hand. 'You have also a right not to know,' he said. 'Dear Margaret, use it.'

She shrank back into the chair and covered her face with her hands.

'No, no, tell me.'

'Will you promise not to believe it?'

'Yes . . . No . . . I can't promise anything.'

'Well, Lauriol said she saw me. She said I looked in at her flat, just before one. The broken clock said one-eleven.'

There was a long pause, then Margaret said,

'And what did you say, Colum?'

'I told the police I did.'

'And they believed you?'

Colum shrugged his shoulders.

'But what about your first story, that you walked straight home. Do they believe that too?'

'Margaret, I'm not in their confidence. They said they appreciated the reason why I hadn't spoken, and why Lauriol didn't speak till the last minute. They are men of the world. They didn't want to see me brought into court, I'm told, and they believed my first story. I didn't ask if they believed my second.'

'Your second! Was it yours or Lauriol's? Or was it Nick's?'

'We concocted it together.'

'But it was his idea? That's how he got you off?'

Colum shrugged his shoulders.

'Darling, he didn't want to see me go to gaol. Can't you understand that?'

'Nick,' said Margaret. 'Do you believe it?'

'Believe what, Margaret?' said Nick, his eyes hardening with irritation. 'What do you want me to believe? That Colum didn't go to Lauriol, or that he did go?'

'Oh,' cried Margaret, 'you sicken me! You stand there, both of you, making things up, as if truth was only something that you pull out of a pigeon-hole! Do you suppose it makes no difference to me whether Colum went to Lauriol's or not?'

'My dear, of course I didn't go,' said Colum.

'You didn't go?' said Margaret. 'But how can I be sure? Why did Lauriol stay at home instead of going to the party? Why did she warn you not to go? Wasn't it a plot, so that you could go to her instead, and no one be the wiser?'

'A very obvious plot, if so,' said Nick.

'Yes, but aren't people obvious, if they're after something they want? Isn't it often the best way of getting it?'

'Darling, you've never been jealous of Lauriol before,' said Colum. 'And why should you be now? Is it because you care for me so much? I wasn't sure you did.'

Margaret's emotions had outstripped her mind. She tried to adjust herself to this new situation. It was one thing to leave Colum in order to marry Nick; it was another to leave Colum in order, in order, well . . . to leave him. But her emotions would not answer to the facts: they went careering on; she felt deceived, betrayed, abandoned by the two people who had meant most to her. They were in league against her. Ever since Colum came into the room he had been edging nearer to Nick; now they were standing almost side by side, two naughty boys being reprimanded by their teacher, mutely supporting each other. It was an unnatural alliance, and she wanted to say something wounding, something in the worst of taste, that would drive a wedge between them. She was aware of their male solidarity working against her, she felt the mortification the sex-shame of a woman whom men have made a fool of. The only answer to them was to rail like a fish-wife; but she had not been brought up that way. She was quivering with resentment, and resented feeling resentful;

especially did she resent the position they had manoeuvred her into, the prig's position of not believing what it would be for her own happiness to believe, chaining herself to a barren rock of principle while the warm tide of humanity flowed by her. Yet she could not entrust her happiness and peace of mind to it when all these questions of plain truth were still outstanding, while she did not know for certain where Colum had been on the night of the party, while she could not believe anything that anyone said to her. Without the magnetic needle of truth love itself was bewildered and disorientated; it could find no mark to aim at.

'If you loved me,' Colum said, as though divining her thoughts, 'you would believe me.'

But he had put the cart before the horse. If she had believed him she would have loved him.

'If you don't believe me,' Colum went on, 'can't you believe Nick? I've always found him a truthful fellow.' He gave Nick a sly glance as he spoke.

Suddenly Margaret felt she couldn't bear their collusion any longer. Though she had little sense of humour she was outraged by the humourlessness of them standing there, like blood-brothers, presenting a common front against her, they who had been at daggers drawn.

'Nick,' she said, 'I think I could talk to Colum more easily if you went away.'

The tableau broke up, but too late; for as Nick, with scarlet face, was visibly wondering how, or whether, to say goodbye, Richards came in. Under arched eyebrows he glanced from Margaret to Colum and back, and said

'Will luncheon be for three, Madam, or for two?'

'It's all right,' said Nick. 'I'm going.' With a stiff nod to Margaret he hurried out.

*

'So you were lunching together?' Margaret said. 'Boys will be boys, I suppose.' She disliked herself for saying it, disliked the tone, disliked the implication.

'Yes,' said Colum simply. 'We were. Would you have minded, Margaret? You were so anxious we should be friends again.'

Margaret couldn't answer. Instead, a twinge of conscience made her say,

'I suppose he'll find somewhere to get lunch? It's rather late.'

The clock showed nearly two.

'Oh yes,' said Colum, 'there's a place he always goes to.'

'And you go with him?'

'Well, yes. That's what you wanted, wasn't it?'

Again he scored a verbal point, and Margaret's silence acknowledged it. But he didn't follow up his victory. He changed his ground and said.

'You want to marry him, don't you?'

Margaret was disconcerted by his frankness. For all her regard for truth candour did not come easily to her.

'I wanted to,' she said at last.

'But now you don't want to?'

His directness was infectious and she said, feeling that she was speaking to a Colum she hardly knew,

'He doesn't want to.'

In the ensuing silence a great many cables as well as cobwebs of feeling seemed to snap.

'I'm sorry,' Colum said at last. 'But Margaret, have I been such a bad husband to you? I haven't been unkind to you, have I?'

Margaret was silent.

'Some husband are, I believe,' he went on, but without sarcasm or even irony. 'They beat their wives . . . Well, I haven't.' He paused. 'I've neglected you, I know, but we went into that and you agreed it wasn't my fault. You like a husband to labour in his vocation, don't you? Nick said you did.'

Margaret couldn't deny it, though she hated to think of them discussing her.

'Come to think of it,' he said reflectively, 'I've been a better husband than I thought I should be, than anyone thought I should be. Much better than I was to poor old Jennifer.'

He tried a smile on her but Margaret didn't return it. She felt she knew this record, and it was playing to an empty room. Get it over, get it over, she thought.

'I know our backgrounds were different,' he said, 'and that's supposed to be important. But we got over it somehow, didn't we? You were marvellously adaptable, Margaret, and I . . . well . . . I hit it off all right with your father, I think. It wasn't difficult – he's a dear old boy.'

He stopped again, but still Margaret couldn't answer; she hadn't contributed a word.

'It isn't that you think I've been unfaithful to you, is it?' he said. 'I haven't, Margaret.'

She believed that he was lying and said miserably,

'What about Lauriol?'

'Lauriol is an old friend of mine,' he countered, 'the sort of friend that most men have. A good friend to me and to you too, Margaret. I shouldn't be a free man but for her.'

'You forget,' said Margaret. 'You wouldn't be a free man if I hadn't lied about the musical-box.' She hated herself for saying it.

'Oh, but darling,' exclaimed Colum, and for the first time his agitation began to show in his voice, 'you don't grudge me that little fib? I'd have done it for you a thousand times, and Lauriol . . .' he broke off.

'Well?' said Margaret.

'Lauriol thought nothing of it. You don't think I really called on her that night, do you?'

'I don't know what to think,' said Margaret.

402

'Oh, but you can't, it isn't possible,' he cried, and the change in his appearance from dapperness to woe was so complete it almost frightened her. He began to pace the room as he used to in their darkest days. Suddenly he stopped in front of her and said:

'What is it you really have against me?'

If she did not tell him she could never leave him; differently as they felt about such matters, she realized that the grievances that had come to the surface so far gave her no excuse. He was trying to by-pass the true explanation and pretend it didn't exist. Yet how could she tell him, how break the secret she had guarded as carefully as though it was her function in life to keep it? And above all how could she do it now, with his professional career hanging in the balance, to be decided perhaps once and for all by to-night performance?

'Colum,' she said rising unsteadily to her feet, 'don't ask me now. I was wrong, I ought never to have come back like this and taken you by surprise. It was most . . . most thoughtless of me. Let me go now, and sometime, another time, I'll tell you.'

But he stood between her and the door.

'No, you'll t—tell me n—now,' he stammered, spreading his arms out like black wings to bar her way.

'No, no, please not, Colum.'

'I won't let you—g—go until you do.'

For the first time in her life she was frightened of as well as for him; and on impulse, because she was afraid, she whispered,

'It's because I don't trust you, Colum.'

'Not trust me?' he repeated, his arms falling to his sides.

'No, I don't trust you. You're a thief.' She dropped back into the chair and clutched its arms.

'A thief?' he said, 'a thief?' The little word wandered about the room, prying into corners like a feather-duster. 'A thief,' he repeated, and his face seemed to hang back in shadow behind

403

his glowing eyes. 'A th—' but the word would not take shape again, though Margaret and the whole room listened for it. 'And you don't tr—ust me.' His look brought back her love for him and seemed to break her heart. He moved away from her, as though to be outside touching distance. 'You're wrong,' he said. 'Whatever I was once, I'm different now, Margaret, you've s— seen to that.' The words popped out of his tormented mouth expressionlessly. You've re—reformed me, Nick said so. And he said you could tr—ust me, but you didn't want to.' With his hand on the door-knob he repeated, 'You didn't want to.'

She didn't see him go, but when she lifted her eyes Richards was standing in his place.

'Will there be two for luncheon, Madam?' he asked with a puzzled air.

'No,' said Margaret, 'only one.'

Later in the afternoon, when Colum did not return, it occurred to her that he might have gone to lunch with Nick.

36

THE great, L-shaped room was slowly filling up. Margaret was one of the earliest to arrive, and an attendant in gold-braided coat and satin breeches conducted her immediately to her seat. Each table was crowned by a letter of the alphabet and every seat was numbered. Margaret's was at table A, some distance from the middle of it, and almost in the corner of the room: it commanded both wings of the L.

Dreamily she watched the Company's six hundred guests settling into their places. She sat passive, drained by the emotions of the day and almost hypnotized by seeing so many people together. All the last weeks, since the inquest in fact, the world outside her had receded to a rumour; she had been scarcely aware of it even as an audience for her private drama. Now it was flooding back, asserting its existence. Her tired mind seemed to have lost the power of selection or withdrawal: she found herself watching how the guests sat down as if every movement this or that one made was of immense importance. In imagination she went through the motions of sitting down a score of times.

Yet from habit her mind was on the watch for someone, and from habit uneasy because he did not come. Colum had stayed behind, unable to shake off the crowd of his admirers. They made a lane for him while he was helping her into the car; once she was safely in they thronged about him. The huddle of bent backs and peering faces reminded her of a picture of the stoning of Stephen.

Colum had come back to the flat just in time to change. When at last he emerged from his dressing-room his ravaged face was so little in keeping with his tail coat and white tie that her resentment against him changed once more to concern. Even in ordinary circumstances, another suit of clothes had the effect of a disguise on him; now she could hardly connect him with the Colum of a few hours before. All the way to the theatre he did not speak; she heard his gusty breathing and felt his hand tremble as it lay in hers.

His nervousness continued long after (as it seemed to Margaret) the film was certain of success. Like all his films it fascinated and repelled her, but it was different from the others and Colum was different in it. In the others he exploited personality, flaunted it, wore it almost as though it was a make-up; his gestures and expressions were deliberately made exuberant to bring out his physical vitality. Now that vitality was reduced to the merest glimmer; his face was like a mask, his gestures sparing. It was his dupes and victims who gave themselves away, breaking themselves upon his steel-smooth surface. They were mostly women, rich, beautiful, sophisticated, no longer young. One after another he enticed them into situations from which they, or their husbands, could extricate themselves only by the payment of large sums of hush-money; the scene in which he stood over one husband, persuading him in the gentlest, deadliest way, to add nought after nought to the cheque he was writing out was a master-piece of under-acting. One of the women looked so like Mrs Belmore that Margaret felt sure the audience must recognize her.

After each coup the blackmailer would disappear. One saw him walking out of the victim's house – yet one did not see him walk – he moved, he covered the ground, he was first in one place and then in another but how had he got there? What had become of Colum's ravishing stride? – into the street, where he mingled with the crowd and was lost to view. The crowd would fade away and gradually be re-formed in another street; an innocent-looking, ordinary crowd from which the figure we know would slowly disengage himself, look round, select another door, not unlike the last, rich, highly polished, well secured with locks; he would ring and be admitted, and the next scene would show him the familiar friend of the family who occupied the house.

It occurred to Margaret that there was no need for him to change his locality; another door in the same street would have served, for his victims never gave him away. There were good reasons for their not doing so, good practical reasons; they all had plenty to hide. But the chief reason was, they did not want to; those women guarded his secret as if it had been their own, as indeed it was. He had no need to keep them in water-tight compartments. Once he slipped up and a lady who had suffered from his depredations warned the current victim of what she might expect. 'He's a devil, you know,' she said. 'Yes, darling,' replied her friend. 'I suspected that he was' (actually she hadn't) 'but he's such a distinguished devil.' She laughed as she said this, and the house laughed too. Before Sir Montagu Willoughby had finished with her she laughed on the wrong side of her face, but even so she did not betray him, or apparently cease to love him, although once he nearly murdered her.

His heart, meanwhile, remained untouched. But having selected as his latest victim a widow with a nest egg and a little boy, a simple, sweet, domesticated woman, he suddenly found that his emotions were involved. It was too late to draw back; he had shown his hand; she knew, and he knew that she knew.

It was a duel of wills and wits between them and Margaret had no doubt who would win. The rest of the audience had no doubt either, for the time-honoured pattern of Colum's films demanded that love should reclaim him in the end.

Almost for the first time there were signs that the piece was losing its grip – relaxing bodies creaked and rustled, coughing that excitement had restrained burst out. Margaret stole a glance at Colum's profile, fearing to see disappointment written there; but no, his look of confidence had increased. Surreptitiously getting out her lipstick she turned her eyes on the film. Wide-eyed, the little boy was watching from the minstrel's gallery while Sir Montagu made discreet love to his mother; and Margaret found, what she had never found before, that she could look at his technique without discomfort, almost critically.

'No, no,' the victim cried, 'I can't, I won't. You mustn't ask me to!' It seemed quite clear what she was refusing, but he stopped her mouth with kisses, murmuring, 'Oh yes, you will, you will, see if you don't,' and other loving threats, until the scene faded and the street door took its place. Out came Sir Montagu with for the first time a touch of jauntiness in his bearing, and mingled with the crowd which was always at hand to aid his exits. It vanished and was reconstituted before a glossier door in a still more imposing street. But where was Sir Montagu? He did not materialize. Once more the audience was stung to silence and all eyes searched the screen. At last, from behind two burly passers-by he appeared, but he was not alone: the widow was tripping at his side. Together they walked up to the door. While they were waiting for the bell to be answered, their hands touched and they looked towards each other.

So they stood, waiting, with their backs to the audience, quite still except for a slight stiffening at the neck and shoulder. The crowd pursued its aimless way, but suddenly, waist-high among the throng, something began to flicker in and out, like a rivulet among pebbles, eddying round skirts and trouser legs and announcing itself with eager, anxious cries. The darting movement took shape; it was a child: the new Lady Willoughby's little boy who had somehow got left behind. Suddenly from across the road he spied his mother and his step-father and made a bee-line for them. Seizing his mother's hand he swung it to and fro, turning his innocent small face up to hers. She bent down and whispered something to him, at which he became as rigid as a statue, his coat puckered between his narrow shoulder blades. So the three marauders stood, facing the doomed house, until the door opened and one by one they were received inside. But the child turned on the threshold and gave the passers-by a little wave and a very naughty smile.

It took the audience a moment to realize that the film was over; they were still expecting the customary ending. Then, with the delighted knowledge that they had been spared that, had been tricked as the victims of the Willoughby family's latest raid were to be tricked, the clapping broke out. It was not the mere volume but the wild gusts of it, breaking out again and again in frantic crescendos, which proved to the most sceptical that Colum had made his come-back, and at a higher level than before.

The applause still reverberated in Margaret's memory, like the distant sound of the sea; and her mind was further lulled by the soft shuffling around her, the decorous, restrained movements of people too polite to push, but obliged to bump against each other. With warm smiles of apology and excuse, they searched for their places at the slowly-filling tables. Margaret listened to the murmur of the excuses and watched the smiles. Every face wore a smile; and it seemed to her that every smile was for Colum, and was an offering of love from his well-wisher and a tribute to his success. Could she not join in? She must at any rate try, and she was forcing her features to relax, when she saw Colum come into the room. At sight of him the smiles redoubled and the shuffling ceased; everyone stood still and some of those who were sitting down stood up. A hush fell upon the room as, moving with Sir Montagu's smooth level gait not with his own springing step, Colum threaded his way through the tables. The two who had come in with him dropped behind, then followed slowly in his wake. Presently they separated and began to look for their places at other tables. They were Nick and Lauriol.

For a moment Margaret took in nothing more, and when she came to herself she found that the chairs on either side of her were being occupied by magnates of the film-world whom she knew slightly. The newcomers were both middle-aged men. One was an Englishman, an agreeable and ready talker, the other was a foreigner, a Central European, well-known for his unpredictable and sometimes disconcerting tongue. The Englishman turned to her and said,

'Well, he didn't let us down, did he? You must be a proud woman to-night, Mrs McInnes.'

'I am,' said Margaret. She sighed as she said it; the sigh was for Truth, once more denied. But her companion did not notice.

'Some of us were a bit jumpy about this film, if the truth is to be told,' her neighbour said. 'Colum wasn't too happy about it himself, but I expect you knew that, Mrs McInnes.'

Yes, I am Mrs McInnes, Margaret thought.

'My husband doesn't tell me much about his film-work,' she said, 'but I couldn't help knowing he was nervous.'

Her neighbour nodded. 'But he needn't have been. The Trade Show went down well, so did the Press Show. You won't have to worry about his reputation for the next three years at least.'

Oh shan't I? Margaret thought, taking the word 'reputation' in another sense from the one he meant. Aloud she said, 'I'm very glad you think so. He needs a rest, I'm sure of that.'

'And you must need one too.'

Margaret smiled. Her condition was too plain for her to feel any embarrassment about it.

The talk went on, the glasses were filled up. Skating about on the surface of conversation at first gave Margaret a feeling of security. But the glow had faded from her mind. Had Colum deceived her, she idly wondered, when he said the film had been so badly received? She heard the pauses in the talk, not its continuous flow, saw dark patches in the air, which the diffused light did not reach, had no wish to eat but was impatiently aware of the waits between the courses. She found herself mentally jumping from moment to moment, as though they were ice floes in a river of unplumbed depth.

Presently she noticed that her neighbour's talk, too, was becoming jerky; he was giving her only half his attention, trying to make a bridge between her and the woman on his other side. The conversation was switching over. She turned to her other neighbour. He had a square, ugly, fleshy poker-face.

'You must be a proud woman to-night, Mrs McInnes,' he said.

She stared at him, wondering if he was mocking her, and said shortly,

'Yes, I am.'

'You are?' he said. 'Then why do you look so miserable?'

Margaret was taken aback and rather frightened.

'Do I look miserable?' she said.

'Not miserable, perhaps,' said he, 'but, how shall I say? Non-participating, as if you were at someone else's party. It is the reaction, yes?'

'Perhaps it is,' said Margaret, grateful to him for finding her a way out.

'And yet you should not be sad,' the man went on. 'On such an evening you should not be sad. But you are not the only sad person here, there is someone else.'

'Someone else?' repeated Margaret, looking at the radiant faces round her.

'Ah, you do not look in the right place – but you have looked two, three, four, perhaps many times?'

'I've been too busy talking,' Margaret said, 'I haven't had time to look about me.'

'Yet he has looked at you so many times,' her companion went on in his slightly sing-song voice. 'He is looking at you now. Have you not looked at him?'

'I don't know who you mean,' said Margaret.

'She doesn't know who I mean,' her companion said, his voice now edged with wonder. 'She hasn't looked at him. Not even once?' he said, addressing her directly.

'I'm afraid I don't know what you're talking about,' said Margaret as politely as she could.

'Oh dear, oh dear,' he said. 'This is more serious than I thought. Now it explains itself. You have not looked at him, and that is why he is sad. And why he neglects his neighbour, for his face is always turned this way.' He leaned forward and looked across her.

'I'm afraid I don't know,' – began Margaret, her voice trembling.

'Oh yes, you know,' her companion said. 'I should be sad if you did not look at me. Lean forward, Mrs McInnes, lean forward just a little, and smile at him down the table, not as an actress would' – he waved his hand from side to side as though discounting an actress's smile – 'but as you would.'

Stiffly, furtively, reluctantly Margaret bent forward, and let her glance travel slowly along the line of guests. She had not far to look, for Colum was sitting only a few places from her. It was true that he was looking in her direction and he seemed to have been looking that way a long time. Their eyes met and she tried to smile. She saw the incredulous gladness leap into his face, transforming it, and her smile became less forced. But still she felt it was opaque, a mask for her real feelings, and with an unconscious shake of her head she turned back to her companion.

'Do it again,' he ordered her, 'and smile more brightly this time.'

'How do you know how I smiled?' asked Margaret. 'You couldn't see.' He was sitting on the side of her away from Colum.

'I could see the reflexion on his face,' he retorted. 'It went out when you turned.'

Submissively she tried again, and as Colum's face lit up she felt its sweetness piercing her as of old. Regardless of what any one might see or think she made grimaces at him, as one child to another; she stretched out her hand and waved. Colum half rose from his chair, thought better of it and sat down again, making an eloquent pantomime of helplessness. At last they released each other's eyes.

'That was better, much better,' her mentor said, his bumpy face beaming at her. 'Now he feels much better, here, inside' – he touched his heart, – 'and you too, you feel better, yes?'

Margaret said she did.

'Quick, quick, now,' he said, 'while you are still in vein, and smile at everyone, yes,' he added impatiently, for Margaret looked blank at this tall order, 'at everyone in the room.'

Mechanically and methodically Margaret obeyed, and the first face her smile lit upon was Lauriol's. Lauriol, too, seemed to have been watching her, for she at once smiled back, a lazy, amused, wide-eyed smile, full of complicity. 'Yes,' her smile said, 'we understand each other; we are what we are, and have done what we have done, for each other's sake and his.' Margaret's eyes travelled on, and every face that she identified – her father's face, Diana's, Stuart's – seemed to give her the same message. 'We are all in this together,' they said. 'You have not suffered for nothing. Everything has come right. Your patience has been rewarded. All the poisons of the past have been absorbed and assimilated by the life-stream, just as a river by the act of flowing purifies itself. Love is the principle by which the life-stream moves. By feeling as we feel now, thankful and happy and elated, we have restored the ulcerous tissues and brought the body back to health. Happiness is the great cure; and happiness is not a static condition achieved by the elimination of its opposites, it is not a negative or an abstraction; it is as complex as life itself and made up of as many ingredients. Therefore no experience is to be rejected, for the spiritual like the physical constitution thrives on the variety that is offered it, The richness, the enhancement of life that we feel now, how could we possess it, if a single item of what we have gone through had been omitted? If we had turned aside and said, this is not for me? If we had drawn up for ourselves a dietary from which certain things should be excluded? If we had doubted the power of life to doctor life, furnish its own medicine, and inoculate the spirit against illness? If we had opposed to life any single principle derived from life? If we had looked askance at its gifts and benefits? If we had seen goodness as something with which these gifts must not mix? Something to be kept apart, in a refrigerator? If we had deprived ourselves of the sunlight, and of the thing which had made life worth living? If we had deprived him of it too? If we had sent him away, like Ishmael, into the wilderness? If we had repudiated Colum? . . .

They were all standing now, and almost automatically Margaret, too, rose to her feet. It was the loyal toast. 'The King,' she heard. 'God bless him.' 'The King,' said Margaret, and clinked glasses with her Central European neighbour. But the King she meant was Colum.

They sat down again. It was the first climax, the preliminary one that left the guests still expectant. Margaret was only half aware of that, for her eyes were still searching the eyes of the company for a confirmation, a reassurance of what she was feeling about Colum. It was a roll-call; no one must be missed out, every answering smile must be recorded. Her smile searched face after face; she had no idea she knew so many people, and face after face gave her the same answer: all is well. Yet one face eluded her and she must find it, and find it now, for someone – yes, the Chairman of the Company, was on his feet and was speaking about Colum. She caught a phrase here and there, but she could not give her attention to the speech until she had located the missing face. To find it was vitally important to her, a compulsive obligation like a quest in a dream. If she did not find it, and before the Chairman proposed Colum's health, she would lose the benefit of all the other recognitions; they would be labour thrown away, like an unfinished sentence, like a story that lacks its final chapter. She heard the speaker's voice deepening, and changing its rhythm: he was marching to his conclusion, he could count the sentences now. It was a race between them. And then suddenly she saw the face she was looking for. He was sitting by a column – not her Colum, not his Colum – a little in shadow, and her gaze must have lighted on him a score of times. And he too had been trying to catch her eye, as desperately as she had his – for the moment when their glances met seemed like a revelation to him. He sat bolt upright, among the relaxed and sprawling diners: and a message of forgiveness, of apology, of congratulation, of complete acceptance of all she had been, was, and might be, flashed across to her, with a meaning far more immediate and overwhelming than any attainable by the human voice. Drinking in bliss, she sank back with closed eyes, feeling that she need never open them again, there was nothing more to look at, now that Nick, too, had bestowed his blessing on her.

'And now I must give you the toast we have all been waiting for, and perhaps you have been a little impatient with me for keeping you so long away from it. You all know his name, his name is known, as they say, all over the civilized world, but this is an intimate informal gathering of his special friends and fellow actors, so I should like to call him by the nickname by which he is known and loved by us, and which he has done and will do so much to make popular. My lords, ladies and gentlemen, I ask you to drink the health of our old, dear, and distinguished friend, the Devil.'

A salvo of laughter and applause broke out, chairs were pushed back, the guests rose shakily to their feet; but long before they had reached the perpendicular the word began to be whispered, spoken, and by some of the more festive diners, shouted, all round the room. 'The Devil! To the Devil! Good old Devil! Long life to him!' such were some of the tributes, half drowned in laughter and slurred by wine, that Margaret heard around her; and she was raising her glass to her lips and had got as far as the D in devil, when her eyes lit on a guest who was sitting down and not responding to the toast. She stared at him in amazement and indignation. 'Why don't his neighbours tell him?' she thought. 'Why don't they make him stand up? Why don't they shake him?' And then she saw who it was; it was Father McBane. His eyes were fixed on hers, just as the eyes of the other guests had been; but there was no smile in them, no exultation; only reproach and sorrow.

The glass slipped through Margaret's fingers and rebounded on the table-cloth, happily without breaking, though the wine spread amber fingers in all directions. Faintness seized her and she sat down suddenly. No one noticed her for they were all beginning to sit down themselves. The word devil was still vibrating in the air, some of its devotees had made a sort of chant of it, a rhythmical barking like an American college cry: 'Devil, devil, devil, devil,' while others were striking up 'For he's a jolly good fellow'. Margaret struggled to keep her senses;

she was aware, even in the act of losing them, how little credit it would do her to slide under the table. She just managed to hang on long enough to see Colum get up. Shouts of 'Satan!' greeted him, but they were drowned by cries of 'hush', and Margaret heard his familiar voice. 'Sir Franklin Pierce,' he began, 'my lords, ladies and gentlemen, and dare I say, my fellow-devils? . . .'

She heard no more before the black-out claimed her.

37

'I'D rather we didn't drive right up to the church, Wilkins,' said Margaret to her father's chauffeur. 'I'll walk the last bit.'

'Yes, Miss, – Madam, I mean.'

Wilkins still could not accustom his tongue to her married state. 'And shall I bring you back?'

'Well, this once, if you don't mind.'

Margaret had had to start before the bus service began, otherwise she would have gone by bus both ways, for she shared her father's prejudice against taking Wilkins out on Sundays, just as she shared his prejudice against rolling up to church in their big old car. He felt that it made a bad impression. 'Not unto us, O Lord . . .' He had never been a great church-goer, but since his daughter had announced her intention of joining the Church of Rome he had taken to going to church quite often. He did not mean it as a protest, and yet in reality it was one.

Indulgent father as he was in many ways, and ready to back her up where material forces threatened her, he had not taken kindly to her proposed change of faith. 'It isn't as if you had been anything much before,' he complained, and could not or would not follow Margaret's reasoning when she said that that made her conversion less of an apostasy. 'It seems so unnecessary,' he said, 'you were quite all right as you were. If you were going back to Colum I could understand it, but you say you aren't. It doesn't make sense.'

'It makes sense to me,' said Margaret with a flicker of spirit.

'But how? The only Roman Catholic you've known at all

well is Colum, and you want to leave him because you don't think he'd be a good influence for Anthony. As I've told you before, I dare say that film-stars don't make ideal fathers, but there's no law against them having children. If being a Roman Catholic hasn't in your opinion made Colum a proper parent, I don't see why you should want to be one. Forgive me for speaking so plainly, my dear child.'

'Colum isn't a good Catholic,' said Margaret with difficulty. 'He said so himself.'

'But surely that's to his credit? It shows he's straightforward, anyhow. And another thing: I know very little about Roman Catholics, but I do know one thing: they make almost a fetish of family life. You'll see they'll want you to go back to Colum.'

Mr Pennefather was right: they did. Father Grantham, to whom Margaret went for instruction, was a large, kindly, elderly priest, with an excellent sense of humour and a considerable knowledge of the world. His sense of humour was a slight barrier, for Margaret was not well provided with that quality. Talking to him was a little like talking to a good-natured Customs House officer, who is anxious to let the immigrant in and ready to overlook trifling irregularities provided the main regulations are complied with. Quite early on he warned her that her unwillingness to return to her husband might be regarded as an obstacle; and Margaret said that if it was she must withdraw her candidature and remain outside the fold of the Church.

It cost her a great deal to say this, for since the birth of her baby, which happened very soon after her collapse at the banquet, her one great desire outside her absorption in the baby was to join the Roman Catholic Church. Indeed, the two objects of her devotion, the spiritual and the physical, soon became identified in her mind. She could not rest until the child had been baptized, and as soon as he was she began to regard him with a new veneration, amounting almost to awe, as if he had already achieved what she was only hoping to attain to. In worshipping him she felt she worshipped something holy, and at moments she even envied him for enjoying a grace which she did not.

For that reason the break with Colum had cost her much less than she feared. The love which was necessary to her, and which had continued to flow towards Colum in spite of so many setbacks, transferred itself automatically to her child; and the longing to trust which Colum could not satisfy found its object in religion and in what seemed to her religion's most enduring stronghold, the Church of Rome. There she would find the authority she was seeking. The need to believe was as much part of her mental and emotional make-up as the need to love, indeed it was another aspect of the same thing, and perhaps circumstances had made it a more important aspect. She felt she needed certitude even more than love.

Superficially Colum made the break easier for her because he would not recognize it. He attributed her wish to leave him to disappointment over Nick's defection and she did not altogether undeceive him. She could not tell him again she did not trust him. If she did his vanity would prevent him from believing her; she wasn't sure whether he hadn't persuaded himself that he was not a thief; he could not for long believe anything that would have lowered him in his own regard. He would be much less wounded if he thought she left him for a whim. While she still loved him she thought she ought to supply reasons for leaving him – reasons that would seem sufficient to herself and him and the world. Now that she no longer loved him, and the stream of her affections was flowing elsewhere, it did not seem so necessary to find reasons. She had her reasons and had lived with them until they became part of her; she no longer thought of them as something external to her.

For never, never more would she join the band of devil-worshippers. When she came round and saw Colum standing over her she gave a weak cry and tried to push him away; to her enfeebled sense of reality he seemed to be what everybody said he was, – the Devil. Little did she remember how only a year before, coming round from another faint, she had looked into his face and lost her heart to it. She would not stay at the banquet, nor would she let him see her home; she would not spoil the party, she said, and accepted the escort of one of many volunteers. And the next day she went by ambulance to Fair Haven.

This step seemed natural enough; it caused no surprise to anyone; and from behind the thick screen of shrubs which sheltered her old home from the road she could treat Colum as a visitor. She was on her own ground and it was not difficult to persuade the doctor to drop him a hint not to come too often. Women were sometimes like that, the doctor told him; after childbirth they shrank from seeing the father. He must not take it seriously, it would pass.

Margaret did not think that she was being cruel to Colum. She had lived so long with her problem, wrestling with it, that Colum had become an abstraction to her, a mere symbol of his own dishonesty. That he should still exist as a man with feelings to be hurt after she had exorcised him hardly crossed her mind. Like many people, she felt that by reaching a decision she had altered everything that went before. The pros and cons that had for so long faced each other on the battlefield of her mind had been swept away like the pieces of last night's game of chess, and the board was clear for another game. She had kept to the rules of the game as well as she could. One of the chief rules was that she must not leave Colum in any sort of misery or disgrace. But he was not, he was on a pinnacle of success, and she was now free to go her own way.

So she thought, but the neighbourhood thought differently. Margaret had to have another confidant besides her father: she told Diana she was meaning to leave Colum and the news spread. It did not spread beyond the locality. Margaret did not receive from strangers letters of congratulation or rebuke. Dittingham was her home town and she commanded the respect there she had always had. The buzz of talk around her never reached her. But it came back to Diana, and after the trial of the Queen's Gate Rangers she decided to have a chat with Margaret. It seemed a suitable moment.

'All's well that ends well, Margaret dear,' she said. 'His name was hardly mentioned.'

Stuart and Diana had been seriously shocked when Colum was cited in the Belmore case. But the withdrawal of the charge had cleared him in their eyes, as it had in other people's, more completely than an acquittal would have done. They now approved of him wholeheartedly; Margaret had not misunderstood the signals of delight they had flashed at her on the night of the banquet.

'Stuart thinks, as I do,' Diana went on, not noticing Margaret's silence, 'that the man who took the things was very lucky to get off with two years. Of course he meant to keep them; if not, why did he take them? His defence, that he always meant to give them back, and only parted with them because he had lost his head and thought he might be suspected was the most awful bunkum. He was just taking a chance. I think it was right to let the others off – they didn't mean the poor old lady any harm – but they must have been a rather nasty crew. Colum is evidently too trusting. Lucky he realized what they were really like and turned back just in time. Darling, how thankful you must be.'

Margaret said she was.

'And how proud of Colum, too. He has simply covered himself with glory. Darling, it can't be true what you told me, that you are thinking of leaving him?'

Margaret looked at her friend despairingly.

'I think I must,' she said.

'But it's incomprehensible to me,' Diana cried, 'and Stuart can't understand it either. If he had been convicted, that would have been another matter. I could understand your wanting to leave him *then* – we all could. If he had been that frightful gaolbird, Ripman, – you saw that he had been convicted for the same sort of offence three times before? – Colum must have got a shock when he read that! – well, naturally you wouldn't have wanted to stay with him. But *now*! It seems so very strange. Darling, are you sure you understand what you are doing yourself?'

'I think it will be for the best,' muttered Margaret miserably.

'But then why are you becoming an R.C.? That seems so inexplicable. Of course nobody exactly *minds* – so many people that one knows are turning Papists, as Stuart quaintly calls them. Only I never thought you were much interested in religion in *that* way – you were always so taken up with good works. In fact you were so *good*, Margaret dear, that we didn't think you had any need of it! Of course, it's your affair, not mine – we shan't feel differently towards you, except that you'll be like a foreigner – what seems so odd is that you should choose this moment to do it. I mean, I should have thought it was a sign you were coming together, not drifting apart. Darling, what is the real reason? I don't believe you've told us.'

'We're too unlike,' said Margaret. 'We . . . we look at things too differently. I cramp him in his professional life and he . . .'

'Yes, darling, what does he do?'

'Well, I can't explain, but he makes me very unhappy sometimes. He doesn't mean to.'

'Stuart has never given me a moment's unhappiness,' said Diana after a pause. 'A little while ago we were all together,' (Diana's frequent use of the first person plural made it seem that she was always at a party) 'and the question of unhappy marriages came up (nothing at all to do with you, my dear), and someone asked what one would find most trying in a husband, and we all suggested different things, infidelity and so on, and somebody said, If he was a thief! Oh dear, we did all laugh.'

'You wouldn't mind that?' Margaret asked.

'Well, darling, it seemed so funny, it doesn't happen in our walk of life, does it? Or if it does, we call it something else. But a real thief who broke into houses and stole things with his own hands, like Colum does in his films, oh that would be too thrilling. I wouldn't regard it as a serious drawback.'

There was a pause, then Margaret said,

'Would you like to look at Anthony?'

'Oh, darling, of course, it was on the tip of my tongue to ask. Who did you call him after?'

'Well, the saint, St. Anthony of Padua.'

'I thought it might be that, because they all do, they all call them by the names of saints. I don't mind it, but of course it's limiting.'

Margaret led the way upstairs to where St. Anthony's namesake lay in his white, peaked, hooded cradle. He seemed to be asleep and only his ear was visible; but when he felt their presences he turned his head and opened blue-grey eyes.

'Why, they're just Colum's eyes!' Diana said, bending over him, near enough to drink in his babyhood, but not so near as to frighten him. 'And his nose, you know, Margaret, when it grows it'll be just like Colum's too. He'll grow up exactly like him. What a lucky little boy. The only thing that's like you is his hair, but of course that may get darker,' she added hopefully. 'What does Colum think of him?'

'Oh, I think he likes him,' Margaret said.

'Likes him? I should hope so. But of course ... well ...' Diana stopped and coughed. In the belief that she was changing the subject she said,

'I wonder what will be the first word he learns to say. I hope not Daddy, for that might lead to an Oedipus complex. But in your case there won't be so much risk . . . I mean, if he doesn't see his father, he can't . . .' Embarrassed, she stopped again, and suddenly the baby, which had been glowering at them, opened its eyes wide and smiled.

'Oh, but he smiles exactly as Colum used to, in those early films of his, I mean, when he hardly ever smiled. If you just put a revolver in his hand . . .' Diana put her finger there instead and the baby's fist closed over it. 'Oh, Margaret, do look how he clutches! I can hardly get my finger away. He'll be as strong as Colum some day.'

The nurse came in, bringing a whiff of professional superiority. 'He's smiling because he's got a touch of wind,' she said. 'Babies that age don't smile.' With more than one backward glance at the recumbent idol the two friends stole from the room. Margaret paused a second in the hall, to give Diana the opportunity to leave, but Diana did not take it and they returned to the drawing room.

'He is too sweet, isn't he?' Diana said, 'your Anthony, I mean. He's a prize baby, I'm afraid Francis looks a most plebeian child beside him. But seriously, Margaret, I think you're making a big mistake, not going back to Colum.'

'I always used to be very happy here,' said Margaret.

'I know, I know, and of course we long to have you. But it won't be quite the same will it, for you, I mean?'

'I think I shall slip into it,' said Margaret. 'There's Daddy – I'm sure he'll be glad to have me, though he hasn't said so. And my good works, as you called them, and the Bench – there'll be quite enough to keep me from being idle.'

'Yes,' said Diana, 'but it won't be quite as simple as that. People will wonder what it means, and ask questions – you know what they're like. They won't accept you on quite the old footing, I'm afraid. A woman living apart from her husband, and all that. You know how conventional Dittingham is. They won't exactly blame you, but they'll criticize. Especially as no one will know why you're doing it – I don't myself, to be frank. Colum's so popular, more popular now than he ever was – I needn't tell you that! – and people will think you are treating him badly – I can't help thinking you are myself. Of course he's been married once, but that's nothing for a filmstar; he's still the Bayard of the film world, though I'm told he doesn't like it said. You would tell me if it was anything of that sort, wouldn't you?'

'Oh no, it isn't,' Margaret said.

'And I'm afraid that changing your religion will make you a bit unpopular. I have lots of Roman Catholic friends, as you know, but none round here, and nor have you – except the Elliots, but they hardly count and anyhow you never liked them. People will think you're trying to make religion a substitute for a husband, and be rather shocked. Goodness of that sort is so unattractive, but then, most goodness is. I'm so afraid you will be lonely and feel yourself left out.'

'Oh no,' said Margaret, who at this moment felt surer of herself than she had at any time since Diana's visit. 'I shan't be lonely. I can't tell you what it will mean to me to belong to the Church. I've always wanted to, you know, and you yourself were quite in favour of it when I married Colum.'

'Oh *yes*,' said Diana, 'we all were when we thought it would bring you and Colum closer. But now it seems as if you were doing it to spite him, to be different from him, almost. And you realize, don't you, that you won't be able to marry anyone else? You could now as you are; you could marry Nick, for instance, any moment you liked, just by lifting a finger.'

'I don't want to marry anyone,' said Margaret, colouring.

'Darling, forgive me – we are such old friends, aren't we? And I hate to see you making a mistake. I've known many women living apart from their husbands, and they don't make a good thing of it. They miss all the fun, they're neither one thing nor the other. Far better be divorced. But you can't be, if you're a Catholic. You're cutting the ground from under your own feet, walling yourself up in a kind of solitude. It isn't natural. I'm sure you'll be most frightfully lonely, a sort of grass widow, always popping off to Church at inconvenient times. I couldn't stand it, I know. I'd rather not have married. One hates to say it, but spinsters often have quite a good time.'

Trying not to sound priggish, Margaret said,

'It's not a good time I'm after, not in that sense. Really, Diana, I know where my own happiness lies. And I shan't be lonely; how can I be? I shall have Anthony.'

Diana pounced.

'But darling, *will* you? That's what I've been wanting to say all along, but didn't like to. Will Colum let you keep him? I don't think he will, and he's the injured party; he doesn't want to live away from you. I'm sure he'll want to have the child with him. He loves children; he's so sweet with them even on the films. I'm sure you mustn't count on keeping Anthony.'

Margaret, who had remained unmoved by all Diana's darts, deliberate and unintentional, protected by the twin shields of religion and her child, now saw one of them snatched away. She opened her eyes in terror, and cried,

'Oh, but he'd never steal him from me!'

'Steal him, darling, but it's hardly stealing, is it? You'll find most people think he has every right to keep him.'

Margaret spent the next two days in misery. Her world was once more turned upside down. She consulted her father; she consulted Father Grantham. Both confirmed Diana's opinion, both seemed astonished that Margaret had imagined there

427

could be any other. 'It all points to one thing, my child,' the priest said. 'You must go back to him.'

If only she could have asked advice of Father McBane! But he had told her they must not meet again, and they could not meet again, for he was dead. He had died, whether after or before the banquet Margaret never learned. But he was not among the invited guests and it was this perhaps more than any other single circumstance that had convinced Margaret that she must part from Colum. It was like a warning from beyond the grave from the one person whom she had trusted implicitly. To her overwrought, exhausted mind it seemed that Colum not only played the Devil's part, he was the Devil, and to be avoided like the Devil. She yearned for a simplification of her affairs, and did not realize that theology, complex as it is, is simpler than life.

Now her confused thoughts, devil-ridden, saw Colum stealing from her either her child, or her religion, or both.

Yet she felt that there must be some answer and that right was not inconsistent with her happiness, if only she knew how to apply it to her own case. She had clung to principles, she had ordered her life by them, she thought; but translated into terms of life, what did they amount to? A way of thinking and behaving that alienated most people. They sterilized life, and by sterilizing somehow poisoned it. Besides, as soon as they were applied to life they changed their tune and became self-contradictory. She had gone to Father Grantham all submission, ready to put her will, her reason, everything under his direction, but the first thing she had done was to behave like an ultra-Protestant and flout him, all for the sake of her principles. All for the sake of a principle she had not told him the one thing that might have put her right with him – that Colum was a thief. That was more, or less, than a principle, it was an inhibition. She knew that she would have to tell him, in her confession when she was received into the Church. She would have to admit that she was Colum's accomplice, an accessory after the fact. But tell him now she could not. Nor would she enter the Church at all if it meant living with Colum. The Church was to be her refuge from him. In the Church she would live according to the Church's rules. No doubt she would commit many sins; but she had Father McBane's word for it, his word from the grave as well as her own conviction, that living with Colum she could not escape the corruption of his nature. He was a liar and the father of lies. Nothing was true about him but his outside, and even his physical appearance changed from hour to hour. One could know nothing about him because he was always keeping something back, or putting something forward. When he told the truth it was because he could not think of anything else to say. One did not know where one was with him, any more than one knew where he was at a given moment, out of sight, on the night of Mrs Belmore's party . . .

She must not let herself think of Colum as a person. As long as she thought of him as an evil influence her way was clear. But sitting with Anthony in her arms, and seeing Colum's face in embryo, she could not but relent a little; the evil influence took on a shape – a human not a diabolic shape, a shape she had loved. Love was one thing but justice was another: all human beings, however evil they might be, were entitled to justice. Colum, she had persuaded herself, would not miss her; he had his fame, his work, he had his secret, incurable passion which she could not bring herself to name. And he had Lauriol – Lauriol who was much better equipped to deal with him than she was. As a husband, with a stake in her, he could be written off. But as a father, no. As a father, he still had his rights, and the more she thought about it the more convinced she was he had a right to Anthony. The Devil must have his due.

So long in conflict, her emotions and her thoughts had blunted each other. Neither would answer to the helm of reason. Perhaps because of her own love for Anthony, it seemed more important now that Colum should have Anthony to love than that Anthony should escape the risk of Colum's bad example.

She wrote to Colum saying that she did not know how such things were arranged, but that as soon as Anthony was old enough he should go to Colum if Colum wanted him. She tried to make it all sound business-like; her letters to Colum were quite formal now.

She had no doubt what his reply would be. While she was waiting for it she spent as much time as she could with Anthony, whom she had quickly come to regard as a visitor in the house, a blessing with a time-limit attached. Deeply as she suffered at the thought of losing him she felt a kind of exultation too, almost as if she had thrown off a burden. The personal had ceased to weigh with her as once it did. It did not matter, for instance, that she did not find Father Grantham particularly sympathetic; he was not a man for her to like or dislike, but a priest, an officer of religion, a pilot who could bring her into port. Her private feelings about him were irrelevant.

When she told him what she had done he neither approved nor disapproved, but looked at her inquiringly.

'I still don't quite understand what draws you to the Church,' he said, in a tone less cut and dried than he sometimes used. 'Though, mind you, I'm not questioning your sincerity. You tell me that your wish to join the Church is nothing new – you had it when you first married your husband. Why didn't you join it then?'

Margaret was silent. Father Grantham had asked her this question before and she had evaded answering it.

'Was it because you were uncertain of your feelings?' Father Grantham asked.

'Partly,' Margaret said. 'I wasn't quite certain of them. And as I told you before . . .'

'Ah, but you didn't tell me.' There was a hint of impatience in Father Grantham's voice. 'I understand that you are still unwilling to rejoin your husband?'

Margaret said she was.

'Any priest would tell you,' said he, 'that that is against the teaching of the Church. You cannot belong to us and keep your private ethical system.'

'Any priest would tell you . . .' but he was mistaken. Father McBane had told her just the opposite. But she did not feel she could tell her instructor this. It would be in bad taste, like quoting the opinion of one doctor to another. And it would be betraying Father McBane's secret, who was not there to answer for himself. If Father Grantham knew what Father McBane had known, he might have given a different answer. At her confession she would tell him, but not till then. She knew that this postponement was illogical, but her deepest feelings were concerned in it.

'But there are Catholic women who live apart from their husbands,' Margaret said.

'They do, they do – it is allowable but we discourage it. I am thinking of yourself. We should like to help you to go back to him. Have you considered what this self-mutilation means?'

'I do not love my husband,' Margaret said.

'Are you quite sure? You loved him once; might not your love come back, when you have the child to bring you together?'

Margaret shook her head.

The priest sighed. 'You must be patient with life,' he said, 'and not expect impossibilities. I think your duty lies with your husband. And while you are in the world it is unwise – I don't say it is wrong – to decline the chances of legitimate happiness that the world offers. Circumstances alter and our feelings alter with them. Do you no longer feel any longing for his love?'

'No,' said Margaret in a whisper.

'Tell me what you want.'

Suddenly Margaret felt that she must testify. By shielding Colum she had let her own case go by default. It was unfair to her, unfair to Father Grantham. She had given him and everyone else the impression that her reasons for wanting to join the Church were frivolous and unreal, but they were not. Her voice and colour rising, she said – and she had no difficulty in finding the words, for she had said them so often to herself—

'I want the liberty to love, without having to ask myself whether what I love is a good thing. I want my love to be centred on something – someone – that I know is true, something that I can trust. Where shall I find it, except in the Church?'

The priest was silent: Then he said, 'You tell me you experience no difficulty in accepting the Church's dogmas?'

'None at all,' said Margaret. She did not add that, for her, to believe in the Immaculate Conception or the Infallibility of the Pope was easy compared with the difficulty of believing any one of the stories of where Colum was on the night of Mrs Belmore's death.

'You say that our ritual does not mean much to you, that you have no feeling for institutional religion, that you would not feel your faith sustained and strengthened by fulfilling the observances laid down by the Church?'

'How can I tell until I try?' asked Margaret. 'All I know is I don't seem to need them. All I seem to need is the opportunity for prayer and . . . and . . . for adoration, and the sense, which your Church can give me – that the experience is real and flawless, that it means everything I believe it means, that I can repose on its truth as absolutely – oh much more absolutely – than I can on the truth of any human relationship.'

'There is more in religion than praying by oneself in churches,' said the priest.

'Yes,' said Margaret, 'But it is a part of religion, isn't it?' She added: 'I don't want to think of sins, my own or any ones. I needn't, need I?'

Father Grantham did not answer. Then he said, 'Perhaps you should have been a nun.'

Margaret stared at him. Had she then proved herself a failure in the world? The world had meant a great deal to her – in a flash she realized how much she owed to it. She had believed she understood it, she had been proud of the part she played in it. At the thought that all along she had been unfitted for it, a tone-deaf dancer dancing to another tune, she wept.

After that Father Grantham softened to her, and he did not again bring up the question of her going back to Colum. He guessed that she had something which she could not tell him. He even made an exception for her: she could make her confession before she was received, though she must wait for absolution until afterwards. 'You think,' he told her smiling, 'that the Church won't want you when it knows what's on your conscience; but it will, believe me.' Margaret was immensely relieved. Her instruction went on smoothly and she felt herself more and more at home in it, more and more delighted with the new landscape that was opening to her view.

Colum's reply was brief:

'My darling,' it ran, 'I will have both of you or neither.

Colum.'

But most messages are brief that change the lives of the recipients. Margaret roamed from room to room feeling her happiness reborn in each. There was no one to whom she could confide it, for her father would not see it as great matter for rejoicing; so she told it to the polished chairs and tables, she even went out and told it to the bees. Then she went up to

Anthony and told it to him: 'My darling, you are mine for ever.' For a moment he scowled at her with his sulkiest expression as if the prospect was hateful to him; he even closed his eyes against her. Then the silver gleam appeared between them; his arms stretched out, his upturned toes made hillocks in his blue silk coverlet and his face became one smile. She laughed back at him and kissed him and took him in her arms. What matter if it was only wind? He had changed her mood from bliss to doubt and back again all in the space of a few seconds.

Would it be always like that? Would she be always subject to his moods, as she had been to Colum's? And which was he, the grim-faced little gangster of one minute, or the angel of the next? How could she tell? I shall have to teach him not to frown, she thought anxiously. He must smile all the time. People will like him better if he smiles. As though he had heard her thought, he frowned in his sleep. 'I am a man,' his frown said, 'and if you think you can dispute my right to frown, you are very much mistaken.'

After many minutes had passed this way, Margaret sat down to write a letter to the father. The father, her child's father, was the Devil, and the Devil was the father of lies. There should be no communication between them and the letter must be merely formal. 'Dear Devil, Good old Devil,' – the phrases that accompanied Colum's toast came back to her. But Margaret could not call him that. 'My dear Colum, I am so very grateful to you . . .' But how could one be grateful to the Devil, even formally? One had nothing to be grateful to the Devil for. Yet she was grateful, or she had been: in the flood of emotions that Colum's note let loose, gratitude had certainly been present. But not gratitude to Colum; gratitude to St. Anthony, perhaps, who had restored what had been so nearly lost . . . She took another sheet. 'I think it is very generous of you, Colum . . .'

That eliminated the word dear; she need not call him dear, need not call the Devil dear, which he was not. But even so she had attributed generosity to him, and how could the Devil be generous? How did one thank a thief for not stealing one's child? She thought again, trying to instil some sense into herself. Why was she finding it so difficult to write? Not because she really thought that Colum was the Devil, but because she did not want to admit that he was a husband with claims on her, or even a man. She could not re-open relations with him: he must remain an abstraction, the X in an equation that had been solved. Despairing, she laid down her pen, and did not take it up again either that day or the next.

Dittingham was now left far behind and they were approaching its larger, commercial neighbour, Bruntisfield. She knew it well, of course. She knew the hotels and the shops and what things could be bought there that could not be bought in Dittingham; it was a useful place but she had never liked it, she always tried not to look at it, and was glad when the time came to go. Now all that was changed; it had become a place of pilgrimage and she was going there for her first communion. There was a Catholic church in Dittingham, but she had chosen Bruntisfield because she shrank from making her début as a Catholic among people who would know her. Her desire for anonymity went deeper than this; she wanted to make her new start in new surroundings, and the very fact that they were uncongenial was somehow a recommendation.

Not for the first time she looked about her to make sure that she had brought with her the things necessary to her devotions, and only those things. They did not include letters, keepsakes, and such odds and ends; these she had taken out of her bag, with Colum's photograph, before she left.

But in her bag was one thing that should not have been

there. She had succumbed to a last-minute temptation. The post had arrived before she left, bringing only one letter. This letter she snatched up and took with her, meaning to read it on the way back. But curiosity overcame her and she opened the envelope.

'Darling Margaret,' began the Devil's playfellow,

'I have been looking after Colum as best I could, and as much as he will let me. You wanted me to, didn't you. Or don't you care what happens to him now.

'He says you want to separate. But why don't you divorce. I don't understand this business of becoming a Catholic and tying yourself to him. Is it a kind of blind – I mean, are you really doing it to make sure you *can't* get rid of him. It's no affair of mine, of course, but I just wondered.

'Margaret, how clever you are. We knew you had other qualities, but didn't think you clever. I mean, it was clever to offer him the baby instead of fighting for it. You guessed he never wants what's offered him. It was risky, I suppose, but it came off. Now he doesn't want the brat at all, or says he doesn't. He did want it before, and he'd have had it.

'I'm not sure, though. He isn't quite the man he used to be. You may not realize it but you have done something to him. He ratted at Mrs Belmore's party because he felt you tugging at him. My theory is, he got so used to having a good angel on the films that he feels lost without one in real life. (Unless you count me.) You don't believe it, do you, and I'd much rather you didn't. You think he went in with the others, which he didn't, or that he came on here to me, which he didn't. He was saved by a good woman's love!!!

'I think he misses you, but really you did lead him a life. I asked him how he stood it and he said, Well, I like hard chocolates and I like hard women. What do you say to that.

'I'm too soft or I shouldn't be writing to you. I shouldn't be writing either if I wasn't pretty sure you'd made your mind up. Are you happy, darling. I am but I'm not sure he is.

'Best love, Lauriol.

'P.S. His boy-friend Burden drops in fairly often. Do you approve of that. I don't. Old Nick, Colum calls him, so now there are two of them – three, counting me, but perhaps I don't count. It's a game, as the servants say, or isn't it. We rub along quite well, all things considered. But why not come back and make a fourth.'

At first she was puzzled by the absence of question marks. Lauriol was too lazy, she supposed, to put them in. But she had put three exclamations after that bit about Colum being saved by the love of a good woman.

Had he been? Had he been? It didn't suit her to think he had – or did it? And was she a good woman?

Slowly she tore the letter up, opened the window and let the wind carry away the pieces.

But try as she would, she could not keep her mind from dwelling on the past. This should have been the greatest moment of her life, but was it? She thought of her departure. It had not been triumphal. Despite the early hour her father had dressed and come down to see her off. It was sweet of him to think of it. Yet, at the last, some scruple must have seized him; he came with her as far as the front door, but did not accompany her to the car itself. 'And you haven't had any breakfast!' he said, reproachfully. He did not wave to her; she thought that, as he turned away, he shook his head. Many heads, she told herself, were being shaken; all Dittingham, as the phrase went, would be shaking their heads. They had not hung out flags for her conversion; they regarded it, those who were aware of it, as an un-English thing to do, an implied criticism of themselves, a slightly ungracious gesture of dissociation from those who had cared for and made much of her.

She had not, they shrewdly felt, found among them what she wanted; by an inexplicable kind of snobbishness, she preferred the Pope to them.

But neither could she regard herself as a martyr. No one had been unkind to her or cut her. Some even said they were glad for her sake. They were not glad for their own, and whether they said they understood, or didn't understand, they meant the same thing – that they disapproved.

'Of course we understand, but it does seem so unnecessary!' that was the usual comment. Unnecessary! Could they but realize what it meant to her, to be free at last from the uncertainties she dreaded and to be anchored to those truths which were as indestructible as Peter's rock!

But it did not constitute martyrdom to exchange one kind of life for another that she liked, or expected to like, better; a showily luxurious existence for one of solid comfort; and the cares and pains of marriage – a husband – for its blessing and reward – a child.

She almost wished it could have been a greater sacrifice, for then, surely, she would have the enlargement of spirit that she hoped for instead of this dull, dry sense of causing other people disappointment. If only she had someone to rejoice with her, if Colum . . .

Father Grantham had warned her not to expect too much. 'We must do our best in an imperfect world,' he had said. 'I suspect you of being an enthusiast, a perfectionist, perhaps.' She had smiled, thinking he was paying her a compliment; but his face showed he was not. 'Are they bad things to be?' she asked. 'Well, yes,' he said. 'You must beware of ecstasy, ecstasy is for the saints, and even they have sometimes mistrusted it. We common mortals are more safely employed in telling our beads.'

She closed her eyes and tried to meditate, but a thought kept coming back to her – how should she answer Colum's letter, his letter granting her the child? The note she had sent him was a bare acknowledgment and he had not replied. She did not want him to reply, she did not want to think about him, and yet . . . Apprised at last of her problem, Father Grantham had told her she must pray for guidance: after her Communion she might see her way more clearly.

When she looked up Bruntisfield was closing round her. She scarcely recognized it. She saw it as a stranger might, shorn of its softening mantle of familiarity, nakedly ugly. Nor did she recognize herself. A tingling started in her mind, the chilly quiver of expectation ran along her nerves. But she remembered where she was and tapped on the glass screen and asked the chauffeur to stop.

'Wait for me here, please, Wilkins,' she said. 'I'll come back in' – suddenly she remembered she did not know how long she would be. 'I'll come back,' she repeated.

But would she, Margaret, come back or would someone else?

She need not hurry, there was plenty of time. Slowly she went down the sunny, empty, Sunday street. Was it an illusion or was her very weight changing, so that at one moment she felt light, and the next heavy? All at once a sense of the gravity of what she was doing assailed her. She tottered; her unrest deepened; loneliness and strangeness weighed her down. In a panic she halted and turned round, hoping to see the car, but it had gone. The past had forsaken her, with its burden of problems solved and unsolved. It was not true that she was returning to her old life; she was entering on a new one, about which she knew nothing. She stared at the horizon above the roof-tops. Beyond lay Dittingham and beyond Dittingham, London. The sky above them looked as smudged and blotchy as if it had been wiped out by a dirty india-rubber. She hesitated, poised for flight. But whither could she fly? The present was a knife-edge between the past and the future. She could not stay on it: she must topple over, one side or the other. She turned her back on Dittingham and looked forward. The street was not so empty after all. People were walking in it, and they were all going the same way, her way. At the end of the street, piercing the clear blue sky, the spire of St. Saviour's Church soared upwards. She did not remember it with her mind, her mind had always dismissed it as just another part of Bruntisfield. But her heart shouted and sang with recognition. Her fellow-worshippers were loitering towards it. They could afford to loiter but she must hasten. Her steps came quicker and she began to run.

From Byron, Austen and Darwin
to some of the most acclaimed and original
contemporary writing, John Murray takes pride in
bringing you powerful, prizewinning, absorbing
and provocative books that will entertain you
today and become the classics of tomorrow.

We put a lot of time and passion into what we
publish and how we publish it, and we'd like to
hear what you think.

Be part of John Murray – share your views with us at:

www.johnmurray.co.uk

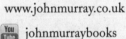 johnmurraybooks

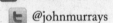 @johnmurrays

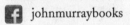 johnmurraybooks